Ecology of the Zombie

Postcolonialism across the Disciplines 28

Postcolonialism across the Disciplines

Series Editors
Graham Huggan, University of Leeds
Andrew Thompson, University of Exeter

Postcolonialism across the Disciplines showcases alternative directions for postcolonial studies. It is in part an attempt to counteract the dominance in colonial and postcolonial studies of one particular discipline – English literary/cultural studies – and to make the case for a combination of disciplinary knowledges as the basis for contemporary postcolonial critique. Edited by leading scholars, the series aims to be a seminal contribution to the field, spanning the traditional range of disciplines represented in postcolonial studies but also those less acknowledged. It will also embrace new critical paradigms and examine the relationship between the transnational/cultural, the global and the postcolonial.

Ecology of the Zombie

World-culture and the Monstrous

Kerstin Oloff

Liverpool University Press

First published 2023 by
Liverpool University Press
4 Cambridge Street
Liverpool L69 7ZU

Copyright © 2023 Kerstin Oloff

Kerstin Oloff has asserted the right to be identified as the author of this book in accordance with the Copyright, Design and Patents Act 1988.

All rights reserved. No part of this book may be reproduced, stored in a retrieval system, or transmitted, in any form or by any means, electronic, mechanical, photocopying, recording, or otherwise, without the prior written permission of the publisher.

British Library Cataloguing-in-Publication data
A British Library CIP record is available

ISBN-978-1-83764-422-3 cased

Typeset in Amerigo by Carnegie Book Production, Lancaster
Printed and bound by CPI Group (UK) Ltd, Croydon CR0 4YY

Contents

Acknowledgements vii

Introduction 1

1 Greening Zombie Theory 19

2 The Sugar-Zombie, Race and Cash-Crop Monocultures 41

3 The Zombie-in-the-House, Nature and the Colonies 67

4 Energy and the Emergence of the Petro-Zombie 95

5 Zombies-of-Waste and Neoliberal Exhaustion 125

Conclusion: Plotting the Routes of De-zombification 159

Works Cited 171
Index 189

Acknowledgements

This book would not exist without the help of the many medical professionals and friends who took care of me after I fell ill following the Covid-19 AstraZeneca vaccine. I would like to thank all of the staff at Newcastle RVI's intensive care unit, particularly Carl and Angela. Thanks, also, to Bishop Auckland Hospital, especially Kathy and June, and to the staff at Walkergate Park, not least Jo for the support she gave me.

Mike Niblett needs to be listed with a special thank you for the many years of friendship and companionship. Thanks, too, to Sharae Deckard, a brilliant friend and interlocutor, always on call for intellectual stimulation. Claudia Nitschke deserves special praise, for her friendship, feedback and constant support. Thanks are due also to my many colleagues and intellectual comrades at Durham and elsewhere whose work and conversations have informed my thinking: Chris Campbell, Sandra Casanova-Vizcaíno, Laura Chuhan Campbell, Abir Hamdar, Santiago Fouz-Hernández, Sorcha Gunne, Neil Lazarus, Treasa de Loughry, Victoria Ivleva, John King, Jason W. Moore, Yarí Pérez-Marín, Simon Pirani, Jane Poyner, Nicholas Roberts, Néstor Rodríguez, William Schaefer, Stephen Shapiro, Janet Stewart and Katrin Wehling-Giorgi. Special thanks to Lucy Potter for her invaluable feedback on the book and incomparable editing skills. I would also like to thank the School of Modern Languages and Culture at Durham for all the support they have provided me with over the years. Thank you also to Stanley Greaves for his generosity in allowing me to use "People of the Garden City" (1962) as the cover image for this book and also to John Torres for allowing me to cite *Undead* (2013).

Thanks are due to my family – my mum, dad, Leon, Lewis and Mike – for all their support and love over the years. This book is dedicated to Leon, Lewis and Mario.

I would like to acknowledge the following publications, in which earlier drafts of several of the arguments elaborated in this book were first published. Portions of Chapter 3 were published as "Zombies, Gender, and World-Ecology:

Acknowledgements

Gothic Narrative in the Work of Ana Lydia Vega and Mayra Montero," in *The Caribbean: Aesthetics, World-ecology, Politics* (ed. Chris Campbell and Michael Niblett, Liverpool University Press) and "Marie Vieux Chauvet's World-Gothic: Commodity Frontiers, 'Cheap Natures' and the Monstrous-Feminine," in *Latin American Gothic in Literature and Culture: Transposition, Hybridization, Tropicalization* (ed. Sandra Casanova-Vizcaíno and Inés Ordiz, Routledge). The second part of Chapter 4 appeared previously as a separate essay, "From Sugar to Oil: The Ecology of George A. Romero's *Night of the Living Dead* (1968)," *Journal of Postcolonial Literature* 53 (2017), pp. 316–28.

Introduction

The zombie is a precarious figure who continues to traverse the earth that can never be his.[1]

Áurea María Sotomayor, 2013

[A]ll progress in capitalist production is a progress in the art, not only of robbing the worker, but of robbing the soil; all the progress in increasing the fertility of the soil for a given time is a progress towards ruining the more long-lasting sources of that fertility.

Karl Marx, 1867

Contemporary zombie apocalypse novels and films are steeped in anxieties around food supplies, infrastructural collapse, environmental disasters and the possibility of human extinction. But zombie narratives are not merely reflective of these fears. A cultural history of the zombie holds many lessons for the contemporary moment, profoundly marked as it is by accelerating climate change, animal extinctions and environmental degradation, as well as the (perhaps terminal) crisis of the capitalist world-system. Indeed, the term "zombie" – now often naming a creature that continues moving long after physical laws should allow it to do so – has become a powerful metaphor for the socio-ecological crisis of capitalism. This is not coincidental: zombie history provides a store of horrifying memories of capitalism's profit-driven destruction of the earth and its human and non-human inhabitants. Yet it

---

1 When the original text is in Spanish or French, I provide my own translations unless otherwise indicated. I base my work on the general translatability of literary devices, figures and metaphors, searching for likeness in situations that are unlike each other.

Ecology of the Zombie

also offers an imaginary of resistance against these processes, continuing the zombie's early association with the Haitian Revolution through the revolutionary fighter Jean Zombi, who, "during Dessalines's massacre of whites [...] earned a reputation for brutality," and was subsequently transformed into a *lwa* (Vodou spirit) (Dayan 1998: 36). The potential of de-zombification plays a role in many of the more critical and self-aware zombie narratives – especially those from the Caribbean.[2]

Monsters both "reveal" (*monstrare*) and "warn" (*monere*). Like many other modern monsters, zombies warn us of capitalism's inherent monstrosity: zombies are "mere bodies" manifesting "recurrent anxieties about corporeal dismemberment in societies where the commodification of human labour – its purchase and sale on markets – is becoming widespread," as David McNally argues (2011: 4).[3] But beyond this, they warn us that capitalism is environmentally unsustainable, as has been plainly visible in the peripheries and semi-peripheries of capitalism for a long time. As I will show throughout this book, zombies reveal the ways in which environmental degradation and the exploitation and appropriation of the gendered and racialised human majority are inextricably imbricated. The figure of the zombie is constitutively marked by life under capitalism and is fundamentally ecological, encoding profound socio-ecological rifts in the relations between humans and the environments they inhabit. The zombie is thus the ideal monster to allow us to think through nature–society relations under capitalism.

My understanding of zombies is shaped by a range of filmic and literary texts from across the Caribbean and the United States. They include both canonical zombie films and narratives as well as texts that are not usually included in zombie studies, thus breaking out of some well-defined disciplinary boundaries. This selection of texts has the advantage of making recent shifts within the mainstream zombie imaginary appear less sudden or unprecedented. Indeed, I would argue that these shifts become legible within a regional context during the "Long American Century." In some ways, this study follows in the footsteps of – but also departs from – important comparative approaches, perhaps most notably Sarah Lauro's *The Transatlantic Zombie* (2015).[4] It is also worth emphasising here what this book is *not*: it is not an anthropological engagement with the zombie as a figure of popular

---

2 De-zombification is a term used for zombies that seek to break out of their state and return to being fully human.

3 The zombie-figure has, of course, become a global phenomenon, and one could provide world-literary analyses of their appearance in contemporary texts from any number of locations: from Colombia to China, Nigeria to South Korea. However, my focus in this study is on the Americas, as the ground zero for the emergence of the modern zombie, and indeed of modernity itself.

4 With regard to comparative approaches, it is worth highlighting here the recent collection *Decolonizing the Undead: Rethinking Zombies in World-Literature, Film, and Media*, edited by Giulia Champion, Roxanne Douglas and Stephen Shapiro, which appeared after the present study had been completed.

oral culture in Haiti, embedded in the country's rich belief systems. There are other critics that are better placed to do this work.[5] This book focusses on the zombie as a literary and filmic figure *informed by* historically embedded oral cultures.

My work is also informed by recent scholarly work on world-ecology, which builds on previous thinking about the ways in which struggles over lands and environments and resistance against racism and sexism need to go hand in hand. As Jason W. Moore (2015) has convincingly argued, capitalism must be understood not only as an economic system, but as a specific way of organising human and extra-human natures in the *oikeos*. This organisation – the capitalist world-ecology – fundamentally depends on the "downgrading or devaluing of nature" (Mukherjee 2010: 66), something that has long been clouded by the fact that, under capitalism, "Society" and "Nature" *appear* as opposites, and capitalism *appears* to belong squarely to the realm of the former while only acting on the latter. In order to reproduce itself, capitalism relies both on the *exploitation* of human workers and the *appropriation* of both unpaid or de-valued work by the racialised and gendered majority and of "Cheap Natures," including natural resources such as minerals in the soil or fossil fuels. The history of capitalism is fundamentally ecological. On an ideological level, however, it relies on constantly redrawing the boundaries between "Nature" and "Society," which is done in such a way as to render invisible the appropriation of gendered and racialised work, tendentially conflated into the realm of "Nature."

Ecology of the Zombie focusses on the zombie in the Long American Century – the century of the figure's thorough globalisation, enabled through the new medium of film in the age of oil. In this investigation, the juxtaposition of Caribbean and US versions of the zombie is crucial, since the figure has been profoundly shaped by its move from Haiti at the periphery of capitalism to the core – and back, in its post-1968 incarnation, to the (semi-)periphery in more recent years. The relation between the Caribbean region and the US is crucial to understanding these trajectories. As Anthony Maingot and Wilfredo Lozano explain:

> No other region of the world has had a relationship with the U.S. similar to that of the Caribbean. For one, the dramatic asymmetry in power, accompanied by geographic proximity, made the region easily accessible to a variety of U.S. designs. Because these two factors, power and proximity, have not changed, there has been a substantial degree of continuity in the fundamental nature of U.S.–Caribbean relations. (2005: 1)

This asymmetric relationship is constitutive of a particular way of organising ecologies in the region, with highly detrimental socio-ecological effects, as we will see over the course of this book. It is this historical situation that

---

5 Paravisini-Gebert (1997), for instance, offers a brilliant take on zombies in their anthropological context.

has profoundly shaped the history of the zombie and its displacements. The challenge to read Caribbean representations of zombie figures alongside and in dialogue with US cinematic representations has been posed in earnest by writers such as Pedro Cabiya (2011), who deliberately juxtaposes Caribbean and US versions of the figure and, in the process, asks challenging questions regarding the meaning of this shape-shifting monster.

The central observation developed over the course of this book is that the zombie turns on the combination of – and shifting relations between – the logics of exploitation and appropriation under capitalism. The former refers to the form that oppression and power relations take when determined by capitalist value relations; the latter "to the various processes through which unpaid work/energy is identified, secured, and mobilized in service to value production" (Niblett 2020: 46). This is why, as we will see, it is difficult to define the zombie, or grasp its logic, since the figure can never represent these dynamics and processes as such.

Both appropriation and exploitation are fundamental to zombie imaginaries. Yet exploitation continues to be the more obvious and easily recognised feature of capitalism – and often also of Marxist accounts of the figure of the zombie. However, as Nancy Fraser writes, "expropriation is an ongoing, albeit unofficial, mechanism of accumulation, which continues alongside the official mechanism of exploitation" (2014: 50). Capitalism as a civilisation relies on the co-dependence of capitalist value – produced by exploitation – and not-value. The zombie has been remarkably versatile in its registration of forms of exploitation *and* appropriation, as we will see in Chapter 3, for instance, as we turn to zombified women.

It is crucial in this context that the zombie has never shed its background conditions of possibility – that is, its mythic roots in a society shaped by slavery. As has often been observed, the figure embodies the long legacies of a society that was structured around a genocidal colonial regime of slavery. Dehumanised and animalised, the zombie is "a being without essence— lobotomized, depersonalized, and reduced through black magic to a state of absolute impotence" (Glover 2010: 59). Yet this figure "of mourning" that carries within it the memory of slavery also embodies "the fear of the first modern industrial workers who were stripped of human dignity" (Murphy 2011: 48). The lives of the enslaved were profoundly modern, as C.L.R. James famously argued: working in industrial conditions, enslaved peoples often consumed imported food while the product of their labour was exported ([1938] 1991: 392). Indeed, it is their "modernity" that provides the key for the zombie's flexibility when it comes to registering both exploitation and appropriation. While producing value (embodied, for instance, in sugar) as living labour for the global market, enslaved Africans were brutally appropriated and transformed into commodities. Moreover, their appropriation was central to the emergence of modern capitalism, as Eric Williams ([1944] 1994) and others have shown.

Unlike historians who see capitalism emerging with the industrial revolution, world-systemic accounts emphasise that capitalism was built on mass murder and plunder as instantiated in the sugar plantations. From an ecological perspective, understanding that Caribbean sugar plantations were fundamental to the emergence of capitalism allows us to see the radical change in socio-ecological organisation that emerged through them. Sugar plantations in the Caribbean enabled, for the first time, global divisions not only of labour but also of natures, as Caribbean environments underwent the profound simplification via mono-cropping (which had disastrous, and now well-documented, short- and long-term effects for local ecosystems). The appropriation of racialised work, foundational to modern racism, is thus constitutively ecological. As a figure that, even in its revived twentieth-century form, still carries these legacies, the zombie therefore allows us to think of racism as a constitutive element of the capitalist world-ecology.

Revived in Haiti during the US occupation (1915–1934), the zombie in its classic form was a figure controlled by a sorcerer. Appropriation also played a central role in the globalisation of the zombie in the 1920s and 1930s – a soulless body that was either raised from the grave or had part of its soul stolen while still alive through the administration of poison. Without an individual will, the zombie thus becomes "a beast of burden that [the] master exploits without mercy, making him work in the fields, weighing him down with labour, whipping him freely and feeding him on meagre, taste-less food" (Métraux 1972: 282). The zombie is an agency-less, thingified being, made to work for someone else on someone else's lands, resonating with the legacies of slavery. But at this time it also registered the contemporary effects of the military occupation and financial takeover of Haiti by the US, including the imposition of a forced labour (*corvée*) system "for the purpose of constructing roads to facilitate military control in the countryside" (Renda 2001: 148). The figure also resonated with the displacement of scores of Haitian farmers by US agricultural projects. Indeed, as I argue in detail in Chapter 2, the emergence of US hegemony and the imperialist appropriation of land and lives in the Caribbean provide the most crucial and immediately relevant context for understanding the zombie over the course of the Long American Century.

So far, I have understood the zombie as a self-evident figure. However, as anyone familiar with zombie studies will know, one problem that plagues the field is precisely the question of definition – a question that I will address in more detail in Chapter 1. In the quest for the figure's origins, anthropologists have traced the figure back to African belief systems pre-dating the Middle Passage (Ackermann and Gauthier 1991). But while one must recognise these roots, there is also, as I have argued elsewhere, something "radically new and historically specific to its emergence in the plantation context" (Oloff 2012: 33). Further, the zombie exists within a whole continuum of figures, both in Haiti itself and the Caribbean more broadly. An important early variation of the zombie-of-the-body are the tales of zombies-of-the-spirit (body-less zombies), which also resemble other spectral figures found in Jamaica, Cuba and Surinam (Ackermann and Gauthier 1991: 484). It is, of course, the zombie-of-the-body

5

that has become the internationally recognised figure, and it is on this figure that my book is primarily focussed. But even this figure has shifted greatly, especially since 1968. This is equally true in Haitian literature, where zombies have ranged from the zombified mass of the population dominated by François Duvalier, to women confined to the "private" realm of the house, to villagers inhabiting a degraded landscape. In the international context, the zombie's instability is highlighted by high-profile debates over whether or when the zombie stops being a zombie.

Within colonial writing, the zombie and zombie-esque figures also do not emerge as unitary but range in type from spectral apparitions to shape-shifters to the animated dead (see Ellis 2000; Garraway 2005; Lauro 2015; Hoermann 2017). Indeed, the zombie "referred to a constellation of gothic properties related to slave culture in the Caribbean" (Ellis 2000: 218). While the zombie-of-the-spirit appeared at the end of the seventeenth century,[6] the zombie-of-the-body only appears from the late eighteenth century onwards in colonial texts. In British colonial ethnographic writing on the Caribbean, myths resembling the zombies-of-the body were embedded within racist depictions of Caribbean life. Bryan Edwards's *History, Civil and Commercial, of the British West Indies* (1793), for instance, focussed on the power of "Myal-men" to induce a "trance or profound sleep of a certain duration" followed by supposed reanimation from death (Edwards 1793: 88–89; quoted in Ellis 2000: 210). In French writer Michel-Etienne Descourtilz's *Voyage d'un naturaliste, et ses observations* (1809), a text equally steeped in notions of "'negro' savagery" (Daut 2015: 82), the "zombie" is also embodied, although it is here associated with severe poverty rather than witchcraft: it is used to describe a diseased, near-skeletal, elderly Haitian woman by her son as he rejects her (Descourtilz 1809: 220). In Irish writer Lafcadio Hearn's story "La Guiablesse" ([1890] 2001), it is a shape-shifting Martinican zombie that takes on the body of a beautiful Black woman, associated with a lost African past and a more "primitive" state, seemingly more in tune with "Nature." The zombie woman lures a cane-field worker away from the plantation and to his death in a ravine, in what we might read as a racialised eco-gynophobic climax. By the late nineteenth century, within the context of full-blown New Imperialism and its racialising ideologies, British colonial writers including Spenser St John and James Anthony Froude would evoke cannibalism and savagery alongside the herbal knowledge that is associated with the induction of a death-like state akin to zombification (see Kee 2011; Lauro 2015).

What this brief summary suggests is that attempts to seek a stable definition or origin of the zombie are not necessarily helpful. Zombies need to be placed

---

6 The earliest known written reference to a zombie spirit entity occurs in Pierre-Corneille Blessbois's *Le Zombi du Grand Perou, ou la Comtesse de Cocagne* (1697), a colonial misogynist satire that takes place on a sugar plantation in Guadeloupe and mocks the creole planter class's belief in local sorcery.

within the context of *zombie effects* – describing zombie-esque figures without the necessary gothic context. What we can say, then, is that zombies – and more broadly zombie effects – are clearly inscribed within a civilisation marked by the brutal objectification and immiseration of the colonised, which was, in turn, entwined with the appropriation and degradation of lands and soils. Further, their presence in colonial writing demonstrates that monstrous figures and zombie myths ascribed to the Caribbean have been circulating outside the Caribbean for a long time. As Lauro writes, "African-born mythology had influenced European culture far earlier than the zombie's introduction via cinema" (2015: 47). The version of the zombie found in Bryan Edwards's text in all likelihood influenced the depiction of the animated dead in two of the most famous Romantic texts – Samuel Coleridge's "Rime of the Ancient Mariner" and Mary Shelley's *Frankenstein* (see Fulford 2022: 3; Lauro 2015: 47; Warner 2002: 152) – in which ecophobia and a fear of the revolutionary potential unleashed by the Haitian and French Revolutions powerfully coalesce. The zombie-esque figure, it would appear, has long been a monster that registers the emergence of the capitalist world-ecology on both sides of the Atlantic.

I begin *Ecology of the Zombie* with an analysis of the classic version of the zombie – that of the working undead – which, I argue, holds clues for the zombie's trajectory across the Long American Century and provides a good heuristic starting point for its later transformations. It was at the beginning of the twentieth century, as a result of the US occupation of Haiti, that the zombie began to circulate in North America and the Caribbean, mainly through the newly emergent medium of film. From that point onwards, it becomes easier to identify spikes in its popularity. The quantity of zombie films in circulation has been mapped by Kyle Bishop in a graph that shows clear spikes in the 1970s, 1980s and from 2008 onwards (2010a: 14). Of course, the weakness of any such graph is what it renders invisible as well as visible: oral tales are excluded, as are texts that refuse to follow genre conventions. But what is most striking about Bishop's graph is that, while zombie films first appear in the 1930s and 1940s, the zombie figure explodes in the filmic imagination from the 1970s onwards. It is no surprise that it is during late neoliberal capitalism that the figure of the zombie-as-system becomes more prominent; we increasingly encounter zombie banks, zombie bankers, the zombie patriarchy, zombie debts and so forth. Why this should be so emerges as one of the most pressing questions of this book, the answer to which can be found in the zombie's trajectory. It is during the era of financialised capitalism that systemic long-term tendencies are coming to the fore, as capitalism increasingly turns inwards, destroying its own conditions of reproduction.

If, as I argue, rifts in ecological metabolisms lie at the very heart of the processes that animate the modern zombie figure, then it is not difficult to see why a figure from Haiti should have gained such international visibility, since it is a place that was subjected to these processes in the most brutal of fashions. Yet metabolic rifts are not limited to Haiti or the Caribbean.[7] While experienced more violently on what Robert Fatton refers to as the "outer periphery" (2014) of the capitalist world-system, they are also fundamental to capitalism more broadly, and are becoming increasingly pronounced. As McNally writes in *Monsters of the Market*, "[f]or capitalism to develop, customary ties between people and the land must be severed and communal obligations among people severed" (2011: 37). Rather than insisting on an original zombie figure, then, I proceed by placing the figure within a range of zombie effects, occurring both in the context of the Caribbean and in the mainland United States. The zombie – as the most paradigmatic of these zombie effects – retrospectively provides both a name and an imaginative device for figuring the intertwining of human and extra-human socio-ecological degradation. This way of proceeding will allow for a different perspective on the figure's journey – one that recognises that the zombie's insertion into American culture was certainly driven by racist and sensationalist ideologies that fed into Jim Crow ideologies at home. But one that also recognises that the zombie resonated with a range of experiences shaping the lives of the American working classes, from displaced farmers in Oklahoma to African American sharecroppers in Mississippi.

The central propositions of *Ecology of the Zombie*, then, can be expressed in the following three points that relate to each other throughout:

1. Zombies figure rifts in socio-ecological metabolisms.
2. Zombies are animated by processes through which capitalism reproduces itself as a historically specific, and environmentally destructive, way of organising natures; they thus figure changing sets of relations.
3. Zombies render visible capitalism's "absolute general law of environmental degradation" (Foster 1992: 77).

As we will see throughout the book, whether it is labouring in fields that she or he does not own, or walking through landscapes in search of human flesh, the zombie is generally disconnected from the body. Indeed, a ruptured connection to the land, to food production, to one's own body (and hence labour-force) and to knowledge production is key to the emergence and continued relevance of the zombie phenomenon. While Métraux's (1972: 282) classic definition of the zombie as a "beast of burden" has clearly shaped my understanding, my analysis soon departs from this specific incarnation of the zombie and reinserts it within a continuum of zombie figures. As McNally writes, "[r]ather than bringing a phenomenon under its demands, dialectical investigations are shaped by the characteristics of the object being explored" (2011: 117). The zombie's shape-shifting ways have partly given form to the chapters of this book, as I move from the sugar-zombie to

---

[7] I take the term "metabolic rifts" from eco-Marxist theory – I will explore this concept in more detail in Chapter 1.

the zombie-of-the-house to the petro-zombie and, finally, to the increasingly unmoored zombie of financialised capitalism.

***

In its different incarnations, the representation of the zombie is part of "world-literature" or, more broadly, "world-culture" (see WReC 2015). Rather than interpreting world literature as somehow defined by (and for) a systematic reader of texts, which would be broad enough to be both "too wide" as well as "too exclusive" (Damrosch 2003), we can think about it in relation to the capitalist world-system itself. If the term world-literature, or world-culture, is defined as registering the processes and logics shaping the capitalist world-system – that is, a system vitally linked through the massively uneven divisions of labour and production of goods, food and raw materials (Chase-Dunn and Grimes 1995: 389) – then a new version of world-literature (now hyphenated) becomes visible. The monstrous offers particularly illuminating ways of conducting world-literary research, since it cuts across a variety of genres, media and high/low divisions, and tends to cluster around the pressure points of the world-system. But this does not mean that all instantiations of the zombie figure are necessarily critical – precisely because the figure is immanent within a number of the processes shaping this world-system. Indeed, it can easily, and regularly does, turn into a justification for racism, sexism and militarisation. Historically, zombies have often functioned as rhetorical devices serving the re-entrenchment of imperial, racial, gender and class divides, racialising and othering already exploited and marginalised groups. Worryingly, zombies are also thoroughly embedded in US gun culture and have been employed by right-wing groups as a justification for gun violence (Baker 2013). And yet, because the figure has been immanent in these processes, it has also functioned as an excellent analytic tool. As Paget Henry observed in his seminal work on Afro-Caribbean philosophy, *Caliban's Reason*, for historical reasons to do with the formation of disciplines under the conditions of colonialism, Afro-Caribbean philosophy mainly unfolded in novelistic form "as an intertextually embedded discursive practice" (2000: 2). This observation holds true for many of the texts examined in this book that employ the zombie figure to examine the logic of world-systemic processes.

What, then, is to be gained from reading zombie movies alongside a range of novels that do not normally occupy the same space of enquiry? Do we not lose some of the specificity that generically or nationally organised studies can produce? Perhaps. But as I will briefly demonstrate with two examples, I believe that much is to be gained as a more multi-layered, world-historical perspective on the zombie emerges. My first example is *Myal* (1988), a zombie novel by Jamaican novelist Erna Brodber that does not follow hegemonic zombie genre conventions, although it does sit squarely within a Caribbean tradition of zombie novels. The second is *Dawn of the Dead* (1978), a classic zombie movie by the US director George A. Romero, which has helped to define the hegemonic form the zombie now takes. Both texts post-date the global oil crisis of 1973 that occurred within the context of a global crisis of capitalism and prepared the way for the emergence of neoliberalism. At a time when Romero had already popularised the cannibalistic zombie hordes within a globally hegemonic US imaginary, Brodber's novel builds on Caribbean literary predecessors, in which the zombie tends to be a victim rather than an aggressor. Romero's zombie apocalypse movie, on the other hand, depicts the zombies as cannibals – as would many of the movies that followed. Yet, famously, it is also highly critical of US society and, as we will see, of the interrelated racial and ecological regimes that define it.

To start, it is important to note that Jamaica and the US were differently affected by neoliberalisation. For countries such as Jamaica, under-developed by decades of colonialism, the global crisis of the 1970s translated into increasing levels of debt, which, in the 1980s, would be turned into a mechanism for further rounds of capitalist expropriation. Through the enforcement of Structural Adjustment Programmes (SAPs) by the US-dominated World Bank and the International Monetary Fund (IMF), local (food) industries were destroyed and austerity measures imposed, including through the devaluation of the Jamaican dollar. Neoliberalisation, which forced the opening of international markets, was marked by the establishment of foreign-owned Free Trade Zones (FTZs) across the Caribbean, largely staffed by women (as cheaper workers) and mainly belonging to the apparel industry. In other words, neoliberalisation is the form that accumulation-by-dispossession took in this period. The US, on the other hand, saw the rise of shopping malls where the garments produced in the FTZs at below average cost would be consumed. These were coupled with the longer trends of ongoing deindustrialisation, outsourcing, rising levels of debt and rising unemployment, especially among African Americans. The shopping mall, which becomes Romero's symbolic location in *Dawn of the Dead*, was reliant on pre-existing American car culture but also intensified metabolic rifts between consumers and producers.

These interrelated realities are registered in both zombie texts. *Myal*, as has been pointed out, represents a community that is both "intensely local and allegorized as national" (Puri 2004: 145). But it is also explicitly allegorised as world-historical – or, one might even say, *world-ecological*. Brodber turns to the early twentieth century (1913–1919), a moment marked by the shift from British and European hegemony to the emergence of US hegemony. The shift is allegorised through the dual zombification of the light-skinned and mixed-race central character, Ella. She is first zombified by the colonial school system, to which she is rendered particularly susceptible by her outsider status within the community and resultant identification with an imagined England that bears little resemblance to actuality. In an evocative scene in the second chapter, we encounter her as a young schoolgirl, unquestioningly reciting two Rudyard Kipling's poems for a school performance. She starts with "Big Steamers" (1899), in which coal-powered steam ships are celebrated for transporting food around the British Empire:

"Oh, where are you going to all you Big Steamers
With England's own coal, up and down salt seas?"
"We are going to fetch you your bread and your butter
Your beef, pork, and mutton, apples and cheese."

"And where will you fetch it from, all you Big Steamers
And where shall I write you when you are away?"
"We fetch it from Melbourne, Quebec and Vancouver
Address us as Hobart, Hong Kong and Bombay." (Brodber 1988: 5)

Kipling's poem unabashedly celebrates the first global food regime (1870–1930), which "combined colonial tropical imports to Europe with basic grains and livestock imports from settler colonies, provisioning emerging European industrial classes, and underwriting the British 'workshop of the world'" (McMichael 2009: 141). The environmental impact of the outsourcing of food production to the colonies and former settler colonies is beyond the conceptual framework (or interest) of Kipling's poem. Monocultural production is highly destructive of local ecosystems and compromised the food self-sufficiency of Caribbean islands, while the over-exploitation of soils in the settler colonies also had dramatic and devastating effects. But to return to *Myal*, Ella's recital continues with the now infamous Kipling poem "The White Man's Burden" (1899), in which the colonised are declared "half devil and half child" and thus in need of paternalistic guidance (Brodber 1988: 6). Her recital, which takes place in the year preceding the conflagration between imperial powers in 1914, is focussed only on performance and not on content. It thus unwittingly and uncritically celebrates the increasing "globalisation" of food-getting alongside the masculinist racism that is woven into the very fabric of imperialist competition between European powers.

The second zombification takes place when Ella is in her twenties and married to a US American called Selwyn, at a time when the US military is occupying Haiti and the Dominican Republic, and US capital is reshaping Caribbean landscapes. While the occupations are not mentioned, Selwyn's treatment of her resembles the repackaging of the Caribbean as exotic commodity in US imperial discourse of the time. Selwyn treats Ella and her memories as entertainment to be consumed by a US audience. Using his inherited wealth, with roots in monopoly capitalism, Selwyn proposes to "expand the family business to movie houses" (Brodber 1988: 80). He transforms the memories he has extracted from Ella into a "coon show," which he plans to bring to the silver screen. As he notes, what "Ella had given him was of the purest gold. He only had to refine it" (1988: 79). The metaphor employed for this process inscribes it clearly within colonial and imperial processes of capitalist extraction and plunder. The resultant show, "*Caribbean Days and Nights*," is vaguely based on Ella's narrative but curiously detached from locality and full of racist stereotypes: "Everybody's hair was in plaits and stood on end [...] Ella was the star. He had given her flowing blond hair. Our heroine was chased by outstretched black hands grabbing at her" (1988:

83–84). While there are no zombies in this "coon show," the set-up here might be read as an implicit commentary on the racial dynamics of the early zombie films, including most famously Victor Halperin's *White Zombie* (1932) and Jacques Tourneur's *I Walked with a Zombie* (1943), which turned on imperial fears about the potential racial contagion of the blonde, white heroine, as we will see in more detail in later chapters. As Cedric Robinson explains, as an "instrument of American capital," the early movie industry was profoundly intertwined with "the stitching together" of a new racial regime "from the remnants of its predecessors and new cloth accommodating the disposal of immigrants, colonial subjects, and insurgencies amongst the native poor" (2007: xv, xiv).

Yet the show also renders visible something else: a drive towards food delocalisation, as knowledge of local ecological conditions and natural cycles become increasingly irrelevant. This delocalisation is very explicitly set within a racist world-order. As Ella observes:

> This Grove town in which Selwyn set his play, had to be the most fruitful place in the whole world and one which respected no seasons. There were breadfruits at the same time as there were star-apples as there were mangoes. Selwyn knew nothing about Easter as star-apple time; mid-summer for mangoes and the end of summer, the breadfruit season. (Brodber 1988: 83)

On the level of plot, this ignorance is specifically Selwyn's. And yet we might say that the ignorance of natural cycles and seasons is also a tendency within capitalist agriculture, as would have been quite noticeable by the time of writing in the 1980s. Supermarkets enable consumers to ignore the seasonal specificities of the places they live in as they buy foods that have been imported from across the globe. The scene also links us back to the poems Ella had recited in her schooldays, with their celebration of imperial foodways and Britain's capacity to transport food around the Empire. These (neo-)imperial links are already present, even if they would become more clearly visible in the 1990s.

In this context, it becomes clear why the novel chooses the zombie as its preferred conceptual device. Zombification is explained as spirit theft, which leaves people as "[f]lesh that takes direction from someone" (Brodber 1988: 108). While firmly inscribed within a regional context, the figure also strongly resonates with Marxist definitions of the alienation of the worker under capitalism found in *Myal*: zombification "separate[s] people from themselves, separate[s] man from his labour" (1988: 37). But most significantly for the present context, the text highlights the ecological character of this separation in a conversation between Ella and Reverend Simpson. Ella has become a schoolteacher and is required to teach her pupils a paternalist colonial fable in which farm animals rebel, only to find out that they cannot survive by themselves and that the farmer supposedly had their best interests at heart. The comparison of the colonised with animals in a fable is built on the intertwined colonialist-capitalist processes of the dehumanisation of colonial subjects and the instrumentalisation of animals. The "difference between human and non-human [is presented] as [one of] inferiority" (Mukherjee 2010: 55), and colonial subjects are inscribed within "Nature" in opposition to the supposedly rational space of civilisation. When questioned by an infuriated Ella, Reverend Simpson explains the animals' fate as one of zombification, in which the author has "[t]aken their knowledge of their original and natural world away from them and left them empty shells – duppies, zombies, living deads capable only of receiving orders from someone else and carrying them out" (Brodber 1988: 107). Echoing the classic definition of the zombie as a soulless body working on a plantation, Reverend Simpson's definition encapsulates the alienation of the colonised from the lands she inhabits, from her own body and from the knowledge her community produces. Brodber's brilliant exposition of zombification as environmental history thus holds crucial clues for our understanding of the ecology of zombies more broadly.

Brodber's novel is not the only text to render explicit the zombie's ecology, however, and I here want to turn to the second example, released only a few years earlier and rarely, if ever, studied within the same context. Romero's satirical *Dawn of the Dead* (1978) – a classic zombie film – was the second of the famous "Dead" trilogy, including *Night of the Living Dead* (1968) and *Day of the Dead* (1985). All three films focussed to some extent on the way in which oil shapes our everyday lives, as well as our increasing alienation from natural environments. As I argue in detail in Chapter 5, the first film of the trilogy, *Night of the Living Dead*, offers a critique of oil-fuelled agro-industrialisation and de-peasantisation as well as the accompanying rise of car culture and urbanisation. Romero's second "Dead" film provides a rather more obvious critique of consumerism: a group of survivors seek refuge from the zombie apocalypse in Monroeville mall in Pennsylvania. While it offers them plenty of food, clothing and a wide array of other commodities, zombies are ironically attracted to the mall by force of habit, by "[s]ome kind of instinct," as one of the characters puts it. Throughout the film, the differences between zombies and humans are eroded as both turn out to be "insatiable consumers" (Paffenroth 2006: 57) drawn to this "cavernous temple to American consumerism" (Russell 2007: 91).

Yet rather than merely a nightmarish vision of consumerism as claimed by McNally, the film also contains a systemic critique of capitalism. José Fernández Gonzalo, for instance, reads the film as exposing capitalism as a system that renews itself through violent expansion and intensification, functioning like a zombie pandemic that expands to "cover everything, raze everything," subordinating "even leisure time" to the logic of the market (2011: 43, 45). I here want to suggest that the film's critique of capitalism is also explicitly ecological. Indeed, the film signposts that the archetypal mall constitutes a new way of organising nature–society relations – one that not only entrenches a militarised notion of private ownership based on violence and racialised inequality, but is also completely dominated by oil and deepening metabolic rifts. From the first aerial shot of the mall surrounded

Ecology of the Zombie

by a massive parking lot, the viewer is reminded of its dependence on and inscription within car culture. The mall functions as a hub through which consumers access a range of commodities, from food to clothes; to each of these commodities spectrally cling concrete labour and bio-physical nature. Neither humans nor zombies "have the need (or perhaps more importantly, the ability) to produce the goods themselves" (Bishop 2010b: 235). This alienation from local environments and production is most memorably symbolised in Romero's zombie hordes that shamble, aimlessly, across fields and streets, without ever stopping to produce or make anything – unlike the zombies of the 1930s who, in *White Zombie* (Halperin 1932), were commandeered by their masters to "work long hours" without complaining. Humans, as Romero's film tells us, resemble these zombies – controlled by the hidden forces of capital – but they also resemble shop mannequins (made from plastic and thus oil), as is visually emphasised through repeated contrasting shots.

If Romero's film is highly allegorical when it comes to its critique of consumerism, this is also true for its critique of petro-fuelled capitalism. In a famous scene set to polka music, in which the viewer is offered a concatenation of different commodities, "Nature" remains conceptually and allegorically at the centre: repeatedly, we see the zombies stumble across the little artificial island at the centre of the mall, which is planted with fake trees and plants assembled around a fountain. While the fields that the zombies walked across in the aerial shots of the shopping mall were also human-produced, this little island flaunts its artificiality, while simultaneously playing on the nostalgia for "untouched nature" at the heart of late capitalist modernity. Money and the commodity form appear to mediate our access to "Nature." To drive home this point, in one metonymic shot, a zombie sits in the mall's fountain, contemplating the coins he has picked up. As if this scene did not make its point clearly enough, it is further spliced with shots of the chiming clock tower, allegorising the domination of abstract time to which all zombies and humans are subordinated.

Fig. 1. *Dawn of the Dead* (Romero, 1978). A zombie, sitting down in an artificial fountain, counting the money that's fallen into the water.

Introduction

Just like in *Night of the Living Dead*, Romero made use of an actual location for the scenes in the shopping mall – a shopping mall located in Monroeville, Pennsylvania. And yet, as it is turned into setting, this location of everyday life becomes something different. As the Warwick Research Collective (WReC) writes, paraphrasing Herbert Marcuse, art "possesses the means to estrange and subvert the quotidian by defying dominant social practices and ordinary modes of consciousness" (2015: 83). The absurdity of the everyday, rendered visible by the zombie proliferation, is thus objectified and becomes graspable. The metabolic rifts of everyday life, widened by oil, which is mostly invisible in its structuring of American lives, are suddenly foregrounded. The alienation from nature, again usually only experienced in muffled form, becomes visible on the big screen.

What is more difficult to grasp in Romero's film is the uneven relation between the Caribbean periphery and the US core, which in Brodber's text was allegorised in the relation between Ella and Selwyn. As briefly mentioned above, with the neoliberalisation of the world-economy, Jamaica, Haiti and other islands had been opened up to foreign assembly manufacturers, who favoured the Caribbean because of the "abundance of cheap labor, the containment of all labor discontent, the generous fiscal concessions of the government, and the proximity […] to the USA" (Dupuy 2014: 84). These garment assembly companies located in the Caribbean function as subcontractors for many popular US chains, including JC Penney (a store featured in Romero's 1978 film). Fredric Jameson has linked this "spatial disjunction" to the "inability to grasp the way the system functions as a whole" from a position at the core ([1988] 2016: n.p.). While Jameson wrote about an earlier colonial moment, his observations here hold true: "daily life and existential experience in the metropolis […] can now no longer be grasped immanently; it no longer has its meaning, its deeper reason for being, within itself" (2016: n.p.). Instead, an increased fetishism of commodities takes hold even as US domination remains plainly visible on the periphery.

In *Dawn of the Dead*, Romero does not explicitly make any reference to the Caribbean as a place where clothing and other items are produced by low-waged labour while local agriculture is eroded. However, the film does, from the very start, highlight that capitalism is inherently racist, unequal and based on violence. In this context, it seems significant that one of the pockets of resistance in the film is associated with Puerto Ricans. Before the surviving characters set out to the famous shopping mall by helicopter, a SWAT team and the National Guard are shown attacking a building in Philadelphia inhabited by Puerto Ricans and African Americans, on the grounds that the latter had refused to kill "their" zombies, to whom they still display an attachment. For them, the police force turns out to be more dangerous than the zombies, as the film plays on the Caribbean tradition of representing the zombie as a victim rather than a victimiser.

If in *Night of the Living Dead* we see resonances of the civil rights struggles of the 1960s, in *Dawn* we encounter echoes of the Puerto Rican struggle for

15

autonomy in Chicago and New York, as fought by the Young Lords in the 1960s and early 1970s. These fights were also anti-capitalist and involved demands for community gardens along with a whole series of other issues, including investment in children's education, self-determination for all Latin Americans as well as Third World countries, equality for women and reorganisation for a socialist society. Consider these lines from Nuyorican poet Pedro Pietri's *Puerto Rican Obituary*, first read out in 1969, in this context:

> They worked
> They worked
> They worked
> and they died
> [...]
> All died yesterday today
> and will die again tomorrow
> passing their bill collectors
> on to the next of kin
> All died
> waiting for the garden of eden
> to open up again
> under a new management
> [...]
> All died
> hating the grocery stores
> that sold them make-believe steak
> and bullet-proof rice and beans
> All died waiting dreaming and hating
> [...]
> They were born dead
> and they died dead ([1969] 2000: 15–19).

In this poem, Pietri laments the destruction of solidarity and collectivity in the context of the individualist ambitions of the American Dream, which turns out to be an illusion. Images of death-in-life and work-in-death abound in this critique of the racism on which the United States is founded. Bound up in this vision of racist America are questions of access to green spaces and food plots, as even the "garden of eden" is subordinated to the logic of capital and healthy food is out of reach. Through its reference to Puerto Rican resistance and their siding with the zombies, Romero's film thus offers a vision of resistance against the racist violence of the police force as well as the state that underpins the capitalist world-ecological regime we find allegorised in the shopping mall.

What I have aimed to show with this juxtaposition of *Myal* and *Dawn of the Dead* is that reading the zombie across the United States and the Caribbean allows us to paint a larger picture of the zombie as a figure embedded in, and shaped by, the unevenness of the capitalist world-system, which becomes visible within this regional context. Rather than narrating the cultural history

Introduction

of the zombie in US cinema, or in specific Caribbean locations, this book thus seeks to put pressure on the ways in which the zombie figure is remade in different contexts, as it responds to the global logics shaping and degrading socio-ecological realities in different locations, with differing effects and results. Inspired by the recent zombie revival in Puerto Rico and Cuba, where writers have tended to emphasise the multiple histories of the zombie and then pitted them against each other, I aim to tell a cultural history of the zombie that is self-consciously world-cultural in the sense that it is placed within the context of an uneven and combined capitalist modernity. This approach enables us to render visible its history as a representational device that gestures towards the capitalist logics shaping the contemporary world-system. The zombie does not simply or passively possess an environmental history; rather, it gestures towards the logics shaping, reshaping and degrading global ecologies and is simultaneously reshaped by them.

***

This book engages with resistant zombie imaginaries as a mode of thought that enables us to think through the relations between extra-human nature and variously racialised, gendered and classed human populations in the capitalist world-ecology. In Chapter 1, I seek to render visible a theoretical framework for the history of the zombie in the Long American Century. Drawing on recent work conducted in the fields of world-ecology, world-literature and social reproduction theory, I read the zombie as a frontier figure that is animated by the interlinked logics of exploitation and appropriation. I contend that the zombie is a figure that narrates relations-in-motion and therefore cannot be defined as a stable transhistorical figure. In Chapter 2, I turn to the 1930s, which saw a proliferation of zombies and zombie effects across a number of different locations and genres. Viewing the crisis of the 1930s, heralded by the Wall Street Crash, from the perspective of today is instructive, since today's economic and environmental crisis has its roots in the former. Reading comparatively, I examine the sugar-zombie alongside zombie-esque figures that map the exhaustion of former commodity frontiers. In Chapters 4 and 5, I turn to the questions of gender and energy, respectively. Significantly, the Haitian tradition of tales of female zombification existed alongside that of tales of workers' alienation. In US films, women-zombies became misrecognised as (or else synonymous with) US culture, coded as white, passive and "under threat" by miscegenation. Yet the texts of several Caribbean and American writers bring out the ecology of the racialised monstrous feminine, seeking to re-visibilise the systemic links between gendered sexual violence, the exploitation of natural resources and unpaid or "cheap-ened" work. Questions of energy – human and extra-human – have also long been implicit in zombie tales, especially since the advent of film, petromodernity's prime art form. But from the mid-century onwards, (non-)access to (particularly fossil-fuelled) energy increasingly becomes a main focus, as illustrated by *Night of the Living Dead*. Chapter 6, finally, turns its focus to the period that has provided the most fertile ground for zombie imaginaries: neoliberal or "late" capitalism, which has seen numerous zombie spikes of unprecedented proportions. The variety of zombie figures is such that many critics have often classed it as untheorisable (Shapiro 2014). Yet, as I argue here, they register the contradictions within late capitalism, as viewed from different locations within a fundamentally uneven world-system. Further, especially after 2008, it is becoming easier to recognise that the crisis of capitalism *is* the crisis of the capitalist world-ecology. Climate change, widespread environmental degradation, animal extinctions, increasing levels of poverty, debt and inequality and the virulent renascence of racism and sexism are all constitutive elements of the crisis of capitalism. The zombie then turns into the most relevant monster of what many commentators call the Anthropocene, but which, following Jason W. Moore, I prefer to term the Capitalocene, for reasons explored in more detail in Chapter 5.

CHAPTER 1

Greening Zombie Theory

> Erosion and deforestation are, for our mountains, what zombification is for the people.
>
> René Depestre, 1979

> It is self-evident that where things and their interrelations are conceived, not as fixed, but as changing, their mental images, the ideas, are likewise subject to change and transformation, and they are not encapsulated in rigid definitions, but are developed in their historical or logical process of formation.
>
> Friedrich Engels, 1894

The imaginative link between zombification and what is broadly called "Nature" is not new. Indeed, I would argue that the zombie is animated by historically specific material, economic, ideological, semiotic and social struggles over "Nature" – a term that, far from being self-evident, is employed to name, codify and help produce shifting sets of relations between humans, non-human animals and the environments they inhabit. As Raymond Williams writes, "the idea of nature contains, though often unnoticed, an extraordinary amount of history" (1980: 67). These struggles over "Nature" have occupied many of the producers – writers, poets and film-makers – of zombie texts for much of the Long American Century. Sometimes, the connection between zombification and "Nature" is drawn consciously and critically, as we have already seen in Erna Brodber's *Myal* (1988) – a text that is part of a literary tradition that links zombification and socio-ecological metabolic ruptures explicitly. At other times, this connection irrupts in a less conscious fashion, as zombies inhabit hostile, degraded landscapes. Often, zombies become themselves a threatening image of humans reduced to their bodies and instincts – to their "animal functions" (Marx 1984: 74). Occasionally they are transformed into examples of "unnatural" monsters defying, as dead but walking corpses, the laws of physics, going against natural cycles and energy flows. In other words, beyond films and texts that consciously address environmental concerns, anxieties around historical ecological regimes might be said to animate even zombie imaginaries that do not seem to be explicitly *about* the environment.

In scholarly research on zombies, the ecology of the zombie figure has recently begun to receive more attention (see, for instance, Lauro 2011; Oloff 2012; Ferrer-Medina 2015). This is no doubt because of the increasing visibility of pressing global environmental issues such as climate change, animal extinctions and environmental degradation, which shed a different light on the history of this figure. Sarah Lauro, one of the most authoritative voices in zombie scholarship, refers to the eco-zombie as a "new phenomenon" of zombie novels and films in which the undead result from "some gross mistreatment of nature," from "the abuses of the planet by capitalist industry," or from the "effects of Global Warming" (2011: 54, 61–62). Yet far from staying within this more limited view of the relation between zombies and "Nature," Lauro then proceeds to embed the eco-zombie within a longer zombie history, evoking what she calls the "natural" zombie as a precursor and tracing a shift from the critique of science to the naming of capitalism as the culprit (2011: 54). Aren't "all zombie stories […] eco-zombie narratives," she asks, for "they are all concerned to some degree with humanity's mistreatment of nature, a broad category which includes at times, mankind itself" (2011: 61). This is, indeed, an excellent starting point for our enquiry into the ecology of the zombie.

Another ecocritical take is proffered by Patricia Ferrer-Medina, who traces the figure to its long ecological roots in colonialism. As she shows, the dehumanised zombie's obsession with struggles over "Nature" must be related to the ideological, material and political struggles over the humanity of indigenous populations during colonialism, as manifested in the Valladolid debate on indigenous peoples in 1550–1551 (2015: 32–33). Following ecofeminists such as Val Plumwood, she reads the appropriation of human lives as constitutive of environmental history: part of humanity is aligned with an externalised "Nature" that is seen as the binary opposite of "Reason" and "Civilisation." For Ferrer-Medina, the zombie comes to embody a radical "ecological alterity" to this order (2015: 30). Yet, arguably, the zombie's registration of capitalist destruction, plunder and the violent reorganisation of "Nature" – which includes the dehumanisation of the majority of humanity – makes it less a figure of "ecological alterity" than one that points towards the historical natures produced by capitalism, which for its reproduction relies on both capitalised and non-capitalised natures.[1]

---

1 On a separate point, Ferrer-Medina also problematically leaves the door open to, and even quotes, a Malthusian vision of the zombie horde as articulated by the director, Marc Forster, of the film *World War Z* (Ferrer-Medina 2015: 37). According

In this initial chapter, I am seeking to clarify my own framework for an eco-materialist understanding of the zombie, which relies centrally on world-systemic and world-ecological critiques of capitalism – the system that has made the externalisation and objectification of "Nature" a central feature of modernity. While Ferrer-Medina correctly embeds the zombie in a longer history of ideological, material and political struggles over "Nature," I argue that it was over the course of the Long American Century that the zombie increasingly turned into a narrative device for the dynamics shaping the capitalist world-ecology, which it registered at times critically and at times unconsciously. I do not offer a stable definition of the zombie beyond my initial starting point of the zombie-of-the-body (and even that definition is eventually abandoned when we examine John Torres' largely immaterial zombies in his poem collection *Undead* [2013]). Instead, I propose the following: what if the "zombie" names not a fixed figurative device, but rather an effort to figure shifting sets of relations? If zombies are animated by the "inner logic of capitalism" (Shaviro 1993: 63), then we must allow for changes to the zombie figure as it is revived at different moments within irreducibly specific contexts. Once we accept a less stable definition of the zombie as a figure that narrates capitalist dynamics, then it has to follow that the zombie cannot be understood as a transhistorical figurative device that, detached from its historical moorings, travels through space and time. Zombies are profoundly dialectical figures that cannot be reduced to an abstracted figurative device – despite having congealed into a recognisable, marketable figure. While I, too, have embarked on my argument from one specific instantiation of the zombie as "the beast of burden" (Métraux 1972: 282), I will proceed to follow its dynamics – moving from the sugar-zombie and the post-sugar-zombie, to the zombie-of-the-house, the petro-zombie and finally to the zombie-as-waste – over the course of this book.

Zombie Logic and World-Literature

One of the central academic contexts for this study is the current debate around "world literature." From the standpoint of hegemonic definitions of this term, a focus on the zombie would seem counterintuitive, given that "world literature" is frequently taken to refer to a canon of so-called masterworks, a select example of "high culture," whereas zombies tend to carry the associative burden of low or "popular culture" (despite the fact that many zombie texts *are* classed as literary fictions, as we have seen in the case of *Myal*). Yet the work done by a network of world-literary

---

to Forster, the zombie apocalypse represents the "problem" of over-population. Yet materialist critics point out that the level of resource utilisation and pollution are not causally linked to population growth and that we instead need to turn our analysis to the system through which resources are consumed (see Pirani 2018).

materialist critics radically changes the parameters of this field of study, leaving behind its idealist and dehistoricising tendencies and pushing beyond the exclusive focus on high literary fictions. The Warwick Research Collective (WReC) repositions the "world" in world literature as referring to the modern capitalist world-system. How might the zombie sit within this world-system? The world-system, they argue, constitutes the ultimate horizon of (the now hyphenated) "world-literature" – or, more broadly, "world-culture" (WReC 2015: 8). In that context, zombies appear less out of place and arguably offer a particularly compelling case study, since they not only help to map the unevenness of the system, unveiling its mechanisms through their travels and transformations, but also gesture towards its constitutive logic.

One of the problems thrown up by this approach is, of course, the sheer volume of texts one might face, since the adjective "world-literary" does not imply a judgement on literary quality and thus opens the door to an immeasurably large body of works. But, as Franco Moretti put it, "world literature is not an object, it's a *problem*, and a problem that asks for a new critical method" (2000: 55). To a certain extent, there is an analogy to be drawn here with zombie scholarship. While academic zombie studies still tend to be confined by generic, linguistic and national boundaries, a world-systemic approach cannot merely be additive as this would not only immediately reach its limits of possibility, but also risk not adding much to currently available insights. The zombie must therefore equally be approached as "a problem," and attention must be paid to its relation to "the underlying structures and conditions produced by the international division of labour," *and* to the logics that shape it (Graham, Niblett and Deckard 2012: 465). Such an approach would follow in the footsteps of work, not only by the WReC, but also by zombie critics such as Dave McNally (2011; 2017), Steven Shaviro (2002) and Sarah Lauro (2011; 2015), who have analysed zombie history in dialectical relation to a theory and history of (colonialist and imperialist) capitalism.

My approach also builds on the imaginative work of a whole range of novelists and film-makers who have employed the zombie to think critically about the processes structuring the capitalist world-system. Zombies, as is well known, are double-edged: they often reinforce dominant racist, sexist and ecophobic ideologies as they are firmly part of the processes that shape capitalist exploitation and appropriation. Over the course of this book, we will encounter several examples of these – even if my emphasis tends to fall on their critical employments. It is, of course, precisely because zombies are often immanent in racist, sexist and environmentally destructive regimes that they also provide an excellent tool for critical texts to disentangle their workings. Further, even texts that work hegemonically never completely erase the zombie's resistant potential; as McNally reminds us, "the process of taming subversive impulses is never total; something always exceeds and resists its grasp" (2017: 125). As we will see, this is demonstrated by the principal zombie text that transported the figure into the US imaginary: William Seabrook's travelogue, *The Magic Island* (1929).

As I argue above, the zombie is essentially modern. But the figure is also essentially *modernist*. Central to the WReC perspective is the notion of a single modernity that names the way in which world-systemic processes and capitalist social relations are lived and experienced. In contrast to often hostile assertions of a supposed Marxist tendency to homogenise, they emphasise that modernity is "everywhere irreducibly specific" (2015: 12), while possessing common structural and systemic characteristics and being shaped by the logics of exploitation and appropriation. One of the fundamental characteristics of the world-system is its "*unevenness,* the historically determinate 'coexistence,' in any given place and time, 'of realities from radically different moments of history – handicrafts alongside the great cartels, peasant fields with the Krupp factories or the Ford plant in the distance'" (Jameson, quoted in WReC 2015: 12). Further, if modernity names the way in which the contradictions of the capitalist world-system are experienced and lived, then modern*ism* in WReC's definition refers to the formal qualities of literary and cultural artefacts through which the structural unevenness of modernity is registered. Unevenness – an inevitable product of the logics shaping the zombie – plays a central role in zombie aesthetics. Whether coded as a difference marked by horror or "primitive" otherness, or historicised as an effect of the imperial takeover of lands, zombie effects are, as we will see, inherently marked by the unevenness of capitalism. In the twentieth-century sugar-cane novel, the zombie-as-enslaved-worker is bound to modern agribusiness fuelled by oil, as brutal, direct exploitation exists alongside technical innovation. By definition, zombie texts – which can take on various different styles and genres – display these temporal disjunctions, literalised in the phantasmagoric tales of the living undead that embody a degraded past that refuses to die.

For the current context, it is also important to highlight that a world-ecological understanding of capitalism underpins much of the world-literary scholarship to date, yoking literary criticism to an understanding of capitalism as a systemically patterned way of organising nature on a global scale. As Michael Niblett writes,

> world literature is also the literature of the capitalist world-ecology: this too is its interpretive horizon. To put it another way, world literature will necessarily register ecological regimes and revolutions [...] since these organize in fundamental ways the material conditions, social modalities, and areas of experience upon which literary form works. (2012b: 20)

Of course, the capitalist world-ecology as interpretative horizon is not always and everywhere easily perceptible. As Fredric Jameson has observed, "[n]o one had ever seen that totality, nor is capitalism ever visible as such, but only in its symptoms" ([2011] 2014: 6). Capitalism is fundamentally built on "structures of denial," which have been analysed by Karl Marx, most influentially perhaps in his examination of capitalism's "hidden abode" in Volume 1 of *Capital* ([1867] 1990; McNally 2011: 6). Yet Marx's "hidden abode of production," structurally occluded by capitalism, represses the even more hidden abode of reproduction (Fraser 2014: 60). It is this interdependence of production and reproduction, of productivity and plunder, that a world-ecology perspective seeks to render visible.

In literary texts, the "registration" of the interpretative horizon of the world-system is, of course, not always coincident with a literary text's conscious mapping thereof. Nor is it (necessarily) related to a critical or even conscious position vis-à-vis the world-system. But as we will see in more detail later, capitalist dynamics do become more graspable at moments of global ecological and economic crisis, or at moments of the rapid intensification and/or expansion of capitalisation, contrasting with our usually "muffled [experience of capitalism] as a result of the hegemony of everyday expectations and interactions" (Shapiro 2014: 202). Hence, we might not be surprised to find that key periods for zombie visibility were the 1930s, 1970s, 1980s and early 2000s onwards, peaking in the current ongoing crisis. Moreover, capitalism's symptoms are more visible, "immediate and pressing" in peripheralised locations, most prominently in the postcolonial (semi-)peripheries, which for centuries have been subjected to the brutal theft of resources and soil fertility (Niblett 2012b: 20). Since the Caribbean is one of the areas most affected by the climate emergency and ecological degradation, it is unsurprising that recent Caribbean zombie texts have tended to inscribe the figure within these threatening realities. As we see in Chapter 5, there is a noticeable tendency for current Caribbean zombie imaginaries to employ multiple time frames, placing current crises in longer contexts and thus offering a history of the present.

From a world-ecology perspective, capitalism's "structures of denial" do not only possess an environmental dimension but are themselves inherently ecological. Central to capitalism is an understanding of "Nature" as external and commodifiable, rather than as the matrix of life including that of human animals and their constructions. This manifests in the (gendered and racialised) separation of the realms of *production*, associated with "Civilisation," and *reproduction* associated with "Nature." Various all-too-familiar dualisms underpin this separation on an ideological level, limiting the ways in which nature–society relations under capitalism are, and can be, understood. The "master model of modernity" organises the modern perception of the world around a series of binaries, including culture/nature, reason/nature, male/female, mind/body, master/slave, rationality/animality, civilised/primitive, public/private (Plumwood 1993: 42–43). These dualisms enable "the denial of dependence on biospheric processes, and a view of humans as apart, outside of nature, which is treated as a limitless provider without needs of its own" (Plumwood 1993: 21). As Ferrer-Medina suggests, in these dualisms, the zombie is situated on the side of "Nature" and reduced to a mere body without rational thought. Tendentially, the zombie is working-class, racialised (including in whiteness) and/or female. But rather than merely reinforcing these binaries, the zombie often registers anxieties around the fault lines between these "Nature" and "Culture" binaries, which can, in critical narratives, be employed to highlight the workings of capitalist dynamics. At stake in zombie narratives, then, is the role of "Nature" (including human natures) within modernising societies.

It bears emphasising here that the modern capitalist binaries of "Nature" and "Society" are, of course, abstractions that environmentalist thinkers would do well to overcome – but they are also real abstractions that structure and organise life under capitalism. While nature is indeed the matrix of *all* life, historical natures under capitalism are organised in ecological regimes that alienate populations unevenly from what is coded "Nature" – that is, food production, their own bodies, knowledge about the natural world, access to non-urban spaces and so forth. Metabolic rifts, which we will discuss in more detail below, are therefore real in this sense – even if, as Jason W. Moore points out, we need to understand that on the level of nature-as-matrix, Wall Street is as "natural" as a field of corn (2011: 39).

In the context of these debates around "Nature," it is interesting to note that zombies are also often conceptualised as human machines – a conceptualisation that needs to be understood within the larger context of hegemonic cultural understandings of the relations between race, technology and nature. Alternative understandings of "Nature" as a living organism, or as anthropomorphically conceived nurturing mother, were gradually being displaced (albeit not completely) by a mechanic conception, as the Scientific Revolution "proceeded to mechanize and rationalize the world view" between 1500 and 1700 (Merchant [1980] 2019: 2). While "Nature" as a space of wilderness is thereby turned into the definitional opposite of the modern, it is paradoxically also reconceptualised using the metaphors of an increasingly mechanised society, disposing of a more complex vision of interconnecting human, plant and animal lives. To this we might add that, in the US context, African Americans have also been represented as machines – as well as being imagined as somehow closer to "Nature." In the nineteenth century, long before the introduction of the zombie figure into the US context (Chude-Sokei 2012: 117), enslaved Africans and African Americans were tragically compared to and even exhibited alongside machines in the United States. Indeed, it was the nineteenth-century plantation, according to Louis Chude-Sokei, "that sealed the relationship between blacks and machines and expressed it in performance via blackface minstrelsy" (2012: 114). The term robot – "meaning serf if not slave labour" (Chude-Sokei 2012: 104) – was introduced into English in the 1920s, around the same time as the zombie. When the zombie entered US culture, it was thus inserted into these discourses around "Nature," race and technology.

What the shifting relations between concepts of "Nature," race and technology demonstrate is that a static conception of binaries will be unable to grasp the evolving role of hegemonic ideology in capitalist power relations. This is true also for our view of zombies. Over the course of zombie history, zombies have appeared as "primitives," driven by "natural" instinct, *and* as human machines working by the value-driven clock; they have been seen as workers *and* as representative of the human-as-waste, expelled as useless. The

Ecology of the Zombie

historical trajectory of zombie figures over the twentieth and twenty-first centuries shows them to be adaptable to gothic contexts, where they figure the return of an undead past, *and* in sci-fi and cyberpunk contexts where they evoke a dehumanised, mechanised future.

Let us now turn for a moment to one of the most (in)famous zombie texts, written by self-proclaimed adventurer W.B. Seabrook during the US occupation of Haiti. Seabrook travelled at the end of the 1920s, when he was 41. His work is often viewed as an origin of sorts for the twentieth-century zombie imaginary, and credited with providing the source material for the first ever zombie film, *White Zombie* (Halperin 1932). *The Magic Island* (Seabrook 1929) is a racist, primitivist travelogue, authored by a white US writer who apparently collected a lot of his information in a hotel bar (Palmié 2002: 65). The book was heavily criticised by important Haitian intellectuals, including Jean Price Mars, who in *Une étape de l'évolution haïtienne* described Seabrook's work as "a bluff, but one that brings in money" (1929: 155). Yet *The Magic Island* influenced not only plenty of US narratives, but also Caribbean depictions of Haiti – most notably perhaps, Alejo Carpentier's *El reino de este mundo* (1949).[2]

In Seabrook's travelogue, Haiti is presented in line with colonial-imperialist stereotypes and tropes of a Caribbean "otherness." The "structures of denial" are, for the most part, firmly in place. Ecophobia and a stereotyped, exoticising perspective on Haitian religion conjoin to produce a space of primitivist difference, which is invested with all the familiar gendered and racialised tropes of imperial discourse. In contrast to patriarchal American culture, coded as masculine and white, Haitian culture is feminised and infantilised, revealing the primitive origins of humankind to the "rational" (read: white, male) visitor. Haiti is thus depicted as a space in which the "dark and mysterious" jungle resonates with the sound of the "Voodoo drums" (Seabrook 1929: 4). It is strange but also familiar, as encapsulated in the narrator's description of his bond with Maman Célie that "went beyond [...] conscious reasoning" as if he had "suckled in infancy at her dark breasts, had wandered far, and was now returning home" (1929: 28).[3] Seabrook's "fantasy of white reinvigoration" (Zieger 2012: 742), through insertion into Black "primitive" culture, plays on Spenglerian notions of "Western" culture in decline. This emphasis on a supposedly primitive origin that might cure the ills of modernity (coded, again, as white) is blind precisely to Haiti's modernity, thus "erasing," as Raphael Dalleo argues, "the impact of the occupation and [Seabrook's] own complicity in it" (2016: 138). In his caricatural

---

2 For an excellent discussion of this, see Raphael Dalleo's *American Imperialism's Undead* (2016).

3 The racism of Seabrook's supposedly sympathetic vision was distilled in the illustrations by European artist Alexander King. Purportedly inspired by African sculpture, King's work demonstrated "how primitivism's ability to critique modern society easily devolved into base racist stereotype," as he regularly employed "distorted facial features, enormous bulbous heads with diminished crania, and ape-like qualities" (Twa 2014: 34).

depictions of sacrificial vodou rituals and "collective ecstasy" – much criticised for their lack of accuracy by Price Mars (1929) – he claims to find the antidote to the modern age, in which "we [have] all become *mechanical, soulless robots*" (1929: 42, emphasis added). Note that robots and zombies are here rooted in opposing contexts, as zombies belong to "primitive" Haiti, robots to the "modern" US. Indeed, in many US texts that would follow, the zombie became a sign for a primitivistically conceived colonial difference.

However, what is interesting in Seabrook's text is that the introduction of zombies breaks with the framework of binarisms (modernity/primitivism, white/black, etc.), and threatens the overall ideological assumptions of both the text and its author. The ideological structures of denial are in direct conflict with the zombie, who brings the world-ecological unconscious disturbingly close to the surface. It is the figure of the zombie itself, born from popular narratives circulating within Haiti, that carries and embodies this understanding. Zombies are introduced in relation to the modern US-owned sugar industry, enabled by the occupation that changed the post-Revolutionary constitution to allow foreigners to own land once again. As "the largest American-owned enterprise in Haiti and foremost icon of the agribusiness that was steadily displacing peasant sharecroppers across these regions by means of land appropriations," the Haitian American Sugar Company (HASCO) was the epitome of how imperialism was brutally reshaping the socio-ecological make-up of Haiti, and a "highly likely object for sorcery discourse" (Ramsey 2014: 173). Indeed, as Kate Ramsey points out, 1918, the year in which the travels of Seabrook's "rational friend" Polynice take place, marked the opening of the HASCO factory in the Cul-de-Sac, as well as intensifying unrest over the *corvée* system (2014: 173). In order to make way for its business venture, the company cleared lands in the Cul-de-Sac and Leogane plains, "marking the beginning of widespread deforestation and erosion" (Miles and Charles 2004: 123). It also displaced thousands of peasants, who "had long farmed the land on these fertile plains, whether independently or for elite landowners through the demwatye (sharecropping) system" (Ramsey 2014: 173–74). The former sharecroppers, who had received 60–75% of the harvest, were reduced to being salaried day labourers as the company divested itself of any responsibility towards them by "subhiring through native gang bosses" (Schmidt 1995: 178). Profit was generated only eventually by underpaying the workers.

In the course of his travelogue, Seabrook recounts a story about a gang of zombies working at HASCO in 1918, as told to him by Polynice. Here is the key passage:

> At this very moment, in the moonlight, there are *zombies* working on this island, less than two hours' ride from my own habitation [...] I will show you dead men working in the cane fields. Close even to the cities, there are sometimes *zombies*. Perhaps you have already heard of those that were at Hasco…"

"What about Hasco?" I interrupted him, for in the whole of Haiti, Hasco is perhaps the last name anybody would think of connecting with either sorcery or superstition.

The word is American-commercial-synthetic, like Nabisco, Delco, Socony. It stands for the Haitian-American Sugar Company – an immense factory plant, dominated by a huge chimney, with clanging machinery, steam whistles, freight cars. It is like a chunk of Hoboken. It lies in the eastern suburbs of Port-au-Prince, and beyond it stretch the cane fields of the Cul-de-Sac. Hasco makes rum when the sugar market is off, pays low wages, twenty or thirty cents a day, and gives steady work. It is modern big business, and it sounds it, looks it, smells it. Such, then, was the incongruous background for the tale Constant Polynice told me [...] As Joseph lined them up for registration, they still stared, vacant-eyed like cattle, and made no reply when asked to give their names [...] They were frightened, he said, by the din and the smoke of the great factory. (Seabrook 1929: 94–95).

For Price Mars, who was reading the book as a pseudo-anthropological account of Haitian culture and religion, "this black magic [...] is the worst of abominations" that finds its expression in the "coarsely vicious and aggressive" illustrations by Alexander King (1929: 128). Price Mars is, of course, correct in his evaluations of Seabrook's text, but the reason so many later commentators would find something of interest in this passage is not to be found in any claims to authenticity, but rather in its registration of the impact of US-led modernisation in Haiti. By linking the "history of chattel slavery and revolution in Haiti to modern wage slavery," the text "sketch[ed] black modernity in a way that diverged from primitivist stereotypes" (Zieger 2012: 740). Much emphasis is placed by Seabrook on the "incongruity" of hearing of the existence of zombies in the vicinity of the HASCO factory, a symbol of US modernity in the text.

In other words, even if the zombie is inscribed within a racist depiction of Haiti, this subversive excess here stems from the fact that the zombie sits at the intersection of connected realities – the expropriation of Haitian farmers and the expansion of capitalist relations – which are expressed through temporal disjunctions, as the supposedly "archaic" zombie erupts within a modernising landscape. It offers a critical view on capitalist unevenness and its reality, "deeply riven with a sense of moral crisis unleashed by a predatory modernity and experienced, chronicled and analysed by its victims in the form of phantasmagoric narratives about how even the bodies of the dead, bereft of their souls, do not escape conscription into capitalist social relations of production" (Palmié 2002: 66). The zombie is, in other words, clearly tied to modernity and modernisation through brutal imperialism, embodied here by agribusiness. Indeed, the fact that HASCO "pays low wages" to expropriated peasants provides a more powerful context for their behaviour than the depiction of a primitive country steeped in superstitions that Seabrook proffers.

In this passage, we thus find the context for the zombie's twentieth-century trajectory, even if the meaning of this context escapes both Polynice and Seabrook. HASCO, a company employing new fossil-fuelled technology sustained by monopoly capital, is here explicitly compared to Nabisco, a large manufacturer of biscuits (including the world-bestselling, sugar-laced Oreo, introduced in 1912), founded in 1909; it is also compared to Delco, an automotive electronics manufacturer founded in 1909, and Socony, a major oil company founded in 1911, which metonymically signals the emergence of US-dominated petromodernity. In other words, while Seabrook sought to offer a paternalist vision of Haiti as "primitive," the zombie story puts pressure on the world-ecological unconscious of the text. Zombies are clearly not archaic. What remains invisible in this brief passage, however, is the internationalisation of Wall Street through New York City-based banks expanding into Haiti (and Cuba) in pursuit of new commodity frontiers and opportunities for plunder – an expansion propped up by racist ideology (Hudson 2017: 10).

In Seabrook's text, the zombie is a modern*ist* figure (in the WReC sense) – even if in its representations throughout the 1930s, the tensions displayed often collapsed back into simplistic, racist, primitivist horror. Unlike the first US zombie movie *White Zombie* (1932), which sought to repress the presence of US machinery and military in Haiti by offering images of antiquated sugar mills and seemingly feudal social relations, the text revels in the seeming disjunctions produced by "modern big business," with its "clanging machinery" and "freight cars," and the supposed Haitian primitiveness captured by folkloric beliefs. As a profoundly world-literary figure, the zombie not only displays and registers all the signs of uneven and combined development, but thrives on the logic of capitalism underpinning it. It is no coincidence that a figure with imaginative roots in slavery is revived at a moment when the *corvée* system reintroduces a racial form of slavery as part of the US occupation of Haiti. The zombie, then, offers us a way into world-literature that is not confined to its most literary forms (in this case, a travelogue), but crosses many boundaries of genre, form and medium.

From "Cultural Appropriation" to "Capitalist Appropriation"

[T]he notion of zombification replaces the theory of alienation.

René Depestre, 1993[4]

The zombie's transition into a US imaginary not only fostered imperialist paternalism but was also lucrative to US writers and film-makers. Price Mars, as we saw above, denounced *The Magic Island* as a money-making "bluff." As Mary Renda observes, Americans in Haiti not only treated servants and

---

4 Cited in Dayan (1993: 146).

prostitutes "as objects of exchange," but also "transformed the very idea of Haiti into an object of value in capitalist exchange," feeding and fuelling "Americans' fascination with the exotic" (2001: 216). In line with this attitude towards Haiti as the lucrative exotic, the first zombie film, *White Zombie*, was "a typical piece of opportunism" (Luckhurst 2015: 75): made for only 100,000 dollars, and recycling used film sets, it became a surprise commercial triumph. As a result of its commercial potential, the zombie's early life in the US was not alien to copyright issues. Ironically for a figure that had been appropriated from Haitian oral traditions as a by-product of colonisation and plunder, US "stakeholders" sought to claim it as intellectual property: the Halperin brothers were sued unsuccessfully by Kenneth Webb, a playwright, in 1932, and again in 1936 by their old production company when filming *Revenge of the Zombies*.[5] Ultimately, however, it was the zombie's previous existence in folklore that made it immune to copyright claims.

In *Myal* (1988), the zombie novel I discussed in the introduction, Brodber offers a brilliant commentary on the appropriation of cultural memories for profit and reflects on its relation to the appropriation of Caribbean lives. The US American character Selwyn treats his Jamaican wife Ella like an exotic trophy who serves his own careerist purposes. He transforms her stories and memories into an exoticist play, mixing caricature with just enough local detail to transform it into a money-making bluff that people might believe. Selwyn's backstory is of interest here: his family owns a pharmaceutical empire. They are thus engaged in an industry which was in the process of being reshaped by patent and trademark law and would increasingly be dominated by considerations of profit, rather than health. Selwyn's caricatural play is similarly oriented towards profit rather than serious cultural reflections; it is not interested in cultural health, as one might put it. The damage done by this misrepresentation to Ella, who realises what Selwyn has done to her, is explored by Brodber through Ella's phantom pregnancy. Instead of giving birth to a child, Ella expels a grey mass that made her sick – a metaphorical symbolisation of her second zombification, following the first when she was acting out Kipling's poems. Her cure is intimately linked to her reinsertion into her community, along with a nascent critical understanding of forms of domination embodied by colonialism and imperialism.

Given the zombie's early history, it is easy to see why charges of appropriation and theft play a role in much thinking about the transition of the zombie from Haiti to the United States.[6] In *The Transatlantic Zombie*, Lauro – while granting that the zombie is never "merely a cultural appropriation, but […]

---

5 The zombie continues to be a lucrative creature. In 2011, the zombie industry was estimated to be worth $5.74 billion by *24/7 Wall Street* (McIntyre 2011).
6 Sascha Morrell discusses the precedents in US culture in a fair amount of detail, concluding that her previous examples "have shown that the Haitian idea of the zombie as a mindless yet animate corpse was by no means unprecedented when it entered U.S. culture" (2015: 117).

also infects its occupying host" – places a lot of emphasis on the fact that the zombie's importation into the United States constituted the "cultural theft of an artefact that was itself about cultural theft" (2015: 5, 98). Even though there is, of course, truth to this claim, she allows notions of authenticity and cultural ownership to become increasingly detached from their historical context. As a result, there are moments in Lauro's argument when the charge of cultural appropriation is applied to uses of the zombie over seven decades after the Haitian occupation, despite the fact that those zombie invocations draw on the by then decades-long tradition of zombie representations in the US. Further, ideologically distinct invocations of the zombie begin to look the same from Lauro's perspective, regardless of whether or not they are critical of imperialist capitalism. Much of the powerful critique of global processes that the zombie originally offered is lost as a result.

The most striking example of this tendency occurs when Lauro turns to Occupy Wall Street's visual employment of the zombie.[7] As readers will recall, the protesters of Occupy Wall Street (OWS), who popularised the notion of "the 99%," dressed as zombie bankers in a protest against the hegemony of Wall Street and its role in the ever-widening gap between the super-rich and the poor majority. "Occupy" as a movement is difficult to define, since it brought together a diverse range of protesters ranging from radical to reformist. But within its spaces of occupation, it opened up loci of debate. It comes as something of a surprise that Lauro ends up on the same side as critics of a different political ilk – as she herself points out – and chastises the protesters for their use of zombie imagery. She brands their "appropriation" of the zombie as "intellectually negligent," and suggests that it "unknowingly parallel[s] the colonial imperialism under which the zombie myth was born(e) even as they propose to critique the global economic system that is its heir" (Lauro 2015: 195, 12). Let's examine her argument in a little more detail:

> the zombie is deeply connected to a colonial and postcolonial history of oppression. This is crystallised in the fraught term Occupy, which here is doubly laden, tacitly bearing the acknowledgment that the zombie only comes into cinema because of the American occupation of the sovereign republic of Haiti (1915–34). Yet this zombie is neither, like its Haitian forebear, a critique of commodity production under a slave economy nor, like its cinematic parent, an allegory of the blind ingestion of the consumer capitalist. Rather, in this setting the spectacle of the zombie was invoked to protest corporate greed, Wall Street's special brand of conjuring: nothing is made but profits; nothing is consumed but dollars. Nevertheless, the Occupy zombie is not so far afield from where the myth began, and even

---

7 Lauro quotes Drew Grant's article from the *New York Observer*, which starts with the rhetorical question: "What better way to engage the pros and cons of the Occupy Wall Street movement that to see it in terms of a zombie invasion?" Grant herself answers with the statement that many of the protesters were indeed conformist zombies (because she is addressing a largely conservative readership).

as it would overwrite the image of the living corpse with a new program (a trick that has been performed time and time again upon the zombie's body), the sight of the dead lumbering down a city block in New York preserves two aspects of the zombie mythology – those [...] forming the center of the zombie myth: the spectre of the colonial slave and the slave's potential for rebellion. (Lauro 2015: 4–5)

The language employed here is purposely tendentious: following the justified criticism of the term and the limits implied by indigenous participants and activists of Occupy Oakland, Lauro sees the very name Occupy as "fraught" and, by implication, associated with the history of oppression. But one ought to distinguish between a valid critique made as part of the discursive space opened up by Occupy, and a move that seems willing to delegitimate Occupy as a form of social protest. The occupation of spaces also inscribes itself in a series of protests (from labour strikes to the Arab Spring) where it is employed as a tactic. Further, for a critique of Wall Street, there is surely no more apt figure than the zombie. Wall Street paved the way for the military occupation of Haiti and continues to build on its legacy. In 1925, Grace Hutchins labelled the occupation "Wall Street's occupation of Hayti" (cited in Keresztesi 2011: 35). The zombie figure is not so much "over-written" with a new program as inscribed within a long history of capitalism, linking its different moments. That authentic zombie, for Lauro, is the figure that denounces slavery while simultaneously carrying the potential for rebellion – something that she refers to as the "zombie dialectic" that would transcend individual zombie manifestations. Since the zombie no longer possesses this particular meaning, it seems to have lost its value as a figure of resistance to her mind.

Lauro goes on to claim that the zombie as a metaphor itself became enslaved: a "slave metaphor," "when it was forced to labour in cinema" (2015: 17, 9). While the transition of the zombie into cinema was indeed problematic on many grounds, it is important to emphasise – even if it may sound pedantic – that a metaphor is a representational device and cannot be literally enslaved because it lacks agency and consciousness. There is a categorical difference between the enslavement of Africans in Saint Domingue, the forced labour regime under US occupation and, on the other hand, the cinematic employment of a figure in different contexts (even if they are employed in support of the occupation). A similar erasure of crucial differences is also found elsewhere when she argues that the employment of zombie imagery by Occupy Wall Street "risks seeming like a kind of second-degree blackface, an appropriation [...] for entertainment purposes [...] by its former colonizers and occupiers" (2015: 11). Surely, the devil lies in the historical and class-specific detail: these are protesters *against* the financial domination of capital embodied and enacted by Wall Street, which, let us not forget, had actively enabled the invasion of Haiti (Hudson 2017). The protesters might have been predominantly US American, but to equate them with the "coloniser" erases any notion of class struggle that would help us compare and differentiate two historical moments. Similarly, to equate their protest with a racist form of entertainment seems a wilful act of misreading that eschews historical context.

Other cultural commentators have read the protest in a much more nuanced fashion. Andrea Shaw, for instance, observed that

> the movement, which is representative of oppressed peoples in contemporary America (the much-touted ninety-nine per cent), is using the supernatural to discredit the oppressor (corporate America) by designating that entity as undead—as a subject or practitioner of sorcery, which has led to its cannibalistic onslaught on the American economy. (2011: 4)

That this onslaught has had powerful repercussions on the level of racial inequalities is also well known. In contrast to Lauro, Shaw is here sensitive to the shifts in meaning of the figure, retaining its potential for critique and resistance. This difference in reading is particularly poignant if we recall the well-known fact that Wall Street used to be an official slave market in the eighteenth century, embedded in the brutal commodification of African and indigenous persons and the denial of their humanity. This fact renders the connections between the legacies of slavery and high finance very tangible. Further, in the context of my argument, one must note that Wall Street is not somehow removed from "Nature"; rather, it is itself "a way of organising nature," as Jason W. Moore asserts (2011: 39). Indeed, whether we think of neoliberal restructuring and the resultant devastation of Caribbean economies and ecologies in the 1980s and 1990s, or of the effect of the Wall Street Crash of 1929 on sugar planters, or of the role of financiers and bankers in slavery as an institution, global finance is deeply embedded in capitalist world-ecology. As a financial centre, Wall Street was involved in bankrolling imperialism and the occupation of Haiti, which profoundly transformed and degraded the country's environments.

This is not a critique of the concept of cultural appropriation as such, which has done important work to expose the colonial-capitalist theft of lives and cultures. Rather, from a materialist point of view, it is important to go beyond "essentialist and ahistorical assumptions" that can sometimes be embedded within contemporary employments of the term (Crane 2018: 6), and to redirect our attention to the global processes that enable cultural appropriation in specific circumstances. Offering a materialist specification of the concept, William Crane defines cultural appropriation as "the *capitalist appropriation* of human labour and lives" (2018: 6, emphasis in original); to this we might add the appropriation of environments, natures and lands. As is well documented, zombies entered US culture as part of the ideological struggle over how to represent US imperialism, which with the help of the military translated into the ruthless appropriation of lives, labour, lands and cultures. Yet, as Crane notes, "[t]he historical violence of appropriation is one moment in the history of a cultural sign which is continually reshaped by the struggle between dominant and emergent cultures. That moment must be understood in the web of world history rather than taken outside it" (2018: 26). The zombie's meaning, in other words, will be reshaped within changing contexts and evolving struggles, and historical contextualisation is crucial to understanding the relation of the figure to structures of racial, gendered and class-based exploitation and appropriation. Further, as we will see in more detail in Chapter 2, while the zombie was certainly a monster utilised in primitivist depictions of Haiti, it also resonated with figures derived from the US context that had responded to processes of appropriation *within* the United States.

What I want to argue, then, is that the zombie's power lies in its ability to give narrative shape to the brutal dynamics and logics of capitalism – that is, the combined logics of exploitation and appropriation. As Haitian writer René Depestre noted in an interview, the zombie is a figure that "means," in a broader context, contributing to and correcting analyses of a Marxist nature, since "the notion of zombification replaces the theory of alienation" (quoted in Dayan 1993: 146). I argue that the zombie does this by gesturing towards changing sets of relations between two logics – between the exploitation of value and the appropriation of non-value. This, however, poses definitional problems: where does one draw the line between the zombie and the no-longer-zombie or not-yet-zombie? Is the line between shuffling zombies and fast non-zombies? Or should one draw the line much earlier, between the folkloric Haitian figure and its different incarnations? The zombie's importance as a cultural figure and myth in Haiti has been described by Haitian scholars and is undeniable; it is likely not exhausted by the dynamics described here. My focus here falls not (directly) on the zombie as a figure of oral and spiritual cultures in Haiti. Instead, it falls on the way the zombie is taken up in literary and filmic texts.

As a literary figure, the zombie is animated by – and gestures towards – global processes. It takes irreducibly specific forms depending on the context. A world-ecological perspective on the zombie necessitates a renunciation of what Stephen Shapiro, in a different context, calls "semiotic essentialism" (2014: 205). Shapiro argues that, in the fan world, the fan fetishistically takes "medium for message," transforming the zombie into an "unalterable, transhistorical figurative device and plot rules" (2014: 205). While his analysis concerns the fan world, Shapiro's observations hold true more generally, as critical interventions sometimes stick to narrow definitions of the figure or confine themselves to a particular genre, medium or national "tradition." Provocatively, Shapiro proposes the following:

> while there are certainly past instances of zombie representations […] it is not useful to read these within a framework of a linear perspective […] Each recurrence of zombies is less a *recitation* or adaptation of the already known than a more or less distinctive *repurposing* of generic, representational devices to consider a specific contemporary process that generates social uncertainty or crisis. (2014: 198, emphasis in original)

Rather than trying to measure each zombie by reference to an original, zombie theory in this argument needs to be able to allow for historical shifts in zombie imaginaries, taking account of world-historic transformations and revolutions. Indeed, changes to form, narrative structure and voice are crucial to their ability to express different social pressures and functions (Shapiro 2014: 199). Since, in my argument, the zombie is animated by the systemic logics of appropriation and exploitation, which take specific and unique form in specific places throughout history, the zombie cannot be reduced to a singular form.

Shapiro's rethinking of zombie history is usefully placed in the context of his earlier work on "[g]othic effects," which are characterised by "periodicity" – or regular recurrences at particular moments in capitalism's boom–bust cycles. Indeed, zombie effects demonstrably proliferate "as capitalism separates laborers from any means of production (agricultural, crafts-oriented) that might sustain them outside of or in tension with a system that produces commodities only for their profit-generating potential," as well as during subsequent turns of the screw (Shapiro 2008: 30; see also Taussig [1980] 2010). Hence, we see the first proliferation during the 1930s, as well as ever-increasing spikes from the 1970s onwards. The logic of this figure cannot be analysed adequately without a dialectical engagement with the conditions and processes that animate zombie effects throughout history.

To return to Lauro's argument, then, one might argue that her understanding of the zombie as a critique of colonialism needs to be more firmly embedded in an exploration of the logics and cycles of capitalism. How were the logics of exploitation and appropriation at work during the occupation of Haiti? How do we move from one specific cultural instantiation of the zombie figure to a different one, which responds to the reorganisation of those logics? A more flexible understanding of the form of the zombie would enable us to draw out the potential ground for comparison between, say, displaced Haitian farmers in the 1920s or 1930s and the OWS protesters. The former were left without plots by US land appropriations and turned into a super-exploited workforce on sugar plantations in Cuba and the Dominican Republic; the latter protested against increasing inequality in the wake of the financial crisis of 2008, which was turned into a mechanism for expropriating the working and middle classes.

But Marxist histories of zombies can similarly run into difficulties. Traditional Marxist explorations of the exploitation of wage labour through abstract labour have tendentially de-emphasised the process of appropriation (Fraser 2016: 165; see also Federici 2004). As my preceding analysis suggests, this would limit our understanding of the range of zombie figures. Our zombie history must ground itself in a revised critique of capitalism that would take on board lessons from anti-colonial, postcolonial, feminist, social reproduction theory (SRT), Marxist and materialist thinkers for thinking through the relations between appropriation and exploitation – relations that are strongly overdetermined by racism and sexism (Fraser 2014; 2016; Dawson 2016; Patterson [1982] 2018; Ralph and

Singhal 2019). The massive and brutal expropriation of "bodies, labor, land, and mineral wealth in the 'New World'" not only preceded but "dwarfed exploitation throughout the phase of commercial capitalism" (Fraser 2016: 174); moreover, racialised appropriation continues to play a fundamental role in capitalism, taking the form of predatory loans, debt foreclosures and prison labor (Fraser 2016: 166–67; Alexander 2010; K. Taylor 2016). Colonial and imperial appropriation likewise remains central to capitalism as a world-ecology. Further, the appropriation of gendered reproductive labour – and the devaluation of care-work more generally – continues to structure the capitalist world-system, just as the division between production (coded as public and value-productive) and reproduction (coded as private and non-value-producing) remains fundamental. In short, our renewed zombie theory must enable us to bridge the difference between the zombie-as-worker and the zombie-as-slave – between the logics of appropriation and exploitation, which are always closely intertwined (Patterson 2018: 22). This renewed zombie theory must, in other words, be value-relational (J. Moore 2015; Jakes and Shokr 2017; Niblett 2020).

Towards a Value-Relational Approach: World-Gothic, Metabolic Rifts and Zombies

Value-relationality offers a new theoretical approach to zombies. To understand this approach, it is first necessary to understand the law of value under capitalism. Although, as many critics have asserted, value as socially abstract labour time is central to the dynamics of accumulation, capitalism also crucially relies on what is *not* valued. World-ecology, like SRT, emphasises that the law of value is highly dependent on non-valued forms of work, energy and resources. As Jason W. Moore phrases it:

> Value does not work unless most *work* is not valued. The law of value under capitalism is, then, comprised of two moments. One is the endless accumulation of capital as abstract social labour. The other, the ceaseless expansion of the relations of exploitation and appropriation, joined as an organic whole. This perspective stresses the historical and logical *non-identity* between the value form and its necessarily more expansive value relations. (2015: 54, emphasis in original)

Central to capitalism-as-civilisation are the shifting relations between paid and unpaid labour and energy, between the logics of exploitation and appropriation, between productivity and plunder (or, what Nancy Fraser [2014] calls the even more "hidden abode" behind Marx's abode of production). The devaluation of certain forms of work under capitalism is enabled by the cultural schemas and knowledge practices that systematically cheapen lives and landscapes. As Niblett argues, "capitalism has mobilized gendered and racialized hierarchies, in tandem with the denigration and reification of non-human nature, to ensure the devaluation" of the work of women, racialised others and Nature (2020: 48). Patriarchal and colonialist-racist ideologies, continues Niblett, "that position women and people of colour as belonging to the sphere of Nature (as a singular abstraction defined in opposition to Society) serve to justify the demarcation of these groups as less than human, all the better to depreciate or invisibilise their labour" (2020: 48).

One of the key geographical expressions of the division between paid labour and unpaid work under capitalism – that is, of the way the system unfolds through exploitation and appropriation – is the "metabolic rift." In his reconstruction of Marx's ecological thought, John Bellamy Foster shows how Marx went a considerable way towards a "historical-environmental-materialism" (2000: 373). Central to this was Marx's analysis of the ways in which the intensive exploitation of the soil by large-scale agriculture under capitalism led to an "irreparable rift" in the "metabolic interaction between man and the earth" (quoted in Foster 2000: 156). Capitalist agriculture exhausts the fertility of the soil, while "capitalist production collects the population together in great centres," in which environmental degradation becomes an increasingly prominent issue (quoted in Foster 2000: 155). "All progress in capitalist agriculture," Marx writes in *Capital* I (1867), "is a progress in the art, not only of robbing the worker, but of robbing the soil; all progress in increasing the fertility of the soil for a given time is a progress toward ruining the more long-lasting sources of that fertility" (1990: 637–38; quoted in Foster 1999: 379). More generally, from the 1450s onwards, the agricultural population was progressively displaced by centuries of enclosures and technical innovations, by the growth of the fertiliser industry and soil chemistry in the 1830s–1850s, and finally in the twentieth century by large-scale agriculture, industrialisation, chemicals and pesticides. The rift is ecological (referring to nutrient cycling); it is social (the dispossession of the peasantry and the pollution of cities); and it is individual (as peasants become alienated from the products they produce). Overall, the separation into industrial cities and declining villages produces an irreparable rift in the interdependent process of socio-ecological metabolism.

Building on Marx's and Foster's work, Schneider and McMichael offer an expanded definition of the metabolic rift, re-embedding it within larger rifts in socio-ecological relations. Marx's understanding of metabolism, they argue, "centres on a particular nutrient pathway, whereby nutrients move from the soil, through humans, and back to the soil in the form of 'humanure'" (Schneider and McMichael 2010: 468). This leaves aside all the other ways in which soils and earths reproduce themselves, including the masses of earthworms, fungi, bacteria, arthropods and algae, making up the "complex soil food web and metabolic reactions between living and non-living soil components" (2010: 468). The metabolic rift thus also names an *epistemic rift* – between people and their knowledge about the soils – that will be lost in the process of their displacement.

This rift occurs most obviously between the colony and its metropole, where of course the zombie originated. Following Moore, we know that a fundamental first step in the emergence of capitalism as world-ecology was the extraction of sugar and silver from the "New World" through the exploitation of enslaved Africans and indigenous peoples (2003: 309). The sugar (and silver) commodity frontiers of the Americas were ecologically central, constitutive moments of an epochal reorganisation of "world ecology." Lands were depleted of soil nutrients and other resources, which were shipped across the Atlantic to the emerging cores of Western Europe. In the Caribbean, the impact of the expansion of sugar plantations was particularly devastating. Sugar required the clearing of lands and destroyed "forests well beyond the plantation," because of the latter's need for large quantities of firewood for the furnaces in which the cane juice would be boiled (Miller 2007: 79). Indeed, one of the chief environmental "legacies of colonialism" in the Caribbean, and particularly of the "plantation economy," has been "compromised deforested environments" (Paravisini-Gebert 2011: 100), the consequences of which are a loss of biodiversity, flooding, soil erosion and related signs of environmental degradation. In tandem with the exhaustion of the land went the degradation of the enslaved; it was not only brutal physical violence to which they were subjected, but also forms of symbolic violence that translated into a "social death" (Patterson 2018). As Sidney Mintz puts it, this social death began "with migration and resettlement, forced transportation, the stripping of kinship and community, [and] the growth of individuality on a new basis" (1996: 301).

The zombie figure emerges in Haiti as an ecological figure that encodes not only the alienation of nature, but also the metabolic rift instantiated by the plantation system in terms of the leaching of resources and nutrients from the land *and* the epistemic rift associated with the social death of the enslaved. The figure registers the shifting logics of exploitation and appropriation, of paid and unpaid work, of value and non-value, which are manifested in the metabolic rifts that characterise capitalist society. And these shifting logics continue to animate the zombie as it shape-shifts over the course of the twentieth century, in Haiti but also system-wide. In Haiti, the zombie has undergone significant changes in literature – from the tales of zombified workers to zombified women and, finally, zombified masses under the Duvaliers.

In *World Literature and Ecology* (2020), Niblett explores the relationship between commodity frontiers and irrealist instances in (irrealist or realist) texts. This investigation builds on Niblett's argument that "zombie effects" – by their very nature, typically irrealist – register recurring shifts in the socio-ecological metabolism, and that the alteration of the effects is driven by the change in relations that move commodity frontiers. Animated by the combined logics of exploitation and appropriation, these symbolic-ecological revolutions turn on shifting relations between value (abstract social labour) and that which is not valued but appropriated (unpaid work/energy). Zombie representations are *world-literary* by definition, insofar as zombies always register the systemic dynamics of capitalism. Representations of exploited labour are thus *only one particular* zombie effect and cannot account for the evolution of zombie aesthetics over the *longue durée*. The zombie is, in other words, not a static figure but one that is animated by "the inner logic of capitalism" (Shaviro 1993: 63), and corresponding revolutions in the capitalist world-ecology. Hence, it is no surprise that the zombie should turn from being a slow-working labourer on the plantations into a (now increasingly fast) zombie-worker that eats human flesh. Or that it would come to take the shape of a zombified proletarianised woman. Or that it would represent the financial elites that parasitically suck money from poorer populations, as it has recently in the context of the fallout from the 2008 financial crisis.

In the chapters that follow, I will explore the ways in which the zombie has shifted over time, as it registers the changing relations between value and not-value in different historical contexts. In the next chapter, I will look mainly at racist depictions of zombies – Black males and white females – and examine how they fit into this paradigm.

CHAPTER 2

The Sugar-Zombie, Race and Cash-Crop Monocultures

> They work faithfully. They are not worried about long hours.
>
> Victor Halperin, *White Zombie*, 1932

> Listen, white world,
> To the salvos of our dead
> Listen to my zombie voice
> In honor of our dead.
>
> René Depestre, "Cap'tain Zombi," 1967

White Zombie (Halperin 1932) translated the oral tales of zombies transmitted via William Seabrook's 1929 travelogue on to the screen. The film was set in an imaginary Haiti, in which all the main protagonists are played by white actors. While a small number of critics see the film's plot as abstractly mythic and the Haitian location as almost incidental (Rhodes 2001), analyses of the film have usually contextualised it in relation to the cultural and ideological consolidation not only of racist imperialism abroad, but also racial regimes at home (Bishop 2010a: 66; Robinson 2007: xv). The film's narrative emphasis lies on a love triangle between the French white plantation owner Charles Beaumont, the equally white American Neil Parker and his fiancée Madeleine Short, who becomes the victim of zombification and functions as a vehicle for racist fears. The "true horror," as Kyle Bishop remarks, lies in the domination, subjugation and "symboli[c] rap[e]" of a white woman (2010a: 66), who stands in for an imagined white imperial culture. Unsurprisingly, the movie was not well received in Haiti, and critics demanded that it should be withdrawn from screening (Plummer 1992: 128). But I here want to pause on one of the film's most famous scenes, which features enslaved zombies working in a sugar mill. As Beaumont visits the "voodoo master" Legendre to enlist his help to win over

Ecology of the Zombie

Parker's fiancée, the camera pans over the inside of the mill in which a range of mostly black zombie workers – played by African American extras (Renda 2001: 227) – slowly push a manually operated mill that crushes the cane. Almost as if in slow motion, one of the lifeless workers loses balance, falls between the spokes and is crushed, apparently without any reaction. He becomes part of the *bagasse* – the crushed leftover of the cane after the juice is extracted. For all the film's imperialist ideological investments, this scene is significant. In most of the later Hollywood-directed films set in Haiti, the concern with the working conditions of those toiling on US-owned sugar plantations had disappeared. Even if responsibility for those conditions is here displaced, this scene graphically shows concern over working conditions. As many critics suggest (Russell 2007; Rhodes 2001), it prompted responses of identification among US audiences who were living through the Great Depression – a global crisis that, as environmental historians now remind us, was not only economic and social in nature, but also profoundly related to the exhaustion of the ecological regimes installed by New Imperialism (Hollemann 2017).

In the 1930s, zombie-esque figures – that is, alienated workers, referred to as having their "soul" or "ego" destroyed – were circulating in realist and regionalist texts from Cuba and the Dominican Republic where Haitian migrants were working in US-owned fields. Unlike *White Zombie*, these narratives were predominantly anti-imperialist, linking the zombification of workers to the modernisation and mechanisation of agriculture led by US

Fig. 2. *White Zombie* (Halperin, 1932). A zombie falls into the archaic sugar-rollers and becomes part of the bagasse.

The Sugar-Zombie, Race and Cash-Crop Monocultures

companies. The zombie, as Raphael Dalleo has astutely remarked, "evoked the same feeling of alienation from mechanized modernity that spurred primitivism in the 1920s, but with the added context of the anxiety over labor's lack of autonomy brought on by the economic crisis of the early 1930s" (2016: 182–83). What I want to propose here, then, is that the zombie spike of the 1930s and early 1940s needs to be embedded within the world-ecological context that surrounds the Great Depression to enable us to read the consolidation of the zombie figure across a regional context. Since the late nineteenth century, well-established "domestic patterns of racial thinking and racist perception" (Hudson 2017: 14), along with practices of appropriating and clearing indigenous lands for capitalist farming, took on a hemispheric dimension as the United States turned outward. In the regional context of the Caribbean, New Imperialism developed through the sugar commodity frontier that accelerated the appropriation of lands. Caribbean environments were rapidly degraded by capitalist techniques of monocultural farming and the extraction of wealth from the soil. By the 1930s, the capital-driven plunder propelled by capitalist ideology had led to major issues of soil erosion and environmental degradation across the mainland United States – the so-called "American Sugar Kingdom" (including Cuba, Puerto Rico and the Dominican Republic) – and Haiti. It is important to highlight that the deep economic crisis felt in the 1930s across the United States and Caribbean was part of a larger crisis of New Imperialism. It led to the growth of fascisms, social unrest, anti-imperialist resistance and nationalist violence. The zombie spike in this context was both backward- and forward-looking, marking the crisis of a cycle of capitalist accumulation and its ecological regime, but also heralding the ascendancy of an oil-fuelled American hegemony that would consolidate into a US-dominated world-ecological regime after 1945. Zombies were invoked in the context of the plantation economy, but they were also frequently linked to the exhaustion of the commodity frontier of monocultural growing. As described in more detail below, this is often the more implicit context for some of the pulp stories and the images of dereliction and nostalgia.

Sugar-Zombies and the Caribbean Regionalist Narrative

It will come as no surprise that the radical transformations of socio-ecological regimes that resulted from the emergence and consolidation of US imperialism was experienced very differently from Caribbean perspectives than it tends to be represented within the US imaginary. Unlike *White Zombie*'s near erasure of the role of the US in Haiti, many (though not all) Caribbean texts have tended to link zombie-esque figures explicitly to US imperial domination.[1] As seen

---

[1] There are examples of Hispanic Caribbean writers, such as Puerto Rican Luis Palés Matos in "Canción festiva para ser llorada" ([1937] 1995) and Cuban Alejo Carpentier in *El reino de este mundo* (1947), who evoke zombies within a more

in the previous chapter, the military occupation of Haiti prompted a revival of popular tales of zombification, registering the realities of a forced labour regime as well as land dispossessions under US-led capitalist modernisation. As independent farmers and sharecroppers were forced out into the Cul-de-Sac plain where HASCO (Haitian American Sugar Company) would operate, day labourers were hired for a fraction – one fifth, or perhaps less as some sources suggest – of what they would have received on Cuban *ingenios* as migrant workers (Ramsay 2011: 385). The day labourers would locally be referred to as *zonbis* (Ramsay 2011: 172; Richman 2005: 111). This idea of zombies working for HASCO contains, as we have previously seen, a strong critique of the impact of imperialist modernisation on Haiti. But we may note here that images of alienation resembling zombification were much more widespread: they were also employed throughout the American Sugar Kingdom of the Hispanic Caribbean, particularly in narratives focussed on predominantly migrant plantation labour in the Dominican Republic and Cuba. Within those narratives, zombies were usually complemented by other monstrous figures, such as the omnivorous sugar mill. While formally these zombie-esque and monstrous figures tended to strain against the realist conventions in which they were evoked, the sugar-zombie in these narratives became a marker of the negative socio-ecological impact of US imperial interventions. Their appearance in these regional texts is not as surprising as it might at first appear: as Ericka Beckman reminds us, "regionalism's turn toward 'nature', and the 'land' marked anything but an escape from commercial culture," but rather an insistent focus on "export-led modernization" (2013: 2995).

The wider context to this is well documented: from the end of the nineteenth century onwards (and especially after 1898), Haiti and the Hispanic Caribbean were radically transformed by US imperialism when, after decades of "industrial development, corporate consolidation and economic expansion that followed the grim history of territorial dispossession that marked the settling of the US West" (Hudson 2017: 5), unproductive US capital began to turn outwards towards the Caribbean to appropriate cheap labour, food (especially sugar), energy (through oil refineries) and raw materials (including timber). As is clear within this context, the liberal fantasy of a world market regulating itself could not be further from the reality. Rather, capital accumulated via violence and dispossession in the United States engendered further possibilities for accumulation and imperial expansion, supported in turn by military might.

---

primitivist mode as they seek to represent Haitian vodou and emphasise the importance of African-descended cultures in the Hispanic Caribbean. As has been documented, Carpentier's vision was influenced by Seabrook's *Magic Island* (1929). The pitfalls of primitivism, tending to deal in racial essentialism to offer a different, non-alienated form of inhabiting the environment, have been amply discussed. Primitivism should, I argue below, be read as another – however flawed – reaction to the deepening of metabolic rifts via US imperialism.

Of course, there were important differences in the ways in which imperial domination impacted Cuba, the Dominican Republic, Puerto Rico and Haiti. As Matthew Casey notes, "[i]n terms of capital investments and scales of production, rural Haiti was on the opposite end of the spectrum from rural Cuba" (2017: 29). While Haitian agriculture was "modernized" with the aim of eradicating "backward," peasant-based subsistence farming (Dalleo 2016: 12), exhausted Haitian soils proved no longer profitable enough for large-scale mono-cropping, which relied on the fertility of newly cleared soils, still available in Cuba. Haiti thus became an extraction zone, mainly for resources other than sugar, including human labour. Proletarianised Haitians were transformed into a mobile workforce and sent to plantations in the Dominican Republic and Cuba. As Valerie Kaussen writes, "a system of indentured servitude was introduced in which the impoverished and now landless Haitian peasants were shipped to more thriving US colonies where plantation production for export was in full swing: Cuba and the Dominican Republic" (2008: xi).

Since Haitian migrant workers in Cuba were earning more than their counterparts in Haiti, returned migrant workers (*viejos*) were often portrayed as flashy, displaying their earnings in their attire, in novels such as Maurice Casseus's *Viejo* (1935). However, sugar-cane workers, and particularly Haitian migrant workers, in the American Sugar Kingdom were also frequently described as zombie-esque in Hispanic Caribbean regionalist narratives – something rarely mentioned in works within the field of zombie studies. These novels and short stories tend to share a commitment to anti-imperialist politics and solidarity with the sugar-cane workers, even if their politics are in some cases limited to a quite conservative vision of national autonomy articulated around the patriarchal national family. And while images of alienation and dehumanisation are also evoked in Puerto Rican narratives in relation to the sugar plantations – one might here refer, for instance, to Enrique Laguerre's *La llamarada* ([1935] 1994) – it is particularly in texts from Cuba and the Dominican Republic that the images of zombification become quite explicit. Cuban and Dominican sugar mills tended to employ migrant workers, many of them Haitian. It bears repeating that these labour migrations occurred within a context of radical socio-ecological transformations, entailed by the sugar revolution and propelled by the invasion of foreign capital. These radical transformations proceeded through the monopolisation and centralisation of lands, enabling industries such as large sugar factories to dominate and exploit the best agricultural land. Between 1900 and 1918, the combined sugar production of the three islands increased at dizzying rates, so much so that by the end of the First World War "the three islands produced close to one-third of the sugar sold in the world market" (Ayala 1999: 5).

While these changes affected all aspects of social life, this was fundamentally and constitutively an ecological process of degradation, propelled by the "first flowering of American ecological imperialism" (Tucker 2007: 16). The latter widened metabolic rifts between consumption and production, as more and more lands were dedicated to exports, resulting in a correlative rise of food scarcity and food dependency which would worsen over the course of the twentieth century, particularly in the case of Haiti and Puerto Rico. Supercharged by fossil-fuelled technologies, US imperialism "surpassed" in intensity and scale the crimes of colonial capitalism's appropriation of natural resources and environments (Tucker 2007: 1). It had devastating socio-ecological effects: landscapes were deforested and soils depleted; most dramatically, in Haiti, forest coverage fell from 60% before the occupation, to 21% by 1945 and down to 12% by 1954 due to large-scale US agricultural projects (Steckley and Shamsie 2015: 185). The market-driven agriculture put in place was highly environmentally destructive owing to the globalisation of metabolic rifts, emphasis on extractivism and monocultural growing. Soil erosion and environmental degradation are a normal by-product of capitalist forms of agriculture, governed by profit rather than local demand and sustainability. These links between imperialist capitalism and environmental degradation were well known and even studied at the time, as Hannah Holleman tells us in *Dust Bowls of Empire* (2018). Perhaps unsurprisingly, the link between racialised figures of zombification and environmental anxieties was also relatively obvious then, just as it is today as we are living through another moment of converging global crises.

In this context, zombie-esque figures offered a crucial narrative figuration of the transformations in working people's lives. Let me start here with a couple of examples of zombie effects in realist narratives, which I will later proceed to embed within the ecological contexts they represent. These zombie effects are predominantly found in descriptions of the working conditions of plantation labourers. In *Over* (1939), Dominican writer Ramón Marrero Aristy refers to the predominantly Haitian labourers on the US-owned sugar plantation, describing them as "ill-smelling mob in rags – with a hunger that never leaves them – on the way to the harvest, like a procession of beings *without a soul*" (1980: 95, emphasis added). The workers are here coded as severely impoverished, to the extent of having lost their spirit or agency. In a similar manner, *Marcos Antilla* (1932), written by the Cuban Luis Felipe Rodríguez, describes a downtrodden Haitian sugar-cane worker called Nicolás Bobó as being reduced to his bodily being and obsessed with food (because of his general lack of it). Rodríguez muses on how Nicolás's ego has seeped out of his body, like water out of a broken jug. Both of these examples – while not using the term zombie – clearly evoke workers subjected to such dire conditions that they become alienated from their own bodies and seem to survive by a form of "split[ing]," as Brodber has termed it, as their spirit, soul or agency evacuates their bodies (1988: 67). It is important to note that, in both texts, the Haitian characters' dehumanisation is represented as a result of the conditions they are exposed to and not as somehow inherent – even if, of course, there are in hindsight obvious problems with the ease with which such figures can flip into the opposite. Regionalist novels and short stories thus arguably provide an important critical archive of the ways in which

The Sugar-Zombie, Race and Cash-Crop Monocultures

zombie-esque figures were mobilised in the interests of thinking through the multifaceted crisis of the 1930s, particularly as they affected migrant workers. These texts also provide an important alternative for thinking through the zombie's internationalisation in the 1930s in ways that go beyond the usual route, via Seabrook's *Magic Island* (1929).

It may seem odd to integrate social realist narratives into a literary history of zombies, but this has everything to do with the commonly held assumptions that inform literary critics' take on genres. Rather than expecting zombie texts to live up to the conventional notions of zombie horror, we might here take cues from the debates around *critical irrealism* – a useful heuristic and capacious term that can include marvellous realism as well as gothic tales. As Michael Löwy has observed, "[t]o some extent, the concept of realism and irrealism should be considered as 'ideal-types' in the Weberian sense; that is, as entirely coherent and 'pure' epistemological constructions: in contradistinction to empirical literary texts, which tend to be an 'impure' combination of both realism and irrealism" (2010: 213). The texts I read here as *zombie texts* offer just such an "impure" combination of social realist conventions and gothic effects. The Haitian writer Jacques Stephen Alexis had made a related point decades before Löwy: in the Haitian context, he suggested, the dichotomy between realism and marvellous realism should be rejected; instead, the marvellous should be understood as an integral element of social realism ([1956] 1995: 197). Similarly, Jamaican writer and theorist Sylvia Wynter suggested that realist aesthetics might be insufficient to capture the brutal forces of the market that subdue Caribbean economies with particular intensity. As Wynter notes, market-driven colonial plantations did not respond to local need and were instead driven by the vagaries of the global sugar market. This created a reality that felt "enchanted, imprisoned, deformed and schizophrenic" (1971: 1): a reality dominated by invisible forces, seemingly governed by sheer bad luck, as suggested by Rodríguez's invocation of "the hands that play the Antillean dice" (1971: 88).

In social realist novels and stories featuring zombie-esque characters, irrealist registers tend to cluster around descriptions of the cane fields that hide unspeakable horrors, the sugar mill that threatens to gobble up lands and people and, as we have seen above, the experiences of the alienated workers. The first example I want to return to is Rodríguez's *Marcos Antilla* – a collection of interlaced short stories that wears its anti-imperialist, and even anti-capitalist, politics on the sleeve. First published in 1932, the collection explicitly links different forms of commodity extraction (of oil, sugar and other commodities) in which both local and foreign elites are involved (Rodríguez 1971: 38), and frames the narrative within a context of international solidarity. The latter is evoked by the narrator Marcos, who recalls working with the oppressed across Latin America and the Caribbean. He worked in Mexico with *indios*, where he learned that "oil was a chain for him and wealth for his neighbour" (1971: 38); in Colombia and Brazil as *cauchero* (a worker in a rubber plantation), "like the hero of *La vorágine*" (1971: 38); in Peru with the miners; in the lesser Antilles and Central America as a banana carrier; and in the Dominican Republic and Cuba as a sugar-cane cutter (1971: 38). His stories, however, focus specifically on the plight of the workers of different nationalities (including Cubans, Dominicans, Jamaicans and Haitians) for the Cubanacán sugar company, a US-owned enterprise in Cuba. While all of the workers are represented as "anonymous being[s]" (1971: 41), plagued by overwork and ill health, Haitians are represented as the most downtrodden. Throughout the texts, they are compared to "mistreated animals," reduced to the experience of hunger to the extent that their awareness has been lulled to sleep (1971: 66–67). Nicolás, who I mentioned above, is described as simple, "primitive," and as having been turned into "a piece of meat with eyes" (1971: 89, 91). While the collection is clear in its representation, and laments the conversion of food-oriented land-use to export-oriented monocultures with dehumanising working conditions, the images of animalisation and zombification are problematic in their replaying of contemporary Cuban stereotypes of Haitians (Sklodowska 2009: 83). Nonetheless, the assembled short stories clearly seek to expose this degradation as part of a liberatory political agenda and attack on US imperialism.

The degradation of the worker is very explicitly framed within the context of the rapid transformation of the Cuban landscape by the sugar companies. In contrast to the mill evoked in *White Zombie*, the mill is here referred to as a form of "economic imperialism and submission of man to the modern slavery of the industrial machine" (Rodríguez 1971: 54). Modernisation and technology are not separate from rural life but rather dominate the landscape: the mill's "very high chimneys" tower over the surroundings, "like incredible fingers of the tentacular hand extended with love towards Liborio by his tall and blond friend Uncle Sam" (1971: 95). This supposedly loving gesture is undercut by the reference to tentacles, which in the late nineteenth and early twentieth centuries was commonly evoked "in political cartoons in the Americas and Western Europe" "to figure the reach and impact of corporate power and imperialist exploitation" (Niblett 2021: n.p.). In this context, the cane fields, too, become spaces of horror, from whose "bossom flow many dark things" (Rodríguez 1971: 47); still resounding with the inhumanities of slavery and the brutalities of the new labour regime, at night, the arms "can emerge" of those whose lives have been extinguished (1971: 52).

The vision offered by Rodríguez is not dissimilar to that of his more famous compatriot Alejo Carpentier, in the opening chapters of his novel, *Ecue-Yamba-O*, first published in 1933 but written six years earlier. As in *Marcos Antilla*, the sugar mill in *Ecue-Yamba-O* is portrayed as both linked to modernity and monstrous, as it "sull[ies] the landscapes" and gobbles up all life in its orbit: "The *ingenio* swallows interminable caravans of carts, loads of cane capable of sweetening an ocean" (Carpentier 2010: 165, 166). Again, the description of the mill emphasises its own fossil-fuelled modernity inscribed in a global world-market as well as the technical innovation that propels the sugar productivity revolution. While the furnaces burn bagasse with

The Sugar-Zombie, Race and Cash-Crop Monocultures

Norwegian coal, the machines – described through many of their component parts – turn, crush, whistle, shake. Indeed, the mill swallows up not only the cane, but also the workers: "Every six hours, hundreds of men would be sent there. She would return them exhausted, sticky and panting" (Carpentier 2010: 166). As this description suggests, workers are subdued by its will and their agency is annulled. They are consumed as labour-power and expelled as wasted, exhausted bodies. Their humanity is truncated, as they become "asexual, almost mechanical" (2010: 165).

Overall, the novel describes the processes by which Afro-Cuban peasants become tenant farmers for US companies while shedding light on the importation of Haitian labour, rendered "cheap" by the US occupation of Haiti and the displacements of peasants. While the novel's primitivist vision of Afro-Cuban and Haitian cultures has rightly been criticised, Dalleo has convincingly argued that its opening chapters offer a useful critique of US capitalism in the Caribbean "by showing Haitians and Afro-Cubans caught up in the exploitative labor networks" (2016: 123). The novel's primitivism is therefore presented as a product of imperialist modernisation.[2]

Zombies are also found in novels that offer the trope of the national family that is thwarted by the American-owned sugar industry, as in Marrero Aristy's *Over* (1939). The problems attendant upon the trope of the national family – which tends to promote a heterosexist, masculinist, often racist vision of a nostalgically conceived patriarchal past – have been amply discussed by a range of critics. In the novels by Marrero Aristy and Laguerre, it is the bourgeois protagonist – "the propertied, educated, white-identified, and heteronormative man as bearer of the political agency of the citizen" (Reyes-Santos 2015: 64) – who ultimately fails to form a family, thwarted by the presence of US imperialists. As we have seen above, Marrero Aristy's narrative very explicitly evokes "beings without a soul" in his descriptions of the migrant workers on the plantations.[3]

In these predominantly realist and regionalist novels, the sugar mills are regularly associated with US capital and fossil-fuelled modernisation. In *Over*, images of the "immense chimneys" of the now steam-powered sugar industry, rising to the sky as if to "stea[l] the clouds" (Marrero Aristy 1980: 27), have ominously threatening overtones. What is striking in *Over* is the insistent

---

[2] In other words, while Carpentier's later novel *El reino de este mundo* (1947) offered a marvellous depiction influenced by the primitivist aesthetics of W.H. Seabrook, in this earlier text primitivism is contextualised within and presented as being produced by capitalist modernity.

[3] As Anne Garland Mahler writes, at "its core are issues relevant – both then and now – to political organising across linguistic, racial, and national lines" (2019: 237). She describes the ways in which Caribbean migrants in the US, as well as African Americans (part of the American Labour movements and the Comintern), behaved towards race and labour after the "Thesis on the Negro Question" that dated to 1919 (2019: 239).

Ecology of the Zombie

emphasis on the unevenness of access to the benefits of technology: fossil-fuel-powered modernity individualises imperialists, while defacing the majority of the workers. Monstrous irrealist imagery thus revolves around chimneys, locomotives and railways, coded not as signs of "progress" but of uneven access and exploitation. In *Over*, the sugar work's locomotive is a "monster of iron," "a beast" that transports the workers, "vomiting" them out again at their destination (1980: 82). The machine triumphs over the workers who become its excretions. Automobiles, on the other hand, individualise and empower the central's foreign managers but are inaccessible to Haitian or West Indian workers, and only barely to the Dominican protagonist. Throughout, they are linked to images of implied violence to land and people, as encapsulated in the image of the car carrying Daniel to his future job down a lane that is like a "scar on the stomach of the cane fields" (1980: 30).

Zombie effects are thus put into the context of a failed struggle for national autonomy, thwarted by imperialist modernisation, which excludes the majority. More interestingly, zombie effects are evoked in relation to the barely grasped logics of capitalism – the drive for surplus value evoked through the notion of "over." As in many texts focussed on plantations, sugar emerges as a structuring force in terms of both the plot and people's daily lives. Yet in *Over*, Marrero Aristy is able to gesture towards the logic that makes sugar such a dominant force through the practice of "over" [in English in the original], explained in the text as a surplus profit extracted through corruption, made possible by the monopolisation of food, necessities and healthcare: "The *over* swallowed your life [...] everything that is yours – conscience, body, heart – belonged to the monster that smothers men in the agony of over [or more]" (1980: 210). The over here emerges as a vampiric force, taking over the protagonist Daniel Compres and his body, his affective life, and his conscience – or perhaps, more disturbingly, his consciousness (the Spanish term *conciencia* can refer to either) – producing yet another zombified worker. While *Over*'s consciously voiced political position is more moderate, it here points towards the "monstrosity" of the imposition of value relations under the conditions of peripheral and dependent capitalism. Indeed, the domination of *over* turns into the "reign of the absurd and the alienation of human sensibility and will" (Pimentel 1986: 194). Overall, then, the sugar-zombies in the regional texts of the time figure the impact of US imperialism, magnified by the Great Depression, environmental degradation and the collapse of the sugar market. Zombie-esque figures are visibly linked to imperialist modernity and its ecological regime that is based on export production of primary commodities and food delocalisation. While the ideological investments of their authors were varied, the labour conditions of cane workers and the environmental degradation wrought by this form of agriculture are linked to US-led modernisation.

One of the main problems of such a registration is, of course, that it can be mobilised for opposing political responses to crisis and foreign domination. Images of dehumanisation and animalisation, especially when not linked to images of agency, can easily feed into negative stereotypes. Further, when uncoupled from a critique of capitalism, within the framework of a patriarchal, often racist and classist nationalism, they can easily be conjoined with fascist and racist ideologies. They can become part of the scapegoating of certain groups, especially Haitian (migrant) workers in the context of Cuba and the Dominican Republic. One might here mention *Over*, which – despite its anti-racist politics – was at least briefly invoked to prop up the dictatorial regime of fascist Rafael Trujillo, who had murdered thousands of Haitians and Haitian-Dominicans only two years earlier. From this, we may conclude that, if zombies do indeed register the crisis of capitalism as a world-ecology, this does not inevitably lead to a critique of capitalism.

Zombies and Plantations in Early Zombie Film and "the Pulps"

While zombie effects abounded in the context of the turbulent 1930s and 1940s, the zombie's most explicit literary and filmic presence beyond Haiti was to be found in American gothic pulp stories and zombie films. Starting with *White Zombie* (Halperin 1932), the zombie quickly became a mainstay of American horror, appearing in movies such as *Ouanga* (Terwilliger 1935), *Revolt of the Zombies* (Halperin 1936), *The Ghost Breakers* (Marshall 1940), *King of the Zombies* (Yarbrough 1941), *Revenge of the Zombies* (Sekely 1943), *I Walked with a Zombie* (Tourneur 1943) and *Zombies on Broadway* (1945). The plot (though usually not the filming) of zombie movies took place in Haiti (*White Zombie*, *Ouanga*), Cuba (*The Ghost-Breakers*), other invented Caribbean islands (*King of the Zombies*, *I Walked with a Zombie*) and Cambodia (*Revolt of the Zombies*). As these films demonstrate, the zombie turned into a figure of horror increasingly detached from Haiti, but with strong associations of racialised difference projected on to colonial/imperial locations or racialised groups in the United States. As Cedric Robinson remarked, "the zombie – dead-brain Black labor – was as perfect a slave as could be conjured up by a racialized imaginary" (2007: 272). For different reasons, the most interesting of these films for my argument are *White Zombie* and *I Walked with a Zombie*.

Through *White Zombie*, the zombie was built into the birth of horror film, albeit as the cheap and belated cousin of the famous trilogy of pre-code horror talkies released a year earlier: *Dracula* (dir. Browning), *Frankenstein* (dir. Whale) and *Dr Jekyll and Mr Hyde* (dir. Mamoulian) (see Peirse 2013: 12). Produced on a small budget as part of Poverty Row,[4] *White Zombie* was inexpensive to make (costing less than $100,000), took only 11 days to shoot and reused sets from a range of films, including *Frankenstein*. In terms of style,

---

4 On Poverty Row, see Russell's *Book of the Dead*, especially pages 33–35. Poverty Row was founded "during the Depression" and the companies involved managed to stay relevant in a market "by churning out exceedingly cheap productions" (2005: 34).

technique and setting, *White Zombie* is marked by a certain anachronism and a sense of déjà vu compared to the earlier horror trilogy. The context of these cost-cutting measures was the Great Depression, which translated into plummeting numbers of moviegoers and the falling stock value of the movie houses on Wall Street (Doherty 1999: 28). The resulting film was, however, remarkably successful by market – though not critical – standards. This might, to a large extent, be down to the zombie being a "perfect monster for the age" since "its vision of a living dead workforce neatly tapp[ed] into the American public's fears" at a time of staggeringly high unemployment rates (Russell 2007: 22). Simultaneously, of course, it resonated strongly with racial anxieties over the US's imperial ambitions. Both in the Caribbean and the United States, monocultural plantations and capitalist ways of farming were plagued by environmental degradation and aridification, as well as labour strikes and unrest. The zombie thus became a nodal figure for the different elements of the multifaceted crisis of capitalism as world-ecology.

Within this context, the zombie became codified as a Gothic horror trope that played on notions of racialised alterity, embedded in primitivist discourses that "often justified denying self-determination to the Caribbean by portraying non-white people as premodern and therefore as incapable of – or at least not yet ready for – self-rule" (Dalleo 2016: 4). Uneven development – which pits "modern big business" against violent practices of appropriation, and orients entire countries or regions around the production of one export crop – is rendered invisible through its recoding as the racialised difference between primitive/barbaric and modern/civilised. The zombie also entered pre-existing discourses around race, nature and industrialisation, in which African slaves were portrayed in a primitivist light as closer to Nature and driven by instinct (Chude-Sokei 2012: 11), but also – paradoxically it may seem – as robotic automatons. Louis Chude-Sokei traces the latter association of enslaved Africans with machines to the plantation regime as a precursor of Fordism (2012: 114). As this shows, discourses surrounding race, Nature and industrialisation are closely intertwined, and the zombie entered them at a stage when feelings of alienation were compounded by the world-economic and -ecological crisis of the 1930s (Dalleo 2016: 182–83).

Frederick Douglass, in *My Bondage and My Freedom* (1855), compared enslavement to "a life of living death, beset with the innumerable horrors of the cotton field, and the sugar plantation," as well as the "reduc[tion of] man to a mere machine" (Douglass 2018: 4805, 464). Yet in the context of fossil-fuelled modernity, it is also crucial to analytically retain the distinction between machines and labour-power. For Marx, machines are famously dead labour and cannot produce surplus value; they can only facilitate the production of relative surplus value as one capitalist gains a momentary advantage through technical/energetic innovation that drives up labour productivity in comparison with their competitors. It is thus only from the perspective of a fetishistic belief in machines as sources of value that the extremity of the continued unevenness of capitalism may seem surprising.

The Sugar-Zombie, Race and Cash-Crop Monocultures

But let us return now to the scene with which I opened this chapter. In Legendre's sugar mill, the zombie who pushes the wheel and falls to his death registers anxieties over race, mechanisation and the exploitation of labourers. *White Zombie* seeks to contain these associations and to ascribe them to a more primitivistic (Haitian and/or Black) realm. But the containment strategies are not as successful as in later films. What would be obvious to anyone familiar with the history of sugar is that the sugar mill here is entirely anachronistic. A contemporary sugar mill would have involved fossil-fuelled machinery, massive chimneys dominating the landscape and trains to transport the cane, usually financed by heavy US investment. As suggested by Seabrook's 1929 text, quoted in the previous chapter, sugar mills were associated with modernity. This modification, then, is not an unimportant detail but is crucial to the representation of Haiti as primitivist and a source of the evil embodied by Legendre, played by Hungarian actor Bela Lugosi wearing darker make-up. It is implied that the scene depicting the utter dehumanisation of the workers has nothing to do with the French and US protagonists, Madeline White and Neil Bellamy. The US military invasion, fossil-fuelled modernisation and the associated forceful rearrangement of local landholding patterns are here erased.

But *why* do Madeline and Neil travel to Haiti in the first place? The crucial detail here is that Neil is a banker. Bankers and banks played an important role in the imperial, and eventually military, takeover of the country. Wall Street's white financial elite – individual bankers as well as the National City bank, in the case of Haiti and Cuba – played a crucial part in this, providing financial mechanisms for primitive accumulation. US bankers had originally offered to consolidate Haiti's foreign debt (which was, to a large extent, a direct or indirect result of the colonial powers' reaction to the Haitian Revolution); this then became a way to direct all profits towards debt servicing. Military forces were eventually deployed to protect financial investments: the long occupation in Haiti "came in response to the urging of the National City Bank" (Dalleo 2016: ix), which forced through a programme of structural adjustment. As the Haitian experience demonstrates, finance capitalism driven by Wall Street, land dispossession and modernisation are tightly intertwined and form part of the same project. Similar patterns revealing the tight relation between US banks, military might and agribusiness can also be found in Cuba and the Dominican Republic.[5] Further, if we extend our purview backwards, they repeat patterns of militarised financial expansion and land takeovers in weakly capitalised areas, as had previously occurred in the American West.

In line with the film's ideological vision, the subtext of *White Zombie* is that Neil has come to modernise (read "civilise") Haiti, viewed as primitive and

---

5 The ventures of bankers such as Samuel Miller Jarvis, who had made a profession out of offering banking services in areas weakly integrated into the financial global market, starting two decades earlier in the US Midwest, "were guaranteed by force" via the "threat of military intervention" (Hudson 2017: 21).

53

barbaric and represented via reutilised sets from earlier horror films. With his genteel manner and apparent lack of connections to the military, one might say that the character of Neil literalises the racist ideology and self-image employed by imperial banking. Nevertheless, we can say that his profession along with the appearance of the alienated workers are remainders of a historical reality that allow us to begin to unravel the film's repressed world-ecological unconscious. Both of these filmic elements, once reinserted into the world-systemic context (in which American imperialism proceeds through the degradation of environments and the dispossession and proletarianisation of small-scale farmers), begin to signify quite differently.[6]

In the US, the zombie was popularised rapidly through film but also in pulp stories. Stories of the racialised worker being oppressed on plantations – whether sugar or cotton – continued to be prominent in the "pulps," although they were not usually invoked to critique the legacies of plantation slavery but dealt with images of nostalgia for the "Old South." Common tropes in the narratives featuring zombie-workers include the association of zombies with primitivist belief systems, as well as with Blackness and/or Haiti; the corruption of white characters by primitivist practices; and white women falling prey to evil influences. The assimilation of the zombie into the pulps did not come from nowhere. Animated dead figures had already been circulating well before the 1930s, and tended to be embedded in discourses around race, Nature and modernisation; in American pulps, for instance, they were steeped in racist imagery and had appeared from at least the 1920s onwards. Further, the figure of the mindless yet animate corpse had already become "a standard figure for describing the conditions of the slave or factory worker in nineteenth-century letters, and the racist denial of black subjectivity" (Morrell 2015: 117). The Haitian zombie was thus quickly assimilated into the pre-existing array of (usually racialised) figures of alienation. In the pulps and many of the films, zombies usually did not challenge the racial and ecological hegemonies of the time, but they nevertheless registered the radical transformations in capitalist ecological regimes, and the emergence and deepening of racialised ecological rifts.

In the pulps, zombie narratives often built on, and accentuated, Lovecraftian "race fantasies" in which "white manhood" was under threat in "a delirium of miscegenation and monstrosity" (Luckhurst 2015: 63). These zombie narratives – whether in the form of film or the pulps – still frequently turned on the socio-ecological violence of mono-crop agriculture, but they either located the violence in the past or recoded it as "primitive." In many of these stories, then, white or light-skinned women occupy a particular role: they are portrayed as fragile and potentially threatened by primitivist

---

6 This marginalised, but nevertheless present, concern with working conditions and banking would disappear in most of the later zombie of films of the decade: in *Ouanga* (1936), for instance, zombies are reduced to the quite minor function of exotic henchmen controlled by the central female mixed-race "voodoo-master."

practices from which they need to be rescued by the white male, and symbolically they stand in for imperial, patriarchal culture coded as white. In an article entitled "I Walked with a Zombie," published in the early 1940s, Inez Wallace wrote that "these things have happened, and are happening today – not many miles from our highly civilised United States, down in the mysterious magic island of Haiti" (1985: 96). Horror, for her as well as for many of her contemporaries, is born from the breaking down of those boundaries, symbolised by the repeated stories of white or light-skinned women being zombified. Thus, the horror in Wallace's article derives from a scene of perceived incongruity: *"in the cane fields, working with the negro slaves, was the corpse of George MacDonough's wife!"* (1985: 98). The horror is created by the depiction of the white middle-class woman as suffering the same fate as the Black captives as a result of zombification at the hands of the Haitian woman, Gramercie, who had been MacDonough's first love but was pushed aside when he met his future white wife. Capitalism's unevenness and the brutal legacies of slavery are here masked by an ideology of civilisational differences. The zombie is associated with primitive, racialised practices that "erupt" in the present; the figure evokes the ideological borderline between the human and the (racialised) not-quite-human or sub-human. Surprisingly, perhaps, a good number of zombie stories in the pulps retain an emphasis on labour conditions – albeit in a way that displaces the blame and obfuscates the workings of capitalism as a racial regime.

"House in the Magnolias" (1932) by August Derleth (a follower of Lovecraft) and Mark Schorer, for instance, is a story set on a plantation in New Orleans, featuring a young, creole woman named Rosamunda, who is living with Abby, her elderly Haitian aunt. Initially attracted by the beauty of the magnolia-adorned colonial plantation house, Jordan, the white male narrator and painter, quickly senses that "something was wrong" (Derleth and Schorer 2011: 148). Alerted by the screams that he hears during his stay, he eventually sneaks out of his room at night to discover the following sight behind the house:

> there were men in the fields, a number of them [...] They were Negroes, and they were working in the fields. Moreover, they were probably under orders. Miss Abby's orders. I understood abruptly that her watching them was to see that they did their work. But Negroes that worked at night! (2011: 151)

While the wording of the discovery of zombies is close to Seabrook's, there is here again a crucial erasure of the link between zombies, modernity and modernisation. Instead, the plantation is characterised by anachronism: there are no electric lights and cars are expressly forbidden. The story almost turns into an allegory of the legacies of slavery as the foundations of present-day America: during the day the slaves are "in the cellars" (2011: 157), or foundations, of the plantation house. But not only does the plot shift emphasis away from the slaves and on to the romance between Jordan and the creole woman, it also shows the enslavement to be the work of a Black Haitian woman, Rosamunda's aunt, who is described as monstrous and as the one in charge of the horde of zombie labourers, whom she had robbed from their graves. Her monstrosity is here very clearly linked to her Blackness: her face is described as "bloodless," "dark, ugly" (2011: 148, 151). The fields, meanwhile, become the site of horror – but a horror that originates in actions coded as primitive, Black and alien, not at home in a white supremacist plantation order. In an act of denial and historical revisionism, "white people are [here represented as] not directly responsible for the evils" of the regime they have imposed (Pulliam 2007: 729). The reader is, in other words, served a dish of colonial nostalgia mixed with horror that is designated as foreign, non-white and primitivist.

One of the aspects of zombie tales from the 1930s and 1940s that might strike the contemporary reader is the ease with which gothic depictions were employed within a conservative and racist ideology, even in stories where zombies are linked to the haunting of the legacies of slavery, and even when they proffer an implicit critique of colonial-capitalist rationalisation. Manly Wade Wellman's story "The Song of the Slaves" (2011 [1940]) is a good example: in the story, a plantation owner from New Orleans in the 1850s, called Gender, sets out to enslave Africans as a means of making money. In the process, he is caught by the British and ends up throwing the captive Africans overboard to their certain deaths. The drowned and shackled Africans turn into zombies who come to seek their revenge on him:

> Figures surrounded him, black, naked, wet figures; dead as to sunken faces and flaccid muscles, but horribly alive as to eyes and trembling hands and slack mouths that formed the strange primitive words of the song; separate, yet strung together with a great chain and collar-shackles like an awful fish on the gigantic line of some demon-angler. (Wellman 2011: 583)

The story clearly registers the horrors of the plantation and of slavery, and links the horrors associated with plantation landscapes to the horrors associated with the Atlantic Ocean and the slave trade.[7] Gender the plantation owner is punished for his crimes in gothic fashion, dragged to his death in the ocean. But it is important to point out that the author himself was a Confederate who defended the institution of slavery along patriarchal lines (presumably, there are then "good" plantation owners, versus "bad" plantation owners). While his story features the punishment of one plantation owner, this clearly did not translate into a view critical of the institution of slavery, or its legacies.

Phrased differently, a lot of these tales are about the crisis of the socio-ecological organisation of space in the American empire. Horror is associated with plantations both in the United States and elsewhere. Let us take Thorp McClusky's "While Zombies Walked" (1939), a clunky story drenched in racism, in which Black characters are entirely flat and used as "props," adding

---

7 I might here note that there is a not-often-discussed strand of underwater zombie narratives, a tradition picked up more recently by the Cuban-Spanish film *Juan de los muertos*.

nothing to the perspective. The story offers another example of the evocation of zombie plantation horror, in this case in relation to cotton planting in the American South. The cotton plantation is isolated in the mountains along a path of deserted shacks that contrast with the house the protagonist Tony finally discovers: a "rambling, pillared house, half hidden by mimosa and magnolia [...] squatted amid broad, level acres lush with cotton" (McClusky 2011: 301), combining a nostalgia for an archaic past with the horror about to unfold. In this case, the zombified "men working, men who were clad in grimy, dirt-greyed garments" are described as "poor white trash" (2011: 301, 304) (and the reader is later informed that the Black workers left when this new regime started). Unlike in the regionalist Caribbean novels, the story quickly shifts into horror mode, as Tony discovers "jagged splinters of bone gleam[ing] through the torn and discoloured flesh," along with "a grey-ish ribbon of brain-stuff hung down beside the man's left ear" (2011: 301). Again, the horror does not derive from agro-modernisation, but is inscribed into a convoluted plot involving the white, bulky, evil and power-hungry Reverend Barnes, who employs, in Lovecraftian fashion, "powers so primitive, so barbaric that the descendants of the higher civilizations utterly disbelieve them" (2011: 308). We learn that the Reverend acquired these powers in a swamp; moreover, they are described by Tony as employing stereotypical images of voodoo dolls that accord with his estimation of Haitian caricatures. Again, the crisis of the sugar plantation – and the horrors associated with it – are displaced.

At once emerging from and questioning the tradition of imperialist plantation zombie depictions, *I Walked with a Zombie* (1943) by the French director Jacques Tourneur and Russian-American producer Val Lewton stands out for its subtlety, ambiguity, obvious narrative gaps and breaks, constant revising of assumptions and, perhaps most importantly, the "breaking of form" (Fujiwara [1998] 2015: 8). It is again notable that this innovative zombie film, too, was the product of a limited budget and the imaginative work of a director and producer who were relatively marginal to the big business of film-making. They took a by then established tradition, weighed down by a whole range of established tropes, and transformed it into what one might see as the *Heart of Darkness* of imperialist zombie films. This is signalled from the opening sequence when, in a narrative voiceover, Betsy (Frances Dee) distances the audience "from the naively trashy expectations raised by the title" (Fujiwara 2015: 88) by commenting on the story as "odd." This break in expectations is repeated when Betsy first encounters the zombified Jessica (Christine Gordon), who very briefly appears threatening – an impression enforced by under-eye make-up (Fujiwara 2015: 91). However, almost immediately the representation shifts in tone.

The history of sugar in relation to North American capital is also highlighted from the start of the film (even if the seat of the sugar company is here displaced from New York to Ottawa). The plot begins in the offices of a sugar company where Betsy is hired to care for the wife of one of the company's most prosperous plantation owners, Paul Holland, on the fictional island of

San Sebastian. The sequence is an early indication of Betsy's role as both the "representative of rationalism and positivism" (Fujiwara 2015: 88) and the purveyor of imperialist discourse about the Caribbean, which she reduces to a romanticised place, mocking the suggestion of witchcraft and evoking a palm tree as the dehistoricised image of the region. Both – the witchcraft and the palm tree – are thrown into doubt, however: while the question of the supernatural remains unresolved, her version of the Caribbean is quickly shown to be uninformed and naïve.

Representations of the Caribbean – as hellish or paradisiacal – are similarly undercut by the film's displaced emphasis on the brutal history of African enslavement, which is shown still to influence present-day cultural practices within the imaginative world of the film, including Alma's (Theresa Harris) weeping at the birth of a child. Paul Holland's (Tom Conway) early descriptions of the Caribbean as a place that looks beautiful but is evil sit uncomfortably with his references to the traditions of the Black population, commemorating the historical genocide perpetrated by the white plantocracy – a history he seems to recognise but never explicitly to link to his own position. Several of the Black characters contribute to highlighting the unreliability of the perspectives we are offered by Paul and the nurse Betsy. One might think of Lancelot's song as an example, revealing not only the love triangle but also the shift in dynamics as a "young" nurse enters the household.

As is well known, *I Walked with a Zombie* loosely reinterprets *Jane Eyre* in a Caribbean setting and, in the process, evokes a lot of the by then quite familiar tropes of zombie narratives: the contrast between the "rational" North America and a "mysterious" Caribbean steeped in rituals; the Caribbean as both paradise and hell; a love triangle ending in the zombification of a white woman (in this specific case, the triangle involves two half-brothers, one English and one American); the representation of "voodoo" being used for evil practices by white characters; and sugar plantations that are linked to fear, religious rituals and the supernatural. And yet, rather than reinforcing these tropes, the film renders them ambiguous. The central mystery of what happened to Jessica, and whether her condition has natural or supernatural causes, remains undecidable as competing explanations are offered from the perspective of various characters.

Significantly, the film's most suspenseful sequence is set in a cane field, as Betsy leads Jessica to the *honfourt* (a vodou temple) to cure her. The scene is conveyed through a long travelling shot as Betsy guides Jessica through the stalks that throw eerie shadows on to the women, transforming the cane field into a site of horror. But is the horror motivated by racial/cultural differences, or the brutal realities of plantation culture? Again, this is quite ambiguous since, on the way, the women encounter signs of rituals: a skull on the ground, a goat hanging from a tree and a completely still Black sentinel, Carrefour, played by Derby Jones. This is in many ways familiar ground for imperialist primitivism. And yet, as Chris Fujiwara (2015: 104) points out in detail, the sequence also resonates with images familiar from protests against US-based racism

– specifically, anti-lynching imagery from the 1930s – and must further be read in the context of the pressure exerted by the NAACP (National Association for the Advancement of Colored People) on Hollywood productions during the Second World War. In this context, the zombie Carrefour turns into a "disturbing figure" who, in his stillness, embodies the links between slavery and zombies (Fujiwara 2015: 103). Overall, one might say that the film consistently undermines the racialised separation of primitive/rational and highlights the brutal legacies of plantation slavery (without, however, being explicit about the realities of working conditions in the American Sugar Kingdom). Simultaneously, the film is discursively and materially marked by profound racial inequalities, attached to hierarchical divisions of plantation labour.[8]

Zombies, then, are very obviously inscribed within the larger crisis of capitalist (colonial and imperial) ways of farming, which, as we have seen throughout, translated into brutal and racialised labour regimes with devastating environmental consequences. They register feelings of alienation as well as racial tensions. It is perhaps no surprise that they should be invoked by so many white Southern writers – themselves in a subordinated

Fig. 3. *I Walked with a Zombie* (Tourneur, 1941). Betsy and Jessica walk through the canefield.

---

8 This becomes all too obvious if we compare the difference in salaries of the actors who played Betsy and Carrefour. The former received nearly 26.5 times the amount of the latter (Nemerov 2005: 114).

Ecology of the Zombie

Fig. 4. *I Walked with a Zombie* (1941). Betsy and Jessica meet the zombie-sentinel Carrefour.

position in relation to the white Northern elite. These writers adopted a marginalised, low-cultural genre that turned into a vehicle for their nostalgia-tinged investment in the plantation order of the "Old South" at a moment of deep crisis and transformation. Zombies have been invoked from very different ideological positions in response to this crisis, ranging from fascism and white supremacist imperialism to socialist and anti-capitalist critique. Undead figures offered an outlet for and a way of articulating the feelings of alienation experienced as the ecological regime of New Imperialism – based on extractive forms of farming and an intense racism – was unravelling.

The Uprooted Undead: The Zombie after the Commodity Frontier

As we have seen thus far, the zombie was frequently evoked in US pulps, as well as in Hispanic Caribbean and Haitian narratives of the mechanised takeover of lands by US companies. It was a modernist figure of alienation that was, in a large number of its incarnations, specifically tied to the plantation and its racial regimes. Read across the Caribbean region and the American South, the zombie registered the uneven development of environments within the expanding US empire. White racial anxieties in the US created these nostalgic fantasies about the plantation order (which could be equally recoded as referring to imperial expansion) as well as registering resistance to racial and imperial ecologies. I now want to turn to two texts that write back to and complicate this tradition, using the zombie figure in a context that evokes the socio-ecological transformations of regional environments. In Jacques Roumain's famous peasant novel *Gouverneurs de la rosée* [Masters of the dew] ([1944] 1988), the protagonist Manuel returns from the Cuban sugar plantations to his birth village in Haiti, which has become arid and treeless. Metaphorical zombification is here not associated with the sugar workers – who were organised into unions and participated in strikes – but with the villagers who are no longer able to sustain themselves (adequately) by working the soil. Richard Wright's *Native Son* (1940), on the other hand, is a novel about African American migration towards the northern cities as a result of massive ecological upheavals, the decline of sugar and cotton and the enclosure of sharecropping lands. Wright makes explicit use of images of zombification that draw upon the imperialist tradition; these are evoked at key moments and intimately linked to thinking through the ecological rifts through which capitalism develops.

Roumain's 1944 novel reimagines zombies in the context of post-occupation Haiti. He does not turn to the zombie figure associated with plantation agriculture, but instead focusses on what one might term post-sugar zombification. In other words, being dead-in-life is here the product, not of an active commodity frontier, but of an exhausted one: having already been massively underdeveloped by imperialist capitalism, and suffering from extreme levels of socio-ecological degradation (from the sugar plantations but also collateral damage, including deforestation and aridification), Haiti was at this stage only able to produce underpaid workers. Historically, the environmental exhaustion of Haiti is the legacy of colonial and imperialist extractivism. While Roumain's novel is relatively unspecific, it appears to be set in the 1920s and 1930s, "likely during or just following the U.S. occupation of Haiti"; the US presence in Haiti may not be mentioned, but the novel clearly inserts itself into "the time period when the U.S. effort to build a productive sugar cane industry in Cuba was partly predicated on cheap labor from Haiti" (Kaussen 2004: 126). Indeed, Roumain was a Marxist and a member of the Communist Party, who wrote extensively on imperialism, the exploitation of the peasantry and the US occupation. Unlike Marrero Aristy and Laguerre, who nostalgically evoke earlier historical moments inscribed within racist-patriarchal relations, *Gouverneurs de la rosée* attempts to marry the cultural nationalism of the foundational romance to the modernising narrative of revolutionary internationalism (Niblett 2012a: 28).

Manuel, the returning migrant worker, is not a zombie – instead he has learned to combat alienation through strike action and other collective endeavours, which he seeks to implement in the village of Fond Rouge. In doing so, he hopes to de-zombify the local community and its relation to the land in the wake of occupation. The insertion of the allegorical Fond Rouge within the very specific historical context of the American empire in the Caribbean is no coincidence. Haiti is portrayed as the underdeveloped, exhausted, devastated periphery that now produces "an inexpensive and flexible labor force" for the US empire (Kaussen 2004: 127). In light of Kaussen's observations, Manuel's travelling back to Haiti might be read as a journey from an active, and contested, commodity frontier in Cuba to one that is already exhausted. This exhaustion translates into severe environmental degradation as well as social and familial erosion, which are mutually entangled (Thésée and Carr 2015: 6).

Roumain invokes the zombification of an entire village as a state that needs to be historicised in order to be overcome. The dead-in-life inhabitants of Fond Rouge perceive zombification as an almost timeless state. As Kaussen notes, "[t]he rural space and its peasants are not represented as pre-modern or primitive here, as much as asleep, dead-in-life" (2004: 132). But fundamental to the text, and the process of conscientisation portrayed, is an understanding of zombification as the effect and legacy of imperialism that needs to be combatted through a transformation of the relations between the population and the land. As told from the perspective of Manuel's parents, the villagers are "already dead beneath this dust, in these warm ashes that covered what formerly had been life" (Roumain 1998: 32); Manuel's mother Délira, who worries over her absent son (who had left fifteen years earlier to work on the Cuban cane plantations), feels that "her heart had petrified in her breast and that she had been emptied of all life save that incurable torment that gripped her throat" (1998: 33).

The lives of the land and the villagers are depicted as profoundly intertwined. The villagers' zombification is at least in part a result of the land's devastation, which in turn is a result of deforestation, drought and erosion. Roumain's devastated landscape is presented in gothic and ecophobic terms:

> a flock of crows swooped down on the charred field, like bits of scattered coal [...] farther away against the sky, another mountain jutted, traversed by shining gullies where erosion had undressed long strata of rock and bled the earth to the bone. (1998: 24)

The landscape described displays obvious signs of erosion and aridification and is dominated by birds of prey. Water, which in the novel functions as a symbol for life, is largely absent or confined to the stagnant, ill-smelling and mosquito-breeding "Zombie Pool" (1998: 141). The villagers, reduced to a life of severe poverty, are forced to sell off more wood in the form of charcoal, intensifying environmental devastation and deforestation. While the novel overall seeks to focus on the Fond Rouge community, the text throughout describes characters belonging to the economic elite as benefiting from their poverty, and as seeking to force the villagers (through debt) to sell their remaining lands. Within this allegory of zombification, class struggle is thus by no means absent – even if it is represented abstractly in this allegory through largely off-stage characters. Instead, poverty and environmental degradation are shown to be profoundly interlinked.

The Sugar-Zombie, Race and Cash-Crop Monocultures

Devastatingly, the socio-ecological exhaustion of the land translates into the collapse of perceptions of time and thereby hope, as life has turned into a purgatorial dusty landscape inhabited by predatory crows. If the commodity frontier turns "abstract time" into the dominant force that subjugates peoples' lives to its temporal logic, its exhaustion leaves behind land and peoples as "waste products" of the system as well as the total collapse of time. Within this context, the former peasants have lost any meaningful connection to the land; they have turned into the destitute reserve army of labour for the neighbouring islands on the commodity frontier. It has been pointed out that the novel does not mention the US occupation and imperialist extraction as one of the prime factors for the land's degradation. Yet the allegory of the transformation of the peasants' relation to the land clearly registers the wider context of the US empire in the Caribbean, and notably highlights US-owned Cuban cane plantations as "a nodal point of the world economic system in which its contradictions are laid bare" (Kaussen 2008: 106).

Since zombification is understood as a historical process in *Gouverneurs de la rosée*, the text is able to imagine – unlike any of the other novels examined here – what de-zombification might look like. The plot is driven by Manuel's desire to find a means to de-zombify Fond Rouge, and ultimately water becomes the metaphorical salt that revivifies the land as well as the population (Kaussen 2004: 134). Further, the re-establishment of a sense of community – and of an understanding of its members as historical actors – is posited as central. This resembles the earlier tales of the zombies' awakening, their recognition of their fate and their communal drive to action. There are several aspects of Roumain's narrative that one might take forward into a contemporary version of de-zombification – notably, his emphasis on the "re-organisation of the state in line with the social needs of the poor" and on the "plot system of the peasantry as the potential basis on which to erect this new order" (Niblett 2012a: 30). Historically, the plot – and the ability to produce food – was associated with resistance to the plantation (Niblett 2012a; see also Wynter 1971). In Roumain's novel, the emphasis on the plot speaks to Manuel's emphasis on the community's alienation from the land and the soil: "Can [man] divorce [the soil] without losing the very reason for his existence, the use of his hands, the taste for life?" (Roumain 1998: 107).

Yet Roumain's vision displays clear limitations. Most easily recognised now is his "retention of masculinist tropes" (Niblett 2012a: 29), inherited from patriarchal-colonial capitalism, which later writers would debunk. Of course, Roumain's novel has been subjected to valid critiques – most deservedly, to the charge of naturalising a patriarchal sexism, which suffuses a text that, in many ways, resembles both nineteenth-century national romances as well as the failed romances of the sugar-cane novels. Roumain's text metaphorically conflates women and the land, offering a vision of the revitalisation, or de-zombification, of community and the land through the finding of water via the messianic sacrifice of Manuel. Symbolically, the revitalisation of the land is mirrored by Annaïse's pregnancy with Manuel's child. Patriarchal

63

dichotomies are here employed to render different ecological regimes: a negatively connoted ex-prostitute is associated with an exploitative approach to land and labour, whereas the young Annaïse, who will give birth to the martyred hero's child, is linked to ecological recovery.[9] Throughout, Manuel's love interest for Annaïse is equated with his love for the feminised land and the soil. Heavily symbolic acts coded as masculine – such as "plung[ing] his machete into the soil" (Roumain 1998: 109) – suggest that the imaginative decolonisation of the relationship to the land is yet to disentangle itself from its constitutive sexism.

Turning now to Wright, I want to suggest that, despite its otherwise quite different focus, his novel *Native Son* (1940) can be read alongside *Gouverneurs de la rosée* for the way that it uses images of undeadness and zombiedom. After his early-career publication of *Uncle Tom's Children* (1938), Wright wanted to ensure that not "even bankers' daughters could read and weep over and feel good about" this text, as he created the anti-hero Bigger Thomas (Wright 2000b: 23). Wright's characters are shown as "famously caught up in forms over which they have little control; *zombies all*, they seem driven by larger ideological forces" (Comentale 2014: 292, emphasis added). *Native Son*'s anti-hero Bigger is the epitome of a character driven by larger forces that he cannot verbalise and that are always pitted against him. But, as I want to emphasise here, Wright also very explicitly renders this history of "undeadness" as one of environmental degradation. Wright's text should be read as a work that is embedded in relational and systemic thinking about large-scale socio-ecological changes, including the previous migration to the Plains (which would end in the Dust Bowl), the Great Migration during the twentieth century and the devastation of the hinterlands wrought by metropolises such as Chicago (Rutledge 2011: 258).

Bigger – who was born in Mississippi but lives in Chicago in the narrative present – is caught up in these larger transformations. His resulting sense of dislocation and lack of direction is palpable throughout. As he is being sued for killing a Black woman called Bessie, the lawyer describes them during the trial as "trees without roots" (Wright 2000a: 427) and explains that the Black Belt of Chicago is a space that is incapable of supporting such rootless plants. Instead, the Black Belt is evocative of death-images, like that of the "snow-covered building whose many windows gaped blackly, like the eye-sockets of empty skulls" (2000a: 261). As has been documented, the Green Revolution had the effect of displacing African Americans, as the sharecropping plantation gave way to the mechanised neo-plantation. Clyde Woods writes that the "rural enclosure movement" in the Delta had destroyed several million African American homes, social networks and centuries of agricultural knowledge and

---

9 This association between prostitution and an ecology based on extractivism also underlies Jacques Stephen Alexis's *L'espace d'un cillement* ([1959] 1995), in which a desensitised – one might say zombified – female prostitute to American marines is re-sensitised by a male Cuban mechanic and labour strike organiser.

skill, and that, by the 1960s, 95% of African Americans were living in urban environments (1998: 87). Thus, the "centuries-old push for ethnic, political, and economic democracy which re-emerged under the banner of civil rights in the 1950s was effectively hollowed out by this revolution" (Woods 1998: 87).

Bigger finds himself in Chicago, in a miserable and insanitary one-bedroom apartment rented from a property mogul (whose daughter Mary he eventually kills by accident). In the run-up to the accidental murder, Wright takes care to paint a picture of the petromodern city – a "world of steel and stone" (2000a: 46) – as characterised by deep inequalities. Like in the American Sugar Kingdom, oil is associated with freedoms that Bigger cannot access. This is epitomised not only by the many cars that pass him, but also in the description of him watching an aeroplane spelling out an advert for "speed gasoline" while he muses on his inability to become a pilot. *Native Son* is obviously an urban novel but, in the context of Wright's oeuvre, it is placed within the changing relations between the plantation South and the urban North. In *12 Million Black Voices* (1941), a photo-documentary text about the Great Migration, Wright saw the changes to Southern life as part of the larger logic of imperialist capitalism: the soil is "bled of its fertility," the "potency of gasoline" is replacing manual labourers, and land is increasingly monopolised by growing agribusiness (2008: 38, 49, 56). While, as a Southerner, Wright had no illusions about the brutal realities of the South that included lynching and Jim Crow segregation, he nevertheless points to the "ecological costs" involved in the Great Migration. As he puts it, "it seems as though we are now living inside of a machine [...] no longer do our lives depend upon the soil, the sun, the rain, or the wind; we live by the grace of jobs and the brutal logic of jobs" (Wright 2008: 100). As Gregory Rutledge observes, Wright understands "American urbanity and modernity [...] as an ecological disaster unfolding on a global scale" (2011: 258). But Wright also makes clear that this fits neatly into the ideological context of racist discourse on "Nature" and race, in which Black people are routinely seen as closer to "Nature" (as seen in the endless comparisons of Bigger to a large range of animals), in a manner that upholds colonial-capitalist binary oppositions between "civilization" and the state of a human "beast" (2000a: 310).

Most explicitly, zombie imagery is invoked by Bigger's lawyer in his plea against the death penalty. Metaphorically describing the history of slavery as a corpse that white America has sought to bury, he shifts into monstrous registers to think through the legacies of slavery and the plantations: "For the corpse is not dead! It still lives! It has made itself at home in the wild forests of our great cities, among the rank and choking vegetation of slums! It has forgotten our language! In order to live it has sharpened its claws!" (Wright 2000a: 420). The zombie-esque creature here resembles the monsters that populated the tales of Lovecraft ([1922] 2011): rather than obedient workers like Seabrook's zombies, the living dead monster is the creation of the urban society it now comes to haunt and threaten with its claws. That this is an ecological story is made amply clear by the lawyer's insistence on natural metaphors to describe urban life. Interestingly, like Wynter (1971) in the context of the sugar plantations of the Anglophone Caribbean, or Alexis ([1956] 1995) in response to Haitian realities, Wright describes irrealist horror as a form of realism in response to the socio-ecological dislocations of a racist, classist society. As he puts it, "if Poe were alive, he would not have to invent horror; horror would invent him" (Wright 2000b: 31).

The novel's depiction of entrenched racial inequalities is clearly reinforced on an ideological level by its references to another industry enabled by oil: the film industry. The novel mentions Bigger watching *Trader Horn* (1931), a typical jungle picture. While the white characters are suitably heroic, the films feature Black characters that offer racist images of African savagery. Again, as in the zombie films, white femininity is seen as being "derailed" by contact with Black characters. As Cynthia Erb writes, the young daughter "Nina's wildness became the centerpiece for promotional spots for *Trader Horn*" (2009: 96). As *Trader Horn* itself illustrates, racist understandings of Blackness are developed alongside notions of white femininity as always under threat from miscegenation and rape. As we have seen earlier in this chapter, these imperial fears around racial contagion are very plainly displayed in films such as *White Zombie*, where the white foreign heroine is afflicted by the sorcery associated with the colonial space, coded as Black or "other." *Native Son* throws a light on these discourses around Black male sexuality and white femininity, as Bigger very quickly realises that he will be falsely accused of rape. Indeed, as Edward Comentale (2014) points out, the posters for the 1951 film version of *Native Son* seek to emulate the aesthetic of zombie films: Bigger is portrayed as carrying the white heroine in an upright fashion – as if he was a zombie himself.

Wright points out in his introduction to the novel that he felt that

> Bigger [...] carried within him the potentialities of either Communism or Fascism. [I don't] mean to say that the Negro Boy [he] depicted in *Native Son* is either a Communist or a Fascist. He is not either. But he is a product of a dislocated society: he is a dispossessed and disinherited man. (2000b: 15)

Wright here suggests that the crisis of the 1930s and the forms of dispossession and disinheritance that it produced – exacerbating long-standing racial and class inequalities – opened the door to two implacably opposed responses. Bigger, as he notes, carries the potentialities of both communism and fascism, and in this way he is very much a figure that resonates with the other zombie figures we have encountered in this chapter, all of whom encode a range of political possibilities – from the reactionary ideologies of imperialism to the energies of anti-imperial resistance. But in in the imagery surrounding Mary, the white murdered daughter, Wright also alludes to the whole history of imperialist-patriarchal anxiety around miscegenation and the vulnerabilities of white women in the colonies. It is to these issues around gender, imperialism and zombification that I turn in the next chapter.

CHAPTER 3

The Zombie-in-the-House, Nature and the Colonies

Zombies have, as we have seen, a long history of functioning as figures of socio-ecological alienation. Working as "beasts of burden" in fields they did not own, they provided an image for the dispossession of the working and peasant classes and the increasing commodification of life under capitalism. Yet, as Zora Neale Hurston suggests in her travel narrative *Tell my Horse* (1938), zombies "are wanted for more uses besides fieldwork" (1990: 182, 197), opening the door to thinking about the ways in which women's gendered dispossession, from rape and sexual violence to other forms of locking women into the realm of the "private," can be understood through zombie narratives. It is worth noting immediately that Hurston's conservatism and "surface collusion with [...] exotic and paternalistic discourses" (Renda 2001: 293) result in a text that in some ways follows in the footsteps of exoticising representations of Haiti and the US occupation. However, *Tell my Horse* has also been discussed for its more subversive subtexts, particularly through its ironic tone, its critique of US racism and its emphasis on sexism.[1] When it comes to zombies, Hurston, like William Seabrook, reports stories of people "set to toi[l] ceaselessly in the banana fields, working like a beast" and bought by plantation owners from *bokors* [sorcerers] (1990: 181). The zombie's

---

1 This was written about her stay in Haiti not long after the end of the US occupation. Some Haitian subjects Hurston portrays confirm the paternalistic representations bolstering imperialism, while others voice virulent criticism in reported speech. In chapter 6, we read that, in the lead-up to the occupation, "[o]ne black peasant woman fell upon her knees" and cried: "The black man is so cruel to his own, *let the white man come!*" (1990: 71). One chapter later, an unnamed Haitian accuses the Americans of having impoverished the country, now "full of beggars and [...] very poor" (1990: 85). As critics note, her writing cannot be taken at face value, as it seems imbued with ironising critique (see Renda 2001: 299).

connection to US imperialism is also strongly suggested;[2] at least partly dismantling ideological claims of the benefits of US occupation, Hurston's text reveals a society with "a hidden slave system [functioning] under neo-colonial circumstances" (Keresztesi 2011: 37). Most importantly for the current context, it is notable that zombie tropes are explicitly inscribed within the context of patriarchal relations. Evoking the context of a society in which women are regarded as "perishable goods" (Hurston 1990: 197), she describes cases of women presumed dead and buried, found in a state of dejection and displaying clear signs of trauma. The most disturbing passage contains her description of "the broken remnant, relic, or refuse of Felicia Felix-Mentor" (1990: 179) – a female zombie found many years after her abduction and sent to a hospital in Gonaives in northern Haiti. With the permission of the male Director General, Hurston photographs her against her will:

> She hovered against the fence in a sort of defensive position. The moment that she sensed our approach, she broke off a limb of a shrub and began to use it to dust and clean the ground and the fence and the table which bore food. She huddled the cloth about her head more closely and showed every sign of fear and expectation of abuse and violence. The two doctors with me made kindly noises and tried to reassure her. She seemed to hear nothing. Just kept on trying to hide herself. The doctor uncovered her head for a moment but she promptly clapped her arms and hands over it to shut out the things she dreaded. I said to the doctors that I had permission of Dr. Léon to take some pictures and he helped me go about it. I took her first in the position that she assumed herself whenever left alone. That is, cringing against the wall with the cloth hiding her face and head. Then in other positions. Finally the doctor forcibly uncovered her and held her so I could take her face. And the sight was dreadful. That blank face with the dead eyes. The eyelids were white all around the eyes as if they had been burned with acid. (1990: 195)

There is nothing in this description that would lead the reader to conclude that we are definitively dealing with a literal zombie created through poisoning. Rather, Hurston presents US readers with a woman who displays signs of trauma and anxiety, and immediately assumes the role of a domestic servant when feeling threatened. In a work that presents its criticism in mostly veiled and allegorical form, this description of the act of taking photos is significant, especially since the photo of Felix-Mentor that is printed in the book – which does not show signs of forceful intervention – is not the one described in this passage. Scholars have taken an interest in Hurston's representation of

---

2 The chapter on zombies begins with a reference to "the shadow of the Empire State building" (Hurston 1990: 179), seemingly in a bid to contrast the US and Haiti. But the invocation of the skyscraper – only built at the beginning of the decade and having already featured in the imperialist horror film *King Kong* (1933) – keeps US imperialism within sight as the author evokes reports of zombification.

zombified women and their allegorical meaning in relation to the operations of gender and race within the interrelated contexts of the US occupation and its dominance over Haiti. As Amy Fass Emery writes, the female zombie "represents the uncanny return in the text of fears Hurston tries to repress – of the dispossession of voice and the loss of the self's autonomy through submission to the will of others, the death-in-life of the tragically silenced black woman" (2005: 330). In this argument, the photograph thus speaks to Hurston's experiences in a racist-patriarchal US, but it also registers patriarchal violence in the context of a society marked by the legacies of the American occupation, which had normalised horrific sexual violence against and rape of Haitian women, thinly masked through racist definitions of sexuality and consent (Renda 2001: 163). Hurston represents herself as complicit in the woman's forced representation, while also insisting on exposing the mechanisms at work. The photo is thus turned into an artefact that speaks strongly to the gendered and racialised violence that is a prerequisite for US ethnographic representation.

The female zombie has, of course, long tended to be marked by extremes of violence, whether the structural violence of poverty which disproportionately affects women, sexist gendered violence, or the symbolic violence occluded in the conflation of women with the land/nature, the nation or abstracted culture. An early female zombie reference can be found in the third volume of *Voyages d'un naturaliste* (1809), "a mixture of observations about natural history and autobiographical narrative," written by a white Frenchman, Michel-Étienne Descourtilz, who became a captive of the revolutionary army and worked as a doctor (Popkin 2007: 270). Descourtilz narrates the re-encounter between a soldier of Toussaint Louverture's revolutionary army and his mother Marie Noël, whom he violently disavows and calls an "old *zombie*" who wants to deceive him (1809: 220). Unlike her son, who is a guide for Toussaint Louverture, Marie Noël is completely destitute, covered only by rags and emaciated to the point of being skeletal. In response to her son's rejection, she throws herself to the ground and calls on death to relieve her. The zombie here clearly emerges as an embodied figure, rather than as a spirit (as in many early zombie texts); indeed, Descourtilz "implies that the son feels compelled to reject his mother because she looks like a dead body" (Murphy 2011: 50). But we also need to place emphasis on gender: accordingly, the critic Raphael Hoermann (2017) situates the description of Marie Noël as a female zombie within the context of a society still marked by the legacies of the colonial system, which had operated through the systemic sexual abuse of Haitian women, as the Haitian historian Baron de Vastey had exposed in *The Colonial System Unveiled* ([1814] 2016: 157).

While Marie Noël is barely afforded a couple of pages in Descourtilz's multi-volume work, a more significant role was given to a fictional female zombie two decades later in Ignace Nau's *Isalina* (1836), the first known work of Haitian prose fiction, in which zombification takes place in the context of a sugar mill plantation associated with "merrymaking" and described as "picturesque" (Nau 2000: 29–30). The eponymous heroine is betrothed to the character Paul, but also desired by his "baptismal brother" Jean-Julien (2000: 31), resulting in a patriarchal power struggle. The violence suffusing gender relations in the aftermath of colonialism is close to the surface, even if the novella does not press on the relations between plantation agriculture and gendered oppressions: "if you don't belong to me you will not be his," Jean-Julien announces to Isalina, after she rejects his advances in a cemetery (2000: 36). He pushes her violently, resulting in a severe head injury as well as a shift of her affections towards Jean-Julien – a somewhat inexplicable effect viewed within the narrowly realist frame of understanding (although certainly less enigmatic from a perspective informed by current research on gender violence). Within the novella, narrative realism gives way to "narrative indigenism" (or *le merveilleux creole*) and the communal understanding that Isalina has been murdered and put under a spell (Brickhouse 2004: 116). Indeed, we learn that "there are zombies in this" story (Nau 2000: 42).[3] Likewise, as Isalina phrases her predicament after her recovery through a ritual performed by a wise Vodun practitioner, she was inhabited by an evil spirit that subdued, but did not fully eclipse, her "feeble consciousness" as she "tried, but in vain, to renounce [the evil spirit], to repel it far from [her]" (Nau 2000: 65).

By the time of the zombie's explosive rise in popularity in the 1920s and 1930s in the context of US imperialism and its racist ideologies, the female zombie – rendered submissive to male desire – was crystallising into an internationally recognisable trope that was strongly inflected by tensions around race and class. In contrast to the earlier female zombies we just encountered, she was now frequently middle- or upper-class and/or lighter-skinned or white, and rendered submissive by "an older dark-skinned man who is of lower class and adept at sorcery" (Paravisini-Gebert 1997: 40). Hurston, for instance, noted that the most famous tale of zombification related to the death in 1909 and subsequent rediscovery of a young, upper-class girl referred to as "Marie M" (1990: 194).[4] Seabrook, who is usually credited with introducing the zombie to US audiences in 1929, tells a version of this story. Young, "light-skinned" Camille, who comes from a "prosperous, but not wealthy" family (Seabrook 1929: 109), marries a much older coffee grower, who was "dark and more than twice her age, but rich, suave and well educated" and "kept his own motor car" (1929: 109–10). Yet he is also adept at black magic – equated with "voodoo" by Seabrook. Asked to attend a dinner with dead guests on her anniversary, Camille loses her sanity while dressed in virginal white. As seen in more detail in Chapter 2, these story conventions

---

3 While it is unclear whether the term "zombie" names Isalina's predicament, or is employed much more loosely (see, for example, Lauro 2015: 127), her subordination to Jean-Julien's will can clearly be found in tales of zombification up to the present day.

4 This story, as Paravisini-Gebert details, was also reported by a Haitian doctor and foreign ethnographers (1997: 40–41).

clearly also influenced early American zombie films and zombie pulp, in which the racialised, white or light-skinned female zombie transmutes into a symbol registering racist imperial anxieties around racial contagion and cultural difference.

How might we relate this figure more explicitly to capitalism's subordination of natures to the pursuit of profit? If, from an ecocritical perspective, it was relatively easy to discern the ecological dimension of representations of the zombie labouring on the plantation, the trope of the female zombie often seems less overtly *about* ecology, since she is associated with the domestic realm and reproductive work. Indeed, the mediation of the female's relation to her surroundings through patriarchal structures tends to background questions of ecology, despite her being indispensable to the production and reproduction of material life. As we saw in Chapter 2, Jason W. Moore's analysis of the capitalist strategy of appropriating "Cheap Natures" – which continues a long tradition of feminist, socialist and world-systemic writings by theorists including C.L.R. James, Walter Rodney, Maria Mies, Sylvia Wynter, Wilma Dunaway and Sylvia Federici – allows us to address connections between the appropriation of the work of racialised and gendered humans and the work of extra-human natures.

What I want to show in this chapter, then, is that cultural producers have for some time been able to make explicit the connections between female zombification – often coded as a forced withdrawal into the realm of domestic service or the "home" – and the horizon of the capitalist world-ecology, particularly its extractive and environmentally degrading practices. In these narratives by a range of (often female) writers, female zombification enables thinking beyond the ideological and material separations that divide the "private" from the "public," and "Society" from "Nature." Indeed, the female zombie has enabled these female writers to render visible connections that were occluded in the colonial-capitalist externalising of "women, nature and the colonies" (Mies [1986] 1994: 77). Marie Vieux Chauvet, Ana Lydia Vega and Pedro Cabiya are some of the writers who press on the relations between female zombification and imperialism/colonialism as ecological regimes; between the subordination of women in capitalist cores and the subordination of "nature and colonies"; between social reproduction and the productive industries; and between the subjection of colonised women, including the regulation of their bodies and control over their reproductive rights, and imperialist extractive regimes.

If the plantation zombie rendered visible the metabolic rifts through which the commodification of labour power proceeds, the female zombie – often represented as monstrously *un*productive – registers the gendered experience of capitalist processes of accumulation, which structurally devalue or undervalue women's work. As social reproduction theorist Tithi Bhattacharya reminds us, if "the spatial separation between production (public) and reproduction (private) is a historical form of appearance, then the labor that is dispensed in both spheres must also be theorized integratively"

(2017: 9). In order to do so, it is important not to confuse labour (the work people engage in) with labour-power (the commodity), a common-sense conflation that occludes the role of the household and women's labour in capitalist production (Seccombe 1993: 7). What is suppressed in the wage form is the fact that, while "labour-power is *consumed* in the workplace [...] it is *produced* apart from capital" (Seccombe 1993: 9). An eco-cultural history of the zombie, which would take account of both the zombie-labourer and the zombie-of-the-house, enables us to write an ecological history of the figure that does not background gendered oppression.

The Reproduction of Material Life, the Commodity Frontier and the Female Zombie

As we have seen previously, female zombies entered the US imaginary in narratives and films that ideologically propped up imperialist extractivism in the Caribbean. But the trope also arguably captured something of the endemic gendered violence against women in patriarchal capitalist societies as well as the devaluation of gendered work performed to reproduce the household and the workforce. This aspect would become central in some key female zombie texts from the late 1960s onwards – most famously, perhaps, in *The Stepford Wives* (1972), by American writer Ira Levin. I here propose to read Levin's novel and its 1975 film version alongside "Love," a novella published in 1968 as part of *Amour, colère, folie* [Love, Anger, Madness], by Haitian intellectual Marie Vieux Chauvet. Both texts introduce significant changes to the female zombie and link her to bourgeois domesticity, while refusing to offer the heterosexual romance plot as her potential escape route. While "Love" presents its protagonist, Claire, a character akin to the Gothic madwoman, as only metaphorically zombified, the suburban wives of Stepford are literally replaced by bosomy robots, "echo[ing] critiques offered a decade earlier by de Beauvoir and by Friedan [...] in which housewives are seen as trapped in a life of pointless repetition" (Elliott 2008: 72). In Levin's text, Joanna's growing awareness creates an atmosphere of increasing (ultimately justified) paranoia; in Chauvet's, zombification and self-alienation are formally expressed through the confessional diary, which dramatises Claire's imprisonment within an internal, private sphere, trapped by gendered, raced and classed oppression that manifests in conventions and patterns of behaviour. Both texts, as we will see, situate this depiction of women's alienation within a larger socio-ecological context, reading patriarchal relations as part of capitalist ecologies. Yet the "ultimate horizon" of the capitalist world-system (WReC 2015) is much more plainly visible, indeed graspable, in "Love." While there is, of course, no simplistic or deterministic connection between place and a consciously world-literary aesthetic, Chauvet's ability to represent world-ecological relations in such a lucid manner is at least partly shaped by the fact that, as Greg Beckett to insert gender inequality within a horizon that pays attention to how class, race and geopolitics affect women very unequally across the world-system.

The Stepford wife has by now become a trope that has come to symbolise the "horrific nature of static time" in the household (Elliott 2008: 72): women waste their time on repetitive tasks that fragment their days and render intellectual activity difficult, if not impossible (see Friedan [1963] 2010). The Stepford wives in the 1975 film are replaced by uniformly sexy and ample-bosomed human-looking robots by the Men's Association. Biological women, it is implied, are only needed until the biological reproduction of the workforce is complete, at which point they can be replaced. Such a valuation invalidates the lives of women – cis and trans – who may not want or be able to bear children. As Levin's novel posits, their role after that is vacuous and their time filled by housekeeping, cleaning and "*buy[ing] more things for the house*" within the context of a post-WWII boom economy (Friedan 2010: 166). As the protagonist Joanna in her pre-zombie state observes, the robot-women of "zombieville" are all "actresses in commercials, pleased with detergents and floor wax, with cleansers and shampoos and deodorants. Pretty actresses, big in the bosom but small in talent, playing suburban housewives unconvincingly, too nicey-nice to be real" (Levin 2011: 65, 49). As suggested in this nightmarish vision of the total domination of patriarchal capitalism, atomisation and imprisonment within the realm of soaps and shampoos has as its desired (though, of course, never fully achieved) outcome radical alienation as well as political apathy. Spiritually dulled by shopping, the zombie-robot-housewife epitomises the myopia at the capitalist core or, put differently, the structural impediments to seeing inequality at the capitalist core (i.e., commodity fetishism). Think, for instance, of the scenes of immaculately styled, hyper-feminine, hyper-sexualised Stepford wives strolling past aisles of supermarket products in Forbes's 1975 film version. The visual repression of the work and stress involved in domestic tasks might be said to mirror the hidden, spectral environmental and social histories of the products, involving agro-industrialisation, dispossession of women and workers, enclosures and monopolisation. It seems almost too obvious to point out, but of course not one of the Stepford wives tends to a plot or grows food herself – something that would put her radically at odds with the system exposed, a system in which her relation to the outside world is mediated by the market.

While its explicit focus is on gendered oppression, Levin's novel is aware of the relation between housewifisation, racialisation and environmental history and goes some way towards linking uneven access to green suburban spaces, not only to housewifisation, but also to zoning and "white flight." The all-white green suburbs are contrasted with the space of the city, associated in the novel with pollution and economic decline, as well as with the struggle against racial inequality. To put this into historical context,

> beginning in the 1940s, the United States' racial geography, especially in the North, was reorganised and transformed due to federal policies,

working in concert with local governments and real-estate developers, encouraging and incentivising White Americans to relocate to a newly created and expanding geography: suburbia. This radical transformation was a response to, in large part, the Great Migration. (Poll 2018: 74)

In *The Stepford Wives*, it is notable that apart from a newcomer family at the end, the suburbanites are all white and middle-class – something that the narrative repeatedly signposts. Further, the access to white-green suburbia comes with a price tag: "Look at the sky," Joanna's husband says, "worth every penny it cost us" (Levin 2011: 6). Later, at an awkward dinner party, one of the couple's city friends "tore into suburban communities that enriched themselves with tax-yielding light industry while fortressing themselves with two- and four-acre zoning" (2011: 57) – an accurate description of Stepford, surrounded by a shopping mall, a McDonald's and biochemical, electronics and computer industries. The ecological and social cost of suburbanisation – underwritten by oil and the increasing dominance of car culture, as well as new racial regimes – is largely repressed by the suburbanites, whose concerns about environmental deterioration and social inequality are displaced and re-contained by worrying about small details, such as buying non-polluting detergent (2011: 1). Similarly, when Bobby and Joanna begin to suspect that something is wrong with the women in Stepford, they first think it might be due to contamination of the drinking water caused by one of the electronic or chemical plants nearby. While they are, of course, wrong as far as the plot is concerned, their suspicion registers the increasing awareness of the environmental damage caused by petro-fuelled capitalist modernisation, as represented by the Men's Association. But while *The Stepford Wives* is able to signpost the ways in which capitalism works through racial, gendered and ecological regimes in the United States, what remains ungraspable is the role of imperialism and the extraction of resources (including labour-power) from places such as Haiti in maintaining the American status quo for the middle classes.

By contrast, in "Love" the relations between the capitalist core and the peripheries, as well as the role of the neo-colonial bourgeoisie in this scenario, are explicitly addressed. Claire's zombification is about gendered confinement to the private space of domesticity: living with her two sisters, Felicia and Annette, and Felicia's husband Jean Luce, she occupies a subordinated role in the family, "at once a servant and mistress of the house, a kind of housekeeper on whose shoulders rests the daily round of their lives" (Chauvet 2009: 5). As a 39-year-old unmarried virgin, she does not conform to what is socially defined as central to womanhood under patriarchal capitalism: biological reproduction as part of a nuclear family. Further, as the darkest-skinned daughter of a light-skinned family of coffee plantation owners, Claire, whose name means "light," has internalised colourism, sexism and classism, instilled in her by her father through physical punishment. The repression produced by the racialised and gendered expectations placed on her as a member of the "mulatto" bourgeoisie structures her life, dominated by bottled-up desires that are only inadequately met by displacement activities, including cradling a doll, looking at pornographic postcards, fantasising about her French, white brother-in-law and about killing her sister. Figuratively zombified by her life without agency, she describes herself as a "soulless body" and refers to "an emptiness within" (2009: 66, 65). Indeed, her predicament can be described both in terms of the burial preceding zombification and in terms of automation: "I lie beneath the last geological layer, at once dead and alive. No, dead, truly dead. A kind of automaton. I no longer have a soul. Is this what despair is?" (2009: 65). As we have seen in previous chapters, the imaginaries of zombification and robotisation overlap – whether we are speaking about work in the fields or in the home.

As Chauvet makes clear, Claire's metaphorical zombification – expressive of her radical alienation, lack of agency and imprisonment within racialised and gendered codes of behaviour – is shaped by history, most notably racist colonial legacies and structures, the US occupation (which caused her father's death) and the emergence of militarised race nationalism represented by the brutal regime of the military strongman, Calédu, who cooperates with foreign capital in the oppression of the lower classes. "Love" emphasises the ways in which both the late 1930s and the Duvalier régime were shaped by the US occupation, which had created a highly militarised society and cemented Haiti's position as a resource extraction zone, forced to provide "cheap" extra-human resources and migrant labour-power. But Claire's backstory, revealed through flashbacks, indicates that she – as a member of the neo-colonial mulatto bourgeoisie – has also been an agent in this violent social order, and continues to be a partial beneficiary of it. Prior to her father selling most of their coffee plantations in a bid to achieve political power, Claire's family's social position used to be upheld by the surplus value brutally extracted from severely underpaid, starved peasant-tenants, "enslaved by [...] meagre wages" (2009: 85). After the death of her father when the US invades Haiti, Claire struggles to uphold this situation and proceeds to ally herself with foreign capital, embodied in the novel by American imperialist Mr Long. She fixes coffee prices at a rate that undercuts the coffee price of the region, with horrific results for the peasant-tenants who are killed in retribution for her actions. As becomes clear through these flashbacks, her "zombification" must be read within the context of Haiti as a resource-extraction zone, and in relation to the functioning of the ruling middle class as mediating between foreign interests, world market prices and a super-exploited peasant class. These racialised class divisions also extend into the space of their household, as Claire's position is far above that of her (now paid) domestic servant Augustine. As Claire notes, under her parents, Augustine's role was that of an unpaid "houseslave who called the babies mademoiselle and conceded their every whim for fear of being beaten" (2009: 59).

But perhaps the most perceptive aspect of the novella is the way it highlights the intertwining of the devastating environmental and gendered legacies of the occupation through Chauvet's insistent linking of the gothic mode to the commodity frontier. In the narrative present, Mr Long, with whom both the French Jean Luze and the Haitian Calédu collude, concentrates his business on lumber export. Long and the American ship are evoked frequently as environment-degrading forces:

> The indifferent ship loads the wood piled high on the pier. Business on that end is booming. M. Long, red as a rooster, manages the operation himself. The peasants have faces like whipped dogs. They sulk and hold out their hands for their payment as they look away into the distance at the devastated hillside. Huge white patches have spread on the mountain like leprosy. Immense rocks stick out of its sides like gravestones. (2009: 46)

Deforestation, and the resultant topsoil erosion, is one of the most damaging legacies of this period. While in the early 1920s "over sixty percent [of Haiti] was still covered by forests," "by 1945, following the American Occupation (a period of intensified lumber exportation), this number had been reduced to twenty-one percent; ten years later, the number was eight to nine percent" (Paravisini-Gebert 2015: 79–80). The gothic and anthropomorphic image of the graveyard in the passage above plainly emphasises the intertwining of the fate of the peasants and the environment they inhabit. On the commodity frontier, the brutality of extractivism and primitive accumulation is nakedly apparent, as is the link with human impoverishment and misery. The gothic here does not merely register the repression of such violence, but instead serves to de-fetishise commodity production and global class relations as well as, arguably, the symbolic enclosure of women within the private sphere. This latter aspect becomes especially apparent in the direct textual contrast of Claire's atomisation and the context of resource extraction, as her confessions often shift quite abruptly from descriptions of "external" extractivism to "internal" obsessions. A full-blown episode of madness, evoking several familiar tropes of the monstrous feminine, occurs just after her observation of Calédu's brutal strike-breaking in support of Long's export business, which she does from the safety of the supposedly removed space of the bourgeois "private sphere":

> This morning, Calédu bludgeoned several peasants. He's furious. I watched the whole scene from behind my shutters. Other eyes in the neighborhood were spying too. I saw curtains moved by trembling hands, eyes glowing behind other blinds; I heard whispering to the right, to the left, and piercing the whispering almost at regular intervals, Calédu's swearing, the peasants' cries of pain and protests: they went on strike against M. Long to demand a better price for their wood. In response M. Long unloaded an electric saw from the boat docked in the harbor for the past two hours, and the commandant made the peasants haul it themselves. It was taking too much time to chop the trees down with axes, and M. Long was in a hurry to buy all of the mountain wood at the price he had fixed. One of the peasants kept talking despite the blows:

"Don't give in!" he yelled. "Hang on, and if I die, don't forget you must stick together."

He was taken to prison dying ...

I clutch my doll against my chest. Alone in the dark, I gaze at the moon and attempt a smile. Desire is fading. I feel purified. I hear the church clock chime an hour. Another sleepless night washes away and the day rises without pity and lines up behind all the other days in my life. My wrinkles deepen and my features wilt. Old age is coming soon. Oh, I want to live, to live before it's too late! (Chauvet 2009: 73, ellipses in original)

Claire's seamless turn to the monstrous-feminine Gothic after the description of the brutalities that accompany primitive accumulation suggests that the gothic mode is partly animated by her recognition of the repression at stake in her social position. She seems to recognise that, while Calédu pushes violence to unseen extremes, she is also part of the same system of oppression. In this context, the possibility of a communal expression of resistance and collectivity – a utopian dream that was still imaginable in Roumain's literary universe – is nearly stamped into oblivion by the methods employed by Calédu that involve militarised violence and rape.

The centrality of gendered violence, including rape, to the contemporary social order is highlighted from the beginning of the novella and thematised through the haunting descriptions of Dora Soubiran in the aftermath of sexual torture, as she appears like a "maimed animal" (2009: 17), only able to walk with her legs far apart. Systemic abuse of women has deep roots, as Claire's reflections on her past and present situation as part of the bourgeois class reveal. Female oppression ranges from beatings to hypocritical expectations when it comes to sexuality. Solidarity, and specifically female solidarity, is fragile in "Love," a fact driven home by a number of female doubles for Claire, who are inscribed in racialised class hierarchies, including Augustine, Felicia and Annette. Although Claire – who has internalised sexism, racism and classism – is unable to form a meaningful relation with any of them, she eventually begins to show public solidarity with the women of her own class who have been raped and violated by Calédu. In this context, the ambivalent ending in which Claire stabs Calédu to death during an uprising of the disenfranchised former peasants is invested with new significance. While this is not a triumphant ending since Claire's killing of Calédu is "hardly treated as heroic" (Dalleo 2011: 139) and Mr Long is left untouched, it nevertheless suggests the possibility of aligning the gendered interests of the abused bourgeois women with the uprisings of the dispossessed.

What might the reader of Chauvet's and Levin's texts learn from a comparative reading? Produced at a crucial moment in global history – 1968 in Chauvet's case, and only slightly later in Levin's – both authors rewrite the female zombie and present the sexism that shaped this trope as fundamental to the existing world-order, and thus also as fundamentally enmeshed in racial inequality and ecological degradation. But while Levin's *Stepford Wives* shows a critical awareness of the environmental and racial regimes underpinning suburban housewifisation in a national context, the role of global imperialism from which the American middle classes benefit remains out of sight. Focusing on Haiti, where US extractivist practices and their extreme human and environmental costs are nakedly apparent, Chauvet, on the other hand, was able to draw the connections between imperialism, the Duvalier regime, environmental degradation, sexual violence and bourgeois housewifisation. In the US imaginary of the Cold War, zombies and zombification have often been associated with mind control and, implicitly, with communism – think, for instance, of *Invasion of the Body Snatchers* (Siegel 1956). In Chauvet's novella, it is the anti-communist dictatorship of Duvalier, accepted and at times supported by the US, with which zombifiers are associated – a theme continued by many Haitian writers, including Frankétienne and René Depestre. Further, and more broadly, in both texts it is patriarchal capitalism that produces zombies, or alienated workers (whether unpaid or paid).

Zombies, Madwomen and Aliens in the Puerto Rican Imaginary

If location has something to do with one's ability to grasp the operations of the world-system, then Puerto Rico – where the "pulse of the world capitalist economy" has been felt through its close but subordinated relation to the United States since 1898 (Ayala and Bernabe 2009: 3) – provides an interesting example of zombie texts, especially when combined with our eco-materialist focus on zombies. As we have seen previously, Puerto Rican society – including its economy and ecology – was rapidly transformed by US imperialism, leaving many small-scale peasants without land as US capital was invested in sugar. Yet, in the context of the Cold War during the global boom years after the Second World War, the "Free Associated State" of Puerto Rico "became (largely through massive federal-government subsidies) a political showcase for the prosperity and democracy promised by close alliance with the United States" (Briggs 2002: 2), a situation that partially and temporarily masked damaging levels of dependency, domination and exploitation by US capital along with permanently lower living standards compared with the mainland US. In this context, I want to focus on two writers – Ana Lydia Vega and Pedro Cabiya – who have both employed female zombies to revise or parody national imaginaries. Evoking familiar tropes of Puerto Rican identity, including the *jíbaro* (the rural peasant imagined as white) and the *gran familia puertorriqueña* (the big Puerto Rican family), Vega and Cabiya pose interesting and challenging questions about the role of social and biological reproduction in both a national and a world-systemic context. Both authors highlight the role culture plays in reproducing or challenging the colonialist-capitalist world-ecological order, with a particular emphasis on the Gothic and genre fiction more broadly.

In "Miss Florence's Trunk" (1991), Vega, a well-known feminist writer in Puerto Rico, turns to the nineteenth century under Spanish colonialism and debunks the racist-patriarchal myth of the big Puerto Rican family as well as "the glorified hacienda that served as its primary metaphor" (Moreno 2012: 95). Suppressing the significance and presence of African cultures, the former was imagined as Hispanic, white and benevolently ruled over by the patriarch. As Marisol Moreno details, it was mobilised and celebrated by the *generación del 30* (members of the 1930s generation) as a symbolic defence against Americanisation, and subsequently revived during the boom years in national discourse (2012: 29, 35). In contrast to this national imaginary, Vega depicts the big family as shaped by the plantation economy and international capital: they are Dutch and American, employ a British governess and enslave the workers on the sugar plantation. In Vega's novella, these social relations zombify both women and enslaved plantation workers, albeit very unevenly. It is through an engagement with European and American Gothic narratives that she thus exposes the ecological unconscious of imperial/colonial Gothic imaginaries and corrects distorted visions of the nineteenth-century hacienda.

"Miss Florence's Trunk" engages with two canonical texts that might be said to belong to the genre of plantation Gothic or "sugar Gothic": Charlotte Brontë's novel *Jane Eyre* (1847) and Jacques Tourneur's film *I Walked with a Zombie* (1943). Through this engagement, Vega evokes a world-systemic context dominated first by British hegemony, and then challenged by the emergence of American imperialism. In *Jane Eyre*, Bertha – the creole wife of Mr Rochester and the madwoman in the attic – might be said to represent British "remnant guilt for the Caribbean slave economy" (Kreyling 2016: 234). In Tourneur's filmic reimagination of *Jane Eyre*, the romantic struggles between an American and a British half-brother over the zombified Jessica register these inter-imperial struggles. Unlike these predecessor texts, which employ romance as a device for plotting the narrative and transcoding power dynamics, Vega's novella is structured around a sugar boom-and-bust arc that is determined by the rise and fall of *La Enriqueta*, a historical plantation near Arroyo. Opening in the US in 1885, when the governess Florence Jane receives news of the death of her former mistress Miss Susan (the daughter of American Samuel Morse and wife of the Danish merchant Edward Lind), part I of the novella focuses on the years Florence spent in Puerto Rico (1856–1959), using the narrative device of journal entries read in the narrative present. Part II focuses on her return to Arroyo in 1885, where she finds that slavery has been abolished, the hacienda is in ruins and her former employers are dead. Through this structure, Vega highlights the fundamental role of the volatile international sugar industry in shaping – though not determining – local and global environments and social dynamics. Revolts and rebellions against the social order (which increased after the collapse of the 1820–1840 sugar boom [Baralt 2007: 62]), soil degradation, deforestation and ensuing water scarcity all contributed to undermining the profitability of the Puerto Rican sugar industry, driven by foreign capital. Vega's attention to this world-systemic context helps render explicit what the two precursor texts could only register through horror and the monstrous, raising questions pertaining to the imperial Gothic's world-ecological unconscious and the role of women within it.

In Brontë's novel, the governess Jane is largely unaware of the colonial Jamaican provenance of Rochester's wealth, which, in displaced form, haunts the house through the "preternatural" laugh of his first wife Bertha Mason ([1847] 1996: 123), "a defeated 'colonia[l]' othered in [her] questionable racial provenance, swarthy and un-English" (Paravisini 2002: 249). The same cannot be said for Miss Florence, however, who lives in close proximity to the cane fields and serves the wife, much like Betsy in *I Walked with a Zombie*. Vega's story turns on the limitations of the viewpoint of the governess – a figure who came to encapsulate ideals of imperial domesticity, bound up with a "civilizing" mission and the production of an "elite whiteness" (Tolentino 2011: 324). Florence's social status is ambiguous: she is both an economically dispossessed female and an agent in the colonial order. Indeed, the story situates Florence amid a series of female doubles – including Miss Susan, Selenia and Bela – defining them "as part of a racialized gender hierarchy" (Tolentino 2011: 322). With the potential racial differences between Florence and Miss Susan erased in Vega's version, both white women are metaphorically transformed into zombies as their willpower has turned into bagasse, the crushed leftovers of sugar-cane production. The Gothic secret thus no longer focuses on the madwoman in the attic and her monstrosity, but rather on the fact that the zombified women's "golden cage" is built on "the bones of so many of God's creatures" (Vega [1991] 1994: 186, 217). In other words, it focuses on the moment of fetishistic disavowal, as they are willing to ignore and perpetuate a brutal system of dehumanisation through their active collusion. In this system, Bela is the enslaved domestic servant, whose agency and ability to live her life is brutally curtailed, while Selenia is forced to serve his sexual pleasure and bear his child.

Within this narrative universe, alternative perspectives are advanced, most notably by Bela when she assumes narrative control via reported speech. Referencing abolition in 1873, her reaction exposes the racism underlying Florence's nostalgia for the hacienda in its heyday. Further, in an earlier key scene taking place in the late 1850s, French doctor and potential love interest René Fouchard leads Florence from the gardens of the hacienda into the slave quarters, a place beyond what she refers to as "the magic circle of the gardens" (1994: 200). As Cynthia Tolentino observes, Fouchard seeks to use this as an educational moment to expose the inhumanity of the system that produces sugar for her coffee, and to instruct her "in the link between slave labour and civilized domesticity" (2011: 328); Florence, on the other hand, reduces the sight of impoverished and abused workers to a moment of terror that needs to be erased from memory, and describes the enslaved in gothic imagery and vocabulary. They form "a long cortège of ragged men and women, their bare feet, covered with mud, stumbling" towards her; they have "grim and hostile countenances that looked like faces from some dark cavern in the bowels of hell," which she is "eager to erase" from her memory (Vega 1994: 200). The gothic mode is here evoked as part of the ideological erasure of inequalities and the violence on which they are based, but it also continues to be haunted by the displaced fears of the white elite of rebellions and uprisings, evoked also through references to the Haitian Revolution.

The scene further functions as a comment on the repression of the ecological exhaustion through which colonialist capitalism develops. "The magic circle of the gardens" is where the human and ecological degradation of the *bateyes* [plantation village] and the surrounding cane fields is forgotten. In Victorian fiction, the garden was usually defined as a "woman's space, a safe boundary between the domestic and the wider world" (Henson 2011: 7), an ideological association explored and exposed by Vega. Florence's racialised femininity, as well as her English domesticity – stereotypically defined through the tea-drinking habits she brings to *La Enriqueta* (Tolentino 2011: 324) – are bound up with the gardens that encapsulate the ostentatious excess of the hacienda. In this space, what matters is her relationship with a transnational slave-holding elite. Her "civilizing" mission in this context translates into her attempts to contain any threat to racial and class boundaries, a threat embodied in the text by her double Selenia, described by Edward Lind as belonging to a "hybrid race [...] born without soul" (Vega 1994: 192). In a similar manner, Charlie, who has grown up in Puerto Rico, knows much about the local flora and fauna and refuses to abide by racial segregation, appears to Florence a "little wild beast" (1994: 170) who needs to be domesticated. The reference to "magic" in the "magic circle of the gardens," then, names the fetishistic moment of the erasure of the gardens' relation to the "non-domestic," "un-civilized" space of the cane fields. That relation is, as we have seen, inextricably racialised and gendered.

Vega portrays a very unevenly developed landscape, as the differences between the cane fields, the gardens of *La Enriqueta* and the environment that surrounds the plantation are very pronounced, just as her descriptions illustrate that "Nature" needs to be understood as a social relation. The "dry monotony of the landscape" beyond the plantations contrasts with the out-of-place, "artistically designed gardens" peopled by Greek and Roman statues (1994: 168), as well as caged animals and flowers that recreate stereotypical images of "pristine" exotic nature. Most remarkable is the contrast between the aridity of these surroundings and the large artificial pools of the gardens that defy the "tireless sun" (1994: 168). These pools mark the height of the plantation's splendour and will be empty after the plantation's demise (Overman 2000: 127). To put the lavishness of landscaping into context, by the mid-nineteenth century the impact of the plantation economy on the local ecosystem was felt in the decline of rainfall and the greater frequency of droughts (Figueroa 2005: 22, 70). The original, sparse lowland forests had been rapidly destroyed by cane cultivation, while the "intensified occupation of the highlands and the wholesale cutting of timber for construction [...] exacted a heavy toll on water-retaining vegetation" (Scarano 1984: 47). That the availability of water was also a concern for the real Edward Lind is attested to by his disagreement with his neighbour, Santiago Ryes, over access to a nearby brook in 1857 (Overman 2000: 108). In Vega's novella, when the hacienda is approaching ruin and Lind is heavily indebted, the conditions for making fast profits are exhausted, as both water and labour after emancipation are scarce. The contradictions that led to the hacienda's decline are encapsulated in the image of it standing "like a soulless body amid the green of the trees" (Vega 1994: 241), metaphorically exposing the zombification at the plantation's core. But it is particularly through her reworking of the white female zombie trope via Susan and Florence that Vega draws out the ecology of the monstrous feminine.

While Susan and Florence's transformation into female zombies precedes the hacienda's ruin, and was conditioned by their subordinated role within patriarchal structures, their zombification only fully emerges after Charlie's suicide, which encapsulates the plantation system's social contradictions. In the early-to-mid 1880s, both keep returning to the cane fields as the site that binds together environmental degradation, racial segregation and patriarchal relations, turning them into versions of Bertha or *I Walked with a Zombie*'s Jessica, "moaning like a soul in purgatory" (Vega 1994: 254). Through the lens of Vega's story, Brontë's Bertha – the madwoman in the attic – is exposed as the figure who registers the repression, not only of racial and gendered exploitation and discourse, but also of the ecological violence and devastation on which Rochester's wealth is based and that allows for the articulation of Jane's Victorian domesticity. Bertha, like the zombie, blurs the boundaries between the "human" and the "animal": "What it was, whether beast or human being, one could not, at first sight tell: it grovelled, seemingly, on all fours" (Brontë 1996: 327). While Jane is identified throughout with the English landscape, "the West Indian landscape (with which Bertha is associated) is given its full infernal meaning, inextricably linked to the unexpurgated sexual female" (Henson 2011: 49). Jane's domesticity – bound up as it is with discourses of gender, "Nature" and race – structurally depends on Bertha, her "wild nature" and the invisible cane fields. Vega's narrative thus portrays patriarchal colonialist capitalism as an environment-making – or rather, environment-exhausting – process, and the Gothic as an aesthetic that registers these dynamics.

While Vega challenges any idealisation of the pre-1898 past by focusing on the plantations of the coast, Cabiya debunks the *jíbaro* – a nostalgic trope that had long been evoked as a romanticised symbol of Puerto Rican identity, problematically associated in the early twentieth century (and beyond) with whiteness, Spanish culture and patriarchal masculinity (Guerra 1998: 14). Known for his irreverent attitude towards the national imaginary of *puertorriqueñidad*, Cabiya created a *jíbara* version of the female zombie in his "weird" sci-fi novella, "Relato del piloto que dijo adios con la mano" [Story of the pilot who waved good-bye] ([2003] 2011), suggesting that some of the female rural inhabitants of Puerto Rico were replaced in the 1910s by alien-produced clones. In the process, he raises important questions about the role of female sexuality, biological reproduction and working-class female bodies within a rapidly changing context under US colonialism. As Néstor E. Rodríguez has argued, for all the playfulness that critics tend to see in Cabiya's writing, the novella is hewn from this historical experience of US colonial imperialism and US-led modernisation, with an emphasis on the role of science, medicine and public health, and debates around (and experimentation on) women and biological reproduction (Rodríguez 2009: 1245, 1249).

While Cabiya's story playfully complicates any straightforward allegorisation, it strongly resonates with the ways in which "the sexuality and reproduction of poor women would become the battleground – symbolic and real – for the meaning of the US presence in Puerto Rico" (Briggs 2002: 51). Of course, this modernising impulse was hardly neutral, as both discourse and practice relating to women's rights and scientific progress were deeply enmeshed in the power relations between mainland US and the island, and employed to support the supposed benevolence of colonialism. Indeed, accounts by US government agencies released in the 1920s suggested that to modernise Puerto Rico, and to implement progress, "required a change in *production and reproduction*" (Briggs 2002: 84, emphasis added). In other words, according to this view (held by US and local elite modernisers), not only industry and agriculture but also families and sexual relations needed "modernising"; the latter would also supposedly help to remedy the alleged issue of overpopulation, blamed largely on working women's sexuality. In this Malthusian discourse, working-class women were made responsible for a whole host of issues that stemmed from US colonisation, including poverty and malnourishment.

It is clearly with this context in mind that Cabiya transforms the zombie – a figure that, as we saw in Chapter 2, has strong associations with the American Sugar Kingdom and sugar *production* – and links it to questions around social and biological *reproduction*. This transformation draws on a large range of allusions to literature and film that refuse any strict divisions between national and foreign imperialist imaginaries: the cloning of the *jíbaras* by aliens pits the fictional universe of American H.P. Lovecraft against national imaginaries associated with the generation of the 1930s, mixing the universe of zombie films such as *Invasion of the Body Snatchers* or Levin's *Stepford Wives* with Rosario Ferré's "La muñeca menor," a saccharine-gothic short story peopled by strange dolls inhabited by shellfish (see Rivera 2019). The Lovecraftian dimension, however, is particularly interesting in this context. After a series of playfully convoluted framing devices and clues pointing in myriad directions, the main story is narrated in the form of a letter written by an aged, male, ex-army, African American meteorologist called Epaminondas Jefries. Like Florence in Vega's story, Jefries is in an ambiguous position as a victim of the racist ideologies that drive US colonial imperialism, as well as a scientist working for the US military. Reminiscent of Lovecraft's mad narrators, he is interned in an insane asylum at the time of writing and claims not to have slept since a crash landing in the 1910s in the Puerto Rican mountains, where the story unfolds. There, Jefries fell in love with a young woman called Inés who, as he tells the reader, used to partake in nocturnal meetings with an alien civilisation in the process of cloning over a hundred young women. Eventually, the revelation that she would go willingly with the aliens and leave behind her clone prompts him to shoot and kill both Inés and one of the aliens in an act of rage seemingly motivated by chauvinism.

Overtones of a Lovecraftian Weird are thinly veiled in many of the scenes involving the aliens.[5] As Jefries observes the women assembling in the inexplicably lit clearing, he sits in a tree described as a "terrible tentacled giant" (Cabiya 2011: 48), evoking Lovecraft's terrifying tentacled Cthulhu, a "monster of vaguely anthropoid outline, but with an octopus-like head" (Lovecraft 2013: 32). The aliens themselves are described as "horrible men of big stature" who seem to lack joints, speak with distorted voices, carry tanks on their backs to be able to adapt to earthly conditions and wear overalls with hoods in the shape of cones (Cabiya 2011: 50, 56). The overalls seem to indicate, according to the narrator, their fear of contamination (2011: 59), whereas the hoods evoke the descriptions of "the Great Race" in Lovecraft's novella "The Shadow Out of Time" (1936). In the latter, members of the Great Race look like "immense rugose cones ten feet high" (Lovecraft 2009: n.p.). Like the aliens in Cabiya's novella, who somehow control whether it is night or day in specific locations, they are incomprehensible to human intellect. Another constitutive element of Lovecraftian fiction – the obsessive, hallucinatory racism that feeds the story "Herbert West–Reanimator," the New York-based "The Horror of Red Hook" or perhaps most famously "The Call of Cthulhu" – is here rendered explicit but also distanced, as Jeffries compares the "cones" to the robes and hoods of the Ku Klux Klan. In stories such as "The Call of Cthulhu," Lovecraft's narrative insisted on presenting the Weird as linked to the primitive and ancient associated with Afro-diasporic cultures; the worship of Cthulhu, for instance, endures in "Voodoo orgies multiply in Hayti, and African outposts report ominous mutterings" (Lovecraft 2013: 30). But as critics note, Lovecraft's "Weird monsters" could be read as figuring not so much the repression or recurrence of an ancient past, as the emergence of a new present "impregnat[ed] [...] with a bleak, unthinkable novum" (Miéville 2009: 513).

Cabiya's story combines this emphasis on monstrosity and threat with an emphasis on the integral role of science in imperialism and colonisation. In Jefries' letter (which makes up most of the narrative), the army meteorologist emphasises the large number of scientists who came with the occupying army, noting that "the government of the United States wanted to benefit as much as possible from the territory acquired as spoils in an easy war and the island offered innumerable opportunities for investigators of all disciplines,

---

5 On the "Lovecraftian weird," see, for example, Miéville (2009).

from geology to botany, to marine biology and astronomy" (Cabiya 2011: 57). This emphasis on science is replicated in his portrayal of the aliens, as the novella draws clear parallels between the aliens and US colonial agents, with both objectifying and experimenting on the bodies of colonial subjects. As the narrator dryly claims, Colonel Bailey Kelly Ashford – a historical US army medic who initiated the campaign against hookworm infection, linked to anaemia, in Puerto Rico (see Trujillo-Pagan 2013) – not only ran around the countryside collecting human faeces to examine under a microscope, but also worked through "*trial and error*" (Cabiya 2011: 58; original in English), experimenting with humans. Through his narrator, Cabiya here implicitly rejects the more celebratory paradigm of Ashford's campaign as benevolent. One might thus read his story alongside more recent scholarly approaches to colonial medicine. Nicole Trujillo-Pagan, for instance, criticises the medicalisation of the *jíbaro*'s malnutrition and anaemia, which she reads as colonisation's erasure of the socio-economic context, including the poverty, malnutrition and hunger caused by US imperialism (2013: 613). Trujillo-Pagan sees the efforts by the colonial administration and local physicians to cure the peasant classes of hookworm disease (rather than, say, eliminating poverty and providing shoes to avoid transmission) as part of a modernisation effort that involved population control and formed part of the larger socio-economic transformation of the island (2013: 619).

But the less-than-disinterested role of science becomes even more obvious when refracted through Cabiya's technologically advanced Lovecraft-esque aliens. Their technological know-how is directed towards reproducing, or cloning, young rural women, resonating with the history of racist and classist social engineering in Puerto Rico (see Rodriguez 2009; Ugarte 2017). In particular, the aliens in the story exert control over *how* reproduction takes place – that is, not via the biological route but through their advanced cloning science that avoids all intimacy as well as the uncertainty involved in procreation. The preparatory steps for the cloning process recall some of those taken in *The Stepford Wives* by the men of the Men's Association: upon moving to Stepford, future Stepford wife Joanna is drawn from different angles by an illustrator and she is asked to record as many words and phrases as possible, all under innocent-sounding pretexts. While the Stepford men seek to reproduce women not faithfully but in line with a sexist imaginary that amplifies bosoms and smooths facial features, the aliens seek to reproduce exact replicas of the young women, spending hours taking measurements down to, quite literally, the last hair. Further, they forbid intercourse and use devices to test if the young women have had sex prior to the meetings. This recalls the racist-patriarchal control and power exerted over the bodies and sexualities of Puerto Rican women. As Laura Briggs writes,

> from the exotic, tropical prostitute (seductive but with disease), to the impoverished, overlarge family (produced by ignorance and brimming brainwashing by the Catholic church), to overpopulation, to the notion

of the "culture of poverty," Puerto Rican sexuality has been defined by its deviance, and the island as a whole has been defined by its sexuality. (2002: 4)

Given that zombie-esque figures in the Caribbean context of that period have tended to be associated with the space of the plantation, this reinvention of the zombie trope highlights the role of gendered subordination in the context of US colonialism, as well as in national elite imaginaries and discourse. The female zombie-replica trope thus highlights the subordination of women's bodies as part of what Jason W. Moore (2015) calls capitalism's Cheap Nature strategy.

There is a twist in Cabiya's story, however, which seems destined to function like a metaphorical spanner in the interpretation machine. The story's end reveals that the aliens were in fact women and that the *jíbaras* willingly join them, leaving behind their clones. But the effect of this revelation is to highlight that the dynamics of gendered exploitation and appropriation, in the context of classism, sexism and violence, span across both the US occupying forces and national elite/professional circles. The women's willingness to leave behind their home is not surprising in the plot, but is a reasonable response given the sexist violence and patriarchal oppression that, as is suggested throughout the story, afflicts Inés as a young woman – from her parents' willingness to offer their daughter up to a US army officer, to the narrator's casual suggestion that she'd probably been raped by his fellow (white) army officer. The larger implication of this narrative, then, is the linking of the denunciation of colonialism to the metaphoric destruction of the mythic *gran familia puertorriqueña* and its sexual, racial and class politics. The *gran familia*, it turns out, is marred by sexism and already invaded by zombified clones, alienated by the operations of sexist and classist population control. As Cabiya observed in an interview, he was "disgusted" by the obvious symbolism of the national imaginary as found in literary works evoking the ideals of the *gran familia* (quoted in Rodríguez 2009: 1244).

Beyond the Female Zombie Tradition

As we have seen thus far, the female zombie tradition has provided writers and film-makers with a formal device to address the relation between patriarchal exploitation, class, race and extractivism. While in the present day the trope of the submissive, often white, woman may have exhausted its ability to function as a challenge to hegemonic ideology, new engagements with the figure have emerged that contribute to the critical tradition outlined in this chapter. In the US context, one might point to the TV series *iZombie* (2015–2019) as a reworking of the female and (very) white zombie figure, but it is Jordan Peele's Afropessimist zombie movie *Get Out* (2017) and the more world-systemic *US* (2019) that stand out as highly allegorical and cine-literate films engaging with the history of Gothic horror, the female zombie tradition *and* the social ills that they register. Peele has described *Get Out* as a "social thriller," "a film [...] in which the 'monster' is society itself" (quoted in Keetley 2020: 2). As has been discussed by many critics, the film exposes the "post-racial" ideology of the Barack Obama years by alluding, from the opening scenes onwards, to tragic events such as the killing of Trayvon Martin in 2012, revealing the murderous legacies of racial inequality in the United States. The white girlfriend Rose here works to expose the structural logic of stereotypical white liberal empathy: parading her pro-Obama stance as a sign of her anti-racism, she is eventually exposed as being invested in Black zombification, sexualisation and commodification. Or, put differently, she exposes liberalism's investment in maintaining a structurally racist status quo. Empathy and liberalism – focussed on the individual rather than collectivity – sit all too comfortably within neoliberal structures, and empathy is also all too easily linked to the pornographic consumption of victimised Black bodies, as the historian Marcus Wood has detailed in a different context (2002).

Peele's *Get Out* – while not featuring a single white female zombie – offers formal and thematic innovations to the critical tradition I have discussed, through an explicit engagement with it. Peele's long-standing interest in horror is, of course, well documented in his own work. In the brief sketch "White Zombies," for instance, the comedy duo Peele and Key had offered a comedic commentary on the racial politics built into horror: while the title offers a clear allusion to the film that marked the beginning of the US zombie tradition, the short is also post-Romero-esque in its depiction of the white zombie masses. The humorous twist is that, unlike in *Night of the Living Dead*, the zombies are not a threat to the protagonists or any other African Americans they meet, who seem to inhabit a parallel world governed by different logics. Or rather, as Michael Jarvis puts it, "the mob of white zombified suburbanites are so racist that they will not eat them" (2018: 103). The short offers a sardonic commentary on the racial dynamics and exclusions of American society, including the American horror film tradition.

Get Out is similarly self-aware of the zombie horror tradition: it very overtly reworks Levin's *Stepford Wives* (1972) and contains clear nods to *White Zombie* (Halperin 1932), *Invasion of the Body Snatchers* (Siegel 1956) and *Night of the Living Dead* (Romero 1968), among others. In a reworking of the zombie tropes of the 1930s and 1940s, Rose (Allison Williams), who is Chris Washington's (Daniel Kaluuya) love interest, turns out to be part of the wealthy white Armitage family, whose home is evocative of the aesthetic of a plantation house. Further, in very visibly old-fashioned clothes, their Black servants' anachronistic apparel visually echoes a pre-civil rights era (Ilott 2020: 119). The visual aspect is matched on the level of content: the family sells zombified African Americans to white elderly neighbours who are looking for younger bodies to host their consciousness. The representation of Rose breaks with zombie genre conventions since, instead of being the innocent passive victim in her family's scheming, she turns out to play a key role in the "family business." After it is revealed that she is deeply implicated in the plot to kidnap and subdue Chris, her demeanour and even appearance change abruptly, as a new version of the white monstrous feminine is revealed: Williams's performance suddenly becomes almost affectless, revealing the social pathology bubbling just beneath the surface of the "post-racial" Obama era. If the monstrous feminine tends to be linked to questions around biological and social reproduction, the horror here derives from its perpetuation of white supremacy in which the white female zombie trope used to have a clear function, as we saw in Chapter 2. Further, the shift to the Gothic in the film "registers the failure of realist frameworks of representation to recognize and critique the systems that perpetuate racial violence in the present day" (Ilott 2020: 115).

This rewriting of the female zombie is further complicated by the film's overtly signposted dialogue with *The Stepford Wives*. It is this overt dialogue with a film about the patriarchal subordination of white middle-class women that counters critiques of the film's "problematic" gender dynamics (Casey-Williams 2020: 69). The ending of male bonding over the body of a woman is indeed something of a sexist cliché, which comes close to reinforcing the constitutive sexism of the horror tradition. The film may also stop "short of envisioning the solidarity of all dispossessed or marginalised individuals in the triumph over this system" (Casey-Williams 2020: 70), though this line of critique is arguably upended if we consider this film in the context of Peele's oeuvre to date. Further, we might note that the death of Rose functions as the film's definite rejection of the "individualising logic of Romcom" (Ilott 2020: 118), which sits comfortably with the logic of neoliberalism that seeks to mask racial (or class, or regional) inequalities through a love-driven plot. But it is particularly the overt dialogue with *The Stepford Wives* that invites us to read racial horror alongside gendered horror, allowing us to think about the relation between gendered and racial oppression. This dialogue is created through overt visual references and similarities of plot and atmosphere: both films feature protagonists who are young photographers at risk of zombification by their respective partners and their families, with the role of the Armitage family echoing that of the Men's Association in *The Stepford Wives*. Further, on a first viewing of *Get Out*, one might read Georgina – a Black woman who works in the kitchen – as a relatively straightforward version of the zombified woman-of-the-house, even if the housewife is here replaced by a domestic servant. The audience first encounters her in an immaculate kitchen through a point-of-view shot over Chris's shoulder, giving the viewer the (false) impression that he begins to suspect that there is something wrong with the house and its inhabitants.

However, as we gradually find out, the horror in this scene does not derive from the woman's subordination to domestic tasks, but rather from the fact that she and all the other zombified characters are no longer themselves, as they are dominated by the implanted consciousness of a wealthy white buyer willing to become a "body snatcher." The zombification is product of an operation, performed by the father and surgeon

The Zombie-in-the-House, Nature and the Colonies

Fig. 6. *Get Out* (Peele, 2017). From a point-of-view shot over Chris's shoulder, we see zombified Georgina.

Dean Armitage (Bradley Whitford), in conjunction with hypnosis performed by his wife and psychiatrist Missy Armitage (Katherine Keener). In a cross of Du Boisian double consciousness with zombie body invasion narratives (e.g. *Invasion of the Body Snatchers*), the white consciousness dominates and subdues the original consciousness, which is banished to the "sunken place," from which they have to watch life as mere spectators (Jarvis 2018: 104). The atmosphere of "paranoid horror" (Jarvis 2018: 101), experienced by a "rational and therefore self-doubting" female in *The Stepford Wives*, is matched in *Get Out* as Chris enters into "hostile territory without knowing it […] lingering in the anti-black social text much as Joanna Eberhart (Katharine Ross) lingers far too long in the murderously patriarchal Stepford" (Jarvis 2018: 101). In both films, the social horror serves to expose structural inequalities, as well as the ideological worldviews that underpin them, which liberal humanism seeks to mask or declare non-existent. Unlike *The Stepford Wives*, however, Peele is careful to avoid the pitfall of representing zombies as merely downtrodden and passive victims, making Chris turn the signs of his objectification against the Armitage family: he uses cotton, once linked to enslavement, to plug his ears, and the antlers of the buck, "a slavery-era term for a powerful black man" (Blake 2020: 44), to kill the patriarch. He is thus represented as carrying on a range of protest actions and rebellions against white supremacy, from slave revolts through to more recent struggles.

Like *The Stepford Wives*, *Get Out* explicitly links zombification to the arrangement and distribution of space through racial coding. The horror in *Get Out* begins with a "symbolic journey into the wilderness" that reverses the Great Migration (Gaines 2020: 164): from the urban space coded as safe, to rural America coded as a space of imminent danger to the life of the Black protagonist, recalling the experience of Wright's Bigger Thomas in *Native Son* and Ben (Duane Jones) in *Night of the Living Dead*. In this horror vision, rural America is coded as temporally distinct and visually linked to the Old South, following in a long line of representations from the early twentieth century that presented the Old South as exceptional and out-of-sync with modernity. Yet in *Get Out*, the "Old South" that is evoked is not actually located in the South but in upstate New York, refusing the easy designation of racism as a Southern problem and thus following in the footsteps of a long line of intellectuals such as Richard Wright, Ralph Ellison and others. Discourses around "Nature" and their entanglement with those around race are signalled explicitly from the opening of the film with a "scene of slave capture" (Lauro 2020: 149), when Andre Hayworth (Lakeith Stanfield) is kidnapped in the leafy suburbs, on Evergreen Way, to the tune of "Run, Rabbit, Run." Shortly after, Chris and Rose on their journey through the forest hit and kill a stag – or buck; the stag's head hung on the wall in the basement of the Armitage plantation house is later explicitly linked to the tied up and hypnotised Chris. In other words, rural America – or, even more broadly, "Nature" – is coded as dangerous for African Americans, who are compared to animals in the colonialist-capitalist discourse evoked and exposed by the film. This goes hand in hand with the Black characters' reduction to their bodily characteristics by the white characters: the visitors to the Armitage house who will bid on Chris's body objectify him along a series of racist tropes, touching his muscles, discussing his physique in relation to the athleticism of African American athletes, and enquiring about his sexual performance. It is Chris's genetic make-up, announces an advert for Coagula, the operation that transplants the consciousness of wealthy white buyers, that makes him attractive as a host body.

To draw all of these thematic strands together, I want to return to the scene reported in *Tell my Horse*. In Hurston's narrative, the camera becomes a means of ethnographic narration – or of the *technics* of imperialism, one might say. Meanwhile, her description points towards the violent dynamics that are repressed in this ethnographic narrative act. Joanna in *The Stepford Wives* is also a photographer, who often chooses children as her subject, fitting with the trope of the housewife to which she will eventually be forced to conform. But her most successful photo, commercially and artistically, is one that she took of an unnamed African American businessman in New York just as he was being snubbed by a taxi driver. While it is read internally as symbolising the contemporary moment, this photo simultaneously seems detached from the suburban reality in which she is now immersed – even if the novel overall questions this appearance of detachment. *Get Out*'s Chris is also a photographer well known for his urban photography, often of Black subjects. It is his talent that makes him particularly desirable to the white body traffickers, as would-be enslavers want to inhabit his artistic vision. Like Hurston, he ends up photographing Black zombified subjects, though in his case this occurs in upstate New York when he enters the world of the Armitage family. While the act of taking pictures with a camera has little impact on them, when he switches to a smartphone, this momentarily aids the struggle of the subdued Black consciousness, as Andre Logan King manages to voice the warning "Get Out!" to Chris. Scholars have been quick to point out the link being made between smartphones, the act of witnessing violence and the struggle against racism and police violence in the United States. As Ryan Poll suggests, "cell phones have become […] political tools to capture state-sanctioned violence against African American men, women and children" (2018: 94).

This is an important point in the context of US struggles against systemic racism and police brutality, but it is also crucial to point out that on a world-systemic level, smartphones are profoundly embedded in, and reinforce, structural racism and sexism. Cobalt mining in the Democratic Republic of Congo, driven by the rising demand for batteries to power digital devices, has been linked to modern forms of slavery and functions as a "catalyst for social, economic, and even regional dispossession" (Sovacool 2021: 271). And it is equally important to point out that these extreme levels of inequality and abuse are gendered. As Benjamin Sovacool writes, "many vulnerabilities—in terms of work, status, social norms, and sexual abuse and prostitution—fall disproportionately on women and girls" (2021: 271). I raise this point, not to invalidate the preceding one, but rather to emphasise the necessity of inserting struggles against racial inequality into the global context. While the world-systemic context seems beyond the imaginative reach of *Get Out*, or is at least only dimly alluded to in the film, Peele's subsequent production– *US* (2019) – signposts this larger horizon, continuing the dialogue *within* the horror tradition that he began in his previous one. In this equally complex work, the slasher horror derives from the uprising of the zombie-esque "Tethered." The film presents us with two sets of people: the middle-class Americans, who are replicated by an underclass of doppelgänger Americans, who are actually individual human replicas or "dolls." These "dolls" are separate in body, but "the Tethered" do not possess their own souls and cannot talk. The film opens in 1986, with a young girl called Adelaide watching a commercial for the "Hands Across America" charitable initiative. Later, she visits a funhouse on the Santa Cruz beach boardwalk, where she encounters *her* "Tethered," who replaces Adelaide in the surface world. The uprising is led by this African American female, called Red and played by Lupita Nyong'o, who smashes the mould of the American female zombie tradition that has long emphasised passive white victims. Unlike her very distant filmic ancestor, Madeline of *White Zombie*, Red leads the zombified Tethered who are a cross-racial collective.

Indeed, the anxieties around cross-racial mixing and miscegenation that were so central to the early female zombie tradition are here relegated to the background. While racist colonialism is kept in view (through filmic references to the commodification of indigenous culture via an earlier incident at the funhouse, when young Adelaide sees a stereotyped caricature of an indigenous person), race in the film is presented as by itself not offering a sufficient explanatory framework for what is again a deeply allegorical narrative, focussed this time on national and global inequality. While *US*, too, should be read alongside and in dialogue with its predecessors (most notably, in this case, *Get Out* and its emphasis on structural racism in the US), it is significant that in this film both the white and the Black middle-class families are equally under attack, listen to songs of commodified Black culture and lead similarly comfortable lives. Adelaide/Red carefully masterminds the zombie uprising down to the symbolism that draws heavily on the "Hands Across America" initiative organised by the musical supergroup "USA for Africa" – ironising the ultimate futility of popular charitable efforts to dismantle inequality without challenging neoliberal policies. Insofar as the film is framed by the historical moments of 1986 and the contemporary period, Red's revenge plot is hatched on the underside of the neoliberal period and its brutal austerity measures and debt regimes at home and abroad. The murderous "Tethered" – who attack their living doubles – not only expose the deep inequalities within America but also gesture towards global inequality through the explicit visual references to US charitable enterprises that did not alleviate inequality or challenge US hegemony. The film notably ends in a shot of the "Tethered" in red overalls holding hands as they are about to be attacked by military helicopters. Helicopters have become highly symbolic of US foreign "interventions," and it is therefore difficult not to read this scene as a direct attack on US imperialism. In this context, the new female zombie is a powerful figure, since she can no longer be used as a justification for imperialism, but has shed her shackles and become a leader in the uprising against the global status quo.

CHAPTER 4

Energy and the Emergence of the Petro-Zombie

In his 1935 essay on "The Work of Art in the Age of its Technological Reproducibility," Walter Benjamin commented on the new media of film and photography as heralding radical changes. Famously, he lamented the loss of art's "unique existence in a particular place" and decried film as the "first art form whose artistic character is entirely defined by its reproducibility," and therefore the "exact antithesis of a work created at a single stroke" (2008: 21, 28). Benjamin's observations as a commentator on the emergence of new art forms and a new culture shaped by fossil-fuelled modernity – including TV and film – are noteworthy from today's perspective, since his sense of loss and alienation has been drowned out by its normalisation. Especially interesting in the current context is his focus on the role of the actor and the "highly productive use of human being's self-alienation" that occurs when an actor's performance is captured by a piece of equipment (2008: 32), rather than being experienced directly by an audience. Unlike in a work of theatre that is performed live, the actor's performance is fragmented, repeated until perfection, corrected by professionals and broken into a "series of episodes capable of being assembled" (2008: 32). The performance thus becomes detached from the person, stripped of the spontaneity and particularity of a theatrical performance. Comparing film-acting with other forms of industrialised labour (perfected under Fordism), in which the worker is detached from the final product, he argues that the actor loses control over his or her performance: the final product. The actor's work is therefore, in Benjamin's argument, an alienated art form, enabled by the new medium of film. As Nadia Bozak comments in *The Cinematic Footprint*, Benjamin puts this in the context of other infrastructural and technological developments, as he follows Paul Valery in comparing film and the way images are transported with the way in which we access water, gas and electricity in our households (2011: 34). Put differently, Benjamin suggestively compares the rift *between* actor and performance to other socio-ecological rifts in metabolism that characterise the modern urbanised world.

Fig. 7. *White Zombie* (Halperin, 1932). A zombified Madeline plays piano next to her would-be-lover, Beaumont.

The filmic zombie was well suited to registering these experiences of alienation. We might think, for instance, of Madge Bellamy's much-criticised, stiff, silent and wide-eyed performance as Madeleine, the zombified bride in the first zombie film *White Zombie* (Halperin 1932). While Bellamy "had been a successful actress back in the silent era" (Russell 2007: 21), her acting in this new format was generally found to be less convincing. She was seen to lack charisma – or one might say "energy," in colloquial terms – even prior to her transformation into a zombie. Her performance might thus be read as one of the most hyperbolic expressions of the actor's alienation from her performance – an alienation that has become so normalised as to become almost imperceptible to us nowadays.

Bellamy's performance thus inadvertently exposes the alienation central to modern film-making processes. It is perhaps ironic, then, that the film's content and plot repress the modernity of the sugar industry and the foreign money that propelled it. The modern processes that brought the characters to the island are largely absent, while the surroundings are as Gothic-archaic as they are curiously misplaced. This misplacement may be in part related to the film's minuscule budget, which forced the director to reuse sets from other films, recycling archaic European-looking castles from films set in Europe (such as *Dracula*, *Frankenstein* and *The Hunchback of Notre Dame*), creating a strong "sense of déjà-vu" (Luckhurst 2015: 75).

Energy and the Emergence of the Petro-Zombie

But for all the film's archaisms, it was, of course, profoundly embedded within modernising technologies. Of immediate relevance in this regard is the integral nature of electricity to the way in which *White Zombie* was filmed. In one sense, this was true for almost *any* film of the time: as Bozak notes, "with its interior workspaces artificially illuminated so as to extend working hours and enhance levels of productivity, Hollywood studios came to resemble any other factory unit" (2011: 33). In *White Zombie*, these conditions were further amplified by the nature of the film: shot at night, on rented sets in Universal Studios, in a mere eleven days (Luckhurst 2015: 75), the movie was completely reliant on electrification. In this sense, *White Zombie* could be said to be representative of the zombie's own entry into the world of film, which was strongly overdetermined by the new technologies and energy sources that enabled the development of the film industry itself.

As we will see in this chapter, the zombie articulates a specific set of *relations* to energy sources – something that would become increasingly explicit in the second half of the twentieth century, from *Night of the Living Dead* (1968) onwards. Since at least the 1930s, zombie imaginaries have registered the profound ways in which the capitalist world-system has been restructured by the emergence of fossil-fuel energy regimes. Indeed, zombies are well suited to thinking through the negative impacts of such regimes, whether coal or oil and electricity. While coal had been the dominant energy resource in the global economy in the nineteenth century, in the first half of the twentieth century it was gradually decreasing in importance relative to oil, eventually becoming subordinate to oil's hegemony after the end of the Second World War.[1] Coal, oil and electricity were new forms of energy that transformed all of modern culture, giving birth to forms of technology, social and spatial organisation, habits and affects. They were not merely energetic inputs fuelling an otherwise unchanged capitalist world-system; rather, capitalism "remade itself through their incorporation" (J. Moore 2011: 22). Fossil fuels and electrification changed the organisation of the capitalist world-system, unevenly transforming the way humans live, work, eat and relate to each other and the extra-human world. They enabled new forms of capitalist expansion, intensification and appropriation, and have become "the sources enabling nearly every index and practice of modernity from artificial illumination to transportation to electronic media to computation" (Boyer 2017: 130). Through a combined focus on these fossil fuels and electricity (Boyer 2017: 128–31), new perspectives may alter how we view zombies.

With this in mind, it is worth emphasising that fossil fuels and electricity are not *per se* at fault for such problems as climate change or for the rampant global inequalities associated with them. It is only in the context of capitalism that a viscous, million-year-old liquid composed of animal

---

1 Regardless, coal continues to generate 35% of global electricity today (Dawson 2016: 83).

and plant remains – in short, fossilised remnants from the Paleozoic era – became a way to produce value at the expense of the majority of the planet's human and extra-human inhabitants. A very similar argument can be made for electricity, a form of energy that – while "fashioned" by Americans "into a metonym for modern life" (Lieberman 2017: 13) – attracted high hopes from early socialist commentators, suggesting its great potential for serving communal interests (Nye 1992: 384). Yet within the existing US economic and political systems, unsustainable fossil-fuelled electrification quickly became the norm. The environmental degradation built into capitalism's petro-fuelled, electrified modernity is, and always has been, deeply bound up with the commodification of the earth's human and extra-human natures in the pursuit of surplus value.

In relation to our analysis of zombie imaginaries, which often revolve around the question of harnessing (human and extra-human) energy, it is crucial here to pause on the concept of energy itself. As Cara Daggett has shown in *The Birth of Energy* (2019), the current understanding of energy is a relatively recent invention: it dates to the mid-nineteenth century and is inextricable from the emergence of machine-powered capitalism. Indeed, energy

> is a thoroughly modern thing that became the linchpin of physics only after it was "discovered" in the 1840s, at the apex of the Industrial Revolution, and then proselytized by a group of mostly northern British engineers and scientists involved in the shipbuilding industry, undersea telegraph cable building, and other imperial projects. (Dagget 2019: 3)

The abstraction of energy from specific contexts, rendering it transportable, was a significant historical change within capitalism that built on the prior emergence of abstract labour-power;[2] indeed, it rendered a barrel of oil comparable with the metabolic energy expended by the worker – whether valued or not-valued.

The concept of energy remains slippery and more difficult to define than a concrete example of energy-to-be-harnessed, such as a barrel of oil. As Brent Bellamy and Jeff Diamanti write, "[y]ou cannot *see* energy in the way that you can see a barrel of oil, because energy in the concrete is still abstract, and an energy system fueled by fossil fuels is more abstract still, even though it is determinate of virtually all economic and political capacities today" (2018: 12). Like capitalist value as "socially necessary labour time," the concept of energy works fetishistically, concealing the sites and historical conditions of energetic imperialist extraction. In their concrete form as historical forces, coal, oil and electricity would foster widening metabolic rifts between sites of production and sites of consumption. In the case of coal, we might here think of the role of steam ships in transporting goods and raw materials

---

2 The splitting of the physical body and the mind was central to capitalist alienation. Bodies are transformed into sources of labour-power disembedded from social relations; they become reduced to their muscle energy.

from peripheries to metropoles; in the case of oil, we might think of the long stretches of pipelines crossing time zones and countries. Historically, oil and electricity have also helped to break the collective power of workers through atomisation, thus enabling the intensified disciplining of the workforce associated with late capitalism.[3]

Within capitalist ideology, new sources of energy have tended to be presented as embodying and realising social "progress." Thus, representations of electricity and oil have often evoked images of an enslaved human workforce rendered anachronistic by fossil-fuelled modernity. Oil was commonly conceived as a replacement for enslaved labour (LeMenager 2014: 5), while the energy generated by electricity was figured in a General Electric advert from 1915 in the form of whitewashed images of slavery, featuring a white man tearing at his chains as a depiction of the energy (Lieberman 2017: 176). Meanwhile, early commentators such as Lewis Mumford in *Technics and Civilisation* would associate coal with the "barbarism" of back-breaking labour in contrast to the supposedly clean oil ([1932] 1955: 71). Yet Mumford's misrepresentation of freedom from slavery is, of course, deeply ideological, since it was due neither to oil nor electricity that enslaved labour was abolished, but rather to the resistance of those who were enslaved. Further, oil, coal and electricity were deeply embedded in new racial regimes (Yusoff 2018); thus, in response to energy sustainability in New Orleans, for instance, Nikki Luke and Nik Heyen argue that "distributing access to renewable and affordable electricity through community solar" would challenge petro-racial capitalism and redistribute racialised fossil fuel infrastructures (Luke and Heynen 2020: 603).

Energy, in both human and extra-human form, has long played a fundamental role in zombie imaginaries. In their first figuration as externally controlled humans, zombies offer an image of the absolute control over another human's energy, harnessed as abstract labour-power. Post-Romero zombies, on the other hand, often walk and expend metabolic energy without having ingested anything that might provide it, seemingly embodying the capitalist fantasy – or nightmare – of energy created *ex nihilo*. Further, even if early zombie films presented zombies as part of a "primitive" world, latent within filmic and narrative representations of zombies lies a profoundly modern understanding of the abstraction of human energy as labour-power under capitalism that, in the twentieth century, became increasingly linked to modern understandings of non-human energy.

---

3 For an analysis of the way the transition to oil as the dominant global energy regime was entwined with efforts by capitalist elites to atomise and discipline labour, see Timothy Mitchell's *Carbon Democracy*. Mitchell points out that oil energy networks were "less vulnerable to the political claims of those whose labour kept them running" (2013: 38) than were those of coal, since the technicalities of "moving carbon stores from seam to surface created unusually autonomous places and methods of work," which gave coal miners greater opportunities to pursue collective disruptive action (2013: 20).

Zombies and Uneven Electrification in Ralph Ellison's *Invisible Man* and René Depestre's *The Festival of the Greasy Pole*

Electricity, like oil and coal, is uneven in terms of distribution and access. However, unlike coal and oil, it can be replicated by harnessing the energy of the sun or the wind. I here seek to place one text from the US (which is now highly electrified, with some occlusions, including Puerto Rico and other underdeveloped zones) alongside another text from Haiti (which still today has a "substantial unelectrified population").[4] As we have seen previously, early zombie narratives that were critical of US imperialism often presented the advantages of fossil-fuelled modernity as being out of reach for the zombified workers, yet the processes reshaping landscapes and social relations as deeply embedded in fossil-fuelled modernisation. Since the emergence of fossil-fuelled modernity, zombies have always been very explicitly inscribed in the unevenness of modern capitalist landscapes, in which zones of underdevelopment are tied to, and produced by, zones of (over)development and capitalist hoarding. The question that our focus on "energy" then raises is how writers and film-makers employing zombie imaginaries have thought through the ways in which human and extra-human relations are remade through new energy regimes. How, in other words, are zombies rearticulated within the electric-oil regime?

The two novels I examine here debunk ideologically weighted narratives of progress as inevitably tied to advances in machinery and energy consumption. They also consider how electrification transforms human relationships to human and extra-human natures. Published in the US and Haiti almost thirty years apart, both novels press on the relation between the trope of the zombie and electrification. In both texts, electrification is inextricably linked to power and is highly unevenly distributed: while in Ellison's *Invisible Man,* electrification is controlled by Monopolated Light & Power Company in a commentary on the role of monopolisation, in Depestre's *The Festival of the Greasy Pole* (originally published in French in 1979), electricity is entirely controlled by the dictator and is employed as a means to control the population. In the Haitian novel, the programme of electrification – the *Electricité d'Haïti* – was institutionalised briefly after the death of Papa Doc (the dictator François Duvalier) in 1971 (Coates 1990: xliii); in a country in which electricity is only available to a small percentage, this access turns into a powerful symbolic metaphor for power. Here, as in *Invisible Man*, the potential for de-zombification is thus explicitly linked to fighting dominant forms of electricity, revealing the protagonist's "vital aliveness" (Ellison [1952] 2001: 7).

Significantly, both of these novels are also deeply shaped by the Cold War and the contextual ideological battle against/for communism. Like other

---

4 Quoted in *Tracking SDG7: The Energy Progress Report* (IEA, IRENA, UNSD, World Bank and WHO 2020: 122).

slightly later zombie narratives, Ellison's *Invisible Man* is notably suspicious of collective action (particularly in the historical form of the Communist Party), favouring individual resistance to corporate power while offering an anti-communist indictment of preceding radical, cross-racial struggles. Hence, as Barbara Foley has observed, *Invisible Man* "both emerged from and contributed to the discursive ejection of reds from the circle of humanity" (2010: 10). The relation of zombies to work – whether paid or unpaid – here recedes into the background, giving way to a focus on racial inequality that is to a degree delinked from class-based inequality. In Depestre's novel, on the other hand, the issue of socio-energetic inequality turns on the corruption of the Duvalier government. The narrative's fictional double of Duvalier, Zachary Zoocrates, is in charge of ONEDA (Office National de l'Électricification des Âmes), the company that controls who is able to access electricity and is literally electrifying all of its subjects. Electricity here turns into the monopolisation of corruption and of a single viewpoint that supports the fascist dictator.

Electricity and capitalism have developed hand in hand. As David McDonald notes in *Electric Capitalism*, "virtually all forms of contemporary industrial, manufacturing and service activity require electricity to operate"; further, it would be almost impossible to function "in today's global economy without access to (cheap and reliable) electric power" (2009: 4). In the United States, moreover, electricity would come to be read as a "symbol for American modernity" (Liebermann 2017: 3). There, in the first half of the twentieth century, electrification made possible "the streetcar suburb, the department store, the amusement park, the assembly-line factory, the electrified home, [and] the modernized farm" (Nye 1992: x), transforming "in a single lifetime between 1880 and 1940 [...] the landscapes of the city, factory, home, and farm" (1992: 381). Like oil, electrification had offered improvements and new possibilities – including increased (social) mobility and an amelioration of farm life – but it had also helped to depopulate farms and thus contributed to de-peasantisation (Nye 1992: 25). New labour regimes – such as Fordism – were shaped by electricity, which enabled the reorganisation of production processes through, for instance, electric conveyor belts. Further, electricity as a technology enabled "new financial and commercial forms" (Nye 1992: 169), such as the holding company, which relied on faster communications through telegrams, telephones, radio and, more broadly, economies of scale. Indeed, the current high-speed financial transactions of Wall Street depend on this instant transmission of information. As Alan Ackerman writes in an edited collection on *Fueling Culture*:

> Electricity is not a thing but a set of phenomena produced by the flows of an electric charge; unlike a lump of coal (the epitome of inertia) electricity is never at rest [...] Coal, natural gas, water, wind and the sun generate the electrical power we need. It is not simply that our electrified culture is substantially different than that of the candlelit Romantics but also that

generating electricity has transformed the socioeconomic order and the physical planet. (2017: 121–22)

If such is the case, then it should be no surprise that electricity reshapes zombiehood insofar as the latter can be understood as animated by the inner logic of capitalism.

Electricity is very prominent in Ellison's 1952 novel, which starts with the protagonist sabotaging Monopolated Light & Power by accessing its electricity, burning 1.369 light bulbs in his basement to feel alive. The first line of the Preface functions as an introduction, with the unnamed narrator proclaiming: "I am an invisible man" (Ellison 2001: 3). Invisibility here turns into the new zombification. The narrator claims that he *does* possess flesh and bones, and might even "be said to possess a brain" (2001: 3). He describes how, on one of the preceding nights, he accidentally bumped into a tall white man, who started to curse him. The invisible man headbutts the blond man, who eventually ends up on the ground, with the invisible man kicking him and drawing a knife. And yet he realises that this man had probably not even seen him. He draws back the knife, and just stares angrily at the man, immediately adding that "[m]ost of the time (although I do not choose as I once did to ignore the violence of my days by ignoring it) I am not so overtly violent" (2001: 5).

Through the notion of invisibility, the novel presents this first-person narrator as a zombified figure. Early on in the novel, a mad veteran (formerly a doctor) describes him as a "walking zombie" and as "the mechanical man" (2001: 94) – imaginative connections that were able to build upon pre-existing conceptual links between the undead and human machines (Morrell 2015; Chude-Sokei 2012). In nineteenth-century US culture, these overlapping imaginaries were employed to "emblematiz[e] how slavery and wage-labour relations reduced persons to things" (Morrell 2015: 101). More specifically in this case, they build on Jim Crow racial relations as they follow the veteran's own explanation of how he ended up not practising medicine after his return to the American South from France, having been driven out of the town by ten masked (white, racist) men, who beat him with whips. As the veteran explains, the invisible man's zombiedom is connected to both electrification and post-Jim Crow racism, as he

> registers with his senses but *short-circuits* his brain… not only his emotions but his *humanity* […] He's invisible, a walking personification of the Negative, the most perfect achievement of your dreams, sir! The mechanical man! (Ellison 2001: 94, emphases added)

Zombification is here transmuted into a racial nightmare, into people internalising racialised opinions of themselves and others and living up to them. As J. Bradford Campbell notes in his commentary on Ellison's rewriting of *The Golden Day* (Mumford 1926), "the neuroses Ellison represents at the Golden Day all find their source in *material* circumstances, namely, the distinctive social conditions of African American life at the time" (Campbell 2010: 453, emphasis in original). Zombiedom is, insofar as it is a neurosis, inherently social.

The zombie is, of course, a figure that has a prominent racialised profile, and as an author Ellison was very deliberate in his use of symbols and tropes. Indeed, if we go back to when *Invisible Man* is set, the vet's use of the zombie trope may even post-date the release of *White Zombie* in 1932, as the novel "brings its protagonist to New York in the junior year in college, perhaps 1933" (Hobson 2005: 371). By 1952, when *Invisible Man* was first published, the image of the "walking zombie" deployed by the vet had already a two-decade-long horror film history, profoundly embedded within racist imaginaries as well as visions of resistance. The zombie is also linked to the woman as a symbol of whiteness – or, as a symbol of what a Black man should desire according to the racist fantasies and fears of the Jim Crow era. As Anne Cheng observes, the "historic discourse of white racial purity tied into the fear of miscegenation, its concomitant idealization of white womanhood, and the fear of black sexuality as a threat against that sanctity" (2005: 127).

Ellison was highly aware of the implication of the movie industry in "the construction of successive racial regimes," as Cedric Robinson would put it many decades later (2007: xv). Writing in 1964, Ellison moves from a discussion of D.W. Griffith's racist rendering of Civil War history to the movie industry more broadly:

> Usually *The Birth of a Nation* is discussed in terms of its contribution to cinema technique, but as with every other technical advance since the oceanic sailing ship, it became a further instrument in the dehumanization of the Negro […] In the struggle against Negro freedom, motion pictures have been one of the strongest instruments for justifying some white Americans' anti-Negro attitudes and practices […] If the film became the main manipulator of the American dream, for Negroes that dream contained a strong dose of *such stuff as nightmares are made of*. (Ellison 2003: 304, emphasis added)

As propagated within realist cinema, hegemonic ideology is full of racialised horror and gothic anxieties in the era of Jim Crow (something that Ellison thematises explicitly in the prologue of the novel). Further, apart from all the examples he offers of gothic tales narrating race, the invisible man refers to himself twice as a "natural resource" *without agency* (2001: 303, 508). This is, in many ways, comparable to Jason W. Moore's "Cheap Natures" argument – completely eliminating the agency of those that have none.

Invisible Man is structured around some very noticeable associations between electricity, racism and mentions of automatism, performed by doll-like people without agency. Most notably, we might here mention the "Battle Royal," where the Black students need to perform a fist fight with each other for an audience of white luminaries. The first scene at the Battle Royal is revelatory for the connections it draws between patriarchal and racial domination: in it, we note that in the midst of the battle "stood a magnificent blond – stark naked" (Ellison 2001: 19); "the hair was yellow like that of a *kewpie doll*, the face heavily powdered and rouged, as though to form an abstract mask, the eyes hollow and smeared a cool blue, the color of a baboon's butt" (2001: 19, emphasis added). One must here note the evident primitivism of the descriptions, evoked within the context of the modern doll industry. The plastic Kewpie doll was based on the cartoons of Rose O'Neill that depicted modern, androgynous and self-sufficient characters who "carried suffrage placards, debated the opposition and watched over their working-class neighborhoods as 'social house-keepers'" (Formanek-Brunell 1998: 118). Yet, as Formanek-Brunell explains, they were transformed by the doll-making industry – and therefore by the "male producers" of the doll-making industry "whose conceptions of gender differed" (1998: 119).

As the woman in the Battle Royal scene dances, the invisible man notices "a certain merchant who followed her hungrily, his lips loose and drooling," while the rest of the men attempt to sink "their beefy fingers [...] into soft flesh" (Ellison 2001: 20). As Maisha Wester demonstrates, gothic imagery is here used to describe all the powerful white men, whose gestures are "obscene" and whose "hunger" for the woman's body takes on near cannibalistic overtones (2012: 108). The "nightmare," then, lies in the racial-sexual regime of the Jim Crow era and is clearly visible to both the woman and the invisible man: "I saw the terror and disgust in her eyes, almost like my own terror" (Ellison 2001: 20). Automatism and doll-making go hand in hand, embracing white lower-class women and Black, predominantly lower-class, men and women. Further, the scene exposes the pornographic dynamics of the films that, like the zombie movies discussed previously, rely on the imagery of the passive woman in white, imagined to be under threat of being "contaminated" by Black populations of the racist imperialist imagination.

This further connects with the depiction in the novel of apparently dancing African Americans and animated automata, as well as a whole range of discomfiting irrealist images engaging in racist imagery (Selisker 2011: 571). As Scott Selisker correctly observes, the figures of the automaton, mannequin, robot (and also the zombie) "became central to a wide range of [twentieth-century] representations of subhumanity" (2011: 572). Selisker goes on to note that "African American automata are a driving force behind Ellison's satire" (2011: 573),[5] commenting in detail on a scene in the hospital

---

5 Selisker begins the article with a reference to one of the novel's closing images, in which the invisible man is dreaming that he is being walked to a bridge by Brother Jack (as well as by Emerson, Norton, Bledsoe, Ras and a number of others he fails to recognise). The invisible man is castrated by them and his "*blood-red parts*" are hung on the bridge (Ellison 2001: 571, original emphasis), which strangely begins to animate, "striding like a robot, an iron man, whose iron legs clanged doomfully as it moved" (2001: 582). For Selisker, this image provides the clue for our reading of the novel, as the invisible man shouts at them: "Now laugh, you scientists. Let's

that is also key for the present reading of zombification and electrification. In this scene, the invisible man is reawakened in a hospital, which belongs to a factory that produces white paint. The factory is a neo-plantation Fordist company, towards which he had previously walked amid a whole group of workers, seeing a "huge electric sign," announcing: "Keep America Pure/ With/Liberty Paint." Electricity here supports the continuation of whiteness, as the company's most important paint is white. Further, it is the Uncle Tom stereotype – Mr Brockway – who inadvertently reveals "how the industrial may hide a new plantation economy, consuming blackness in order to produce 'perfect whiteness'" (Wester 2012: 127).

After the invisible man falls out with Mr Brockway and ends up with a head injury from an explosion caused by the latter, he is transported into a part of the hospital. Sitting in a glass frame, from which he is forced to listen to the doctors discussing "primitives," he suffers through electric shocks as part of a "prefrontal lobotomy" – without any of the "negative effects of a knife" (Ellison 2001: 236). But then the description switches from a medical discourse to a judicial one: the apparent beneficiary of this procedure would be society in its entirety because *it* would not suffer any "traumata on [the invisible man's] account" (2001: 236; see Campbell 2010: 456). As Campbell notes, "[t]he electroshock 'therapy' the narrator receives is not designed to make him 'all better' but literally to make him a 'new man', a project that deeply implicates psychiatry in the racial fantasies of an increasingly paranoid America" (2010: 456). Douglas Ford further explains the ways in which "technological systems in this novel often signal the more subtle workings of social systems of domination and power, even as literal networks of electricity reinforce the social networks that maintain a disenfranchised body of people while sustaining the empowerment of a privileged white middle class" (1999: 888). The invisible man is thus declared "cured" when he can no longer remember his name. As Campbell convincingly observes, it is here obvious that Ellison was criticising psychiatry (and Freud) for being too focussed on the familial, rather than the social (2010: 453). In his short story "Out of the Hospital and under the Bar," published eleven years after *Invisible Man* (despite leading up to it as a story), Ellison makes the link between "electroshock identity erasure" and racist motifs even clearer. In the story, the protagonist wakes up in an empty-looking room prompted by a Black nurse; when he moves, he feels that the "nodes come with [him] and [he's] becoming aware of the danger of electrocution" (Ellison [1964] 2003: 264). Further, linking blackness and energy extraction, he screams about the joining of blackness and the extractive logic of energy consumption: "you took my energy. That's it, you probably have a hospital full of us. Using our energy to run your stupid

---

hear you laugh!" (2001: 582). Selisker reads this in relation to Ellison's critical review of Gunnar Myrdal's *An American Dilemma* (1944), and his own attempt not "to define and solve social problems by manipulating them from afar" (Selisker 2011: 572).

Ecology of the Zombie

machinery" (2003: 265). Here, he is turned into a "natural resource," linking in a different way to the issue of enslavement.[6]

The novel is not normally read as contributing to environmental thought. However, one might justifiably argue that it *does* make "a considerable contribution to environmental thought in its own right," and "speaks to the theoretical foundations of what is now known as the environmental justice movement" (Rozelle 2016: 60). When Brother Jack talks to the invisible man after his powerful speech to the people assembled during the ejection of the old couple, he refers to Richard Wright's essay "Death on the City Pavements," stating that "[t]hey're living but dead. Dead-in-living ... a unity of opposites" (Ellison 2001: 290). As Lee Rozelle notes, for Brother Jack, "the agrarian zombie or uprooted self must be exterminated to allow for the march of social progress" (2016: 71). The reference to Wright's essay in conjunction with the status of being dead-while-alive – or zombified – places Brother Jack's argument within an environmental tradition that is interlaced with the Great Migration towards the cities by African Americans. The "rural enclosure movement" destroyed several million African American homes and social networks along with centuries of agricultural knowledge and skill, and, by the 1960s, 95% of African Americans were living in enclosed urban environments (Woods 1998: 87). As Wright puts it in the essay cited by Brother Jack: "[t]he spick-and-span farmhouses done in red and green and white crowd out the casual, unpainted ginger-bread shacks. Silos take the place of straggling piles of hay. Macadam highways now wind over the horizon instead of dirt roads" (2008: 98). This is emblematised in Ellison's novel by Bledsoe's Southern Black college, binding together petromodernisation (macadam highways) with "piles of hay" and "dirt roads." Students in the college are prepared for life in the United States under Jim Crow – but equally this seems to hold true on the other side of the Mason–Dixon line, even if in less explicit form. In any case, the structural environmental damage that accompanies these changes is felt most strongly by Black populations who tend to live in the areas most ravaged by environmental destruction (Wright 2008: 101). The Great Migration, then, is also an environmental movement, determined by racial laws and losses. Ellison links electricity to zombies throughout, whether through the invisible man's sabotage of the monopoly, or through his toying with prefrontal lobotomy.

In the Haitian novel, the link between zombies and electricity occurs somewhat differently. For instance, in Depestre's *The Festival of the Greasy Pole*, zombies are linked with corruption, anti-communism and the power surrounding these political forces. Zoocrates Zachary – a thinly veiled version of François Duvalier (and, implicitly, his son Jean-Claude Duvalier) – controls electricity in Haiti. This control is symbolised by the pole that is erected by

---

6 This links back to my reference above to natural resources in the "Cheap Nature" debate (see Chapter 2).

ONEDA. The Duvalier dictatorship (1957–1986) sat comfortably within the capitalist world-system in a context overdetermined by the Cold War. Duvalier did not seek to challenge Haiti's dependence on foreign capital or radically alter class structures. Indeed, he "was willing to offer all the necessary advantages to foreign capital, such as tax exemptions, an abundance of cheap labour, and a climate of labour peace due to the suppression of all independent labor organizations and the banning of all strikes" (Dupuy 2014: 2192). As a consequence, zombification has also altered somewhat: now, people are zombified-by-mediation via the debt of the state incurred via electrification. In Depestre's 1979 novel, Henri Postel (who we learn has been zombified for five years) is not transformed into a racially coded zombie; rather, he is forced to look after Noah's Ark, a shop that is under the control of ONEDA. Zoocrates has created a new version of the zombie who is "conscious of his state to the very end" (Depestre 1990: 6). As Carrol Coates notes in her introduction to the novel, there are three meanings of electricity evoked in the text: first, it allegorically refers to the process of zombification, as "the control of thought and mind as well as of body" (1990: xlii); second, it references the ongoing process of Haitian electrification, or "the literal project of electrifying Haiti through the construction of a network of dams and generating stations for the production of energy" (1990: xliii); and third, the novel understands electricity as a vital life force – related, it seems, to the older understanding of energy as *energeia* – which we witness through the "good black electricity" of Valéry (Depestre 1990: 80). These three reference points come together in ONEDA's pole, which Henri Postel commits to climbing, and which is located at the centre of tensions between different approaches to the natural world. Depestre seems to suggest, not unlike the Haitian novelist Marie Vieux Chauvet before him, that the dictatorship is fundamentally environmentally degrading. The dictator's pole is frequently referred to in terms suggesting its death; for instance, "a tree that has lost its vegetable innocence, its sap and its song, could become a motionless, bald and sticky monster" (Depestre 1990: 15). The festival with the pole, turned into an event meant to celebrate the dictator, is suggestive of the impoverishment of human relations to their environments. In this context, the heavily allegorical invocation of electricity signifies the brutality of the François Duvalier dictatorship, which, as we will see, was invested in modernisation through electricity for its own ends.

In contrast to Duvalier's reliance on elite discourses of modernisation, Depestre evokes a range of different understandings of the natural world that rely on spiritual connections between humans and extra-humans. Indeed, in a later essay, Depestre adopts a far more accusatory tone that denounces the zombification/immiseration of the Americas, writing that the explosion of "blacks in the plantations and in the workshops of the Americas rendered possible the age of enlightenment, waterpower and electricity, and other discoveries of the first industrial revolution of the industrial modern world" (Depestre [1980] 2018: 7). He later adds that "[t]he gap between the opulence of a small number of countries and the decline of the majority of other countries is getting worse" (2018: 11). This is obviously the new version of violence that supports the "fascism of underdevelopment" (Depestre 1990: 63) enacted by François Duvalier.

In *Festival*, zombification is mockingly adapted to technological advances. The zombie as beast of burden, lacking consciousness of his own oppression and exhibiting a "dazed stare," no longer fits in "with our electronic times" (Depestre 1990: 6). As Zachary elaborates in the novel, the "electrification of souls attains a new metaphysical dimension: a death resembling life more than anything else" (1990: 6). This metaphorical meaning of electrification-as-zombification is connected to the literal electrification of Haiti, rendering explicit the embeddedness of electricity in the unevenness of capitalist (under-)development. It is thus no coincidence that the novel references the "Veligre Dam" (a thinly disguised version of Haiti's Peligre Dam): as announced on propaganda posters, only ONEDA "could conquer electricity at Veligre Dam and in the souls of citizens to bring light to the state of President Zachary" (1990: 123). For Duvalier, the Peligre Dam, which he had seized from the ODVA (Organisation de Developpement de la Vallée d'Artibonite), offered a potential avenue to legitimate his dictatorship through modernisation (Silvia 2016: 88). According to Duvalier's aide Clovis Désinor, "'every program [and] development plan [was] based on energy,' while hydroelectricity was the 'sine qua non of industrialization' that would 'increase the country's revenues and employ excess [population]'" (Silvia 2016: 88–89). However, the actual distribution of electricity would remain profoundly uneven. And employment was similarly uneven: as Wien Wiebert Arthus observes, "[w]hen François Duvalier took office in 1957, he started a policy that would be known as the *macoutisation* of public administration" (2013: 138). With this, Duvalier discarded most of the competent employed officials and replaced them with his own supporters, despite their being largely unqualified for their new positions. Indeed, as Arthus notes, after ousting competent members of the Black elites and replacing them with followers, "important tasks" were given to "foreign experts, especially individuals and companies from the United States" (2013: 139). This tendency worsened in the 1960s due to the out-migration of the professional classes.

Henri Postel is a new type of zombie who is completely aware of his state, but zombies are counterposed in the novel with another Gothic figure: the vampire. While Bram Stoker's *Dracula* associated the vampire with the aristocracy, the vampire has become a standard monstrous trope in critical efforts to expose capitalism's "systematic assaults on bodily and psychic integrity that define the economic infrastructure of modernity" (McNally 2011: 5). In *Capital* Volume I (1867), Karl Marx famously put it as follows: "Capital is dead labor, which, vampire-like, only lives by sucking living labor, and lives the more, the more labor it sucks" (1990: 342). If Duvalier's subjects are zombified, then Duvalier and members of his dictatorial regime are the new vampires within a highly uneven capitalist world-system, in which they suck their subjects' blood only to export and sell it to buyers abroad. This is literalised in the novel when ZAAMCO – the Zacharian American Company – "exports human blood at $3 dollars a liter" (Depestre 1990: 19). This blood is usually extracted from "out-of-work zombies" who are forced to sell it instead of their labour-power. During intense political repression, ONEDA vampirised Henri Postel, his family and partisans as political opponents, but now this enforced form of labour is switched for the "voluntary" submission of blood (1990: 118).

As mentioned in previous chapters, Depestre explicitly links zombification to environmental degradation and, more specifically, deforestation. As he writes: "Erosion and deforestation are, for our mountains, what zombification is for our people" (1990: 41). As we read through the perspective of the narrative voice, where before there was plenty, there are now only "gutted slopes [that] exposed the jutting bones of their flanks, whitened by wind and storms" (1990: 41). But Depestre does not only present the processes as parallel, but as thoroughly intertwined through the symbolism of the pole at the festival organised by ONEDA. Called the "Electrifier of Souls," this pole is often satirically presented as a phallic allegory for the dictatorship of Zachary. In this sense, the frequent association of the pole throughout the text with death and monstrosity is quite straightforwardly symbolic.

In a brief interview on the marvellous real, Depestre stated that vodou is for him "enriching" – a view that is clearly reflected in the novel through the character of Cisa. As practised by her, vodou is seen as "generally wholesome" (Munro 2007: 113) and, when linked to zombies in a positive way, seems to enable a positive embeddedness in the natural world. When Cisa sees Pancho, for instance, she reminds him that the tree "always remains a *pied bois* [a tree as altar or resting place for loas] – even without its roots and branches, it remains a living being that has grown straight, an altar of repose for other living creatures that need its tenderness and peace" (Depestre 1990: 50). She adds that Papa Loko "can assume at will the form of a chameleon, a climbing bird, a lizard, a butterfly or the shadow of a man, woman or child" (1990: 52), revisiting a famous passage from *El reino de este mundo* by Alejo Carpentier (from chapter 6, "The Metamorphoses"), when the narrator mentions Mackandal, who is also positively using vodou, as transforming into the green iguana, the nocturnal moth and the implausible dog as mere disguises (2010: 39). However, this "enriching" understanding of vodou very much clashes with the way in which it is mobilised and instrumentalised by the state under Zoocrates, just as it was under Duvalier. As Carrol Coates writes, vodou "became such an instrument of repression and political abuse with the Duvaliers, father and son, that there was an eruption of vengeful attacks on *oungan*, *manbo*, and the Vodou sanctuaries following the ousting of Baby Doc in 1986" (2006: 184). As rendered in this text, Nildevert, who was sent by Zoocrates, invokes several such negatively connoted gods to hinder Postel from climbing up the phallocentric, death-bringing tree: Baron-Samedi, Baron-la-Croix or Baron-Cimetière, the loas of death.

Ecology of the Zombie

Reading *Invisible Man* alongside *The Festival of the Greasy Pole* allows for an instructive comparison: in one novel, electrification works to zombify the population at large, while in the other, certain white middle- and upper-class people have created racialised access to electricity, while a large majority of African Americans are excluded. Ellison and Depestre are both, to differing degrees, sceptical of collective solutions in the fight against zombification, for reasons that are unevenly rooted in the Cold War context. Ellison's *Invisible Man* is marked by an anti-communist de-emphasis on proletarian cross-racial solidarity and class struggle, favouring instead individual resistance to corporate power. Depestre, by contrast, mocks quests by individuals to defy power single-handedly; indeed, Henry Postel's resistance is increasingly associated with the possibility of sparking wider revolution. Yet *The Festival of the Greasy Pole* is ultimately pessimistic about the ability of an individual to initiate collective action that might lead to change, with the dictatorship killing, raping and brutally decimating those associated with Postel.

Zombies provide a useful entry point for thinking about energy "as a changing category of human experience" (Nye 1992: 85). How to think human and extra-human energy together was slowly becoming a more explicit focus of zombie imaginaries in the twentieth century, as electrification was widely established and petromodern lifestyles became the norm across the US. Yet global energy regimes are experienced very differently depending on one's location in the world-system, as well as on one's class, race and gender. Haitian texts produced under the Duvalier dictatorships view the relation between zombies and non-human energy from the perspective of capitalism's periphery. The dominant energy regime reinforced unequal relations between Haiti and the US, and electrification in Haiti remains to this day incomplete, and accessible primarily to the wealthy and powerful, while access to oil remains an equally important issue. In Depestre's *The Festival of the Greasy Pole*, these forms of energy are explicitly thematised in relation to zombification and the dictatorships. The novel reflects on how zombification has itself changed within the context of twentieth-century forms of energy. Read alongside the US text, the Haitian novel offers a more complex and, one might say, "combined and uneven" picture of the zombie's relation to global energy regimes that have not erased global inequalities. The Haitian novel, far from sticking to the original zombies-as-beasts figuration, has here transformed the zombie and, in doing so, offers a biting critique of the status quo. Examining the zombie phenomenon across various disciplinary and canonical boundaries, then, can yield insights into its world-cultural dimensions.

Zombies and Petromodernity

George A. Romero's 1968 film *Night of the Living Dead* presents a turning point – one might say a symbolic revolution – in the history of zombie representations. Earlier films, such as Victor Halperin's *White Zombie* (1932) and

Energy and the Emergence of the Petro-Zombie

Jacques Tourneur's *I Walked with a Zombie* (1943), featured slow-moving zombie workers as well as zombified white females, reflecting imperialist anxieties of an expanding empire. It was Romero's film that famously featured the first cannibalistic zombie hordes, making it, as Jamie Russell writes, a "watershed movie" (2005: 71). Critical analyses have rightly placed much emphasis on the overdetermined year of the film's first screening: 1968 was the year of the Tet offensive in Vietnam; of student revolutions; of the assassination of Martin Luther King Jr; of the Chicago riots. More broadly, the 1960s was the decade of the civil rights movement, decolonisation struggles and industrial strikes. Romero's film was notably invested in these anti-systemic struggles, as demonstrated by its visual and audio references to the Vietnam War, as well as its attacks on the nuclear family and institutionalised racism in the US. Yet from the vantage point of recent research on "petrocultures," combined with insights derived from work on "world-ecology," this symbolic revolution can be re-read in terms of systemic upheaval and energy transition within the capitalist world-ecology (see Bozak 2011; Macdonald 2013; J. Moore 2015; Niblett 2015). For there is arguably an even more fundamental shift at stake that is rendered visible in the film: from the end of the nineteenth century, oil had emerged as the new energy vector of the world-system, completely reorganising nature–society relations around the logic of oil extraction.

Oil is not just a natural resource. It is an entire web of political, economic and socio-ecological relations whose emergence has reshaped landscapes,

Fig. 8. *Night of the Living Dead* (1968). Ben and Tom try to get oil from the local pump.

111

cultures and socio-economies; created new opportunities and freedoms marked by profound asymmetries; and given rise to a newly integrated world-food-system via petro-fuelled transport and the Green Revolution. As Imre Szeman writes, oil is not only "an input that can easily take other forms, but […] a substance that has given shape to capitalist social reality" (2010: 34). From *Night of the Living Dead* onwards, zombie aesthetics began to register these changes, giving rise to a new and soon-to-be dominant figure: the petro-zombie. Best escaped from in motorised vehicles, these flesh-eating zombie hordes are by now familiar to movie audiences, yet they only emerged in 1968 – just five years before the 1973 global oil crisis – with Romero's landmark production. To grasp the nature of this symbolic revolution, it is necessary to read the zombie as a figure that turns on successive revolutions in the dialectical relations between human and extra-human natures under world-capitalism. In Marxist readings, the slow labouring zombie has long been understood as representing the exploitation of alienated workers: David McNally, for example, reads the zombie as manifesting "recurrent anxieties about corporeal dismemberment in societies where the commodification of human labour […] is becoming widespread" (2012: 4). However, unless we grasp capitalism as a *world-ecology*, certain aspects of the trajectory of this figure, and specifically the shift towards the petro-zombie, remain open to misreading.

While the petro-zombie registers the ecological revolution that began in Titusville in 1859, the zombie figure has its origins in the colonial sugar plantations of Haiti – plantations that were fundamental to the development of capitalism. The sugar-zombie was described by Alfred Métraux as a "beast of burden" with no autonomous will, forcibly reduced to his labour-power and ceaselessly toiling for a zombie master (1972: 282). Decades later, Romero's zombies engendered a fundamental break with these representations. His "ghouls" do not work for anyone but instead wander across the farmlands of Pennsylvania, driven by an insatiable, cannibalistic hunger displaced on to human flesh. Romero's zombies are the creatures of a new, petromodern world-ecology that took shape through the rise of suburbia and automobile culture; through the development of oil-fuelled global transport networks; through the destruction of (often African American) smallholdings in the American South; through the gradual transformation of wheat and cattle into "rivers of seeds and flesh" (Friedmann 2000: 508). Romero's film offers a critical view on the emergence of the US as an imperial power, epitomised at the time by the destruction of Vietnamese lands and lives in a war fuelled by oil. His zombies clearly borrowed from, but ultimately transcended, the US Cold War imaginary and its recurrent tropes, as exemplified in two oft-cited influences: the black-and-white film *Invasion of the Body Snatchers* (Siegel 1956) and Richard Matheson's *I am Legend* (1955). Both of these texts featured contagious humanoid monsters: in the former, these are mass-bred in pods on farms; in the latter, they are masses of vampires that lack the aristocratic individualism of Dracula. Apart from the more obvious political and ideological differences between the anti-communist *Invasion of the Body Snatchers* and Romero's movie, the latter imaginatively grasps the relation between changes to the agricultural landscape and the rise of automobile culture and urbanisation as mutually constitutive, unlike the former, which presents motorised modernity as the salvation from farming gone awry.

Many have commented on the 1968 revolution in zombie aesthetics, but what this means for the figure's relation to capitalism has often been misrecognised. For McNally, this symbolic revolution comes at the expense of "the hidden world of labour and disparities of class" and is only ever able to offer a "critique of consumerism, not capitalism" (2011: 261). This curious failure to appreciate what is at stake in Romero's film is to a large extent due to McNally's understanding of "Nature" and its relation to capitalism. McNally argues that "the utter uniqueness, some would say perversion, of capitalist society consists in the way money replaces nature as the essential condition of human life" (2011: 148). Yet, to state the obvious, money can never literally replace nature as this essential condition, even if this is the illusion on which the current world-system is premised. As Harriet Friedmann writes:

> by linking and displacing local ecosystems, the modern worldsystem *obscured* humans relations to the rest of nature. It created the first basis for human illusions about markets and money as the apparent basis of life. The second basis came with industry, which was made possible by world markets and specialized agriculture. Industrial agriculture not only displaced and obscured earthly cycles, but *ignored* them. (2000: 502)

If capitalism is understood as world-ecology, developing through periodic revolutions in nature–society relations, then oil can be seen as not just as an energy input but a vector through which the entire system remakes itself. McNally reads the zombie as a figure that encapsulates the alienation of labour as a result and effect of commodification; yet as previously argued, we need to read the zombie not merely as a metaphor for a specific relation, but as being animated by the "inner logic" of capitalism (Shaviro 1993: 63). As a figure, it gestures towards processes and sets of relations, which are completely (albeit unevenly) remade by the emergence of oil-as-commodity. It registers not only the human cost of alienation, but also the delayed and displaced consequences of the suppression of local material cycles and of the exhaustion of so-called "natural" resources. As Judith Halberstam explains, gothic economies function by rendering the mystificatory processes of capitalism visible in the monstrous: they construct "a monster out of the traits which ideologies of race, class, gender, sexuality, and capital want to disavow" (1995: 102) – a definition to which we have to add gothic "ecophobia" (Oloff 2012).

To put it differently, Romero's zombies respond to a fundamental change in agricultural relations and food-getting, referred to as the Green Revolution (that is, the introduction of industrial techniques into agriculture from the 1940s onwards, including the use of chemical fertilisers and pesticides, machinery as well as hybrid seeds). The Green Revolution gave rise to today's endless monocultural fields and terrifyingly cramped animal farming; it was made possible by fossil fuels and developed through the deepening of the existing rifts between humans and non-human environments. It displaced family farms with transnational corporations, favouring the "big mechanized farms [that] were hooked on oil not only for the fertilizers and pesticides that produced their super-sized crops but also for the machines that would harvest them and the oil-fired transport that would speed crops to distant markets" (Shah 2004: 18). As a result, the energy input was increased by "an average of 50 times" (Pfeiffer 2013: 7). The mid-twentieth-century productivity revolution was therefore paid for by cheap oil, by the exhaustion of soils and water reservoirs, by ignoring traditional farming knowledge and disregarding natural limits. The zombie's aesthetic shift from a figure rooted in the political ecology of sugar to that of oil is one that responds to these systemic changes, belatedly registering the shift from the globalised ecological regime that originated in the conquest period. One might speculate that the reason the figure lent itself to this shift is that there exist certain parallels between the political ecologies of oil and sugar. Like oil, sugar is a global commodity that provides energy, the production of which has historically been marked by social violence and ecological devastation (see Mintz 1986). Entire societies were structured around it, and bound to its place in the uneven capitalist market, with devastating consequences. Sugar's own link with oil is also highly significant. Oil has brought about fundamental changes in food production and consumption – especially of sugar, as this has become a fundamental ingredient of highly processed foods – yet this relation is indirect, intensifying the fetishism surrounding food commodities. Oil, then, is different from sugar in terms of both scale and function: oil saturates the entire infrastructure of modernity, producing an intensification of commodity fetishism on a global scale.

What does this mean for the aesthetics of sugar and oil respectively? Sugar aesthetics – like oil aesthetics – have tended towards the phantasmagoric, the gothic and the irreal, registering a feeling of unreality, the violence of production and the intense fetishism surrounding the product. Commenting on the differences between saccharine irrealism and petro-aesthetics, Niblett notes that what is different about oil is that:

> to think oil is to think the world-system [...] And this is where the problem lies; for to attempt to make oil the direct subject of a narrative is to attempt to subjectivize the world-system – to make it representable in terms of ordinary (subjective) experience. But whereas the lived experience of the effects produced by the system's petro-driven dynamics would be representable in this way, the system *as such*, as an immense bundle of human and extra-human relations in movement, could not be reduced to such subjective experience. (2015: 275)

In Romero's *Night of the Living Dead*, we see this very contradiction at work. Oil saturates everyday reality; it is the main visual and plot-based obsession of the film, and thus a "direct subject" of the narrative. Yet it is also more than this: it features as a violent dynamic that exceeds comprehension and that seeks to devour everything in its path. Oil-as-relation, or oil-as-system, is difficult to cognitively map. It therefore surfaces in the economy of the monstrous that threatens to bring life as we know it to a halt. The unpaid debts of cheap oil, of water exhaustion and soil erosion and of increasing social inequality return to collect their due. Perhaps somewhat "crudely," one might say that the zombie revolution is one that involves a shift from being a figure that was representative of a relation within a system that consumes his humanity to one that – awkwardly, ambivalently – points towards the world-system itself. There is no longer an easily identifiable zombie-master who can be blamed as events spiral out of control and the world comes to an end. Zombies are no longer represented as alienated producers of food energy; now, they are driven by a never-ending cannibalistic hunger that feeds on the (actual or potential) labour-force of petromodernity.

To the extent that zombies register shifts in nature–society relations under capitalism, landscape and setting – as well as how these are inhabited by humans – are crucial aspects of zombie aesthetics. A concern with how nature–society relations are reshaped in the car-dominated, petro-fuelled twentieth century is prominent throughout *Night of the Living Dead*. Unlike the sugar-zombie, Romero's zombies would never stop in their path to till the land or work on a plantation. Indeed, the aesthetics of sugar plantations and toiling bodies are explicitly replaced by iconic shots of bloodthirsty ghouls wandering across an otherwise deserted rural landscape, culminating in their instinct-driven mass attack on the farmhouse. While the horror of the movie unfolds in and around this dilapidated farmhouse in the south-western Pennsylvanian countryside, almost all of the protagonists have arrived from elsewhere by car. The film thereby places consistent visual emphasis on fossil-fuelled transport, registering the widespread abandonment of the countryside under petro-capitalism.

This emphasis on travel is evident from the start: the film opens on a slightly shaky long shot of a deserted country road, winding through an autumnal landscape of fields and leading past three distant farmhouses. A car appears in the far distance and gradually – over the course of over half a minute – makes its way into the foreground. As the car exits the frame, the camera cuts to another long shot in the opposite direction, and the car proceeds to move through the frame for, again, almost half a minute. This is followed by a concatenation of further shots of the car advancing along the winding road, eventually entering a rural cemetery as the camera focuses on a US flag, symbolically positioned in the foreground.

The prolonged sequence of the car's journey with the cemetery as destination metonymically evokes Johnny and Barbra's 200-mile migration from Pittsburgh – where Gulf Oil, US Steel, Westinghouse and Alcoa all had their headquarters – to the countryside, which the visual economy of the movie links to a national past signalled by the flag. The visual introduction of

Ecology of the Zombie

the car passengers is purposely delayed. As Tony Williams notes: "A low-angle shot frames the car before we see the occupants. This angle emphasises a vision of the dominant technology which most Americans place their trust in" (2003: 23). The importance of cars is thus evoked from the very opening scene, as the camerawork subordinates the individual to a culture knitted together by petro-fuelled transport.

In Romero's film, oil is curiously what both protects and ultimately destroys human life. Fuel-driven transport could potentially enable the escape of the protagonists, registering Stephanie LeMenager's observation that, in the lives of those with regular access to cars, "driving" is habitually associated with "being alive" (2012: 70). This point is literalised in the opposition between fast-driving humans and the slow, stumbling zombies that defy the linear temporality of petromodernity and its ideals of speed and progress. The zombie's inability to compete with functioning cars is rendered visually explicit when Judy and Tom drive their truck to the notorious gas pump, while the zombies fall limply behind; further, as Ben observes, when one drives straight into zombies, they "scatter like bugs." Throughout the film, zombies are simultaneously attracted to and repelled by cars, by petroleum and by artificial light. Zombies are frequently shot in the same frame as cars, often shown trying to access vehicles, meaning the gas pump becomes the prime site of terror. The film's infamous scene of cannibalism takes place just after Judy and Tom's failed attempt to get petrol from the pump, resulting in the young couple being blown up in their car. Canted shots and shaky handheld camera movements here recreate the sense of panic, as the car – and, metonymically, normalised car culture – explodes. This association between zombies, oil and car culture quickly became the new dominant, as Romero's iconic exploding petrol station emerged as a well-established cinematic trope.

Throughout *Night of the Living Dead*, the semi-peripheral landscape and population of rural Pennsylvania are seen as anachronistic, cut off from metropolitan centres, while news footage of Washington DC positions the seat of power elsewhere. Even prior to the outbreak of the zombie apocalypse, the region is marked by stasis and death, symbolised by Barbra and Johnny's visit to the cemetery in remembrance of their long-dead father. Williams explains that even their relation to his memory is now mediated through consumerism, as they place a manufactured wreath on the grave as part of a ritual visit that has long lost its meaning (2003: 24). This sense of anachronism regarding the countryside continues to be central to the plot. Barbra escapes the zombies by taking refuge in a dilapidated farmhouse – a claustrophobic site of horror that evokes a certain type of agricultural relation (family farming), rendered obsolete by agro-industrialisation. This is made explicit in the visual association of the farmhouse with a gas pump through a sequence of shot-reverse-shot: in between two shots of the farm, we are offered two of Barbra holding on to the gas pump, metonymically emphasising the centrality of oil to the new agricultural and social order.

While recent critical analyses of the film tend not to focus on ecology or environmental degradation, this context was clearly visible to Romero's

Energy and the Emergence of the Petro-Zombie

Fig. 9. *Night of the Living Dead* (1968). Barbara holding onto a petrol pump.

contemporaries. Only a few years prior to the film's release, fellow Pennsylvanian Rachel Carson had published *Silent Spring* (1962), the opening fable of which uses a gothic lexicon to invoke the impact of pesticides on the countryside:

> a strange blight crept over the area and everything began to change. Some evil spell had settled on the community [...] Everywhere was the shadow of death [...] No witchcraft, no enemy action had silenced the rebirth of new life in this stricken world. The people had done it themselves [...] A grim spectre has crept upon us almost unnoticed. (2000: 21–22)

Here, the industrialisation of the countryside and its detrimental effects generate a sense of rupture and ecological catastrophe in a vision strikingly similar to that presented six years later by Romero. Similarly, in 1974, the Spanish director Jorge Grau released *No profanar el sueño de los muertos* [*The Living Dead at the Manchester Morgue*], shot in Manchester and the Lake District; with clear visual nods to *Night of the Living Dead*, this film offers an environmentalist message that is made visually explicit from the beginning. The underlying reflection on socio-ecological changes in Romero's opening sequence is echoed in a concatenation of shots of Manchester, an urban environment dominated by car fumes, interspersed with shots of a rotting bird and a lone female streaker making a peace sign. As Russell concludes, "the hippie dream has given way to pollution, ennui and the beginning of the strike-filled, unemployment-soaring 1970s" (2005: 81). The two protagonists are thus pitted against reactionary government officials who ignore the threat posed by industrial agribusiness, as symbolised by a giant orange machine: a reified technological agent of oil-based power which, together with the agri-entrepreneur, has replaced the small-scale farmer and further irradiated the ground following the use of DDT. The radioactive machine produces violent behaviour in animals, babies and dead humans, especially the displaced rural poor, thus becoming the twentieth-century equivalent of the zombie-master. But where Grau's film offers a relatively simple vision in which the threat can be easily decoded, Romero's zombies are complex, uncontainable figures of excess whose cannibalistic terror is strongly overdetermined by multiple entangled histories.

Critical reception of Romero's film has rightly focussed on his strong critique of race relations in the US, as well as of the core-hegemon's imperialist war against North Vietnam. Ben, the African American protagonist, is gunned down at the end of the film by an all-white police force, in a scene that visually resonates with the brutal methods employed by the US military in Vietnam (see Higashi 1992). Yet the film also invites reflection on the political ecology of these very social relations. Though environmental and Cold War historiographies have long been "like two ships passing in the night, dimly conscious of one another but unable or unwilling to engage each other" (McNeil and Unger 2010: 4), more recent accounts have emphasised the role of the Green Revolution in the US's Cold War strategy – for example, mobilising wheat and rice to win "hearts and minds" – as well as the intertwined histories of exploration, research and environmental warfare. For not only was the Vietnam War fuelled on both sides by oil provided by Shell (see Wesseling 2000), but the systematic environmental destruction caused by the agrochemical warfare became so integral to US strategy that, as Greg Bankoff writes, "a photograph of a US Air Force C-123 transport aircraft dispensing defoliants over the emerald green tropical forest below has become almost iconic of how the war is remembered" (2010: 215).

At the national level, the Green Revolution was similarly integral to the large-scale displacement of African Americans, as sharecropping agriculture gave way to the mechanised neo-plantation. As Woods explains, the "centuries-old push for ethnic, political, and economic democracy which re-emerged under the banner of civil rights in the 1950s was effectively hollowed out by this revolution" (1998: 87). The socio-ecology of African American history – specifically the Great Migration and exodus towards US cities – also provides the larger, national context for the role of Ben, a character who was decisively reshaped by the actor Duane Jones. Originally conceived as a white truck driver, "a redneck kind of guy" (Keough [2010] 2011: 171), Jones recoded Ben as a well-educated, presumably urban, white-collar labourer. Partly for this reason, Ben is the most complex character in the film: heroic but flawed, sharply contrasting with the history of African American actors portraying zombies in earlier US films, but also subverting the Sidney Poitier-like character he initially seems to evoke (Bruce 2011: 62). He is also more deracinated than any other character, as nothing is revealed about his family, origins or destination. Notably, the first attempt to verbalise the horror of what is happening comes from Ben, as he relays his encounter with the zombies at Beekman's Diner:

> a big gasoline truck came *screaming* right across the road! There might have been ten, fifteen of those things chasing after it, grabbing and holding on [...] I guess ... guess the driver must've cut off the road into that gas station by Beekman's Diner. It went right through the billboard, ripped over the gas pump, and never stopped moving. But now it was like a moving bonfire! [...] I still hear the man ... *screaming*. These things, just backing away from it! [...] by now there were no more *screams*. I realized that I was alone, with fifty or sixty or sixty of those things just ... standing there, staring at me! (IMDb, emphases added)[7]

As this passage reveals, the "gasoline truck" is symbolically at the centre of the famous gas station chase. In Ben's monologue, "screaming" is at first anthropomorphically associated with the sound of the gasoline truck's screeching tyres. The second time, it names the sound of a man trapped in the burning vehicle. The third time Ben mentions "screams," it is their absence, which now demarcates the victory of dehumanising horror, one that is the product of the bond humans have to their vehicles through oil. The racial dynamics here are not difficult to miss, as Ben's encounter carries horrific resonances of lynch mob violence, in which gasoline was commonly employed to burn the victims. The symbolic importance of oil is so strongly overdetermined – figuratively, culturally and historically – because oil has simultaneously reshaped landscapes and restructured social relations, and the history of the latter cannot be extricated from that of the former. The sliding signifier of the "screams" thus points to their entanglement, just as the underlying threat of cannibalism signals that which exceeds representation: the inexplicable horror of oil-as-relation, oil-as-the-system, which cannot be easily encapsulated by either the cars or the petrol pump. The "scream" not only resonates with and within the zombie horror, that is, but it gestures towards an intensification of oil-fetishism throughout the petromodern world-ecology.

The rise to hegemony of the petro-zombie can usefully be placed within the history of film-making. Like any modern industry, the film industry is itself drenched in fossil fuels: from the materials used for filming and the infrastructure required for distribution, through the drive-in cinemas where Romero's film was first screened, to the film stock itself which, "like the ink used in modern print media, is essentially petroleum" (LeMenager 2014: 100). Zombie movies frequently involve the breakdown of modern media communication – as in Romero's film, when the TV eventually stops transmitting – imaginatively threatening the very possibility of film-making: if petromodern infrastructure breaks down, so will the possibility of communicating through

---

7 https://www.imdb.com/title/tt0063350/quotes/qt0398603 (accessed 11 March 2021).

TV and film screens. Yet from its early days, film-making in general displayed a strong self-awareness of its link to (petro)modern industry, to fossil fuels and to the enhanced speed, light and transportation they enable. For instance, the early films of the Lumière Brothers famously include *The Arrival of the Train at La Ciotat* (1895), capturing the arrival of a train filmed in a single shot, and *Oil Wells of Baku: A Close View* (1896), showing "huge flames and black smoke streaming from the burning oil wells in Baku" (Murray and Heumann 2009: 19), thus highlighting the spectacular quality of the giant oil gushers. The opening scene of *Night of the Living Dead* could be read as an intertextual reference to *The Arrival*, with visuals of the slow-moving car inviting the viewer to reflect on the shift from coal to oil by foregrounding the individualised "freedoms" of petro-transport. But where hegemonic representations of "the spectacle of [oil] gushing from the earth suggests divine or Satanic origins" (LeMenager 2014: 92), Romero's film clearly does not offer a view of oil-as-spectacle. Instead, it re-embeds oil within socio-ecological relations, gesturing towards its history of violence and dispossession, and warning against capitalism's fetishistic reliance on energetic extraction. Like oil – which, as Vaclav Smil reminds us, derives from ancient "dead biomass, the remnants of terrestrial and aquatic plants and heterotrophic organisms" (2008: 58–59) – zombies rise up from the earth as dead but seemingly animated matter, containing within them the remnants of former life. Oil's powers are likewise so great as to seem fantastic: one barrel of oil is equivalent to 25,000 hours – or 12.5 years – of human labour-power. If crude oil appears to rise "magically" from the ground, oil-as-commodity thus gives rise to an intense form of fetishism that reifies the abstract social and physical labour of petrolic commodity production. Yet as is plainly visible from peripheral sites of extraction, oil is neither free – its environmental and human costs are, in fact, skyrocketing – nor is it attained without work. Rather, as has been amply documented, oil extraction is among the most brutal, exploitative and deadly of modern industries. If the energetic labour-power of the sugar-zombie was easily controlled, therefore, this is no longer the case for the multiplied energies of petro-zombie hordes.

According to Hugh Manon, *Night of the Living Dead* was able to tap into larger developments in a way that sprang, perhaps paradoxically, from its "unusually strong investment in the local" (2011: 317). This local "investment" is the polar opposite of contemporary Hollywood's location shooting, which typically employs familiar visual reference points – often tourist attractions – in order to evoke a certain geographical or socio-economic setting. Instead, Romero's film supplies what Manon describes as "a profusion of pointedly unrecognizable local details to create a sense of familiar nonfamiliarity" (2011: 320). This is partly due to the fact that Image Ten was a small, Pittsburgh-based production company, meaning the film's strong local investment was bound up with the economic realities of making a low-budget independent film costing 114,000 dollars (Block [1972] 2011: 15). Further, it was shot in south-western Pennsylvania, using real houses and pastures as setting, meaning the material conditions of locality take on a significant, shaping role. The central farmhouse around which all the action revolves, for instance, was an abandoned building about to be ripped down, adding to the sense of dilapidation and the downturn of family farming in rural Pennsylvania, where the farming population had decreased from over 1 million in 1900 to 303,000 in 1970 (Klein and Hoogenboom 1980: 481). It is perhaps no coincidence that the most significant shift in zombie representation since the Haitian sugar-zombie was first articulated in another peripheralised space, where the socio-ecological costs of exhausted lumber and oil frontiers were acutely, if unevenly, felt.

Despite its peripheral status, however, Pennsylvania was a key site in the emergence of petromodernity. The advent of petro-capitalism can be dated to the discovery of oil in Titusville – a small and impoverished town in north-western Pennsylvania – in 1859. At the time, this lumber town was expected eventually to disappear with increasing deforestation, but the onset of the oil boom changed its fate overnight, as land prices and population rates skyrocketed. By the 1870s and 1880s, moreover, Pennsylvania was suddenly in the position of being the sole producer of a global commodity whose emergence almost miraculously reshaped the region's landscapes, populations, fortunes and imaginaries. As one local editor commented in 1865:

> The oil and land excitement has already become a *sort of epidemic* […] they neither talk, nor look, nor act as they did six months ago […] all our habits, and notions, and associations for half a century are turned *topsy-turvy in the headlong rush for riches*. (quoted in Yergin 2012: 17, emphases added)

The editor paints the oil boom as highly disruptive, erasing social habitus, morals, categories and distinctions, and in the process lays the imaginative foundations for the petro-zombie.

It is not hard to see how Pennsylvania's oil boom made Romero's de-individualised zombie hordes thinkable. During this first boom, it was not gasoline but kerosene that was able to penetrate the market most effectively, the groundwork for its emergence as a global product having already been laid by coal-oils. Kerosene provided an inexpensive but high-quality illuminant, meaning that "man was suddenly given the ability to push back the night" (Yergin 2012: 13), thereby extending the working day. It is unsurprising, then, that Romero's zombies are simultaneously associated with the night and repeatedly shown to be afraid of – but also attracted to – light and fire. Early on, for instance, a bottle of lighter fluid becomes central as Ben soaks an entire sofa in the liquid, creating some respite from the zombie attack but also inevitably attracting more zombies to the house. His experience is later confirmed by one of the experts interviewed on TV, who recommends that all dead bodies should be "soaked with gasoline" and burned immediately. Oil again plays a major role in their attempt to escape: Molotov cocktails – made with the kerosene that Tom discovers in the basement – are important in the attempts of the survivors to take possession of the truck. The film's distinction between light and dark, human and zombie, is repeatedly reinforced by high-contrast lighting – a technique that plays a vital role in photography and cinematography more generally. As Bozak explains, the "photographic camera works by capturing and ultimately controlling doses of light, which, when applied to the light-sensitive emulsion of raw film stock [made of oil], are fixed or fossilised into the latent image" (2011: 31). Simultaneously repelled by and attracted to oil-based light, zombies are thus once again linked with the very possibility – as well as impossibility – of image-making in an age of oil.

By the turn of the century, kerosene would be replaced by electricity and the illuminant market for oil would be replaced by the automobile industry and its demand for gasoline. Pittsburgh, where the film's protagonists originate, was the site of the first drive-in service station in the US, located on Baum Boulevard, which was also known as "automobile row" owing to the high number of car dealerships there (see Wells n.d.). The service station was operated by Gulf Oil, and offered free air and water as well as selling maps. This conjunction of maps and petrol gestures towards the emergence of a car culture whose transformative impact included restructuring space, transforming landscapes and creating affective contexts that were, as Mimi Sheller observes, "deeply materialized in particular types of vehicles, homes, neighborhoods, and cities" (2004: 61). Romero's zombies are clearly a product of this petrolic culture. They are attracted to oil and cars, but they are also inherently mobile and free to roam large territories, unbound by attachments to a particular locality. Unlike plantation-era zombie-labourers, they are no longer producers of value but creatures whose attack on petromodern infrastructure threatens the very possibility of value-production (see Shaviro 1993). Romero's zombies thus simultaneously express the cultural logic of oil and energy transition *and* anticipate growing anxieties about petromodernity's potential collapse.

Since its origins the zombie has disturbed the categorisation of colonialism, racism and plantation as solely socio-economic phenomena, instead revealing these complex bundles of power and production as fundamentally environment-making processes. As a figure that turns on the world-ecological transformations through which capitalism develops, socio-ecological revolutions, crises and the emergence of new energy regimes have tended to produce new zombie effects. The zombie was fundamentally reshaped as a result of the emergence of petromodern world-ecology, at once registering the systemic shift in energy regime and anticipating the global oil crisis of the 1970s. In *Invisible Man* and *The Festival of the Greasy Pole*, we saw that the connection to electricity was also easily made and that it linked zombies to racial and class-based fantasies. In more recent years, sugar has itself re-emerged as a caloric-energy input in petro-zombie films such as *28 Days Later* (Boyle 2002). Such films are visually obsessed with junk food and sodas in a world dominated by zombified consumers and a lack of access to healthy foods (see Newbury 2012). Nevertheless, it is important to acknowledge that the petro- and sugar-zombie continue to exist side by side, just as the "older" saccharine zombie lives on in many Caribbean novels, where it continues to register the legacies of colonialism. This simultaneity and multiplicity of zombie figures arises from a world-system that is profoundly unequal, one in which the spectacular benefits and liberties made possible by oil and other energy sources are only unevenly accessible, and in which paid and unpaid work are rearranged in extremely destructive fashions. As a figure that has crossed from the world-systemic periphery to its new hegemonic core, the zombie is one that – perhaps like no other – is inscribed with local and global inequalities. Both the older and the newer figure strongly register the metabolic rifts through which the world-system developed; however, unlike the sugar-zombie, the petro-zombie gestures towards representing the unrepresentable: towards the multifaceted and, it would seem, terminal crisis of the capitalist world-system.

CHAPTER 5

Zombies-of-Waste and Neoliberal Exhaustion

In Kettly Mars's eerie horror story "Paradise Inn" (2014), a Haitian police officer is sent by the High Command to a small town named Gokal in the north-west of the country, since he is about to uncover a big drug trafficking operation as well as, inadvertently, maleficent police corruption. Having accepted his transfer without suspicion, Commissaire Vanel books into a hotel called Paradise Inn, which he will never leave again, as he is gradually drained of all energy and willpower and eventually, even, his bodily presence. The inn – a Caribbean version of the horror trope of an isolated hotel-turned-death-trap (e.g. Stanley Kubrick's *The Shining*, 1980), or of the witch's house stuck in time (e.g. Carlos Fuentes's *Aura*, 1962) – runs on the energy of its all-male guests in a very literal sense: there are no generators or solar panels to provide electricity for the inn; instead, it vampirically consumes its guests' life forces. The entire village is subject to this life-draining, manifesting in "dull looks on [the villagers'] faces" (Mars 2011: 57). It also produces a strange collapse of time; the narrator observes that the inn "seemed dead; everything was covered in a thin layer of dust" (2014: 58). These monstrous forces are somehow connected to the village's extreme peripheralisation as an exhausted commodity frontier (a former sugar-producing area in the outer periphery): the villagers are isolated from most of the energy-based advantages of modernisation, without cars, phones or a perceptible energy infrastructure. The only trace of economic activity (and even connection to the outside world) is the suggestion that "the sale of charcoal" – which is made by rural dwellers from the last remaining trees – "must still support the dying economy of the town" (2014: 61). The landscape, which is dry and treeless, has turned into a haunted purgatory.

Focussed on one of the most isolated regions in Haiti, with the highest levels of poverty and very little energy infrastructure, the story thus offers a nakedly allegorical representation of the legacy of imperialist plunder, resource appropriation and environmental degradation. In many ways, "Paradise Inn" indexes the conditions in Haiti under neoliberalism and the reign of the NGOs: the US's half-hearted support for the Duvalier dictators after the occupation of 1915–1934; the liberalisation of markets, causing the destruction of the rice industry in the 1980s and cumulative food crises; the shunting of Haitians into production centres where they would produce at rates below the cost of living; and the explosion of an internal drugs market – these details form the general context for the story.

In 1971, Jean-Claude Duvalier succeeded his father, François, as the president of Haiti. The transfer of power from father to son also signalled a shift to neoliberalism, along with a

> new mode of integration of Haiti in the capitalist world economy and the surrendering of the formulation of economic policy to the international foreign institutions – principally the World Bank, the International Monetary Fund, the Inter-American Development Bank (IDB), and the United States Agency for International Development. (Dupuy 2007: 814)

This also set the country on course for the 2010 earthquake. As Alex Dupuy states elsewhere, "we can consider the 1970s as having marked a major turning point in creating the conditions that existed on the eve of the earthquake and contributed to its devastating impact" (2010: 15).

Let us here pause to consider the difference between Commissaire Vanel's transformation into an agency-less being and the classic zombie-worker: though magic powers are involved, the commissaire is not exploited for his labour-power. Instead, Mars's commissaire might be read as an example of the "new zombie" – a phenomenon that can be contextualised within formal shifts that have emerged in recent years. As Junot Díaz notes, "[o]ld zombies were expected to work around the clock with no relief. The new zombie cannot expect work of any kind—the new zombie just waits around to die" (2011: n.p.). Díaz has consistently emphasised the importance of genre imaginaries for thinking through the legacies of colonialist and imperialist capitalism.[1] The shift in generic conventions is, from this perspective, clearly significant. While working zombies have not disappeared from cultural imaginaries, the non-productive zombie – or the zombie registering the "human-as-waste" (Yates 2011) and the devaluation of workers – is now relatively frequent. While the "new zombie" registers the crisis of the neoliberal regime, which is often dated back to the early 2000s and became very visible with the global recession in 2007/8, it has its medium-term roots in the crisis of global capitalism of the 1970s and the reassertion of the power of local and global capitalist elites. Within these "new zombie" imaginaries, capitalism's

---

1 Interviewed by Taryne Taylor: "Alien invasions, natives, slavery, colonies, genocide, racial system, savages, technological superiority, forerunner races and the ruins they leave behind, travel between worlds, breeding programs, superpowered whites, mechanized regimes that work humans to death, human/alien hybrids, lost worlds—all have their roots in the traumas of colonialism" (2014: 101).

tendency towards socio-ecological degradation and exhaustion has become impossible to miss.

This chapter turns to several recent examples of such "new zombie" imaginaries, reading US and Caribbean texts alongside each other. As discussed in previous chapters, the the forceful opening of the Caribbean to US capital was embedded in imperial expansion and (ongoing) colonisation, underwritten and propped up by recurring military invasions. Neoliberalism has functioned as a continuation – and intensification – of this longer history, even if the means have shifted in some contexts. Indeed, openly repressive patterns continued in places such as Haiti long after colonial powers were ousted, including the US backing of pro-neoliberal dictator Jean-Claude Duvalier.[2] As in other peripheralised countries, this opening of markets had the effect of further dismantling the local economy and thus created a damaging dependence on imports. Throughout the 1970s, "the massive influx of transnational corporations in Haiti, with around 240 mainly US-based corporations (specialising mainly in textiles, electronics, toys and sports goods)" (Blakely 2009: 191), further deepened metabolic rifts by accelerating longer trends of de-peasantisation and urbanisation. Haiti was thus even more thoroughly peripheralised in the capitalist world-system through intensifying foreign domination (with the support of local capitalist elites) and the destruction of the local economy, most notably, perhaps, its rice production.[3] Even before the 2010 earthquake, Haiti was experiencing high levels of poverty (80%), and even abject poverty (54%) (Abrams 2010: 444), as well as a large degree of un- and under-employment. As a result, (mostly female) workers were forced into extremely low-paid jobs in foreign-owned businesses in the Export Processing Zones; workers were forced into informal industries, resulting in the growth of the drug trade and tourist sex work; child slavery and trafficking through the *restavek* (unpaid female labourer) system continued to be a significant social issue. Mars's commissaire, the victim of corruption and criminal networks, is thus one of a series of zombie figures registering the impact of neoliberalism on the local population, ranging from zombie *restaveks* to mass starvation.

As previously discussed, capital has historically overcome regularly occurring crises through a combination of productivity revolutions and new forms of plunder, which together unfold through massive transformations in socio-ecological relations. What distinguishes the *neoliberal* regime of accumulation has been the relative failure of this dialectic of plunder and productivity to revive the underlying stagnation in profit rates that has characterised the world-economy since the 1970s. As Jason W. Moore observes, neoliberalism

---

2 Raoul Cédras, the leader of the military coup that ousted the first democratically elected Aristide, was also trained in the United States.
3 The irony here lies in the fact that Bill Clinton, in a much-publicised video testifying to the US Senate Foreign Relations Committee on 10 March 2010, acknowledges responsibility for the rice issue (Dupuy 2010: 14).

broke with [the] world-historical pattern of productivity and plunder. Accumulation revived by the early 1980s, but it did so on a much different basis than during the postwar golden age, or the mid-nineteenth-century zenith of British industrialization. The frontiers that could yield a cornucopia of nature's free gifts were fewer than ever before, and the scientific-technological revolution in labor productivity, greatly anticipated in the 1970s, never materialized. (2010: 229)

Moore goes on to emphasise that

it is precisely the *absence* of a scientific-technological revolution—one that advanced labor productivity and reduced the costs of production—that characterizes the history of neoliberalism. Annual labor productivity growth in the OECD declined from 4.6% in 1960–73 to 1.8% in 1973–79 and just 1.6% in 1979–97. (2010: 244, emphasis in original)

Thus, for example, GMO technologies, which introduced further metabolic rifts into the way in which food is planted and produced, were not able to replicate the (by now exhausted) productivity revolution unleashed by the oil-fuelled Green Revolution. Instead, extra-human and human natures have increasingly reached the point of exhaustion or even extinction, manifesting in a range of global problems: from the 2007–2008 food crisis to the current climate emergency and a whole series of mass extinctions. Moreover, the combination of stagnant profit rates and a continuing increase in the ratio of fixed capital to living labour – that is, the growing dominance of the dead labour of machines over human beings – has generated a surplus population for whom capitalist civilisation has nothing to offer: a permanent surplus, "little more than the human-as-waste, excreted from the capitalist system" (Yates 2011: 1680). As metabolic rifts and resource extraction intensify, the zombie's gesturing towards capitalism's inbuilt law of socio-environmental degradation has become very pronounced.

Contemporary zombie imaginaries register the exhaustion of the forms of plunder and primitive accumulation that emerged from the 1970s onwards, including austerity measures and the erosion of workers' rights; outsourcing of labour to the peripheries and deindustrialisation of the cores; and the escalation of debt imperialism alongside the growth of informal internal economies. Zombie texts thus register a regime of accumulation that is "badly wounded today, dominant but dead" (N. Smith 2010: 54). While the dead ends offered by neoliberalism were clearly visible for many before the present crisis, the post-2007 moment has spawned a range of new zombie imaginaries and effects as the intensification of capitalism's contradictions is more acutely felt in the context of systemic crisis. We encounter the zombie-as-waste, alongside the threatening (petro-)zombie hordes associated with dictatorships in Haiti and the US tradition; we also see the figure evoked more frequently alongside the notion of temporal collapse, as dead labour (capital or debt) increasingly colonises even the future life-forces of the living. Further, zombies begin to invade Cuban cinema of the new era, revamping previous zombie films that coded collectivity as negative.

"New Zombies" in the Capitalist Cores and the (Semi)-Peripheries

Much has been written about how zombie imaginaries have expanded and shifted, both in the Anglo-American tradition over the course of the last five decades but also abroad. Nourished by peripheralised oral cultures, the zombie engages the world-cultural imaginary through a range of B-movies, semi-peripheralised literary traditions and popular sensationalist travel writing, but it is not until the late neoliberal period that the zombie begins to proliferate in mainstream high-budget films and high-literary fiction from the core. In current genre traditions, zombies are portrayed as the detritus of humanity, and are usually met with a band of zombie-slayers, shotguns in hand. In the hegemonic Hollywood tradition, the text that perhaps best marks the transition to the neoliberal phase is George A. Romero's *Land of the Dead* (2005). The zombies are here represented as "exhausted sources of value-producing labour, still recognizable by the clothing of their former day jobs" (Apel 2015: 2937).

It is significant that the zombies in Romero's more recent films are not merely a monstrous threat but, more strongly than in the previous films, register the human-as-waste. This is mirrored also in the human characters, who have moved beyond initial responses to the zombie outbreak to adapting to a new post-apocalyptic social order, within which there is no productive activity, since they merely live off food and other commodities produced prior to the outbreak. Inhabiting an exhausted landscape, in which social infrastructure has decayed and everyday tasks like food-getting become a life-threatening endeavour, their future has collapsed into a nightmarish present dominated by an undead past that refuses to relinquish its grasp. In the film, Dennis Hopper plays the one percenter Kaufman, who has managed to flee to Pittsburgh's Golden Triangle area. He is hemmed in by zombies and is also attacked by the ones he employs. As Linnie Blake observes, "Hopper's Kaufman (a thinly veiled impersonation of Donald Rumsfeld) is CEO of Fiddler's Green, a luxury apartment complex and home to the new one per cent, beneath which huddle an ethnically mixed Green Zone of survivors, hemmed in by the zombies outside" (2015: 30). What Romero's film shares with many of the texts I discuss is an emphasis on inequality, as the extremely wealthy one per cent exclude both the zombies and the less-wealthy humans. This prepares the way for a potential zombie/working-class alliance, as suggested at the film's end. Key here is the zombie character Big Daddy, an African American former petrol station employee, who gradually becomes semi-conscious, grasps a weapon, and turns the unproductive zombie horde into a resistant collective against the elite of Fiddler's Green.

Further, the dystopian setting evokes the real-life landscapes of cities such as Detroit, suggesting that the apocalypse is not (only) to be found in the future but is also inscribed in the neoliberal history of deindustrialisation, automation and outsourcing. In a similar way to how deindustrialisation and suburbanisation are represented in *Land of the Dead*, Colson Whitehead's novel *Zone One* (2011) frames the zombie apocalypse as the product of the global crisis of the 1970s, specifically invoking the case of New York City, and the neoliberal restructuring that followed in the wake of the city's devastating 1975 fiscal crisis. Its management "pioneered the way for neoliberal practices both domestically under Reagan and internationally through the IMF in the 1980s" (Harvey 2007: 48), prioritising financial institutions, specifically Wall Street banks, and the capitalist class over the social well-being of New York's inhabitants. (In)famously, President Gerald Ford refused the city a federal bailout, which the *New York Daily News* couched in the memorable headline: "Ford to City: Drop Dead." While, like many other zombie apocalypse novels and films, *Zone One* takes place in the future, it is also stuck in the past, replaying this particular moment of highly financialised disaster capitalism. This is epitomised by Whitehead's zombie "stragglers," who are trapped in a particular moment of their lives, like the ex-realtor, who is stuck with his proposition for what to do after the end of the apocalypse (sell more houses, ironically).

The novel strongly resonates with and replays the realities of the 1970s. At this time, New York City was being reshaped by white flight and deindustrialisation as a result of "intensifying competition from low-wage regions (especially in the garment trade) and the migration of plants to the south and overseas" (Phillips-Fein 2020: 82). Within this context, many of the poorer inhabitants of places such as the Lower East Side and the South Bronx (mostly African Americans and Puerto Ricans) were ideologically recoded as an "unproductive" underclass and "as holding the city back from a bright future of finance, insurance, and other globally-oriented sectors" (Strombeck 2017: 260). In Andrew Strombeck's reading, it is the "stragglers" and the "skels," as Whitehead calls them, who are evocative of this "unproductive underclass" – the (un)dead Puerto Ricans of Piedro Pietri's "Puerto Rican Obituary" that we encountered in Chapter 1. They are displaced by financialised gentrification and ambitious redevelopment projects – or, in the case of the novel, zombie "sweepers" such as the protagonist Mark Spitz, whose only goal in life prior to the apocalypse was to inhabit an apartment like his uncle – characterless and filled with gadgets, symbolically functioning "as a placeholder for future streams of capital" (Strombeck 2017: 266).

A sense of ambivalence emerges about how the reader should feel towards zombies. This ambivalence is modelled by the characters' diverging attitudes towards the skels and stragglers. White, upper-middle-class Kaitlyn has no qualms about killing zombies – the "rabble who nibbled at the edges of her dream: the weak-willed smokers, deadbeat dads and welfare cheats, single moms incessantly breeding, the flouters of speed laws, and those who had only themselves to blame for their ridiculous credit-card debt" (Whitehead 2011: 213). Here, we see a revival of the "ideological surge against the perception of the city as a safe haven for lazy welfare cheats, liberal intellectual elites, unproductive union workers, and morally depraved miscreants" (R. Moore 2010: 3). Kaitlyn becomes the embodiment of neoliberal ideology, as she seeks to blame the strugglers and the skels for their own condition in the same way that neoliberal ideology locates the blame for increasing inequality, poverty and rising debt on those who supposedly lack motivation. Mark Spitz, on the other hand, comes to view the dead as "his neighbours" (Whitehead 2011: 214), recalling the reaction of the Puerto Rican characters in *Dawn of the Dead* (1978), a film famous for blurring the differences between zombies and humans. Spitz, too, holds up a mirror to the neoliberal destruction of communities and notions of collectivity, as symbolised in "his utter unmooring from all things" (2011: 178). There are clear stirrings of solidarity towards the strugglers and skels. He seems to observe a spark of consciousness in the fortune teller, the straggler who unexpectedly causes the death of his teammate after being cruelly mocked by him (2011: 228). His last action, furthermore, is to immerse himself into the "sea of the dead," or the sea of rabid skels (2011: 259), which clearly deploys the vocabulary of climate change scenarios and rising seas swallowing up cities.

A long view of the zombie apocalypse – often even longer than that suggested by *Land of the Dead* and *Zone One* – is central to many critical zombie texts. Thus, we might revisit Díaz's reflections on the "new zombie" in the context of his analysis of the devastating Haitian earthquake of 2010, which cost the lives of hundreds of thousands of people. The disaster was, as he emphasises, by no means "natural." As comparative analyses show, disasters play out very differently, depending on the context in which they unfold (Díaz 2011). The Haitian tragedy therefore has to be understood as the outcome of centuries of colonialist and imperialist plunder that had left Haiti – particularly its infrastructure, buildings and landscapes – fragile and vulnerable. It is in this sense that the earthquake was also revelatory of larger, world-systemic dynamics, as Díaz argues:

> This is what Haiti is both victim and symbol of – this new, rapacious stage of capitalism. A cannibal stage where, in order to power the explosion of the super-rich and the ultra-rich, middle classes are being forced to fail, working classes are being re-proletarianized, and the poorest are being pushed beyond the grim limits of subsistence, into a kind of sepulchral half-life, perfect targets for any "natural disaster" that just happens to wander by. It is, I suspect, not simply an accident of history that the island that gave us the plantation big bang that put our world on the road to this moment in the capitalist project would also be the first to warn us of this zombie stage of capitalism, where entire nations are being rendered through economic alchemy into not-quite alive. (2011: n.p.)

Zombies often tend not to be taken very seriously; they might therefore be considered inappropriate when dealing with human suffering of this scale. However, Díaz's analysis here helps us understand the continuities and changes that have shaped the world-system over the past five hundred years, from the plantation "big bang" (a phrase reminiscent of Brathwaite's "ongoing explosion" [McSweeney and Brathwaite 2005: n.p.]) to the current "zombie stage of capitalism."

Ecology of the Zombie

In what follows, I demonstrate how the emergence of "new zombies" reveals something about the ways in which the global neoliberal regime renders certain places particularly vulnerable to earthquakes, hurricanes and other disasters; second, I argue that the "new zombies" are still related to the "old zombies," even if the means of domination and appropriation have shifted. To do so requires me to read the zombie alongside a category that has gained visibility since 2000. Biologist Eugene Stoermer and chemist Paul Crutzen coined and popularised the term "Anthropocene" as a way of referring to the contemporary geological period. The term was created to suggest that humanity itself has now become a geological agent, leaving an indelible imprint on the earth such that the naming of a new planetary epoch is necessary. While the term has rapidly gained mainstream currency, and may therefore be useful to a certain extent to rally resistance, it has been sharply criticised by materialist critics for erasing the question of responsibility. As Jason W. Moore (2016) and others emphasise, it is not humans in the abstract that bear responsibility for the climate emergency and related global issues, but rather the value-system under which we live. Not identifying the root cause of geo-ecological change – capitalism and its emphasis on unlimited growth – leaves the door open to mere techno-fixes and geo-engineering. Even when a differentiated responsibility for the climate emergency is acknowledged, the solution is often naïvely formulated as a move towards ethical stewardship. The Anthropocene is thus unconvincingly presented by commentators such as Christian Schwägerl as an "open-ended design project in which everyone [...] commits to considerate and far-sighted behaviours" (2014: 94–95).[4] While Schwägerl accepts the responsibility of often white and always rich people in setting up and maintaining the structures that dominate the "anthropos" – an "ancient Greek word for human beings" at large (2014: 92) – he rashly proposes the term "Westocene" as an alternative. This term not only pays scant if any attention to class, but obviously cannot do the work of the much more nuanced "Capitalocene" – how capitalism-as-system is doing the reshaping, not an imagined geographical entity called "the West."[5]

In the language of the "Anthropocene," we encounter a universalisation of the white man that erases long, violent histories of racism and leaves the colonial underpinnings of geo-ecological change unquestioned. As Kathryn

---

4 I have no desire to add to the growing number of alternative terms for the Anthropocene. The Capitalocene proposed by Moore is the most convincing alternative (see particularly J. Moore 2016). This term functions as a conceptual tool for thinking the present, proposing the emergence of capitalism in the fifteenth century as its starting point and challenging us to adopt anti-capitalism as a response to the climate emergency. It suggests that the culprit is capitalism as an extractive system that degrades its own conditions of reproduction, as it vampirically feeds on extra-economic sources in the realm designed by capitalism as "Nature."

5 See Moore's book *Anthropocene or Capitalocene? Nature, History and the Crisis of Capitalism* (2016). See also Neil Lazarus on the fetish of the "West" as a concept in postcolonial studies (2002).

Yusoff writes, "the origins of the Anthropocene are intensely political in how they draw the world of the present into being and give shape and race to its world-making subjects" (2018: 24–25). As we have seen, capitalism as a system is both fundamentally and structurally racist. Yusoff continues to explain that the "geologic origin stories function as [an] identity politics that coheres around an exclusive notion of humanity (coded white)" (2018: 24). This assertion is nicely illustrated by the increasingly common appeal to "stewardship" and ethical behaviour – an inadequate, and not entirely race-blind, response to global inequalities.[6] If we shifted culpability for climate warming and pollution from the universal generic "Anthropos" to capitalism specifically (as proposed in the "Capitalocene"), the zombie would then draw attention to the conditions and status of racialised, gendered and/or proletarianised populations.

Let us here turn to zombie apocalypse narratives that explicitly imagine Haiti as a crucial site in the emergence both of capitalism and of resistance to its racialised logics – narratives which, for perhaps obvious historical and geopolitical reasons, tend to link the histories of climate change, environmental degradation, economic peripheralisation and plunder in a very lucid way. They also tend to be strongly aware of the unevenness of the climate apocalypse, which does not impact everyone equally or at the same time. Indeed, as we have seen throughout this book, environmental catastrophe has been closely linked with zombie aesthetics throughout the twentieth century. The two short texts that I will consider here – written by Haitian Rodney Saint-Éloi and Dominican-American Junot Díaz – offer interventions into current debates around climate change and environmental degradation. Both highlight that the apocalypse is *always* uneven – temporally, geographically and socially. If our present feels apocalyptic to us now, it has already been experienced as such in different locations for some time – the environmental apocalypse particularly has never been confined to the future and its impacts have been profoundly racialised.

Díaz's short story "Monstro" (2012) is a particularly compelling example of this. It shows how zombie cli-fi narratives are capable of connecting issues of climate change to those of economic and racialised inequalities, militarisation and deadly pandemics. The story in many ways appears strangely prophetic: the reason why it is so prescient is, of course, that these tendencies have long been visible from the peripheries – both those within, and outside of, the capitalist core countries. It is, then, no coincidence that Díaz turns to the zombie in this context. Indeed, he renders visible one of the key claims of this book: that the zombie figure is inherently ecological, offering a way into thinking about the different ecological regimes of capitalism, from the plantation to the neoliberal world-order. In his brief but impactful short

---

6 When I write "not entirely race-blind," I refer to Schwägerl's essay (2014) that notes the obvious racialisation of poverty that underpins global capitalism.

story published in the *New Yorker*, zombies are explicitly situated within a narrative of climate catastrophe and global environmental degradation. In the dystopian future, the oceans have risen, heat records are being broken every month, deforestation has exceeded critical levels, droughts are reshaping the landscape, and new viruses proliferate. Simultaneously, the global economy has hit rock bottom. Amid these crises, an infectious zombie disease breaks out. Referred to as "la negrura," or "the Darkness" (Díaz 2012: 107), the disease not only makes its victims "blacker" but also manifests in strange coral-like outgrowths on their skin, "as if some sort of somatic substitution [has taken] place" for the reefs that once existed in the oceans (Rosenthal 2020: 281).

The apparently climate-driven disease affects mainly impoverished Haitians, while a small Dominican elite is ensconced in air-conditioned buildings and able to turn a blind eye to what is going on. Eventually the infected turn into zombie-esque, cannibalistic creatures that are met with the excessive might of the US military, which bombs the place into near oblivion. It is not particularly difficult to see that this is a story about environmental justice and the role of racism, colonialism, imperialism and fascist militarisation in the creation of the present crisis of capitalism as manifested by the climate emergency that, alongside the extinction crisis, is "the leading edge of contemporary capitalism's contradictions" (Dawson 2016: 13). Capitalism not only fails to reproduce the worker but also the environment. Yet the handling of crises such as mass extinction privilege measurable effects "rather than a cause, and thereby obscure key questions of violence and inequality in humanity's relation to nature" (Dawson 2016: 19).

Mainstream zombie narratives often at least partly present the apocalypse in the terms suggested by the Anthropocene: while zombie hordes are often created by scientific hubris, humanity as a whole is under threat from these hordes. Critical zombie narratives, however, tend to emphasise inequalities in the way the apocalypse unfolds and offer a critique of capitalism in the process. Díaz's short story, for instance, carefully inscribes itself within the context of uneven relations on Hispaniola, evoking the racist anti-Haitianism mobilised in right-wing Dominican political discourse, narratives of invasion, and brutal genocidal actions under dictators Rafael Trujillo and Joaquin Balaguer. More recently, such discourse has been used to legitimise the denationalisation of Dominican-Haitians. But "Monstro" also takes care to inscribe Haitian–Dominican relations within the context of US imperialism, climate change and environmental degradation (which is far more advanced in Haiti, owing to US imperialism).

Díaz's zombie apocalypse incorporates elements of the Lovecraftian Weird, which in the 1920s gestured towards the emergence of the US's fossil-fuelled domination of the global seas (Deckard and Oloff 2020). While the Old Weird was firmly inscribed in the racist imperialist discourse of the time, as Deckard and I demonstrate, the weird today has become, for many writers, "a means of coming to consciousness about the intersection of racial domination and capitalist exploitation" (Shapiro 2021: 56). In light of these new employments of the weird, note the strangeness of Díaz's evocation of zombies. Initially, the plot emphasises the undecipherability of zombie behaviour, as they increasingly begin to group together and even "fuse" with one another. Their weird ability to communicate with one another without saying anything – "[a]nything *human*, that is" – is soon complemented by their joining together into collective daily shrieks three times a day, known as "the Chorus," which becomes notably "unnerving" for the uninfected (Díaz 2012: 109).

Of course, as has long been remarked upon by zombie scholars, the fear of zombie uprisings historically echoes the fears of the Haitian Revolution as experienced by the slave-holding elites. More broadly, it also resonates with anxieties concerning collective resistance of the exploited classes, recoded as masses, from the perspective of the powerful. A reader aware of the long history of zombie narratives, in which the non-zombified characters emerge as less trustworthy and more frightening than the zombies, will probably note the story's ambivalence towards its protagonist. This is a story in which all the main characters are characterised by a shallow outlook and hold, to varying degrees, views shaped by hegemonic racism, classism and sexism (even if their lives have been affected to a differing degree by these relations). With the exception of the narrator, they all firmly inhabit upper-class spaces reserved for the international elites. This allows them to treat landscapes devastated by drought as their playground. The narrator's friend Alex is the "son of the wealthiest, most priv'ed-up family on the Island," whose mother regularly flies to Miami for shopping and whose grandfather is the "ninety-ninth-richest man in the Americas" (Díaz 2012: 110). The position of those affected by the zombie disease is the exact opposite, even prior to infection, as is made clear through the example of Henri Casimir, who, while formerly working as manager in a utility company has been "reduced to carting sewage for the camp administration" (2012: 113).

The protagonists' position shields them from the worst excesses of the unfolding chaos (even if, as the story makes clear through Misty, this does not protect the female characters from sexist violence and rape). The representation of the zombies, on the other hand, is self-consciously inscribed in racist discourse about Haiti and the lower classes, culminating in the reported "hysterical" sightings of "[f]orty-foot-tall cannibal motherfuckers" and Polaroids of a so-called "Class 2 in the process of putting a slender broken girl in its mouth" (2012: 118). Combining centuries-old tropes of Caribbean cannibalism and imperialist tropes of fragile women threatened in spaces coded as barbarous, these monstrous evocations also mutate into something new and weird, emerging in a context where "incredible heat [is] rolling in from the dying seas" (2012: 118). How cultural production might help us to process global crises becomes the explicit focus of the story, as two clashing examples are offered through Alex and the narrator.

Extremely wealthy Alex seeks rapid fame through photography or documentary-making, focussing on sensationalist reporting, whether by taking pictures of disappearing beaches or of the monstrous infected. His unthinking approach is marked by the masculinist, sexist and racist attitudes that characterise his endeavours. On the other hand, the narrator – while unreliable to the extent that he is immature and sexist in his portrayal of women – is able to offer this monstrous-weird tale. As Stephen Shapiro argues, the weird is not simply about understanding the ontology of otherness (often coded as non-human); regardless of their stated difficulties in rendering difference, weird tales "rarely find it difficult to then do so" (2021: 64). He argues that something altogether different is at stake:

> Weird tales instead highlight the difficulty that official institutions, and their curation over what are admissible truth statements, have in acknowledging the presence of incongruity within their normative speech. This tension arises since these institutions seek to avoid not only a discussion of exploitation and domination but also their own complicity in the traces of past and ongoing violence. (2021: 64)

Díaz's story operates on this level. As he writes in the aforementioned article, the Haitian earthquake – by no means a "natural" disaster, to echo Neil Smith – revealed the extent to which Haiti had been rendered vulnerable as a result of centuries of European colonialism and US imperialism that have subjected the country to the most intense forms of plunder and appropriation. International reporting on the "poorest country in the Western hemisphere" and international aid efforts are blind to this long history, to which the only adequate response would be restoration, compensation and the complete withdrawal of the military presence and disaster capitalists (see Díaz 2011). In Díaz's story, a monstrous and weird new reality emerges from Haiti, but its consequences are global and uneven. In other words, this is not so much a story about Haiti and the Dominican Republic as it is one of capital's pillaging and destruction in the profoundly marginalised countries of the periphery, in which a local capitalist-necrotic elite benefits from the disenfranchisement of the masses.

Another story that similarly approaches the Haitian earthquake within a larger context of global ecological degradation and exploitation by capitalist elites is "The Blue Hill," by Rodney Saint-Éloi, published a year before Díaz's story as part of the anthology *Haiti Noir*, edited by Edwidge Danticat. In "The Blue Hill," we encounter the transformation of Haitians into "blue hill-digging zombies" (Saint-Éloi 2011: 306), but the cause is here much more immediate and well defined: it is the result of the dumping of toxic waste by foreign powers, by a "friendly country" with "an overload of chemical refuse" (2011: 302), allowed to do so by a corrupt government. The specific historical incident that this alludes to – albeit in an allegorical fashion – is the unloading of toxic waste by the US cargo ship *Khian Sea* on the beach of Gonaïves in 1987, after sailing the "high seas for over a year, until the right combination of bribes and lawlessness brought it to port not far from a Haitian slum called Raboteau" (Farmer 2005: 80). The incident would become an international affair in 1995, exposing the Jean-Bertrand Aristide government of the time. In the story, the toxic waste has a severe effect on the inhabitants of the nearby village and on the local flora and fauna:

> the stench of sulfur mixes with the reeking blue toxic trash that was dumped on the hill that January day. It has been named the "blue hill" ever since. Everyone is afraid to say who is responsible for this open gash in the earth that poisons everything and will, eventually, eat up the legs of children and rot the roots of plants, cause the dogs, the flies, and the fish to disappear. Even the mosquitoes won't survive. (Saint-Éloi 2011: 302)

Here, human and environmental degradation are intertwined as the entire country is transformed into a graveyard. Zombification features as a "blue body-and-mind disease" that spreads "quickly as mad grass" (2011: 303), evocative of zombie narratives of toxic pollution, such as *Let Sleeping Corpses Lie* (also known as *The Living Dead at the Manchester Morgue*) (dir. Jorge Grau 1974), but also the viral spread associated with the Anglo-American zombie tradition, which has been read as registering the "ever-accelerating viral nature of global capitalism" (Boluk and Lenz 2010: 126). Further, zombification in "The Blue Hill" acquires weird overtones, as the disease affects the brain of the narrator, Detective Simodor, who "immediately began to feel his mind slipping" (Saint-Éloi 2011: 304). In the detective's gradual descent into madness, and the absence of rational explanations for the disease, we again see echoes of weird tales, and their frequent evocations of madness as characters are confronted with alien ontologies and their worldviews are upended.

The "blue invasion" ends in an all-encompassing apocalypse that in its monstrous spirituality transcends mere eco-destruction:

> The agony of the earth is beginning today [...] That's when the beast of the thousand horns appears. It sets up its gigantic legs on the clouds, trampling down whatever is still on earth: limbs, faces, and human traces. (2011: 309)

The blue hill and its disease come to allegorise centuries of imperial-colonial environmental degradation and colonial plunder in general. Addressing the war god Ogun, Simidor sings: "we inhabit an isolated, pristine, gentle island with vegetation that escapes human comprehension [...] Before the blue hill, you could rest here in peace" (2011: 308). After the "Blue Hill," however, the extra-human environment becomes threatening, as oceans erupt into oil gyres and "large mouths of flame," the "sky [sweeps] down on us like a vulture" (2011: 305), birds assume beaks of fire and the sun dies. This surreal apocalypse crescendos and ends very abruptly as Simidor turns to the clock, which shows the time to be 4.53 p.m. – the exact time when the earthquake began to shake Haiti. As Martin Munro writes, Saint-Éloi evokes "the allegorical, apocalyptic surrealism of Frankétienne and Depestre" to capture "the full, desperate absurdity not only of pre-earthquake conditions in Haiti but of the broader world and its profit-driven slide towards ecological disaster" (Munro 2015: 79). The pre-earthquake socio-ecological and political degradation is here presented as central to understanding the catastrophe.

Ecology of the Zombie

Most notable perhaps is the temporal collapse the story enacts. In their militaristic brutality and racist attitudes, the men who unload the toxic waste are clearly an "ech[o] of previous foreign occupiers" (Munro 2015: 78), evoking the Haitian occupation at the beginning of the twentieth century. But the unfolding apocalypse evokes not only religious and surreal images, but also those of "gallons of oil spilling from the Earth's core, from deep beneath the sea" (Saint-Éloi 2011: 305). As with Whitehead's novel, the Deepwater Horizon oil spill that occurred three months after the Haitian earthquake provides a reference point as an event of such magnitude that it is almost impossible to conceptualise (Munro 2015: 78). In "The Blue Hill," the spill binds together a series of seemingly unconnected events as leading up to the earthquake: the US military occupation of Haiti; the frenzied search for offshore oil by multinational oil companies (in this case British Petroleum, a company registered in London); US waste imperialism that uses peripheralised countries as "free sinks." The "slow" process of environmental destruction is here sped up into an all-encompassing, frenzied apocalypse, in which the time of imperialism has collapsed in on itself, eradicating the future.

Zombification in the Semi-Periphery

Puerto Rico's experience with US imperial power has been quite different from Haiti's: the island became a colony in 1898, and then a "Free Associated State" of the United States in 1952. It is noticeable, however, that in the years leading up to the devastation wrought by hurricane María in 2017, an increasing number of Puerto Rican writers turned to zombies and zombie metaphors in their work. This zombie spike includes work by writers such as Pedro Cabiya (who now lives in the Dominican Republic), Ana María Fúster Lavin, Josué Montijo, John Torres, Angel Rivera, Jotacé López and Alexandra Pagán Vélez. As is well known, the global recession has hit the island particularly hard since 2006, translating into a spiralling and devastating debt crisis that worsened in 2008 and now reaches 72 billion dollars. This debt crisis has been described as "unnatural" (de Onís 2018: 1), rapidly exacerbating the legacies of a history of colonial exploitation and of more recent rounds of disaster capitalism and neoliberal austerity. Such extreme levels of debt are linked to the power relations that have tied Puerto Rico to the US in a supposed "Commonwealth" relation since the 1950s. This has benefited mainland American corporations for whom Puerto Rico has long functioned as a tax haven. In the Puerto Rican context, however, it was not the 2008 debt crisis but the amendment of Section 936 of the Inland Revenue Code as part of the Tax Reform Act of 1976 that "marked the incorporation of the island into new patterns of US extensive capitalist accumulation and increasingly neoliberal deregulation" (Benson Arias 2007: 33), thus transforming the island's industrial, economic and social landscape. While debt imperialism took off early in the 1970s, it went viral due to the phasing out of Section 936 (between 1996 and 2006) and the onset of predatory lending, enriching Wall Street at the expense of the Puerto Rican population.

While many writers have turned to zombie tropes to help navigate this devastating debt relation, not all contemporary zombie narratives are explicitly critical of the status quo. In the mainland American context, moreover, the recourse to zombie tropes has often served to prop up a violent pro-gun agenda, along with the rampant individualism that accompanies it. This move was exposed by another Puerto Rican writer, Josué Montijo, in his novel *El killer* (2007). In this text, a sociopathic narrator called Juan Aybar shoots defenceless homeless people addicted to drugs, justifying their brutal shooting to himself by describing them as urban zombies, or the "living dead" (Montijo 2007: 35). Montijo's narrator takes the logic invoked by many uncritical deployments of the zombie to their extreme conclusion, shooting nineteen people over the course of a year. While Juan might embody an extreme, the danger of employing zombie tropes is all too apparent in other cultural texts (even when they do not call for mass murder). We might think here of episode 8, series 2 of the sensationalist docu-series *Drugs Inc.* (2012), produced by *National Geographic*, which focusses on drug trafficking in Puerto Rico, offering voyeuristic footage of people hooked on horse tranquillisers, portrayed as sleep-walking "zombies."[7] Combine this dehumanisation of the drug-addicted in the Caribbean context with the use of exploding zombies by the American pro-gun lobby in the form of shooting practice targets (see Baker 2013: 1397), and one will inevitably end up with (a lower-middle-class) Juan B. Aybar, "prepared" to shoot-to-kill those perceived as a threat in real life.

Montijo's main narrative, presented as a diary, is explicitly mediated through Juan's consciousness. This negative protagonist is designed to turn the familiar zombie-film dynamic of the zombie-slayer on its head: rather than heroically saving a group of leftover humans from threatening zombies, Juan sets out to kill nineteen defenceless and homeless addicts over the course of a year, and graphically details their murders. Of course, many zombie films problematise the killing of zombies: should you kill a loved one in self-defence? Does killing zombies transform humans into monsters, too? But while films such as *Dawn of the Dead* (1978) create unease over humans' behaviour, in many other films and series the evocation of a moral dilemma only serves to reaffirm the killing of zombies as the morally correct action given the circumstances. In Montijo's novel, on the other hand, there is little doubt that the zombie-slayer's actions are brutal and immoral, and they are only justified internally by the narrator's own narrative and logic. Juan's 120-page diary, in which we are presented with his skewed account of the murders, is followed by two other texts: a brief text

---

7 For all its documentary pretence, *Drugs Inc.* "is little more than tabloid television"; while the "Zombie Island" episode does highlight the connection to US drug consumption, the way in which the topic is treated serves to conceal "the fundamental inequalities of late capitalism" (Linnemann 2016: 285).

about Juan, written by a journalist who exposes the sociopathology of his murderous logic, and Juan's letter to this journalist by way of response. While thinking of his victims as zombies might serve as an ideological distancing device for the narrator, the reader is always reminded that the people he kills are *not* actual zombies. And yet the monstrous register he uses, comparing his pale complexion to that of vampires and describing his guns with references to cannibalism (Montijo 2007: 63, 11), is, of course, revelatory in other ways that exceed the consciousness of the narrator.

Through Juan as unreliable narrator, Montijo presents us with an examination of someone who has internalised neoliberal ideology and hegemonic narratives – much like Kaitlyn of *Zone One* – and thinks of his actions as a form of "social cleansing" (Casanova-Vizcaíno 2015: 120). And yet Juan's actual stake in the dominance of neoliberal capital is much lower than Kaitlyn's, as his aimless existence makes clear. Communal solutions to the problems he faces are conceptually (and materially) out of reach; instead, Juan is a profoundly lonely individual, alienated from the community and the urban environment he inhabits. The extent to which his internal world has been reshaped by the privatisation of the commons is exemplified by his observation that "hope […] is a bank account (without funds)" (Montijo 2007: 48). Even moral values are here evacuated and replaced by monetary ones. The irony of Juan's metaphoric use of zombies as a justification for his actions is highlighted in the novel, even if the irony is missed by the narrator himself. Cleaning his "hungry" guns, Juan listens to "Haitian Fight Song" (1957) by Charles Mingus, who explicitly placed his music in the context of the international struggle against racism (Montijo 2007: 56–57); indeed, the title of his song is overtly political, "root[ing] the civil rights movement in a 150-year old struggle" (Dunkel 2013: 76). While Juan does not grasp its significance, he is here engaging with the artistic fruits of the communal struggle for equality. Montijo, then, exposes the ways in which neoliberal ideology – constitutively racist, classist and sexist – attempts to shift the blame for the rise of social inequalities to the groups that most strongly feel the impact of austerity policies and the privatisation of the commons.

The devastating social effects of debt imperialism in Puerto Rico have been registered in a range of images and metaphors involving death and the undead. The undead, in particular, gain in symbolic significance, figuring the past's refusal to die as dead labour (capital) colonises the population's life-forces and atrophies the country's future. In this regard, John Torres's long poem *Undead* (2010) is very useful. Here, the zombification has reached all aspects of life in San Juan, which is dominated by the "reverberation of the living dead" that "pursues" the narrator-poet into the very recesses of his imagination (2013: 27). The zombies mock this narrator-poet and perform a bizarre carnival dance, as life itself is transformed into a zombie flick that feeds on the appropriation and commodification of time: "Life should not be this film/ of walking rags that consumes us/ fattening itself up on our/ hours and minutes and seconds" (Torres 2013: 29). Zombification is all-pervasive in a colony subdued by the fetishism of debt, which serves to misrepresent the power relations in place under capitalist imperialism and, in the process, expropriates the life-forces and futures of its colony. In this topsy-turvy world dominated by fetishism, inanimate objects, concepts and "things" – such as debt – seem to have a life of their own.

In her foreword to *Undead*, Sotomayor defines the zombie as a "precarious figure who continues to traverse the earth that can never be his" (2013: 9). In other words, the zombie figures the alienation produced by the privatisation of the commons, which, in the context of Puerto Rico, is overdetermined by its double colonisation. The Long American Century has propelled a rapid process of urbanisation and delocalisation of consumption in Puerto Rico, alongside the growing monopolisation of land on the island. While we may encounter zombie-esque figures in the literature of the first half of the twentieth century (Oloff 2021), the alienation is here further intensified in the context of an increasingly deindustrialised economy, in which the proletariat turns into the human-as-waste and exploitation and plunder proceed through the impersonalised mechanisms of debt, trapping people within the "radical uselessness of their post-existence," as Torres (2013: 43) puts it. The zombie is here rendered "hygienic," having shed the dirt of the plantations and entered the "frame of cyberculture, the algorithms, the molecules and virtuality" (Sotomayor 2013: 10). This zombie manifests an economy which bit off more "toxic debts than it can chew, [and] just keeps on chewing" (Botting 2013: n.p.). Throughout, Torres's narrator-poet is isolated, living in a computerised virtual world in which relations are largely dematerialised, and the economy is seemingly unbound from the labouring body of the zombie. As Jossiana Arroyo notes, the collection transforms San Juan "into a space from where the living dead in a carnivalesque fashion perform 'la inanida historia' of suspended time" (2015: 37). The annihilation of space by time has here collapsed into stasis: space is homogenised and "annihilated," as the subject withdraws into the virtual but has no time. The landscape evoked in *Undead* is urbanised and devoid of hope and agency. The promises and dreams that modern city life once held are shattered, and the failure of the urban project is compared to a "hanged man who looks at us" (Torres 2013: 32).

In Torres's poem, zombification colonises selfhood itself: the narrator is the "deadest of them all" (2013: 33), and lacks the ability to act or effect change, while still being able to reflect on his own alienation. The zombie is not only the speaker, then, but he is conscious of his own predicament. In particular, he sheds light on the way in which the poet – as, and like, the worker – is replaced by the "spying spirit" (2013: 30) of the machine, by the codes that will enable it to reproduce infinite copies of "your sordid/ searches and acquisitions/ your existential mathemes" (2013: 30–31). The poetic commonplace of the failed lyric voice is hereby inscribed within the particularities of the present, as alienation – not only from the surroundings, but from one's own craft – reigns supreme. This zombification of poetic form also takes the shape of the integration of a range of lines from a range of other poems and texts. What in the past would have been read as postmodern playfulness here transmutes into a zombified form of expression that has lost all agency and capacity for change. The references to Georges Batailles, Sigmund Freud, Reinaldo Arias and many others risk losing their meaning in a context where "language is dispersed, without a brain to which it could refer" (Torres 2013: 14). And yet the fact that the narrator-zombie remains conscious and critical, and able to invoke often highly relevant passages from past authors, also harbours the potential for critical resistance.

In Jotacé López's story "Caffea Arabica+" (2016) "the Corporation," a transnational coffee producer that accounts for 67% of global coffee consumption and dominates most of the island, employs a horde of zombified coffee harvesters who hail from different islands and are unable to show emotion or pain. As Sandra Casanova-Vizcaíno notes, there are plenty of "tropos del hombre-robot o cíborg, la distopía, el zombismo y el canibalismo" [tropes of the human-robot or cyborg, dystopia, zombification and cannibalism] (2021: 146). The brutally exploitative culture created by the sugar industry is replaced in this fictional universe by one structured around coffee-growing, dispensing with any potentially remaining nostalgia for the latter (at least as grown for the global capitalist market and under conditions imposed by monopoly capital). By returning to the aesthetics of these earlier sugar narratives, the story points towards the similarities between the crises of the 1930s and the present, including the untrammelled power of capital in the form of multinationals; increasing militarisation and extreme disciplinary surveillance at the disposal of capital; the super-appropriation of the workers within an export-driven market; and an intensifying racialising discourse that seeks to naturalise their appropriation as one that afflicts an "underdeveloped species" (López 2016: 23). Central to this story are tropes of zombification that, as in the narratives from the 1930s, register a heightening of exploitation, appropriation and accompanying feelings of alienation. The story is told by a narrator who, it becomes clear, is unreliable owing to his gradual zombification by a cocktail of injections that are changing his emotional responses and their physical manifestations. He is increasingly unable to express emotions or show dissent, not even responding to his boyfriend's apparent attempts to rescue him. After a blow on the head and the mutilation of his arms as an implicit punishment for not volunteering to collaborate in the trafficking of human limbs, the narrator is confined to a hospital bed and connected to an "exaggerated quantity of stands and tubes," a treatment paid for by the Corporation's "excellent" medical insurance plan (2016: 11, 12). While he had been originally part of the military surveillance class, after his downfall he is eventually released (as a water carrier) into the army of lower-class coffee pickers, who are equally unable to express emotions and are confined in crowded *caserios* (low-cost residential buildings) surrounded by barbed wire.

Throughout, the story registers in style and form the realities of uneven and combined capitalist development, which produces an experience of multiple, coexisting temporalities. It thus mixes elements that are traditionally associated with the gothic's backward-looking fascination with magic and the "primitive" with sci-fi's investment in technological advances such as holograms, new computerised weaponry or, indeed, the novel techniques used to create zombies via injections. The Corporation possesses highly advanced technological weaponry and has developed ways to manipulate the growth process of coffee bushes to such an extent that they produce mature grains within three days. Technological "progress" here translates into the extreme intensification of capitalist agriculture at the expense of the zombified workers, who are employed to harvest all year round.

López's story registers in literary form the socio-ecological plunder of Puerto Rico at the hands of US imperialists, as well as by local collaborators through profiteering and money-laundering. One might argue that the relations between "[g]othic spikes," which are of particular interest to gothic scholars (Shapiro 2008; Bishop 2010a), and the difficult-to-grasp world-food-system come into sharper focus in cultural productions from certain locations (see also Niblett 2012b). Puerto Rico is one such location. Here, under US imperialism, food delocalisation and alimentary underdevelopment have been particularly pronounced – so much so that the island nowadays imports over 85% of its food, an arrangement that benefits US food corporations. "US food power," to borrow Allison Carruth's (2013) term, has had a devastating socio-ecological impact on Puerto Rico.

From this short story of a debt-riddled Free Associated State and US tax haven, we will now turn to the first release of a zombie film in Cuba – the antithesis of all that the Unites States represents – in a co-production with Spain from 2011 titled *Juan de los muertos* [Juan of the Dead].

Fearing the Walking Reds: Cuban Zombies and Socialist "Threat"

Filmed in Havana by Cuban director Alejandro Brugués, with a majority of Cuban actors, *Juan de los muertos* was announced as the first Cuban zombie movie. As such, the release of the film marks a momentous cultural event in both Cuba and in Spain. Indeed, the film's position and role in zombie film history in Cuba speaks for itself: it received the audience award at the International Festival of New Latin American cinema in Havana, as well as the 2012 Goya award in Spain for the best Spanish-language foreign film. Its novelty was striking in terms of international film history: first, since zombie movies are generally classed as more commercially oriented, *Juan de los muertos*, a Spanish-Cuban co-production, was (seen as) both a product and symbol of the new era in Cuban film-making.[8] Secondly, while the undead have long worked as figures

---

8 This collaboration was between the Cuban independent production company La 5ta Avenida and the Spanish La Zanfaña Producciones. See Stock's (2012) article on the continued relations of these companies to the Instituto Cubano del Arte e Industria Cinematograficos.

Ecology of the Zombie

that register the fear of communism, Brugués's film announces from the start a head-on parodic take on questions surrounding the zombie's shifting relations to the capitalist world-system and actually existing communism. *Juan de los muertos* is thus, among other things, a film about zombie (film) history and the ideological struggles over the encoding of the zombie figure. Of course, zombie figures in the mainstream dominated by Anglophone cinema have shifted quite radically over time – from the slow-working alienated worker popularised in the aftermath of the Great Depression to the threatening, first slow then accelerating zombie masses that have come to dominate in the era of late capitalism. Brugués – who is very well versed in the zombie's history – puts (light-hearted) pressure on this aesthetic by offering a whole range of zombie effects and references in dialogue with Cuban (film) history and communist iconography. The resulting film offers a biting satire of the Cuban government alongside a trenchant critique of global capitalism and its post-Cold War erosion of socialism, expressed through an engagement with global zombie history and the circulation of left iconography.[9]

It is not wrong to state that the zombie figures and plotlines evoked in *Juan de los muertos* "owe more to the sensibilities of George Romero's *Night of the Living Dead*, Jack Finney's *The Body Snatchers* as well as the dark humor of Edgar Wright and Simon Pegg (*Shaun of the Dead*) and Sam Raimi (*Evil Dead*), than to Caribbean folklore" (Armengot 2012: n.p.). But we might still want to highlight the zombie's prior Haitian and Hispanic Caribbean history in order to underscore the extent to which the figure is overdetermined by this context. With the onset of the Cold War, the dynamics of post-war zombie representations in the US were further inflected by anti-communist fears of mass indoctrination, invasion and what has been referred to as "agency panic" (Johnson 2014: 74). In 1951, Senator Joseph McCarthy infamously described communism as "a conspiracy so immense, an infamy so black, as to dwarf any in the history of man" (quoted in Grant 2010: 65). Don Siegel's *Invasion of the Body Snatchers* (1956), in which ordinary Americans are gradually duplicated and replaced by alien pod people, is perhaps the most famous US example of the shift towards sci-fi inflected invasion narratives. The film is read within the Cold War context as registering fears of "invading Communists" as well as the increasing alienation of post-WWII America, when viewed through a window offered by the 1950s version of socialism (Grant 2010: 68).

---

9 Many scholars argue that the critique articulated via the zombie apocalypse changes direction, from the drudgery of capitalism highlighted in films such as *Shaun of the Dead* (Wright 2004), to a critique of "ideological consumerism" under communism (Cardentey Levin 2014: 5), and an exposition of the monstrosity of "revolutionary fervor itself" (Maguire 2015: 180). Others, including Carla Grosman (2013) and Chera Kee (2020), argue (correctly, I believe) against the emphasis of such a reading, highlighting the film's recommitment to socialism and the conscious situating of Cuban socialism – with its undeniable and serious flaws – within a capitalist world-system that is profoundly unequal.

Kaufman's 1978 remake of Siegel's classic – also entitled *Invasion of the Body Snatchers* – offers an example of how this fear of invasion is recoded after the end of the global boom years and the shift towards neoliberalisation. Here, the duplication and replacement of humans by alien zombies bred in pods registers the incipient hollowing out of late capitalism, as illustrated in the spreading zombification of the San Francisco Health Department. But it is interesting to note that, in both films, the true horror lies in industrialised, monocultural agriculture, petro-fuelled distribution networks and global metabolic rifts – aspects of modernisation that were shared by actually existing communism, which saw itself within the gravitational pull of the capitalist emphasis on growth and development. In the 1956 version, Dr Miles Bennell (Kevin McCarthy) discovers with horror the scale of pod agriculture and, later, of its distribution network when he reaches the highway, where he sees a truck full of pods from a trucking company servicing "the major cities of the American west coast" (Grant 2010: 18). In the 1978 version, this horror is further intensified, as the trucks are replaced by big merchant ships full of pallets, ready to travel across the oceans.

Cuban writers have responded in interesting ways to invasion and body takeover narratives, frequently reversing their ideological coding. One might here think of Agustin de Rojas's cult novel *The Year 200* (2016), originally published as *El año 200* in 1990, which takes place in a communist (but imperfect) planetary future in which anti-heroes from the capitalist past invade the minds and bodies of a range of post-capitalist subjects through time travel in an entirely self-interested attempt to recolonise the future. Or one might think of Yoss's "system of Body Spares" in *A Planet to Rent* – originally published as *Se aquila un planeta* in 2001 – in which the human inhabitants of an impoverished planet Earth can rent their bodies to non-humanoid alien tourists with large bank accounts and "credit appendage[s]" (Yoss 2014: 3):

> All of the parameters of the "client" (memory, personality, intelligence quotient, motor skills) were computer-encoded and then introduced into the brain of a host human. The xenoid gained both mobility and access to all the skills and memory of the "spare body." There was just one "minor" detail: forty percent of the time, the person whose body and brain were occupied by the extraterrestrial remained conscious. (2014: 5–6)

On this dystopian planet Earth, the industrial centres are dismantled to restore the ecological balance and tourism becomes the only source of income, as Yoss takes zombification narratives into the age of mass tourism and the post-Cold War context of the "Special Period" (1991–2000)[10] in Cuba.

Within this longer context, *Juan de los muertos* signifies like a relatively straightforward, if tongue-in-cheek, allegory of the effects of US imperialism

---

10 After the falling apart of the Soviet Union, which had been the main trading partner of Cuba, Castro declared Cuba to be in a special period in times of peace.

and the penetration of Cuba by capital in post-Cold War times. Despite the film's mocking of the government's formulaic diagnosis of the zombies as "American dissidents," the irony is that the signalling of the key role of the US in the spread of zombification is not wrong. Not only are the zombies that populate the film clearly of the variety shaped by a US imaginary (and the only person in the film able to identify them is an American preacher), but the first zombie that Juan and Lázaro encounter is at sea, wearing the orange jumpsuit associated with the controversial maximum-security military prison at Guantánamo Bay (see also Eljaiek-Rodríguez 2015: 97). Since 2002, Guantánamo has been used for detainees from the so-called "War on Terror," launched after the justification for illegal invasions in the Middle East was provided by 9/11 (an event irreverently alluded to in the film when a helicopter randomly crashes into the Capitolio, and when, later, the FOCSA [*Fomento de Obras y Construcciones, Sociedad Anónima*] towers collapse). But Guantánamo's role at the heart of US imperialism preceded the invasion of Iraq by over a century, as it was first occupied by the US military in 1898 and subsequently served "as a staging ground for the invasions of Puerto Rico (1898–present), Haiti (1914–1934), and the Dominican Republic (1916–1924), as well as military interventions in Cuba (1912), Nicaragua (1926–33), and Guatemala (1960)" (Walicek and Adams 2017: 11–12). Within this context, Haiti – with its never-forgotten history of resistance to the colonial-capitalist world-system – became the pretext for the US presence in Guantánamo: over the course of the twentieth century, the base enabled the surveillance of and, at times, provided direct support for right-wing dictators such as François Duvalier, while refusing Haitian asylum seekers the right to escape this dangerous context (Walicek and Adams 2017: 76, 80). It is thus no surprise that Fidel Castro, in an essay published in *Granma* in 2008, argued that Guantánamo was "at the core of the struggles between U.S. imperialist designs and the freedom of others" (quoted in Whitfield 2017: 149).

In *Juan de los muertos*, the zombie invasion caricatures the dissolution of social bonds characteristic of the spread of capitalism, turning neighbours against neighbours and melting everything that is solid into air, to recycle Marx and Engels's famous phrasing. But the movie breaks with the conventions of the genre as established in Anglo-American cinema, emphasising that the apocalypse was not sudden, but had been already ongoing to the extent that it is hard to tell the difference between pre- and post-apocalypse Cuba. "Yo lo veo igual que siempre" [it looks the same to me as always] is the sentiment expressed throughout, with explicit reference to Cuba's Special Period in the years 1991–2000, which was marked by a severe economic crisis. Accordingly, several characters change very little: Vlad California, for instance, who is symbolic of the post-Cold War conditions of mass tourism decried by Yoss, acts the same "before" and "after" the apocalypse (first stealing from tourists, and then from zombie tourists). More in line with familiar zombie conventions is the fact that the behaviour of the survivors increasingly renders them similar to the zombies and what they signify. Thus, in a parody of the Special Period expansion of the range of self-employed *cuentapropista* activities, Juan and his gang survive by self-interest, by killing indiscriminately and by commercialising their assistance by charging others to kill their unwanted zombie relatives: "Matamos a sus seres queridos, ¿en qué podemos servirle?" ["We will kill your loved ones, how can we help you?"] Ultimately, however, the narrative arc of the film sees Juan recommit to socialism and stay on the island. This marks perhaps the most significant break with Anglo-American zombie conventions, which, as Jennifer Rutherford notes, tend to "take the ideal of the unfettered mobile modern worker to new heights as [the survivors] travel across the country stripped of their homes, families and communities" (2013: 6). Indeed, Juan's decision to stay (followed, in the credits, by his friends rejoining him) significantly impacts the meaning of the film (see also Kee 2020).

What might need further examination – despite its rather explicit presence – is the film's overt emphasis on playfully testing the zombie's relation to actually existing communism *within* the capitalist world-system. While many scholars have been quick to emphasise the satire of the communist state apparatus, from the government down to the local CDRs, far fewer have reinserted this within the film's sharp critique of global capitalism and its erosion of socialism. Struggles over the ideological coding of zombies are, of course, far from new. Since the 1950s, the zombie has been firmly inscribed in Cold War dynamics through films such as *Invasion of the Body Snatchers* (1956), which – whether expressive of fears over communism or McCarthyism – was profoundly ambivalent and suspicious of the zombie mass as representing mass indoctrination. Zombies subsequently became commonplace in US anti-communist discourse around the threat of Soviet invasion, supposed communist methods of indoctrination and even surgical brain-altering operations such as prefrontal lobotomies (see Johnson 2014).[11] It is thus no surprise that scholars of 1950s popular culture describe zombies as profoundly conservative figures. Yet *Juan de los muertos*' engagement with zombies in the ocean (on which more later) demands an approach that moves beyond the ideological coding of zombies as simply anti-communist, and instead examines how zombie horror enables the film to offer more specific criticism of communism in Cuba within a larger critical vision of the capitalist world-system.

There are scenes in *Juan de los muertos* that echo Tomas Alea Gutierrez's 1968 classic *Memorias del subdesarrollo* [Memories of Underdevelopment],[12] in which bourgeois intellectual Sergio surveys Havana, and a range of women, through

---

11 The undead have long worked as figures that register the fear of communism, especially in the post-war US, where zombies "were deployed as a trenchant political critique of lobotomy's power to alter the individual personality" (Johnson 2014: 91).

12 *Memorias del subdesarrollo* (1968) also includes a surprising reference to zombies: the bourgeois character Pablo denounces the revolution as leading to Cubans "go[ing] hungry, like the Haitians," who, as he claims from his vantage point as

a telescope. But in *Juan*, the ideological underpinnings of this framing device are exposed through sleazy Lázaro's simultaneous, rather pathetic-looking act of masturbation, which renders the sexism and voyeurism excessive. Further, Juan's violence towards the trans character "La China" after she has turned into a zombie and attacks him on the Plaza de la Revolución, with the large figure of Guevara looming in the background, renders obvious Guevara's alleged homo- and (presumably) transphobia.[13] Unlike Raimi's films, which are more postmodernist in their revelling in tropes and stereotypical types, *Juan* does end on a rather more serious recommitment to a socialist vision, which is pronounced by a male, heterosexual, mestizo Cuban coded as an "everyman," who has not only just set up a new heterosexual national family that includes the diaspora, but also, in probably the crudest "joke" in the film, has seen a zombie being anally impaled, while calling him a "sodomite." The film thus stages a clash between the postmodern, decidedly B-movie aesthetic of Raimi's zombie horror-comedy and the commitment characteristic of many Cuban films produced by the Instituto Cubano del Arte e Industria Cinematograficos that ends up reinscribing, rather than merely exposing, the problems inherent in both aesthetics when it comes to sexuality and gender.

Perhaps more seriously, the reinscribing of problematic sexual and gender politics is made most explicit through the circulation of revolutionary iconography that is constantly contrasted with zombies for comedic effect. Often, this involves the juxtaposing of slogans – for instance, *Revolución o muerte* – with the undead and the massacre that the zombie-slayers leave behind. Most interesting and far-reaching, however, is the visual engagement with the iconography surrounding Ernesto "Che" Guevara during the film's climax, situated on the Plaza de la Revolución, where the survivors are surrounded by a growing number of bloodthirsty zombies. The square is one of the film's many heavily overdetermined locations: home to a massive Guevara sculpture by Enrique Ávila González, installed during the Special Period on the exterior wall of the Ministry of the Interior, it has offered space for communist rallies, commemorative events led by Fidel Castro and other public events of historical importance. Guevara's image is iconic, "dense with symbolic accretions" (B. Ghosh 2011: 116), with an auratic presence that seems to merge the signifier and the signified – however much the latter has shifted over the course of the second half of the twentieth century. The reasons for his ascent into iconicity are, of course, multiple: from his early death on the eve of the student movements, through his political writing and activism, to the (copyright-free) availability of a great photo taken in 1960 by the

---

a white male, went from having a successful sugar industry to being "descalzos convertidos en zombis" (barefoot, converted into zombies).

13 Despite the mediation via the extreme and excessive aesthetic of splatterstick, the film falls flat in its gender, sexual (and racial) politics, and ends up semi-reinscribing sexist, homo- and trans-phobic hegemonic norms (see Fehimović 2018).

photographer Alberto Díaz Gutiérrez, better known as Alberto Korda. Korda's iconic image of Guevara came to "institute the 'cognitive map[...]' of globality (Fredric Jameson's unforgettable formulation of the impossible imaging of social totality)" (B. Ghosh 2011: 27–28).

Guevara theorised the ways in which communism should seek to move beyond the alienation of labour. He wrote cogently about the ways in which communism should seek to overcome alienation and private property – embodied aptly, even if negatively, in the figure of the zombie – stating that, "in capitalist societies individuals are controlled by a pitiless law usually beyond their comprehension. The alienated human specimen is tied to society as a whole by an invisible umbilical cord: the law of value" (quoted in Deutschmann 2001: 215). He thus placed emphasis on de-commodifying and de-linking work from surplus-value production and replacing it with voluntary labour for the community. Indeed, in his work on economy and labour, Guevara argued that:

> A socialist economy without communist moral values does not interest me. We fight poverty but we also fight alienation. One of the fundamental aims of Marxism is to eliminate material interest, the factor of "individual self-interest" and profit from man's psychological motivations. Marx was concerned with both economic facts and their reflection in the mind, which he called the "fact of consciousness." If communism neglects the facts of consciousness, it can serve as a method of distribution but it will no longer express revolutionary moral values. (quoted in Yaffe 2009: 63)

With the image of "Che" looming over Plaza de la Revolución, the film thus presents the audience with a metonymic shorthand for the opposition between the face of anti-capitalist resistance (Guevara's) and the zombified masses. This pits the figure of the zombie – often read as embodying capitalist

Fig. 10. *Juan de los Muertos* (Brugúes, 2011). A horde of zombies massing on the famous Plaza de la Revolución, in front of the image of Che Guevara.

alienation in a world dominated by the drive for surplus value – against the iconic face of 'el Che' in a struggle against anti-capitalist resistance. Indeed, it is in the historic square that the apocalypse survivors are attacked by a familiar mass of Romero-esque zombies. They win out against the zombies, but only with the help of an American preacher, who knows no Spanish and ineptly communicates with them in (heavily accented) English.

Seemingly opposing messages are quite commonly voiced in the film, and are perhaps the result of a range of pressures (from the government, from the actors, and from the people themselves). In the promotion materials as well as quite a few scenes, this multiplicity of voices regarding communism is replicated in ways that echo the scene described and pictured above. In general, Cuban uses of Che Guevara imagery were historically tied to the idea of international solidarity and "exporting the Revolution" (Cushing 2012: 62). Between 1966 and 1990, OSPAAAL (Organisation of Solidarity with the People of Asia and Africa and Latin America) – "once a primary source for solidarity posters produced in Cuba and aimed at activists around the world" – also produced "*Tricontinental*, a monthly magazine" (Cushing 2012: 10). Together OSPAAAL and *Tricontinental* were profoundly inscribed in the country's socialism, which was notably internationalist in tenor. In the magazine posters shown in figures 10 and 11, one can clearly see the visual evocation of emanation as the spreading

Fig. 11. Alberto Gutierrez Korda's photo of Che Guevara.

Fig. 12. Tricontinental Poster of Che Guevara, 1967.

of Guevara's ideas and vision beyond the continent. The posters thus carry within them a message of international roll-out that fights against capitalist zombification across the globe, to the furthest reach of the magazine.

Juan de los muertos' engagement with zombies through the Che Guevara iconography demands an approach that moves beyond the ideological coding of the zombies as straightforwardly anti-communist, and instead examines how zombie horror enables the film to offer a more specific criticism of communism in Cuba within a larger critical vision of the capitalist world-system. Yet perhaps the most interesting engagement with the history of zombie genre conventions occurs through the film's evoking of oceanic zombie horror, in which the violent foundations of the capitalist world-system are registered and attempts made to re-contain them. Global capitalism, as Liam Campling and Alejandro Colas remind us, "is a seaborne phenomenon" (2021: 1): its history can be traced from the brutal transatlantic slave trade to issues of overfishing, ocean depletion and global warming, alongside the continued dehumanisation of those seeking to cross the ocean as migrants. Further, oceans have played a particular role in US dominance, since the US came "to exercise global hegemony through its unassailable naval and commercial primacy over the high seas" (Campling and Colas 2021: 14). Film critics have pointed out the overdetermination in *Juan de los muertos* of the scenes that take place in the sea near the Malecon, reading them as clear references to historical events, including the Mariel exodus in 1980.[14] I want to add to these observations by emphasising how the film engages with oceanic *zombie* horror and its relation to capitalism as a seaborne phenomenon. The latter, which one might call a sub-genre of the zombie tradition, runs through a range of twentieth-century short stories and films.

In terms of stories, we might turn to Manly Wade Wellman's "The Song of the Slaves" ([1940] 2011), in which a monstrous villain throws 49 enslaved

Fig. 13. Poster by Elena Serrano, 1968. Reproduced with thanks to the Lindsay Webster Collection of Cuban Posters, Wofford College.

---

14 In his book *Machos, Maricones and Gays: Cuba and Homosexuality*, Ian Lumsden describes Mariel as the last instance of "*institutionally* promoted homophobia" (1996: 78).

individuals to their deaths in the sea in the mid-nineteenth century, while being pursued by a British ship;[15] the zombies then pursue him to land and take him back into to the sea with them. In film history, the first oceanic zombies (Kay 2008: 29) are found in *The Zombies of Mora-Tau* (Cahn 1957), even if previous films such as *I Walked with a Zombie* (Tourneur 1943) had thematised the trauma of the Middle Passage through the motif of the ship's crying figurehead. *The Zombies of Mora-Tau* follows a group of white underwater zombie sailors who guard the lost treasures of a sunken ship off the West African coast, attacking anyone attempting to approach the diamonds. Advertised as "a tide of terror [that] floods the screens," the film was unsuccessful and low-quality, combining exoticising racism and sexism in a story of "colonial anxiety" over European plunder and pillaging (Russell 2007: 49). Nonetheless, it proved a "milestone" in zombie cinema as it introduced to the screen, not only the underwater zombie, but the zombie mass that is able to zombify the living.

In *Juan de los muertos*, the most explicit reference to the sea occurs on the seafront in Havana, when a killer whale snaps up Lázaro's female friend. This scene was made away from the main shooting locations:

La escena de los zombies bajo el agua se filmó en la sala Avellaneda del Teatro Nacional, hicimos un croma (fondo verde que se usa para los efectos digitales) enorme en el escenario, teníamos ventiladores gigantes para mover el pelo y la ropa de los actores. Lo filmamos en cámara lenta, para que diera la sensación que lo filmamos bajo el agua. Luego, en la computadora se agrega el fondo marino, el agua, y se combinan los diferentes grupos de zombies.[16]

[The scene with the zombies underwater was filmed in the Avellaneda Hall of the National Theatre [of Cuba]: we made a big *cromo* (a green background that can be used for special effects) on the stage, we took giant ventilators to move the hair and the clothes of the actors. We filmed it in slow motion, to give the impression that they were moving in the water. Then we added the marine bottom, the water and we combined different groups of zombies.]

The scene itself echoes the underwater zombie scenes of Italian director Lucio Fulci's *Zombie Flesh-Eaters* (1979), which opens with a boat approaching New York harbour with a zombie on board. Gory and influenced by 1970s Italian cannibal movies, Fulci's film represents the zombie outbreak that

---

15 Poole also notes that to defend his ancestor Wade Hampton, Manly Wade Wellman claimed that he had "refused to free his slaves because emancipated slaves 'were often unhappier than slaves under good masters'" (cited by Poole 2004: 94).

16 Quote from an interview with the cast of *Juan de los muertos*, published by Juventude Rebelde [Rebel Youth], online at: https://www.juventudrebelde.cu/cultura/2011-12-06/protagonistas-de-filme-cubano-juan-de-los-muertos-dialogaron-con-nuestros-lectores-fotos-y-video (accessed 14 March 2022).

Zombies-of-Waste and Neoliberal Exhaustion

will infect the global city as starting on the fictional Caribbean island of Matul, stereotypically rumoured to be steeped in "voodoo" and depicted as exotic to the almost permanent background of drumming. A mysterious disease – or perhaps "voodoo" rituals, as one character suggests – awakens

Fig. 14. *I Walked with a Zombie* (Tourneur, 1941). A shot of the crying figurehead, representing the traumas of slavery.

Fig. 15. *Zombies of Mora Tau* (Cahn, 1957). Zombies emerging from the sea.

Ecology of the Zombie

Fig. 16. *Zombies 2* (Fulci, 1979). A zombie is attacked by a shark underwater.

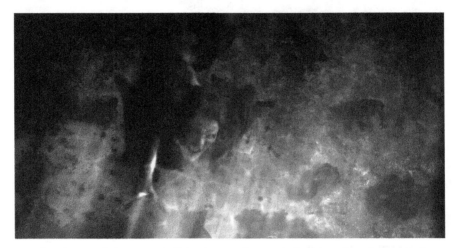

Fig. 17. *Juan de los Muertos* (Brugúes, 2011). An underwater Sara is snapped up by a digitally added white orca.

the dead on the island, including those buried in a colonial-era cemetery, in a thinly disguised allegorical emphasis on colonial legacies. On their way to the island, a (gratuitously) topless female diver who travels with the central characters encounters an underwater zombie, who ends up fighting a shark. The sequence was filmed underwater in Santo Domingo, using a real shark to tear off a fake zombie limb (Kay 2008: 115). In *Juan de los muertos*, by contrast, the underwater zombies were shot in a studio and the image of the female zombie being snapped up by an orca was digitally added.

While perhaps jarring in its approach to such serious subject matter, *Juan de los muertos* builds on several narratives of oeanic zombie horror that register the repressed trauma of the transatlantic slave trade as well as the colonial plunder and genocide at the foundation of capitalist modernity. Further, the film takes on more recent anxieties as it gestures towards the environmental degradation wrought by the industrial-scale fishing associated with contemporary capitalism. Tellingly, industrial-scale fishing was also once central to communist Cuba and the former Soviet Union; under the Cuban communist government, "fisheries were to be part of the [...] development strategy, most notably via industrialisation" (Doyon 2007: 83). In the 1960s, Castro advocated for privileging centralised, industrialised deep-sea fishing over small-scale and subsistence-oriented fishing. This transformation, which secured Cuban fisheries some of the largest catches of the region, benefited from "the strong support of the Soviet Union through preferential rates for fuel and mechanical parts" (Doyon 2007: 86). With the collapse of the Soviet Union, the Cuban fisheries went into dramatic decline during the Special Period, returning "to a small-scale, low-tech, coastal, and regionally-organised fishery" (Doyon 2007: 84), and more people (re-)engaged in subsistence-level fishing. Accordingly, *Juan de los muertos* starts with Juan and Lázaro fishing at sea – which, without a licence, is illegal, though tolerated in Cuba (Doyon 2007: 91) – with Lázaro complaining that the sea "está pelado" [is completely empty], in what appears to be an implicit reference to overfishing and threats to marine biodiversity. Indeed, while Cuba has "the highest marine biodiversity in the region," the whole area is nevertheless under serious threat (Perera Valderrama et al. 2018: 424).

Whether explicitly or implicitly driving formal conventions, environmental anxieties are never far from the surface in zombie apocalypse narratives, as illustrated by the eco-apocalyptic landscapes commonly inhabited by zombie survivors. Since at least 1968, zombies have been associated with the menace of a revived past that threatens to obliterate and devour the future. To put it differently, zombies embody the fundamental crisis of social reproduction within capitalism. While the potential destruction of a sense of futurity (and often the planet) has been central to many post-Romero zombie apocalypse films, the connection with issues around climate change and environmental degradation has become more mainstream in recent years.[17] Indeed, since the early 2000s, "the ominous recognition that we might actually choose the death of nature over the death of capitalism" has become ever more pronounced, and this is increasingly visible in literary-cultural texts (Wenzel 2019: 2). The destructive drive animating zombie aesthetics is rendered visible in the proliferation of zombie apocalypse scenarios that turn on resource anxieties, infrastructure collapse and the increasing degradation of the earth. Climate warming and anxieties around the collapse of foodways, for both environmental and economic reasons, feature particularly prominently. Zombies are thus particularly apt figures to think through the historical context in which capitalist value-relations have made significant forays into

---

17 As discussed in Chapter 1, zombies have long registered capitalism's "absolute general law of environmental degradation" (Foster 1992: 77), though this has become even more obvious in recent times.

the way in which individuals understand their relation to society, to their bodies and to their food.

To return to the United States, in *Zone One* (2011), the link between zombie aesthetics and ecological anxieties is presented in a self-conscious and often parodic way. Indeed, Whitehead places emphasis on the role of apocalyptic imaginaries and their changing meanings, which shift and vary depending on the times (most notably, from the Cold War era to that of "globalisation") but also on one's social position. The anxieties of nuclear fallout and acid rain, evoked in the films Mark Spitz's father used to watch, have thus given way to fears of the eco-apocalypse wrought by capitalism's destruction of natural ecosystems. The zombie, in other words, has been recoded from a marker of terror within the Cold War imaginary (where it resonated with fears of communism and the environmental destruction seen as part of these conflicts), to an ominous if precarious figure registering fears of planetary collapse and potential systemic implosion. One of the characters in *Zone One*, dismissed by Mark as "boring" (Whitehead 2011: 125), sees the apocalypse not only as a form of "moral hygiene" but more specifically as punishment for capitalist excesses:

> the dead came to scrub the earth of capitalism and the vast bourgeois superstructure, with its doilies, helicopter parenting, and streaming video, return us to nature and wholesome communal living [...] the human race deserved the plague, we brought it on ourselves for poisoning the planet, for the Death of God, the calculated brutalities of the global economic system, for driving primordial species to extinction. (2011: 124–25)

This caricatural and somewhat indiscriminate version of an ecological critique of capitalism is regarded sceptically from the perspective of the narrator. But it is also worth remembering that the narrator is not exactly portrayed as ideologically "reliable": before the apocalypse, his goal in life had been to live in an apartment like his uncle's – "a city gadget," the product of gentrification and a class war that sought to evacuate the "underclass" and to function "as a placeholder for future streams of capital" (Strombeck 2017: 265, 266). One might also draw on the novel itself to grasp the nature of this ideological provocation, as we learn that the "intent of the caricature [...] is to capture the monstrous we overlook every day" (Whitehead 2011: 239). While the eco-zombie-apocalypse may be something of a cliché, then, this does not make it any less reflective of the everyday monstrosity of capitalism and unfolding environmental catastrophe.

The gentrification of the imagination permeates Whitehead's critique of the shift to immaterial jobs in the mainland US under neoliberal capital. Thus, Mark Spitz's job, "in Customer Relationship Management, New Media Department, of a coffee multinational [...] doesn't require any skills" (2011: 149). As has been noted, this coffee multinational is a satirical portrayal of Starbucks, with the company starting "in the Pacific Northwest with a single café," and "metastasiz[ing] into an international franchise entity," priding itself on where its "enchanted beans were organically farmed and humanely picked" (Whitehead 2011: 149). While the novel says nothing about the actual farming conditions of the company's coffee producers – though Starbucks has been linked again and again to brutally expropriative forms of forced and child labour – it does make it very clear that what is being sold is a fantasy: a nostalgic, but false and universalisable vision of intimacy that is associated with knowing who produces and makes one's food. The company thus seeks to replace these relations with an immaterial and imagined "nation" of like-minded consumers. Aided by computer programs that spot mentions of the franchise, Mark Spitz's job – a "bullshit job" in David Graeber's terminology (2018) – is precisely to "nurture feelings of brand intimacy" and nostalgia for an imagined, more intimate past (Whitehead 2011: 149), while engaging in meaningless conversations with strangers to create positive associations with the brand. Branding through nostalgia is one of the key themes in Whitehead's novel, best embodied, perhaps, in the "stragglers": zombies that are forever stuck in one particular moment of time, "inhabiting [their] perfect moment" (2011: 158). Compare this to the Puerto Rican version of coffee-harvesting presented in "Coffea Arabica+" (2016), in which López depicts peripheralised bean-picking as opposed to core activities such as selecting the right brand. Or compare these stories of zombified workers to *Juan de los muertos*, which resolves the zombie from the tie to anti-communism without falling victim to capitalist fantasy. Reading these texts comparatively adds to our understanding of the zombie as a world-literary figure, registering world-systemic crises.

While the link to global warming and an eco-critique of capitalism is initially introduced in a parodic tone in *Zone One*, the zombie plague is ultimately firmly reinscribed as linked to climate change, environmental destruction and what one might term "nature's revolt." Throughout, the zombies are increasingly talked about in natural metaphors, as being like a "kind of weather" or "just another species of weed" (Whitehead 2011: 178) – and one cannot help but think of the effect of "superweeds" in recent years on the availability of food crops – while the ashes produced by zombie cremations are compared to the devastating effects of the BP oil spill (2011: 63).[18] Further, the final destruction of Zone One, and apparently all the other camps, is narrated metaphorically as the devastating effect of climate change and rising oceans: "the ocean had overtaken the streets, as if the news programs' global warming simulations had finally come to pass"; "the black tide had rolled in everywhere [... and] everyone was drowning" (2011: 243, 250). *Zone One*'s zombies are particularly interesting in their ambivalence. The zombies point towards the transformation of the Fordist proletariat into "unproductive" human waste, which the forces of gentrification and financial

---

18 This spill occurred in April 2010, when the BP-operated Deepwater Horizon "exploded and sank," and "[s]ome five million barrels in all spewed into the Gulf, making it the largest accidental oil spill in history" (McNeil and Engelke 2014: 15).

Ecology of the Zombie

capital seek to displace. Yet they are also inscribed within the destruction of global environments by industrial, oil-fuelled capitalism. More specifically, they resonate strongly with the exhaustion of global ecosystems since the 1970s, as the "success" of the Green Revolution gave way to the problem of superweeds (J. Moore 2010), while ever more risky offshore drilling (financed by oil companies with growing investment pools [McNeil and Engelke 2014: 14]) has made accidents such as the BP oil spill a regular occurrence.[19]

The recent zombie spike is further animated by the fact that the neoliberal regime itself is by now zombified, living on borrowed time given its failures to solve the capitalist world-ecology's systemic crisis. This is perhaps best reflected in the zombie figures that are not representative of the working classes or the human-as-waste, but that form part of the capitalist class themselves. As David McNally writes, in a paraphrasing of Marx: "[i]n strictly economic terms, it is capital that rules, not capitalists; the latter are mere bearers of capital's imperatives [... so] capitalists too function as the living dead. Colonized and directed by things, they live hollowed out lives, spiritually poor for all their plenty" (2017: 131). Or, as Chera Kee puts it in relation to *Juan de los muertos*: "things also end with Juan clinging to pre-apocalyptic ideals – but instead of those being the ideals of the capitalist world, they are communist ideals [...] The last image asks us to consider, though, if the revolution might be born anew with Juan" (2020: 46).

---

19 In fact, climate warming has even been recognised as a growing issue by the oil companies themselves since the 1970s.

Conclusion: Plotting the Routes of De-zombification

Over the course of the many years it took to complete this book, an ecological history of zombies has become an all the more pressing endeavour even if, in many ways, some of the issues I address have become so obvious that they now barely need stating. Zombie narratives – clearly – evoke fears over the looming environmental catastrophe. Many zombie apocalypse films only thinly disguise their terror at the prospect of a future when the earth has become barely habitable. And this is hardly surprising: the global future, while unknowable, looks terrifying. Propelled by the logic of profit, capitalist civilisation is hurtling towards this catastrophe. As Eddy Yuen summarised:

> The growing body of evidence is alarming. In addition to the well-known crisis of climate change, leading scientists have listed eight other planetary boundaries that must not be crossed if the earth is to remain habitable for humans and other species. These interrelated calamities include ocean acidification, the disruption of the nitrogen cycle, and the sixth mass extinction in planetary history. (2012: 15)

Within the last few years, the urgency and alarm of the scientific community and environmentalist activists around the globe has entered more strongly into mainstream discourse, driven by the increasingly visible impact of climate change and the strength of numerous movements around the globe; in the UK, where I write, XR and Fridays for the Future are part of this movement. The feeling of anxiety over the future is by now palpable for a large section of society and forms part of everyday conversations. It's almost inevitable, it seems, that zombies should be embedded within these contexts.

However, what is important to restate here is that, while the feeling of despair at a loss of futurity is relatively new for the wealthier sections of the world, zombie narratives of devastation from the (semi-)peripheries have long registered the unevenly felt socio-ecological devastation wrought by imperialist capitalism. Throughout this book, we have encountered many zombie texts that – critically or uncritically – narrate both our alienation from and capitalism's destruction of the environments and bodies we inhabit. Critical zombie narratives have long sought to convey the insight that capitalism as a civilisational system is socially and environmentally unsustainable. From enslaved zombies on Caribbean plantations that wreck the local ecosystem, to bourgeois zombie housewives and maids as the flipside of extractive regimes, these texts offer plenty of warnings about the "absolute general law of environmental degradation" that is inherent in capitalism (Foster 1992: 77), and that also, by extension, underlies zombification.

The zombie is the perfect figure for our age: it is the nightmarish creation of the capitalist world-ecology. It is dehumanised, racialised, gendered and alienated from its own body and the surrounding ecosystem, imagined as silent and without agency. Central to the figure is the "dream of silencing the nonhuman [that] has never been completely realized, not even within the very heart of contemporary modernity" (A. Ghosh 2016: 65). And the non-human has been quite a capacious category over the course of capitalist history, as we have seen. The zombie is neither the enemy, nor a representation of the enemy. It is merely the product of – and often a critical reflection on – the dynamics of the system that has led us into the current abyss that is culminating in the climate emergency. Or rather, it is the nightmarish, embodied representation of the exploitation and the plunder that drive capitalism in its relentless pursuit of profit and destruction of communities along with the earth as a habitable planet.

In *The Great Derangement*, Amitav Ghosh reflects on how he has come to

> recognize that the challenges climate change poses for the contemporary writer, although specific in some respects, are also products of something broader and older; that they derive ultimately from the grid of literary forms and conventions that came to shape the narrative imagination in precisely that period when the accumulation of carbon in the atmosphere was rewriting the destiny of the earth. (2016: 7)

While literature's capacity to deal with climate change is arguably not as limited as Ghosh seems to imply, insofar as his critique is ultimately aimed at the hegemonic culture of capitalist modernity and the commonsense narratives it produces, his argument carries weight. "Culture," he writes, "generates desires – for vehicles and appliances, for certain kinds of gardens and dwellings – that are among the principal drivers of the carbon economy" (2016: 9–10). If, as Ghosh implies, the narrative forms embedded in capitalist modernity – from their representation of "Nature" as inert, to their emphasis on the sovereign individual over the collective – not only pose a challenge for the imagination but are also designed to disable or hinder radical action on climate, then we need to resurrect or remember those forms and narratives that capitalist modernity seeks to silence. Specifically, we should focus on the literary-cultural forms and stories relating to collective action, cross-racial and cross-class solidarities, and sustainable forms of living. In our contemporary moment, this must involve redressing what Sara Salem refers to as the "amnesia of radical critique," whereby "the amnesia of empire has erased the role of imperialism in creating our contemporary world; [while we] also seem to suffer from an amnesia that erases the radical forms of resistance to foreign aid and foreign capital" (2020: 729).

The erasure of histories of left radical resistance and their forms of engagement limits our critique of the current moment. This becomes apparent in the ways in which the concept of "cultural appropriation" is evoked, as becomes clear in my discussion of Sarah Lauro's *The Transatlantic Zombie* (2015). A related example of such erasure might be the way in which, in certain Anglophone political circles, the term "ally" has taken the place formerly reserved for "comrade." This reshapes our understanding of the (at times) radical past. While an innocuous term such as "ally" might by itself seem unworthy of debate, Jodi Dean has traced the important political implications of this shift:

> rather than bridging political identities or articulating a politics that moves beyond identity, allyship is a symptom of the displacement of politics into the individualist self-help techniques and social media moralism of communicative capitalism. The underlying vision is of self-oriented individuals, politics as possession, transformation reduced to attitudinal change, and a fixed, naturalized sphere of privilege and oppression. (2019: 21)

Allyship can thus be a limit to, rather than the precondition for, cross-racial, cross-class, cross-gender solidarity. In its fixing of individuals in their identities (as black/white/cis-woman/trans-woman, etc.), allyship is also strangely ahistorical, erasing pre-existing histories of communal struggle. By contrast, the term comrade "indexes a political relation, a set of expectations for action toward a common goal" (Dean 2019: 2); that common goal would function as an alternative to the hegemonic horizon of the world-system. Socialism links comrades together in the emancipatory struggle against the absolute dominance of capitalist exploitation and appropriation in (or of) our lives. In the context of the climate crisis, this struggle has to be explicitly *eco*-socialist and reject the "logic of bureaucratic authoritarianism, within the late departed 'actually existing socialism'" (Löwy 2005: 18). This struggle needs to rebuild the globe, where plunder has destroyed so much, and reject the destructive logic of value relations.

Zombie texts from the (semi-)periphery of the world-system should be distinguished from some of the mainstream zombie narratives circulating in the current moment (e.g. *The Walking Dead*, 2010–2022), which tend to depict an all-encompassing zombie-apocalypse that resounds with anxieties over a looming eco-catastrophe. These anxieties are expressed – more often than not – through the main characters' difficulties in finding food, through the collapse of social structures and through the threatening nature of the environment as embodied by the zombies themselves. Many of these films and texts might be accused of an "undifferentiated environmental catastrophism" – a charge levelled at mainstream environmental movements by Yuen (2012: 22). While his claim that catastrophist rhetoric does not generally lead to dynamic social movements has by now been overtaken by new social and political realities, his concerns remain valid, particularly when he writes that an awareness of global catastrophe is often answered with "inadequate solutions" that may end up serving the interest of corporations (2012: 16). This must be understood within a context in which capitalist modernity is presented in mainstream discourse as the "best of all possible worlds, but [one that is] is currently facing some *exceptional* problems" (2012: 17).

As we have seen throughout this book, a history of the zombie over the Long Twentieth Century offers an understanding of the present crisis as having its roots in the fundamental dynamics driving capitalism, particularly in its monopoly form. Critical zombie texts often depict dystopian arid landscapes inhabited by zombie-esque creatures, but – unlike some of the current zombie-apocalypse imaginaries – they tend to be quite specific about the system that creates these conditions. This is particularly the case in texts from peripheralised locations or positions, where monopoly capital has rapidly and brutally dismantled and transformed socio-ecological relations. Further, as we have seen, many have employed the zombie to think through the relationship between racialised and gendered inequalities and environmental degradation. No one reading Marie Vieux Chauvet's *Amour, colère, folie* (1968), for instance, would ever be able to argue that she would have recommended "pausing" issues of race, class and imperialism while dealing with deforestation in Haiti. Nor can we read Jacques Roumain's 1944 tale of devastation in *Gouverneurs de la rosée* [Masters of the dew] without recognising his indictment of a fully Anthropocentric mistreatment of Haitian ecosystems.

The question of how to de-zombify and, further, to abolish zombification altogether is central to a number of these critical zombie texts. The very first US zombie film – *White Zombie* (Halperin 1932) – features de-zombification as a romantic resolution: the protagonists kiss and Madeleine is de-zombified. De-zombification, however, is here confined to the white, bourgeois woman of the house, while the zombie workers remain zombified, one presumes. Since then, in the filmic tradition, the zombie has become ever more shackled to his/her dehumanised state, and filmic plots often focus on the zombie's extermination – even if the latter is problematised in some of the best zombie films, including, of course, George A. Romero's classic takes – such as *Dawn of the Dead* (1978) – which emphasise the similarities between humans under capitalism and zombies. Yet I would argue that the overwhelming absence of any serious imaginative investment in de-zombification in mainstream cinema may be related to the broader impoverishment of the political imagination since 1989. As Neil Smith famously wrote:

> One of the greatest violences of the neoliberal era was the closure of the political imagination. Even on the left, perhaps especially so, the sense became pervasive that there was no alternative to capitalism. Revolutionary possibility was generally confused with utopianism, the history of revolutions notwithstanding, and revolution was collapsed into a caricature of inevitable failure. (2010: 56)

Until the present crisis, alternatives to the feeling of being "locked into the system" (Foster, quoted in Triantafyllou 2019) – a system driven by the accumulation of surplus-value and oblivious to socio-ecological sustainability – were often missing from mainstream narratives.

Stephen Shapiro has highlighted a crucial shift from about 2010 in mainstream Anglo-American zombie tales towards conscious zombie narrators. Citing Raymond Williams's argument that the "formal transformation of narrative voice [is] the chief signal of a new structure of feeling trying to express itself" (Shapiro 2014: 216), Shapiro speculates that the zombie form – the "longing to be a zombie" (2014: 217) – might in those texts work as a laboratory for the emergence of new class alliances, specifically between the (increasingly eroded) professional-managerial classes and the working classes. How do the new non-zombies come to realise "that *they* are the modern zombie class" (2014: 225)? What does this interpretation look like from a world-ecological perspective focussed on Haiti, the Hispanic Caribbean and the United States? Some shifts, such as the shift in narrative voice and perspective, are not so new in this expanded context. Others, whether the earlier shift towards the cannibal horde or the later shift from slow to fast zombies, are overdetermined by overlapping contexts and processes. The recent shift towards empathy with the zombie in some Anglo-American narratives may be read within a global context of shifting class alliances. They function as a rehearsal or a shift in empathy between (middle and lower) classes. Many of the authors of the *critical* zombie texts studied in this book *are* strongly aware of the "combined and uneven" nature of capitalism, which they put pressure on through their employment of multiple zombie imaginaries. Moreover, a large proportion of the contemporary narratives I have considered seek to provide a cognitive map for the current moment of neoliberal exhaustion. Zombies, that is, provide a register of all that is wrong with the capitalist system as it unfolds.

Increasingly, the zombie is seen in a more sympathetic light in US narratives, as a classic figure narrativising the plight of the disenfranchised masses. Complementing this development has been the shift of referents for zombie figures: from naming the masses (perceived as the "mob" from the dominant position), they now often name the system or the dominant classes (the so-called 1%), as was powerfully demonstrated by the Occupy Wall Street zombie protest. Further, unlike shows such as *The Walking Dead*, in which the formal logic of the suspense-driven serial format propels the murderous imperative, many critical zombie texts have long avoided proposing the destruction of zombies, but rather pointed towards the need to eliminate the processes that zombify. To think de-zombification means to think and work beyond the realities created by capitalism as an ecological regime.

What would it mean to live in a post-capitalist world *after* it has been remodelled by a world-ecological critique of capitalism? It would mean seeking to heal metabolic rifts by re-localising a large part of food production, shifting away from agribusiness and towards smaller scale agro-ecology. It would mean breaking the monopolisation of big food companies. It would mean "leaving fossil fuel in the ground," as so many popular movements demand (and should ask for with more force, as per Andreas Malm), decentralising energy production in order to reclaim the energy commons. History has, of course, no shortage of examples of people refusing to participate in the capitalist system and seeking to transform their relations to their environments and bodies. In a passage from the *Grundrisse* discussed in detail by Orlando Patterson, Karl Marx points out that Jamaican ex-slaves evaded the relations of domination created and determined by capital: "they ceased to be slaves [...] not in order to become wage labourers, but instead self-sustaining peasants working for their own consumption" (Patterson [1982] 2018: 2). Refusing to move from a system based on direct force to one based on indirect force, they sought to sustain themselves through an independent form of small-scale agriculture. They knew that freedom was not to be found on the plantation. Or we might point to examples such as the traditional *lakou* system in Haiti, which integrated individuals into communal practices of agricultural labour and food-sharing (J. Smith 2001: 80), or Cuban urban agricultural practices following the Special Period. While these examples derive, of course, from very different traditions, they share an emphasis on the (re)organisation of society around an effort to localise (food) production. We might also think of all the countless rebellions and revolutions against the colonial-imperial-capitalist world-order, from the Haitian Revolution to the Morant Bay Rebellion, as well as the overthrow of Baby Doc Duvalier (which began through food riots). The no-longer-zombies might, however, become involved in "agroecological initiatives" that "aim at transforming industrial agriculture partly by transitioning the existing food systems away from fossil fuel-based production largely for agroexport crops and biofuels towards an alternative agricultural paradigm that encourages local/national food production by small and family farmers based on local innovation, resources and solar energy" (Altieri and Toledo 2011: 588–89). Imaginaries of de-zombification often draw on these stores of anti-capitalist alternatives and histories of resistance.

What is the role of literature in this? In a similar way that unions and movements can create the spirit of resistance and an understanding of one's position within a global struggle, so too can literature create narratives that resist the poverty of the imagination and question the way things are. Indeed, good art, as Herbert Marcuse wrote, "fights reification, by making the petrified world speak, sing, perhaps dance" (1978: 73). Ignoring the culturally dominant narratives that propose the military, or at least armed, annihilation of zombies – an impulse that can play straight into the logics of fascism – one can find a wide range of approaches to de-zombification. Indeed, critical zombie texts propose a range of solutions, from a revolution against monopolistic landowners, to anti-colonial teaching about how to inhabit and relate within one's own country; from a reimagining of the relation between the population and the land they inhabit, to a re-spiritualisation of the body. The figure of the zombie, as I have argued, has powerful revelatory potential since its imaginative roots lie in the direct force employed as part of capitalist plunder and appropriation; when zombies are employed on their own small-scale farms and are thus de-zombified, they shatter the illusion of freedom and unveil the unequal power relations concealed by the way capital operates.

Let us here (re)turn to some of the zombie texts I have considered and examine how they have imagined de-zombification or, in plainer terms, how they envision alternatives to the capitalist world-ecology. While the huge array of zombie texts that are globally available do not, of course, share a political or ideological horizon, and not all zombie texts even seriously approach the question of de-zombification, select zombie texts – generally by authors embedded within leftist traditions – have been able to work towards a blueprint for positive ways of resisting the capitalist world-ecology. It might not come as a surprise that I here start with Jacques Roumain's *Gouverneurs de la rosée* ([1944] 1998). Roumain was a committed communist who, as we saw in Chapter 3, portrays the Haitian rural landscape as devastated by an unnamed, though continuously present, imperialist world-horizon that has sucked sugar out of the Caribbean islands. De-zombification is here linked to a renewal of sustainable growing, water redistribution and the promise of romanticised reproduction via Annaïse.

Next, we might turn to Franketienne's novel *Dézafi* ([1975] 2018), written after Baby Doc Duvalier had come to power. As we have seen throughout this book, even zombie texts with progressive politics are often marred by sexism. The romance narrative – with its containment of race and class struggles via the heteronormative couple – contains serious conceptual limitations. In Franketienne's allegorical text, however, several strands of zombie tales interlink and overlap, and there is a serious engagement with the tradition of the *restavek* (unpaid female labourer). The central narrative of the novel tells the story of the rural despot and zombie-master Sintil who, with a right-hand henchman called Zofé, keeps a mass of workers zombified and forces them to work on his rice swamps – until they are liberated by eating salt. It is a familiar story, resembling the one William Seabrook offered to his US readers with *The Magic Island* (1929). But Franketienne's narrative is one of many interwoven strands in *Dézafi*, painting a picture of zombification as a much broader phenomenon. While Sintil allegorises the Baby Doc Duvalier dictatorship as well as its neoliberal unevenness, Franketienne interweaves the story of authoritarian oppression with a range of related experiences of zombification, including un- and underemployment, migration to the city and abroad, and women's entrapment within patriarchal structures. Further, all of these stories unfold in a landscape that is experienced as profoundly threatening: it is arid, lacking in water and food sources, and degraded through erosion and flooding. The timeframe in which the narrative takes place is kept deliberately ambiguous: references to the Société Haitiano-Américaine de Développement Agricole (SHADA) and the MacDonalds railway – which played a significant role in displacing farmers – situate it in the 1940s, while the implicit Duvalier context obviously evokes a later historical period. As Régis Antoine observes, within this "dystopian environment" the Haitian character appears completely "destructured" (1998: 67); it is this "destructuring" that leads to the replacement of worthy women and men with the zombie allegory, which takes the place of the praised heroes of previous writers, such as Manuel in Roumain's *Gouverneurs de la rosée* (Antoine 1998: 68).

While Frankétienne's novel is embedded within a very specifically Haitian context, the narrative resonates beyond its specificity. Frankétienne himself sees it that way:

> All countries where there are people who are enslaved, who cannot think, who cannot act, who cannot react, they are zombies […] The globalization that pretends to be a system of globalization is also a system of zombification but a zombification of the whole planet. (quoted in Merriam 2015: 25)

Within this context of global zombification, Frankétienne's narrative offers an allegorical tale of liberation in which salted food plays a crucial role:

> "Alibé, my brother, salt gives soul. When salt gets into a zonbi's bloodstream, it slaps its body, shakes up his guts, wakes up his brain. Once a zonbi gets a taste of salt, he stops being passive, he becomes a bouanovo, he sees clearly, he becomes strong. That's when he gets enraged and wants to break loose. You understand, Alibé? You understand why Sintil says salt is poison?"
> "I sort of get it now."
> "But, my old brother, salt is life." (Frankétienne [1975] 2018: 126)

As in Seabrook's version of the tale, it is salt that liberates the zombie. However, in Frankétienne's tale, the consumption of salt has much more far-reaching symbolic consequences. *Dézafi* beautifully represents what it would mean to de-zombify bodies, senses, memories and thought processes. Zombie narratives often (explicitly or implicitly) emphasise the zombie's lack of taste – either because their food must contain no salt (*Dézafi* and *The Magic Island*), or because they cannot taste anything (*iZombie* [2015–2019], directed by Rob Thomas and Diane Ruggerio-Wright), or because they just blindly, unthinkingly eat anything in their way. In Frankétienne's narrative, tasting salt becomes symbolic of reconnecting with the world around us in its concrete objectivity, in its specific textures, smells and particularities. In other words, what Frankétienne's narrative attempts is the de-reification and reanimation of "relations amongst things and persons via the liberation of things, as well as persons, from the circuits of abstraction" (McNally 2017: 132). Liberation via romantic de-zombification – an option offered by Siltana's infatuation with Klodonis and her offering of salt – is rejected in the plot development: rather than escaping with Siltana, Klodonis opts to liberate his fellow zombies and join forces with the previously zombified village in the rebellion against Sintil. Liberation, then, turns into the liberation of the masses.

In his depiction of the relation between the zombie of the plantation and the zombie servant in the house, Frankétienne may well have followed Chauvet, with whom he attended literary salons in the 1960s. In *Dézafi*, he includes several stories of zombification – the most central revolving around a rice plantation, on which zombie labourers are forced to work by the zombie-master Sintil, who many critics have associated with Baby Doc Duvalier, who pushed neoliberalisation further in Haiti. However, unlike the plantation zombie imaginaries of the 1930s, the zombification of the labourers and entire villages occurs in his novel in parallel to the zombification of Rita, who is a *restavek* in her uncle's house. While the central story reworks pre-existing zombie stories in relation to plantation labour, the story of Rita suggests that a related dynamic is at work in the oppression of women. Rita works for no pay, receives beatings from her uncle, and has little to no formal education, as suggested by her inability to read. Throughout, she is depicted in terms that suggest a high level of zombification: she is described as a "mechanical doll" and works like a "draft animal" (Frankétienne 2018: 84, 25). In these descriptions, we see that Frankétienne joins the imaginary of the plantation zombie with that of female zombification, as he highlights the informal, gendered work of the *restavek*, performed under often extreme conditions. His novel, like Chauvet's, thus offers an integrative understanding of work that refuses the early twentieth-century conflation of women with the land and with the reproduction of community.

Now consider another literary text that has focused on de-zombification via a similar concern with gender dynamics. I opened this book with a reflection on Erna Brodber's *Myal* (1988), a novel that also has plenty to offer for thinking beyond colonialist-capitalist conceptualisations of nature and human animals. *Myal*, as we have seen, effortlessly weaves together the history of European colonialism and emergent US imperialism with the history of fossil-fuelled transport, food regimes and food delocalisation, while also probing the role of the literary in the hegemony of colonial and imperial plunder. Its commitment to pushing beyond the narrative of zombification is underlined in its first chapter, which opens with a Myal spiritual ritual that seeks to reground Ella's body in the island's environment and to extract a strange "grey mass" from her belly. Here, successful de-zombification involves the re-spiritualisation of the body and the environment it inhabits; in other words, it involves the overcoming of the capitalist binary of the immaterial world of the soul and the material world of nature and the body. In many ways, this scene attempts a similar healing process as the one envisioned at the end of Roumain's *Gouverneurs de la rosée*, without, however, falling into the masculinist trope of conflating women with nature.

Myal not only starts with a ritual of de-zombification, but also Ella's music recitation, which splits her mind from her body and indirectly parallels Anita's response when she practises piano. Ella, the mixed-race protagonist, separates from her body through her reading of music, which "splits the mind from the body and both from the soul and leaves each open to infiltration" (Brodber 1988: 28). As Neil ten Kortenaar explains, "the guardian spirits of Grove Town call the process by which such a disembodied other gains control over the embodied self 'zombification'" (2011: 3112). Anita – a young black girl – is physically abused by Mass Levi, who throws stones at her house. This is, as Pin-Chia Feng explains, the "evil internal to the community," supposedly mirroring the male US character Selwyn's "evil from without" (2002: 157). Mass Levi used to be a DC, or district constable (Feng 2002: 158), whereas Selwyn embodies the emergence of US imperialism. In relation to the threat Mass Levi represents, only communal action will suffice, hence the title of the novel, which is evocative of communal spiritual practices: towards the end of the novel, all the spiritual "animals" come together to defend Ella's anti-colonial reading of the school text. Further, the novel also alludes constantly to Morant Bay, where in 1865 there occurred "one of the largest uprisings in Jamaican history, [with] far-reaching consequences for an interpretation of the novel" (Puri 2004: 164). This uprising pitted plantations against plots and was invested in alimentary sovereignty. The whole novel is thus turned against the global food-system and market relations, which, when they come to predominate over use-value, exhaust and devastate nature, as well as reinforcing racial and gendered relations.

Zombies occupy the overlapping relations of capital's reworking of nature; they register capitalism's structuring of histories of alienation, of value and non-value, of natures and "civilisation." They are eco-monstrous figures that embody capitalism's degradation of natures and the domination of profit over all life. From *White Zombie* onwards, representations of zombies have encoded the unfolding of capitalism's classist, sexist, racist and ecocidal dynamics, often doing so in unconscious or reactionary ways. But as I have shown, zombies in (semi-)peripheral texts in particular – such as those depicted in George A. Romero's *Night of the Living Dead* (1968) or Richard Wright's *Native Son* (1940) or Erna Brodber's *Myal* (1988) or indeed Pedro Cabiya's "Relato del piloto que dijo adios con la mano" [Story of the pilot who waved good-bye] ([2003] 2010) – have long been mobilised to more critical effect. Recent zombie imaginaries cannot help but speak to our dystopian present of economic, geopolitical and environmental crisis. Propelled by the deranged logic of capital, the mass of humanity finds itself shuffling (or speeding) towards a living death of ecological collapse. Since the early 2000s, however, in works such as *Juan de los muertos* (2011) and *Land of the Dead* (2005), a shift has occurred in how the relationship between the zombified and non-zombified is represented. These works rehearse the possibility of a new cross-class, multi-ethnic alliance against the depredations of global capital. While zombies neither would, nor could, ever stop to till their own farm and produce their own food, they are increasingly aware of their own predicament. Some are also quite explicitly looking out for some kind of "salt" that would de-zombify them and free their souls.

Works Cited

Abrams, Jennifer S. 2010. "'The kids aren't alright': Using a Comprehensive Anti-trafficking Program to Combat the Restavek System in Haiti." *Temple International and Comparative Law Journal* 24(2): 443–75.
Ackerman, Alan. 2017. "Electricity." In *Fueling Culture: 101 Words for Energy and Environment*, edited by Imre Szeman, Jennifer Wenzel and Patricia Yaeger, pp. 120–23. New York: Fordham University Press.
Ackermann, Hans W. and Jeanine Gauthier. 1991. "The Ways and Nature of the Zombie." *Journal of American Folklore* 104(414): 466–94.
Alexander, Michelle. 2010. *The New Jim Crow: Mass Incarceration in the Age of Colourblindness*. New York: The New Press.
Alexis, Jacques Stephen. 1995 [1956]. "Of the Marvellous Realism of the Haitians." In *The Post-Colonial Studies Reader*, edited by Bill Ashcroft, Gareth Griffiths and Helen Tiffin, pp. 194–98. London: Routledge.
Altieri, Miguel A. and Victor Manuel Toledo. 2011. "The Agroecological Revolution in Latin America: Rescuing Nature, Ensuring Food Sovereignty and Empowering Peasants." *Journal of Peasant Studies* 38: 587–612.
Antoine, Régis. 1998. "Le réalisme mérveilleux dans la flaque" [Marvellous realism in a pool]. *Littérature de 1960 à nos jours, Notre Librairie* 133 (October–November): 64–72.
Apel, Dora. 2015. *Beautiful Terrible Ruins: Detroit and the Anxiety of Decline*. New Brunswick, New Jersey: Rutgers University Press.
Armengot, Sara. 2012. "Creatures of Habit: Emergency Thinking in Alejandro Brugués' *Juan de los muertos* and Junot Díaz's 'Monstro.'" *TRANS-. Revue de littérature générale et comparée* 14: n.p.
Arroyo, Jossiana. 2015. "Cities of the Dead: Performing Life in the Caribbean." *Latin American Studies Association* XLVI(2): 35–40.
Arthus, Wien Weibert. 2013. "The Alliance for Progress: A Case Study of Failure of International Commitments to Haiti." In *The Idea of Haiti: Rethinking Crisis and Development*, edited by Millery Polyné, pp. 135–64. Minneapolis, Minnesota: University of Minnesota Press.
Ayala, César J. 1999. *American Sugar Kingdom: The Plantation Economy of the Spanish Caribbean, 1898–1934*. Chapel Hill, North Carolina: University of North Carolina Press.

Ayala, César J. and Rafael Bernabe. 2009. *Puerto Rico in the American Century: A History since 1898*. Chapel Hill, North Carolina: University of North Carolina Press.
Baker, Kelly J. 2013. *The Zombies are Coming! The Realities of the Zombie Apocalypse in American Culture*. Chapel Hill, North Carolina: Blue Crow Books (Revised Kindle Edition).
Bankoff, Greg. 2010. "A Curtain of Silence: Asia's Fauna in the Cold War." In *Environmental Histories of the Cold War*, edited by J.R. McNeill and Corinne R. Unger, pp. 203–26. Cambridge: Cambridge University Press.
Baralt, Guillermo A. 2007. *Slave Revolts in Puerto Rico*. Princeton, New Jersey: Marcus Wiener.
Beckett, Greg. 2013. "Rethinking the Haitian Crisis." In *The Idea of Haiti: Rethinking Crisis and Development*, edited by Millery Polyné, 1115–588. Minneapolis, Minnesota: University of Minnesota Press (Kindle Edition).
Beckman, Ericka. 2013. *Capital Fictions: The Literature of Latin America's Export Age*. Minneapolis, Minnesota: University of Minnesota Press (Kindle Edition).
Bellamy, Brent Ryan and Jeff Diamanti. 2018. "Phantasmagorias of Energy: Toward a Critical Theory of Energy and Economy." *Mediations* 31(2): 1–16.
Benjamin, Walter. 2008 [1935]. *The Work of Art in the Age of Its Technological Reproducibility, and Other Writings on Media*. Edited by Michael W. Jennings, Brigid Doherty and Thomas Y. Levin. Cambridge, Massachusetts: Belknap Press of Harvard University Press.
Benson Arias, Jaime. 2007. "Sailing on the USS *Titanic*: Puerto Rico's Unique Insertion to Global Economic Trends." In *None of the Above: Puerto Ricans in the Global Era*, edited by Frances Negrón-Muntaner, pp. 29–38. New York: Palgrave Macmillan.
Bhattacharya, Tithi. 2017. "Introduction: Mapping Social Reproduction Theory." In *Mapping Social Reproduction Theory*, edited by Tithi Bhattacharya, pp. 1–20. London: Pluto Press.
Bishop, Kyle William. 2010a. *American Zombie Gothic: The Rise and Fall (and Rise) of the Walking Dead in Popular Culture*. Jefferson, North Carolina: McFarland.
— 2010b. "The Idle Proletariat: *Dawn of the Dead*, Consumer Ideology, and the Loss of Productive Labor." *The Journal of Popular Culture* 43(2): 234–48.
Blake, Linnie. 2015. "'Are We Worth Saving? You Tell Me': Neoliberalism, Zombies and the Failure of Free Trade." *Gothic Studies* 17(2): 26–41.
— 2020. "Burning Down the House: *Get Out* and the Female Gothic." In *Jordan Peele's Get Out: Political Horror*, edited by Dawn Keetley, pp. 36–46. Columbus, Ohio: Ohio State University Press.
Blakeley, Ruth. 2009. *State Terrorism and Neoliberalism: The North in the South*. Abingdon: Routledge.
Block, Alex. 2011 [1972]. "Filming *Night of the Living Dead*: An Interview with Director George Romero." In *George A. Romero: Interviews*, edited by Tony Williams, pp. 8–17. Jackson, Mississippi: University of Mississippi Press.
Boluk, Stephanie and Wylie Lenz. 2010. "Infection, Media, and Capitalism: From Early Modern Plagues to Postmodern Zombies." *The Journal for Early Modern Cultural Studies* 10(2): 126–47.
Bonniol, Jean-Luc. 2005. "Entretien avec René Depestre" [Interview with René Depestre]. *Gradhiva* 1: 1–21.
Botting, Fred. 2013. "Undead Ends: Zombie Debt/Zombie Theory." *Postmodern Culture* 23(3): n.p.

Boyer, Dominic. 2017. "Energopolitics." In *Fueling Culture: 101 Words for Energy and Environment*, edited by Imre Szeman, Jennifer Wenzel and Patricia Yaeger, pp. 128–31. New York: Fordham University Press.
Boyle, Danny, dir. 2002. *28 Days Later*. DNA Films/British Film Council.
Bozak, Nadia. 2011. *The Cinematic Footprint: Lights, Camera, Natural Resources*. New Brunswick, New Jersey: Rutgers University Press.
Brickhouse, Anna. 2004. *Transamerican Literary Relations and the Nineteenth-Century Public Sphere*. Cambridge: Cambridge University Press.
Briggs, Laura. 2002. *Reproducing Empire: Race, Sex, Science, and US Imperialism in Puerto Rico*. Berkeley, California: University of California Press.
Brodber, Erna. 1988. *Myal*. London: New Beacon.
Brontë, Charlotte. 1996 [1847]. *Jane Eyre*. New York: Penguin.
Bruce, Barbara S. 2011. "Guess Who's Going to be Dinner: Sidney Poitier, Black Militancy, and the Ambivalence of Race in Romero's *Night of the Living Dead*." In *Race, Oppression and the Zombie*, edited by Christopher M. Moreman and Cory James Rushton, pp. 60–73. Jefferson, North Carolina: McFarland.
Cabiya, Pedro. 2011 [2003]. "Relato del piloto que dijo adios con la mano" [Story of the pilot who waved good-bye]. In *Historias Atroces*, pp. 17–93. Barcelona: Zemi Books.
Campbell, J. Bradford. 2010. "The Schizophrenic Solution: Dialectics of Neurosis and Anti-Psychiatric Animus in Ralph Ellison's *Invisible Man*." *Novel: A Forum on Fiction* 43(3): 443–65.
Campling, Liam and Alejandro Colas. 2021. *Capitalism and the Sea: The Maritime Factor in the Making of the Modern World*. London: Verso.
Cardentey Levin, Antonio. 2014. "La revolución zombificada. La alegoría del trauma cubano en Juan de los muertos, de Alejandro Brugués" [The zombified revolution. An allegory of Cuban drama in *Juan of the Dead* by Alejandro Brugués]. *Alambique. Revista académica de ciencia ficción y fantasía/Jornal acadêmico de ficção científica e fantasía* 2(1): 1–13.
Carpentier, Alejo. 2010 [1933]. *Ecue-Yamba-O!* Madrid: Ediciones Akal Sa.
Carruth, Allison. 2013. *Global Appetites: American Power and the Literature of Food*. New York: Cambridge University Press.
Carson, Rachel. 2000 [1962]. *Silent Spring*. London: Penguin.
Casanova-Vizcaíno, Sandra. 2015. "'Matar a todos los tecatos', revivir los géneros modernos: gótico y splatterpunk en la literatura puertorriqueña actual" [Killing all the drug-addicts, reliving the modern genres: gothic and splatterpunk in contemporary Puerto Rican literature]. *Letral* 14: 110–23.
— 2021. *El gótico transmigrado: narrativa puertorriqueña de horror, misterio y terror en el siglo XXI* [The transmigrated Gothik: Puerto Rucan narrative of horror, mystery and terror in the twenty-first century]. Corregidor (Kindle Edition).
Casey, Matthew. 2017. *Empire's Guest Workers: Haitian Migrants in Cuba during the Age of US Occupation*. Cambridge: Cambridge University Press.
Casey-Williams, Erin. 2020. "*Get Out* and Zombie Film." In *Jordan Peele's* Get Out: *Political Horror*, edited by Dawn Keetley, pp. 63–71. Columbus, Ohio: Ohio State University Press.
Chase-Dunn, Christopher and Peter Grimes. 1995. "World-Systems Analysis." *Annual Review of Sociology* 21(1): 387–417.
Chauvet, Marie Vieux. 2009 [1968]. *Amour, colère, folie* [Love, Anger, Madness]. Trans. Rose-Myriam Réjouis and Val Vinokur. New York: Modern Library.

Cheng, Anne Anlin. 2005. "Ralph Ellison and the Politics of Melancholia." In *The Cambridge Companion to Ralph Ellison*, edited by Ross Posnock, pp. 121–36. Cambridge: Cambridge University Press.

Chude-Sokei, Louis. 2012. "The Uncanny History of Minstrels and Machines, 1835–1923." In *Burnt Cork: Traditions and Legacies of Blackface Minstrelsy*, edited by Stephen Johnson, pp. 104–32. Amherst, Massachusetts: University of Massachusetts Press.

Coates, Carrol F. 1990. "Introduction." In *The Festival of the Greasy Pole*, by Rene Depestre, pp. xv–xlvii. Translated by Carrol F. Coates. CARAF Books. Charlottesville, Virginia: University Press of Virginia.

— 2006. "Voudou in Haitian Literature." In *Voudou in Haitian Life and Culture: Invisible Powers*, edited by Claudine Michel and Patrick Bellegarde-Smith, pp. 181–98. New York: Palgrave Macmillan.

Comentale, Edward P. 2014. "Zombie Race." In *The Year's Work at the Zombie Research Center*, edited by Edward P. Comentale and Aaron Jaffe, pp. 276–314. Bloomington, Indiana: Indiana University Press.

Crane, William. 2018. "Cultural Formation and Appropriation in Merchant Capitalism." *Historical Materialism* 26(2): 242–70.

Crutzen, Paul J. and Stoermer, Eugene F. 2013. "The 'Anthropocene.'" In *The Future of Nature: Documents of Global Change*, edited by Libby Robin, Sverker Sörlin and Paul Warde, pp. 479–90. New Haven, Connecticut: Yale University Press.

Daggett, Cara New. 2019. *The Birth of Energy: Fossil Fuels, Thermodynamics and the Politics of Work*. Durham, North Carolina: Duke University Press.

Dalleo, Raphael. 2011. *Caribbean Literature and the Public Sphere*. Charlottesville, Virginia: University of Virginia Press.

— 2016. *American Imperialism's Undead: The Occupation of Haiti and the Rise of Caribbean Anticolonialism*. Charlottesville, Virginia: University of Virginia Press.

Daut, Marlene. 2015. *Tropics of Haiti: Race and Literary History of the Haitian Revolution in the Atlantic World. 1789–1865*. Liverpool: Liverpool University Press.

Dawson, Ashley. 2016. *Extinction: A Radical History*. New York: OR Books.

Dawson, Michael C. 2016. "Hidden in Plain Sight: A Note on Legitimation Crises and the Racial Order." *Critical Historical Studies* 3(1): 141–61.

Dayan, Joan. 1993. "France Reads Haiti: An Interview with René Miss Lou's Colonisation in Reverse." *Yale French Studies* 83(2): 136–53.

— 1998. *Haiti, History and the Gods*. Berkeley, California: University of California Press.

Deckard, Sharae and Kerstin Oloff. 2020. "'The One Who Comes from the Sea': Marine Crisis and the New Oceanic Weird in Rita Indiana's *La mucama de Omicunlé* (2015)." *Humanities* 9(3): 86.

DeLoughrey, Elizabeth. 2019. *Allegories of the Anthropocene*. Durham, North Carolina: Duke University Press.

de Onís, Catalina M. 2018. "Energy Colonialism Powers the Ongoing Unnatural Disaster in Puerto Rico." *Frontiers in Communication* 3(2): 1–5.

Depestre, René. 1990 [1979]. *The Festival of the Greasy Pole*. Translated by Carrol F. Coates. CARAF Books. Charlottesville, Virginia: University of Virginia Press.

— 2006 [1967]. "Cap'tain Zombi." In *Rage de vivre: Œuvres poétiques complètes*, pp. 192–93. Paris: Seghers.

— 2018 [1980]. *Bonjour et adieu à la négritude*. FeniXX réédition numérique (Kindle Edition).

Derleth, August and Mark Schorer. 2011 [1932]. "The House in the Magnolias." In *Zombies! Zombies! Zombies!*, edited by Otto Penzler, pp. 634–52. New York: Vintage Crime/Black Lizard.

Works Cited

de Rojas, Agustín. [1990] 2016. *The Year 200*. Translated by Nick Caistor and Hebe Powell. Brooklyn, New York: Regan Arts (Kindle Edition).
Descourtilz, Michel-Étienne. 1809. *Voyages d'un naturaliste, et ses observations* [Travels of a naturalist, and his observations]. Volume III. Paris: Dufart père.
Deutschmann, David. 2001. *Che Guevara Reader: Writings on Politics and Revolution*. Melbourne: Ocean Press.
Díaz, Junot. 2011. "Apocalypse." *Boston Review*, 1 May. http://bostonreview.net/junot-diaz-apocalypse-haiti-earthquake (accessed 4 August 2021).
— 2012. "Monstro." *The New Yorker* (accessed 28 May 2021).
Díaz-Zambrana, Rosana. 2012. "Zombis and chupanalgas en la Isla del Espanto: La comedia del horror en el cine de culto puertorriqueño" [Zombis and buttsuckers on the Island of Horror: Horror comedy in Puerto Rican cult cinema]. In *Horrorfílmico*, edited by Rosana Díaz-Zambrana and Patricia Tomé, pp. 211–29. Santo Domingo, Dominican Republic: Isla negra editores.
Doherty, Thomas. 1999. *Pre-Code Hollywood: Sex, Immorality, and Insurrection in American Cinema, 1930–1934*. New York: Columbia University Press.
Douglass, Frederick. 2018. *The Complete Works of Frederick Douglass*. Madison & Adams Press (Kindle Edition).
Doyon, Sabrina. 2007. "Fishing for the Revolution: Transformations and Adaptations in Cuban Fisheries." *MAST* 6(1): 83–108.
Dunaway, Wilma A. 2001. "The Double Register of History: Situating the Forgotten Woman and her Household in Capitalist Commodity Chains." *Journal of World-Systems Research* VII(I): 2–29.
Dunkel, Mario. 2013. "Duke Ellington, Charles Mingus and the Aesthetics of Pan-Africanism." In *Music, Longing and Belonging: Articulations of the Self and the Other in the Musical Realm*, edited by Magdalena Waligórska, pp. 64–81. Newcastle: Cambridge Scholars Publishing.
Dupuy, Alex. 2007. *The Prophet and Power: Jean-Bertrand Aristide, the International Community and Haiti*. Lanham, Maryland: Rowman and Littlefield.
— 2010. "Disaster Capitalism to the Rescue: The International Community and Haiti After the Earthquake." *NACLA Report on the Americas* 43(4): 14–19.
— 2014. *Haiti: From Revolutionary Slaves to Powerless Citizens: Essays on the Politics and Economics of Underdevelopment, 1804–2013*. Abingdon: Routledge.
Edwards, Bryan. 1793. *History, Civil and Commercial, of the British West Indies*. London: J. Stockdale.
Eljaiek-Rodríguez, Gabriel. 2015. "El retorno de los muertos vivientes (al Caribe). Juan de los muertos y los zombis en el cine cubano contemporáneo" [The return of the living dead (to the Caribbean). *Juan of the Dead* and contemporary Cuban cinema]. *Hispanic Research Journal* 16(1): 86–102.
Elliott, Jane. 2008. *Popular Feminist Fiction as American Allegory: Representing National Time*. New York: Palgrave Macmillan.
Ellis, Markman. 2000. *The History of Gothic Fiction*. Edinburgh: Edinburgh University Press.
Ellison, Ralph. 2001 [1952]. *Invisible Man*. London: Penguin.
— 2003 [1964]. "Out of the Hospital and under the Bar." In *Black Voices: An Anthology of Negro Writing*, edited by Herbert Hill, pp. 244–90. New York: Alfred A. Knopf.
Emery, Amy Fass. 2005. "The Zombie In/As the Text: Zora Neale Hurston's *Tell My Horse*." *African American Review* 39(3): 327–36.
Engels, Friedrich. 1991 [1894]. "Preface." In *Capital. Volume III*, by Karl Marx, pp. 91–111. London: Penguin.

Erb, Cynthia Marie. 2009. *Tracking King Kong: A Hollywood Icon in World Culture*. Detroit, Michigan: Wayne State University Press.
Farmer, Paul. 2005. *Pathologies of Power: Health, Human Rights, and the New War on the Poor*. Berkeley, California: University of California Press.
Fatton, Robert. 2014. *Haiti: Trapped in the Outer Periphery*. Boulder, Colorado: Lynne Rienner.
Federici, Silvia. 2004. *Caliban and the Witch: Women, the Body and Primitive Accumulation*. New York: Autonomedia.
Fehimović, Dunja. 2018. *National Identity in 21st-century Cuban Cinema: Screening the Repeating Island*. Cham: Springer.
Feng, Pin-Chia. 2002. "Afro-Caribbean Religions in 'Myal' and 'It Begins with Tears.'" *MELUS* 27(1): 149–75.
Fernández Gonzalo, José. 2011. *Filosofía zombi*. Barcelona: Anagrama.
Ferrer-Medina, Patricia. 2015. "El zombi caníbal entre la colonialidad y la diferencia ecológica: una breve arqueología de ideas" [The cannibal zombie between coloniality and ecological difference: a brief archaeology of ideas]. In *Terra zombie: el fenómeno transnacional de los muertos vivientes*, edited by Rosana Díaz-Zambrana, pp. 29–45. San Juan, Puerto Rico: Isla Negra editores.
Figueroa, Luis A. 2005. *Sugar, Slavery and Freedom in Nineteenth-Century Puerto Rico*. Chapel Hill, North Carolina: University of North Carolina Press.
Foley, Barbara. 2010. *Wrestling with the Left: The Making of Ralph Ellison's Invisible Man*. Durham, North Carolina: Duke University Press.
Ford, Douglas. 1999. "Crossroads and Cross-Currents in Invisible Man." *MFS Modern Fiction Studies* 45(4): 887–904.
Formanek-Brunnell, Miriam. 1998. *Made to Play House: Dolls and the Commercialization of American Girlhood*. Baltimore, Maryland: Johns Hopkins University Press.
Foster, John Bellamy. 1992. "The Absolute General Law of Environmental Degradation under Capitalism." *Capitalism Nature Socialism* 3(3): 77–81.
— 1999. "Marx's Theory of the Metabolic Rift: Classical Foundations for Environmental Sociology." *American Journal of Sociology: Environmental Sociology* 105(2): 366–405.
— 2000. *Marx's Ecology: Materialism and Nature*. New York: Monthly Review Press.
Foster, John Bellamy and Brett Clark. 2018. "Marx and Alienated Speciesism." *Monthly Review* 70(7): 1–20.
Foster, John Bellamy, Hannah Holleman and Brett Clark. 2020. "Marx and Slavery." *Monthly Review* 72(3): 96–121.
Francis, Donette A. 2004. "'Silences Too Horrific to Disturb': Writing Sexual Histories in Edwidge Danticat's *Breath, Eyes, Memory*." *Research in African Literatures* 35(2): 75–90.
Frankétienne. 2018 [1975]. *Dézafi*. Translated by Asselin Charles. CARAF Books. Charlottesville, Virginia: University of Virginia Press.
Fraser, Nancy. 2014. "Behind Marx's Hidden Abode: For an Expanded Conception of Capitalism." *New Left Review* 86: 55–72.
— 2016. "Expropriation and Exploitation in Racialized Capitalism: A Reply to Michael Dawson." *Critical Historical Studies* 3(1): 163–78.
Friedan, Betty. 2010 [1963]. *The Feminine Mystique*. London: Penguin.
Friedmann, Harriet. 2000. "What on Earth is the Modern World System? Foodgetting and Territory in the Modern Era and Beyond." *Journal of World-Systems Research* 1(2): 480–515.

Works Cited

Fujiwara, Chris. 2015 [1998]. *Jacques Tourneur: The Cinema of Nightfall*. Jefferson, North Carolina: McFarland.
Gaines, Mikal J. 2020. "Staying Woke in Sunken Places, or the Wages of Double Consciousness." In *Jordan Peele's* Get Out: *Political Horror*, edited by Dawn Keetley, pp. 160–73. Columbus, Ohio: Ohio State University Press.
Garraway, Doris L. 2005. *The Libertine Colony: Creolization in the Early French Caribbean*. Durham, North Carolina: Duke University Press.
Ghachem, M. 2012. *The Old Regime and the Haitian Revolution*. Cambridge: Cambridge University Press.
Ghosh, Amitav. 2016. *The Great Derangement: Climate Change and the Unthinkable*. Chicago: Chicago University Press.
Ghosh, Bishnupriya. 2011. *Global Icons: Apertures to the Popular*. Durham, North Carolina: Duke University Press (Kindle Edition).
Glover, Kaiama L. 2010. *Haiti Unbound: A Spiralist Challenge to the Postcolonial Canon*. Liverpool: Liverpool University Press.
— 2013. "'Black' Radicalism in Haiti and the Disorderly Feminine: The Case of Marie Vieux Chauvet." *Small Axe: A Caribbean Journal of Criticism* 17.1(40): 7–21.
Graeber, David. 2018. *Bullshit Jobs*. New York: Simon and Schuster.
Graham, James, Michael Niblett and Sharae Deckard. 2012. "Postcolonial Studies and World Literature." *Journal of Postcolonial Writing* 48(5): 465–71.
Grant, Barry Keith. 2010. *Invasion of the Body Snatchers*. BFI Film Classics. London: British Film Institute.
Grau, Jorge, dir. 1974. *No profanar el sueño de los muertos* [Let sleeping corpses lie]. Star Films S.A./Flaminia Produzioni Cinematografiche.
Grosman, Carla. 2013. "Zombis utópicos" [Utopian zombies]. *Cinémas d'Amérique latine* 21 (December): 96–109.
Grove, Richard. 1995. *Green Imperialism: Colonial Expansion, Tropical Island Edens, and the Origins of Environmentalism, 1600–1860*. Cambridge: Cambridge University Press.
Guerra, Lillian. 1998. *Popular Expression and National Identity in Puerto Rico: The Struggle for Self, Community, and Nation*. Gainesville, Florida: University Press of Florida.
Guéry, François and Didier Deleule. 2014. *The Productive Body*. Winchester: Zero Books.
Halberstam, Judith. 1995. *Skin Shows: Gothic Horror and the Technologies of Monsters*. Durham, North Carolina: Duke University Press.
Halperin, Victor, dir. 1932. *White Zombie*. Edward & Victor Halperin Productions.
— dir. 1936. *Revolt of the Zombies*. Academy Pictures.
Harvey, David. 2007. *A Brief History of Neoliberalism*. Oxford: Oxford University Press.
— 2010. *A Companion to Marx's Capital*. London: Verso.
Hearn, Lafcadio. 2001 [1890]. "La Guiablesse." In *Two Years in the French West Indies*. Oxford: Signal Books.
Henry, Paget. 2000. *Caliban's Reason: Introducing Afro-Caribbean Philosophy*. New York: Routledge.
Henson, Eithne. 2011. *Landscape and Gender in the Novels of Charlotte Brontë, George Eliot, and Thomas Hardy: The Body of Nature*. The Nineteenth Century Series. Farnham: Ashgate.
Higashi, Sumiko. 1992. "*Night of the Living Dead*: A Horror Film about the Horrors of the Vietnam Era." In *From Hanoi to Hollywood: The Vietnam War in American Film*, edited by Linda Dittmar and Gene Michaud, pp. 175–88. New Brunswick, New Jersey: Rutgers University Press.

Hobson, Christopher Z. 2005. "'Invisible Man' and African American Radicalism in World War II." *African American Review* 39(3): 355–76.
Hoermann, R. 2017. "Figures of Terror: The 'Zombie' and the Haitian Revolution." *Atlantic Studies* 14(2): 152–73.
Holleman, Hannah. 2017. "De-naturalizing Ecological Disaster: Colonialism, Racism and the Global Dust Bowl of the 1930s." *The Journal of Peasant Studies* 44(1): 234–60.
— 2018. *Dust Bowls of Empire: Imperialism, Environmental Politics, and the Injustice of Green Capitalism*. New Haven, Connecticut: Yale University Press.
Hudson, Peter James. 2017. *Bankers and Empire: How Wall Street Colonized the Caribbean*. Chicago: University of Chicago Press.
Hurston, Zora Neale. 1990 [1938]. *Tell my Horse: Voodoo and Life in Haiti and Jamaica*. New York: Harper Perennial.
IEA, IRENA, UNSD, World Bank and WHO. 2020. *Tracking SDG 7: The Energy Progress Report*. World Bank, Washington DC.
Ilott, Sarah. 2020. "Racism that Grins: African American Gothic Realism and Systemic Critique." In *Jordan Peele's* Get Out: *Political Horror*, edited by Dawn Keetley, pp. 114–27. Columbus, Ohio: Ohio State University Press.
Jakes, Aaron G. and Ahmad Shokr. 2017. "Finding Value in Empire of Cotton." *Critical Historical Studies* 4(1): 107–36.
James, C.L.R. 1991 [1938]. *The Black Jacobins: Toussaint L'Ouverture and the San Domingo Revolution*. London: Allison and Busby.
Jameson, Fredric. 2014 [2011]. *Representing Capital: A Commentary on Volume One*. London: Verso.
— 2016 [1988]. "Modernism and Imperialism." Verso blog, 17 February. https://www.versobooks.com/blogs/2504-modernism-and-imperialism-by-fredric-jameson (accessed 10 October 2020).
Jarvis, Michael. 2018. "Anger Translator: Jordan Peele's *Get Out*." *Science Fiction Film and Television* 11(1): 97–109.
Johnson, Jenell. 2014. *American Lobotomy: A Rhetorical History*. Ann Arbor, Michigan: University of Michigan Press.
Kaufman, Philip, dir. 1978. *Invasion of the Body Snatchers*. United Artists.
Kaussen, Valerie. 2004. "Slaves, Viejos, and the Internationale: Modernity and Global Contact in Jacques Roumain's *Gouverneurs de la rosée*." *Research in African Literatures* 35(4): 121–41.
— 2008. *Migrant Revolutions: Haitian Literature, Globalization, and US Imperialism*. Lanham, Maryland: Lexington Books.
Kay, Glenn. 2008. *Zombie Movies: The Ultimate Guide*. Chicago: Chicago Review Press.
Kee, Chera. 2011. "'They are not men … they are dead bodies': From Cannibal to Zombie and Back Again." In *Better Off Dead: The Evolution of the Zombie as Post-human*, edited by Deborah Christie and Sarah Juliet Lauro, pp. 9–23. New York: Fordham University Press.
— 2020. "'If You Leave, You'll Have to Work for a Living': Economic Fantasies of the Dissident Undead." Conference paper. https://scholar.uwindsor.ca/cgi/viewcontent.cgi?article=1020&context=zombiesarchive (accessed 26 October 2021).
Keetley, Dawn. 2020. "*Get Out*: Political Horror." In *Jordan Peele's* Get Out: *Political Horror*, edited by Dawn Keetley, pp. 1–23. Columbus, Ohio: Ohio State University Press.

Keresztesi, Rita. 2011. "Hurston in Haiti: Neocolonialism and Zombification." In *Race, Oppression and the Zombie: Essays on Cross-Cultural Appropriations of the Caribbean Tradition*, edited by Christopher M. Moreman and Cory James Rushton, pp. 31–40. Jefferson, North Carolina: McFarland.

Key, Keegan-Michael and Jordan Peele, dir. 2012. *White Zombies*. Comedy Central.

Kortenaar, Neil ten. 2011. *Postcolonial Literature and the Impact of Literacy: Reading and Writing in African and Caribbean Fiction*. Cambridge: Cambridge University Press (Kindle Edition).

Kreyling M. 2016. "Uncanny Plantations: The Repeating Gothic." In *The Palgrave Handbook of the Southern Gothic*, edited by Susan Castillo Street and Charles L. Crow, pp. 231–43. London: Palgrave Macmillan.

Laguerre, Enrique A. 1994 [1935]. *La llamarada* [The Flare]. Rio Piedras, Puerto Rico: Editorial cultural.

Lauro, Sarah J. 2011. "The Eco-Zombie: Environmental Critique in Zombie Fiction." In *Generation Zombie: Essays on the Living Dead in Modern Culture*, edited by S. Boluk and W. Lenz, pp. 54–66. Jefferson, North Carolina: McFarland.

— 2015. *The Transatlantic Zombie: Slavery, Rebellion, and Living Death*. New Brunswick, New Jersey: Rutgers University Press.

— 2020. "Specters of Slave Revolt." In *Jordan Peele's Get Out: Political Horror*, edited by Dawn Keetley, pp. 147–59. Columbus, Ohio: Ohio State University Press.

Lazarus, Neil. 2002. "The Fetish of 'the West' in Postcolonial Theory." In *Marxism, Modernity, and Postcolonial Studies*, edited by Crystal Bartolovich and Neil Lazarus, pp. 43–64. Cambridge: Cambridge University Press.

LeMenager, Stephanie. 2012. "The Aesthetics of Petroleum, After Oil!" *American Literary History* 24(1): 59–86.

— 2014. *Living Oil: Petroleum Culture in the American Century*. New York: Oxford University Press.

Levin, Ira. 2011 [1972]. *The Stepford Wives*. London: Corsair.

Lieberman, Jennifer L. 2017. *Power Lines: Electricity in American Life and Letters, 1882–1952*. Cambridge, Massachusetts: MIT Press.

Linnemann, Travis. 2016. *Meth Wars: Police, Media, Power*. New York: NYU Press.

López, Jotacé. 2016. "Coffea Arabica+." In *Arboretum*, pp. 11–28. San Juan: Instituto de Cultura Puertorriqueña.

Lovecraft, H.P. 2009. "The Shadow out of Time." https://www.hplovecraft.com/writings/texts/fiction/sot.aspx (accessed 12 October 2021).

— 2011 [1922]. "Herbert West – Reanimator." In *Zombies! Zombies! Zombies!*, edited by Otto Penzler, pp. 227–44. New York: Vintage Crime/Black Lizard.

— 2013. *H.P. Lovecraft: The Classic Horror Stories*. Oxford: Oxford University Press.

Löwy, Michael. 2005. "What is Ecosocialism?" *Capitalism Nature Socialism* 16(2): 15–24.

Luckhurst, Roger. 2015. *Zombies: A Cultural History*. London: Reaktion Books.

Lumière, Auguste and Louis Lumière, dir. 1895. *The Arrival of the Train at La Ciotat*. Société Lumière.

— dir. 1896. *Oil Wells of Baku: A Close View*. Société Lumière.

Macdonald, Graeme. 2013. "Research Note: The Resources of Fiction." *Reviews in Cultural Theory* 4(2): 1–24.

Maguire, Emily. 2015. "Walking Dead in Havana: *Juan of the Dead* and the Zombie Film Genre." In *Simultaneous Worlds: Global Science Fiction Cinema*, edited by Jennifer L. Feeley and Sarah Ann Wells, pp. 171–88. Minneapolis, Minnesota: University of Minnesota Press.

Mahler, Anne Garland. 2019. "South–South Organizing in the Global Plantation Zone: Ramón Marrero Aristy, the novela de la caña, and the Caribbean Bureau." *Atlantic Studies* 16(2): 236–60.

Maingot, Anthony P. and Wilfredo Lozano. 2005. *The United States and the Caribbean: Transforming Hegemony and Sovereignty*. New York: Routledge.

Malm, Andreas. 2020. *How to Blow Up a Pipeline: Learning to Fight in a World on Fire*. London: Verso.

Manon, Hugh S. 2011. "Living Dead Spaces: The Desire for the Local in the Films of George Romero." In *Taking Place: Location and the Moving Image*, edited by J.D. Rhodes and E. Gorfinkel, pp. 317–37. Minneapolis, Minnesota: University of Minnesota Press.

Marcuse, Herbert. 1978. *The Aesthetic Dimension: Toward a Critique of Marxist Aesthetics*. Boston: Beacon Press.

Marrero Aristy, Ramón. 1980 [1939]. *Over*. Santo Domingo, Dominican Republic: Ediciones de Taller.

Mars, Kettly. 2011. "Paradise Inn." In *Haiti Noir*, edited by Edwidge Danticat, pp. 50–70. New York: Akashic.

Marshall, George, dir. 1940. *The Ghost Breakers*. Paramount Pictures.

Marx, Karl. 1976 [1867]. *Capital. Volume I*. Translated by Ben Fowkes. London: Penguin.

Matheson, Richard. 2007 [1955]. *I am Legend*. London: Gollancz.

McClusky, Thorp. 2011 [1939]. "While Zombies Walked." In *Zombies! Zombies! Zombies!*, edited by Otto Penzler, pp. 300–15. New York: Vintage Crime/Black Lizard.

McDonald, David. 2009. "Electric Capitalism: Conceptualising Electricity and Accumulation in (South) Africa." In *Electric Capitalism: Recolonising Africa on the Power Grid*, edited by David McDonald, pp. 1–49. London: Earthscan.

McIntyre, Douglas A. 2011. "Zombies Worth Over $5 Billion to Economy." *24/7WallSt*. https://247wallst.com/investing/2011/10/25/zombies-worth-over-5-billion-to-economy/ (accessed 16 November 2022).

McMichael, Philip. 2009. "A Food Regime Genealogy." *The Journal of Peasant Studies* 36(1): 139–69.

McNally, David. 2011. *Monsters of the Market: Zombies, Vampires and Global Capitalism*. Chicago: Haymarket.

— 2017. "Ugly Beauty: Monstrous Dreams of Utopia." In *Zombie Theory: A Reader*, edited by Sarah Juliet Lauro, pp. 124–36. Minneapolis, Minnesota: University of Minnesota Press.

McNeil, J.R. and Corinna R. Unger. 2010. "Introduction." In *Environmental Histories of the Cold War*, edited by J.R. McNeil and Corinna R. Unger, pp. 1–18. Cambridge: Cambridge University Press.

McNeil, John Robert and Peter Engelke. 2014. *The Great Acceleration: A Great Environmental History Since 1945*. Cambridge, Massachusetts: Belknap Press of Harvard University Press.

McSweeney, Joelle and Kamau Brathwaite. 2005. "Poetics, Revelations, and Catastrophes: An Interview with Kamau Brathwaite." *Rain Taxi Online Edition* (Fall). https://www.raintaxi.com/poeticsrevelations-and-catastrophes-an-interview-with-kamau-brathwaite/ (accessed 1 March 2020).

Merchant, Carolyn. 2019 [1980]. *The Death of Nature*. London: Wildwood House (Kindle Edition).

Merriam, Michael W. 2015. "'Haitian Is My Language': A Conversation with Frankétienne." Translated by Wynnie Lamour. *World Literature Today* 89(2): 22–25.
Métraux, Alfred. 1972. *Voodoo*. London: André Deutsch.
Mies, Maria. 1994 [1986]. *Patriarchy and Accumulation on a World Scale: Women in the International Division of Labour*. London: Zed Books.
Miéville, China. 2009. "Weird Fiction." In *The Routledge Companion to Science Fiction*, edited by Mark Bould, Andrew M. Butler, Adam Roberts and Sherryl Vint, pp. 510–15. Abingdon: Routledge.
Miller, Shawn William. 2007. *An Environmental History of Latin America*. Cambridge: Cambridge University Press.
Mintz, Sydney. 1986. *Sweetness and Power*. New York: Penguin.
— 1996. "Enduring Substances, Trying Theories: The Caribbean Region as Oikoumene." *The Journal of the Royal Anthropological Institute* 2(2): 289–311.
Mitchell, Timothy. 2013. *Carbon Democracy: Political Power in the Age of Oil*. 2nd rev. edn. London: Verso.
Montijo, Josué. 2007. *El killer*. San Juan, Puerto Rico: Ediciones Callejón.
Moore, Jason W. 2003. "The Modern World-System as Environmental History? Ecology and the Rise of Capitalism." *Theory & Society* 32(3): 307–77.
— 2010. "Cheap Food & Bad Money: Food, Frontiers, and Financialization in the Rise and Demise of Neoliberalism." *Review* 33(2/3): 225–61.
— 2011. "Transcending the Metabolic Rift: A Theory of Crises in the Capitalist World-Ecology." *The Journal of Peasant Studies* 38(1): 1–46.
— 2015. *Capitalism in the Web of Life: Ecology and the Accumulation of Capital*. London: Verso.
— 2016. *Anthrophocene or Capitalocene? Nature, History and the Crisis of Capitalism*. Oakland, California: PM Press.
Moore, Ryan. 2010. *Sells like Teen Spirit: Music, Youth Culture and Crisis*. New York: NYU Press.
Morejón Guerra, Roberto. 2011. Interview with the protagonists of *Juan de los Muertos*. *Juventud Rebelde*, 6 December. https://www.juventudrebelde.cu/cultura/2011-12-06/protagonistas-de-filme-cubano-juan-de-los-muertos-dialogaron-con-nuestros-lectores-fotos-y-video (accessed 18 December 2021).
Moreno, Marisel C. 2012. *Family Matters: Puerto Rican Women Authors on the Island and the Mainland*. Charlottesville, Virginia: University of Virginia Press.
Moretti, Franco. 2000. "Conjectures on World Literature." *New Left Review* 1: 54–68.
Morrell, Sascha. 2015. "Zombies, Robots, Race, and Modern Labour." *Affirmations: Of the Modern* 2(2): 101–34.
Mukherjee, Upamanyu Pablo. 2010. *Postcolonial Environments: Nature, Culture and the Contemporary Indian Novel in English*. Basingstoke: Palgrave Macmillan.
Mumford, Lewis. 1926. *The Golden Day: A Study in American Experience and Culture*. New York: Boni and Liveright.
— 1955 [1932]. *Technics and Civilization*. London: Routledge and Kegan Paul.
Munro, Martin. 2007. *Exile and Post-1946 Haitian Literature: Alexis, Depestre, Ollivier, Laferrière, Danticat*. Liverpool: Liverpool University Press.
— 2015. *Writing on the Faultline: Haitian Literature and the Earthquake of 2010*. Liverpool: Liverpool University Press.

Murphy, Kieran. 2011. "White Zombie." *Contemporary French and Francophone Studies* 15(1): 47–55.
Murray, Robin L. and Joseph K. Heumann. 2009. *Ecology and Popular Film: Cinema on the Edge*. Albany, New York: SUNY Press.
Nau, Ignace. 2000 [1836]. *Isalina ou une scène créole* [Isalina or a Creole scene]. Port-au-Prince, Haiti: Editions Choucoune.
Nemerov, Alexander. 2005. *Icons of Grief: Val Newton's Home Front Pictures*. Berkeley, California: University of California Press.
Newbury, Michael. 2012. "Fast Zombie/Slow Zombie: Food-writing, Horror Movies and AgriBusiness Apocalypse." *American Literary History* 24(1): 87–114.
Niblett, Michael. 2012a. *The Caribbean Novel Since 1945: Cultural Form, Practice and the Nation-State*. Jackson, Mississippi: University of Mississippi Press.
— 2012b. "World-Economy, World-Ecology, World Literature." *Green Letters* 16(1): 15–30.
— 2015. "Oil on Sugar: Commodity Frontiers and Peripheral Aesthetics." In *Global Ecologies and the Environmental Humanities*, edited by Elizabeth DeLoughrey, Jill Didur and Anthony Carrigan, pp. 268–85. New York: Routledge.
— 2020. *World Literature and Ecology: The Aesthetics of Commodity Frontiers, 1890–1950*. London: Palgrave Macmillan.
— 2021. "The 'Catastrophic Consciousness of Backwardness': Culture and Dependency Theory in Latin America and the Caribbean." Unpublished article.
Nye, David. 1992. *Electrifying America: Social Meanings of a New Technology*. Cambridge, Massachusetts: MIT Press.
Oloff, Kerstin. 2012. "'Greening' the Zombie: Caribbean Gothic, World-Ecology and Socio-Ecological Degradation." *Green Letters* 16(1): 31–45.
— 2021. "Alimentary Gothic: Horror, Puerto Rico, and the World-food-System." In *Literary and Cultural Production, World-Ecology, and the Global Food System*, edited by Chris Campbell, Michael Niblett and Kerstin Oloff, pp. 193–214. London: Palgrave Macmillan.
Overman, C.T. 2000. *A Family Plantation: The History of the Puerto Rican Hacienda "La Enriqueta."* San Juan, Puerto Rico: Academia Puertorriqueña de la historia.
Paffenroth, Kim. 2006. *Gospel of the Living Dead: George Romero's Visions of Hell on Earth*. Waco, Texas: Baylor University Press.
Palés Matos, Luis. 1995 [1937]. "Canción festiva para ser llorada" [A festive song to be mourned]. In *Tuntún de pasa y grifería y otros poemas*. Madrid: Trinidad Barrera.
Palmié, Stephan. 2002. *Wizards and Scientists: Explorations in Afro-Cuban Modernity and Tradition*. Durham, North Carolina: Duke University Press.
Paravisini-Gebert, Lizabeth. 1997. "Woman Possessed: Eroticism and Exoticism in the Representation of Woman as a Zombie." In *Sacred Possessions: Vodou, Santerí, Obeah and the Caribbean*, edited by Margarite Fernández Olmos and Lizabet Paravisini-Gebert, pp. 37–58. New Brunswick, New Jersey: Rutgers University Press.
— 2015. "'All Misfortune Comes from the Cut Trees': Marie Chauvet's Environmental Imagination." *Yale French Studies* 128: 74–91.
Patterson, Orlando. 2018 [1982]. *Slavery and Social Death: A Comparative Study*. Cambridge, Massachusetts: Harvard University Press.
Peele, Jordan, dir. 2017. *Get Out*. Universal Pictures.
Peirse, Alison. 2013. *After Dracula: The 1930s Horror Film*. London: I.B. Tauris.
Perera Valderrama, Susana et al. 2018. "Marine Protected Areas in Cuba." *Bulletin of Marine Science* 94(2): 223–442.

Works Cited

Pfeiffer, Dale Allen. 2013. *Eating Fossil Fuels: Oil, Food and the Coming Crisis of Agriculture*. Gabriola Island, British Columbia: New Society Publishers.

Phillips-Fein, Kim. 2020. "Political Austerity: The Moral Economy of 1970s New York." In *Neoliberal Cities: The Remaking of Postwar Urban America*, edited by Andrew J. Diamond and Thomas J. Sugrue, pp. 78–97. New York: NYU Press.

Pietri, Pedro. 2000 [1969]. *Obituario puertorriqueño* [Puerto Rican obituary]. Trans. Alfredo Matilla Rivas. San Juan, Puerto Rico: Isla Negra Editores.

Pimentel, Miguel. 1986. *Ideología de la Novela Criolla, 1880–1944* [Ideology of the Creole Novel, 1880–1944]. Santo Domingo, Dominican Republic: Editora Universitaria, Universidad Autónoma de Santo Domingo.

Pirani, Simon. 2018. *Burning Up: A Global History of Fossil Fuel Consumption*. London: Pluto Press.

Plummer, Brenda Gayle. 1992. *Haiti and the United States: The Psychological Moment*. Athens, Georgia: University of Georgia Press.

Plumwood, Val. 1993. *Feminism and the Mastery of Nature*. London: Routledge.

Poll, Ryan. 2018. "'Can One Get Out?' The Aesthetics of Afro-Pessimism." *The Journal of the Midwest Modern Language Association* 51(2): 69–102.

Poole, W. Scott. 2004. "Confederates and Vampires: Manly Wade Wellman and the Gothic Sublime." *Studies in Popular Culture* 26(3): 89–99.

Popkin, Jeremy D. 2007. *Facing Racial Revolution: Eyewitness Accounts of the Haitian Insurrection*. Chicago: University of Chicago Press.

Price Mars, Jean. 1929. *Une étape de l'évolution haïtienne* [An era of Haitian evolution]. Port-au-Prince, Haiti: La Presse. http://classiques.uqac.ca/classiques/price_mars_jean/etape_evolution_haiti/etape_evolution_haiti.pdf (accessed 8 October 2021).

Pulliam, June. 2007. "The Zombie." *Icons of Horror and The Supernatural: An Encyclopedia of Our Worst Nightmares* 2: 723–53.

Puri, Shalini. 2004. *The Caribbean Postcolonial: Social Equality, Post-Nationalism, and Cultural Hybridity*. New York: Palgrave Macmillan.

Ralph, Michael and Maya Singhal. 2019. "Racial Capitalism." *Theory and Society* (48): 851–81.

Ramsey, Kate. 2014. *The Spirits and the Law: Vodou and Power in Haiti*. Chicago: University of Chicago Press.

Renda, Mary A. 2001. *Taking Haiti: Military Occupation and the Culture of U.S. Imperialism, 1915–1940*. Chapel Hill, North Carolina: University of North Carolina Press.

Reyes-Santos, Alaí. 2015. *Our Caribbean Kin: Race and Nation in the Neoliberal Antilles*. New Brunswick, New Jersey: Rutgers University Press.

Rhodes, Gary D. 2001. *White Zombie: Anatomy of a Horror Film*. Jefferson, North Carolina: McFarland.

Rivera, Dina Lisel. 2019. "Gothic Childbearing, Monstrous Reproduction, and a Science Fiction Turn: Rosario Ferré's 'La muñeca menor' and Pedro Cabiya's 'Relato del piloto'." *Revista de Crítica Literaria Latinamericano* 7(13): 281–326.

Robinson, Cedric. 2007. *Forgeries of Memory and Meaning: Blacks and the Regimes of Race in American Theatre and Film before WWII*. Chapel Hill, North Carolina: University of North Carolina Press.

Rodríguez, Luis Felipe. 1971 [1932]. *Marcos Antilla: relatos de cañaveral* [Marcos Antilla: stories of sugar-cane plantations]. Havana: Instituto Cubano del libro.

Rodríguez, Néstor E. 2009. "Espectros, alienígenas, clones: los sondeos poscoloniales de Pedro Cabiya" [Ghosts, aliens, clones: the postcolonial explorations of Pedro Cabiya]. *Revista Iberoamericana* LXXV: 1243–51.

Romero, George A., dir. 1968. *Night of the Living Dead*. Image Ten/Laurel Group/Market Square Productions.

— dir. 1978. *Dawn of the Dead*. Laurel Entertainment.

Rosenthal, Debra J. 2020. "Climate-Change Fiction and Poverty Studies: Kingsolver's *Flight Behavior*, Díaz's 'Monstro,' and Bacigalupi's 'The Tamarisk Hunter.'" *Interdisciplinary Studies in Literature and Environment* 27(2): 268–86.

Roumain, Jacques. 1998 [1944]. *Gouverneurs de la rosée* [Masters of the dew]. Paris: Le Temps des Cerise.

Russell, Jamie. 2007. *Book of the Dead: The Complete History of Zombie Cinema*. Godalming, Surrey: FAB Press.

Rutherford, Jennifer. 2013. *Zombies*. New York: Routledge.

Rutledge, Gregory. 2011. "The 'Wonder' Behind the Great-Race-Blue(s) Debate: Wright's Eco-Criticism, Ellison's Blues, and the Dust Bowl." *ANQ: A Quarterly Journal of Short Articles, Notes and Reviews* 24(4): 255–65.

Saint-Éloi, Rodney. 2011. "The Blue Hill." In *Haiti Noir*, edited by Edwidge Danticat, pp. 302–309. New York: Akashic.

Salem, Sara. 2020. "Fanon in the Postcolonial Mediterranean: Sovereignty and Agency in Neoliberal Egypt." *Interventions* 22(6): 722–40.

Scarano, Francisco A. 1984. *Sugar and Slavery in Puerto Rico: The Plantation Economy of Ponce, 1800–1850*. Madison, Wisconsin: University of Wisconsin Press.

Schneider, Mindi and Philip McMichael. 2010. "Deepening, and Repairing, the Metabolic Rift." *The Journal of Peasant Studies* 37(3): 461–84.

Schwägerl, Christian. 2014. "Shared Planet: An Epoch of Global Injustice?" In *Welcome to the Anthropocene: The Earth in our Hands*, edited by Nina Möllers, Christian Schwägerl and Helmuth Trischler, pp. 91–95. Munich: Deutsches Museum and Rachel Carson Centre.

Seabrook, William B. 1929. *The Magic Island*. New York: Literary Guild of America.

Seccombe, Wally. 1993. *Weathering the Storm: Working-Class Families from the Industrial Revolution to the Fertility Decline*. London: Verso.

Sekely, Steve, dir. 1943. *Revenge of the Zombies*. Monogram Pictures.

Selisker, Scott. 2011. "Simply by Reacting? The Sociology of Race and Invisible Man's Automata." *American Literature* 83(3): 571–96.

Selsam, Howard and Harry Martel (ed.). 1987. *Reader in Marxist Philosophy from the Writings of Marx, Engels and Lenin*. New York: International Publishers.

Shah, Sonia. 2004. *Crude: The Story of Oil*. New York: Seven Stories Press.

Shapiro, Stephen. 2008. "Transvaal, Transylvania: Dracula's World-System and Gothic Periodicity." *Gothic Studies* 10(1): 29–47.

— 2014. "Zombie Healthcare." In *The Year's Work at the Zombie Research Centre*, edited by Edward P. Comentale and Aaron Jaffe, pp. 193–226. Bloomington, Indiana: Indiana University Press.

— 2021. "Woke Weird and Cultural Politics of Camp Transformation." In *The American Weird: Concept and Medium*, edited Julius Greve and Florian Zappe, pp. 58–71. London: Bloomsbury Academic.

Shaviro, Steven. 1993. *The Cinematic Body*. Minneapolis, Minnesota: University of Minnesota Press.

— 2002. "Capitalist Monsters." *Historical Materialism* 10(4): 281–90.

Shaw, Andrea E. 2011. "Zombie Occupation." *The Caribbean Review of Books*, 28 November. http://caribbeanreviewofbooks.com/crb-archive/28-november-2011/zombie-occupation/ (accessed 13 October 2020).

Sheller, Mimi. 2004. "Automotive Emotions: Feeling the Car." *Theory, Culture and Society* 21(4–5): 221–41.
Siegel, Don, dir. 1956. *Invasion of the Body Snatchers*. Allied Artists.
Silvia, Adam M. 2016. "Haiti and the Heavens: Utopianism and Technocracy in the Cold War Era." Doctoral dissertation. Florida International University.
Sklodowska, Elzbieta. 2009. *Espectros y espejismos: Haití en el imaginario cubano* [Ghosts and Mirages: Haiti in the Cuban imaginary]. Madrid: Iberoamericana Editorial Vervuert.
Smil, Vaclav. 2008. *Oil*. London: Oneworld.
Smith, Jennie Marcelle. 2001. *When the Hands Are Many: Community Organization and Social Change in Rural Haiti*. Ithaca, New York: Cornell University Press.
Smith, Neil. 2010. "The Revolutionary Imperative." *Antipode* 41(1): 50–65.
Sotomayor, Aurea María. 2013. "La escritura, fuego fatuo (reflexiones sobre *Undead*, de John Torres)" [Writing, a Chimera (reflections on the *Undead*, by John Torres)]. In *Undead*, by John Torres, pp. 9–15. Trujillo Alto, Puerto Rico: Gato Malo editores.
Sovacool, Benjamin K. 2021. "When Subterranean Slavery Supports Sustainability Transitions? Power, Patriarchy, and Child Labor in Artisanal Congolese Cobalt Mining." *The Extractive Industries and Society* 8(1): 271–93.
Spear, Thomas C. 2015. "Marie Chauvet: The Fortress Still Stands." *Yale French Studies* 128: 9–24.
Steckley, Marylynn and Yasmine Shamsie. 2015. "Manufacturing Corporate Landscapes: The Case of Agrarian Displacement and Food (in) Security in Haiti." *Third World Quarterly* 36(1): 179–97.
Stock, Ann Marie. 2012. "Resisting 'Disconnectedness' in *Larga distancia* and *Juan de los muertos*: Cuban Filmmakers Create and Compete in a Globalized World." *Revista canadiense de estudios hispánicos* 37(1): 49–66.
Strombeck, Andrew. 2017. "*Zone One*'s Reanimation of 1970s New York." *Studies in American Fiction* 44(2): 259–80.
Szeman, Imre. 2010. "The Cultural Politics of Oil: On *Lessons of Darkness* and *Black Sea Files*." *Polygraph* 22: 33–45.
Taussig, Michael T. 2010 [1980]. *The Devil and Commodity Fetishism in South America*. Chapel Hill, North Carolina: University of North Carolina Press.
Taylor, Keeanga Yamahtta. 2016. *From #Blacklivesmatter to Black Liberation*. Chicago: Haymarket.
Taylor, Taryne Jade. 2014. "A Singular Dislocation: Interview with Junot Díaz." *Paradoxa* 26: 97–110.
Terwilliger, George, dir. 1935. *Ouanga*. George Terwilliger Productions.
Thésée, Gina and Paul R. Carr. 2015. "L'environnement et l'identité écologique dans le roman *Gouverneurs de la rosée* de Jacques Roumain" [The environment and ecological identity in the novel *Masters of the Dawn* by Jacques Roumain]. *Éducation relative à l'environnement*, volume 12. http://journals.openedition.org/ere/407 (accessed 20 November 2021).
Tolentino, Cynthia. 2011. "'A Deep Sense of No Longer Belonging': Ambiguous Sites of Empire in Ana Lydia Vega's *Miss Florence's Trunk*." In *Strange Affinities: The Gender and Sexual Politics of Comparative Racialization*, edited by Grace Kyungwon Hong and Roderick A. Ferguson, pp. 316–35. Durham, North Carolina: Duke University Press.
Torres, John. 2013 [2010]. *Undead*. Trujillo Alto, Puerto Rico: Gato Malo editores.
Tourneur, Jacques, dir. 1943. *I Walked with a Zombie*. RKO Radio Pictures.

Triantafyllou, Vaios. 2019. "Interview: John Bellamy Foster on the 'Green New Deal.'" *Climate & Capitalism*, 12 February. https://climateandcapitalism.com/2019/02/12/john-bellamy-foster-on-the-green-new-deal/ (accessed 29 September 2021).
Trujillo-Pagan, Nicole. 2013. *Modern Colonization by Medical Intervention*. Leiden: Brill.
Tucker, Richard P. 2007. *Insatiable Appetite: The United States and the Ecological Degradation of the Tropical World*. Berkeley, California: University of California Press.
Twa, Lindsay J. 2014. *Visualizing Haiti in US Culture, 1910–1950*. Farnham: Ashgate.
Ugarte, Ana. 2017. "Ficciones hipocondríacas: Laboratorios y síndromes en la narrativa de Pedro Cabiya" [Hypochondriac fictions: Laboratories and syndromes in the narrative of Pedro Cabiya]. *Revista de Estudios Hispánicos* 51(2): 395–416.
Vastey, Baron de. 2016 [1814]. *The Colonial System Unveiled*. Liverpool: Liverpool University Press.
Vega, Ana Lydia. 1994 [1991]. "Miss Florence's Trunk." In *True and False Romances*, pp. 163–261. Translated by Andrew Hurley. London: Serpent's Tail.
Walicek, Don E. and Jessica Adams (ed). 2017. *Guantánamo and American Empire: The Humanities Respond*. Cham: Palgrave Macmillan.
Wallace, Inez. 1985. "I Walked with a Zombie." In *Stories of the Walking Dead*, edited by Peter Haining, pp. 95–102. London: Severn House.
Wellman, Manly Wade. 2011 [1940]. "The Song of the Slaves." In *Zombies! Zombies! Zombies!*, edited by Otto Penzler, pp. 575–83. New York: Vintage Crime/Black Lizard.
Wells, B. (ed.) n.d. "First Gas Pump and Petrol Station." Washington, DC: American Oil and Gas Historical Society. http://aoghs.org/transportation/first-gas-pump-and-service-stations/ (accessed 1 May 2017).
Wenzel, Jennifer. 2019. "Evicted from the Future." *Alienocene: The Journal of the First Outernational* 6: 1–15.
Wesseling, Louis. 2000. *Fuelling the War: Revealing an Oil Company's Role in Vietnam*. London: I.B. Tauris
Wester, Maisha. 2012. *African American Gothic: Screams from Shadowed Places*. New York: Palgrave Macmillan.
Whitehead, Colson. 2011. *Zone One*. London: Vintage.
Whitfield, Esther. 2017. "Guantánamo and Community: Visual Approaches to the Naval Base." In *Guantánamo and American Empire: The Humanities Respond*, edited by Don E. Walicek and Jessica Adams, 3409–874. Cham: Palgrave Macmillan (Kindle Edition).
Williams, Eric. 1994 [1944]. *Capitalism and Slavery*. Chapel Hill, North Carolina: University of North Carolina Press.
Williams, Raymond. 1980. "Ideas of Nature." In *Problems in Materialism and Culture: Selected Essays*, pp. 67–85. London: Verso.
Williams, Tony. 2003. *The Cinema of George Romero: Knight of the Living Dead*. New York: Wallflower Press.
— 2015. *The Cinema of George A. Romero: Knight of the Living Dead*. New York: Wallflower Press.
Wood, Marcus. 2002. *Slavery, Empathy and Pornography*. Oxford: Oxford University Press.
Woods, Clyde A. 1998. "Regional Blocs, Regional Planning, and the Blues Epistemology in the Lower Mississippi Delta." In *Making the Invisible Visible: A Multicultural Planning History*, edited by L. Sandercock, pp. 78–99. Berkeley and Los Angeles, California: University of California Press.

Works Cited

WReC. 2015. *Combined and Uneven Development: Towards a New Theory of World-Literature.* Liverpool: Liverpool University Press.

Wright, Richard. 2000a [1940]. *Native Son.* London: Vintage.

— 2000b. "Introduction: How 'Bigger' Was Born." In *Native Son*, pp. 1–31. London: Vintage.

— 2008 [1941]. *12 Million Black Voices.* New York: Basic Books.

Wynter, Sylvia. 1971. "Novel and History, Plot and Plantation." *Savacou* 5(1): 95–102.

Yaffe, Helen. 2009. *Che Guevara: The Economics of Revolution.* Basingstoke: Palgrave Macmillan.

Yates, Michelle. 2011. "The Human-As-Waste, the Labor Theory of Value and Disposability in Contemporary Capitalism." *Antipode* 43: 1679–95.

Yergin, Daniel. 2012. *The Prize: The Epic Quest for Oil, Money and Power.* New York: Simon and Schuster.

Yoss (Jose Miguel Sanchez Gomes). 2014. *A Planet for Rent.* Translated by David Frye. Brooklyn, New York: Restless Books.

Yuen, Eddie. 2012. "The Politics of Failure Have Failed: The Environmental Movement and Catastrophism." In *Catastrophism: The Apocalyptic Politics of Collapse and Rebirth* by S. Lilley, D. McNally, E. Yuen and J. Davis, pp. 15–43. Oakland, California: PM Press/Spectre.

Yusoff, Kathryn. 2018. *A Billion Black Anthropocenes or None.* Minneapolis, Minnesota: University of Minnesota Press.

Zieger, Susan. 2012. "The Case of William Seabrook: Documents, Haiti and the Working Dead." *Modernism/Modernity* 19(4): 737–54.

Index

28 Days Later 122

accumulation 4, 10, 36, 43, 44, 53, 71, 78–79, 128, 138, 163
   see also dispossession
aesthetics *see* zombie aesthetics
agriculture
   capitalist (plantation/monocrop) 12, 15, 37, 54, 59–61, 70
   Caribbean, mechanisation/modernisation of 15, 42–45, 50, 85
   industrial/industrialisation of 112–14, 118, 145
   neoliberal intensification of 143, 145
   post-capitalist potential 164
   see also Green Revolution; plantation
Alexis, Jacques Stephen 47, 64n9, 66
alienation
   feelings of 43, 52, 59–60, 75, 95, 142
   of labour/workers 12, 17, 37, 42, 47, 54, 80, 96, 98n2, 112–13, 115, 141, 149
   from land and nature 13–15, 38, 42, 63, 67, 141, 160
   and modern film-making 95–96
   potential to combat through collective action 61, 149
   and, as or resembling zombification 12, 17, 29, 34, 44–45, 72, 77, 141
   and unpaid (house)work 17, 72, 75, 77, 80
   zombies as figures of 43, 54, 59–60, 67, 80, 113, 149–50, 160, 168
America (US mainland)
   "Great Migration" 65, 76, 91, 106
   New York 16, 29, 57, 86, 92, 130, 152
   "Old South" 54, 56–60, 65, 91–92, 102
   Pennsylvania (rural) 13–15, 112–16, 120–21
   post-war 73–75, 144, 147n11
   see also Long American Century; Wall Street; zombies, world-cultural trajectory
American Sugar Kingdom 43–45, 59, 65, 85
   see also US imperialism
the "Anthropocene" 18, 132–34
   see also Moore, Jason W.
appropriation
   colonial-imperialist 5, 7, 27, 35–36, 43, 46, 52, 125, 136, 165
   cultural versus capitalist 29–31, 33–35, 161
   and exploitation as fundamental to zombie imaginaries 2–5, 17, 22–23, 34–35, 38, 142, 165
   gendered and racialised (as world-ecological) 2, 5, 36, 71, 74, 88, 142
   see also capitalism, law of value and value-relationality

Benjamin, Walter 95
Bhattacharya, Tithi 71

Bishop, Kyle 7, 41, 143
Boyle, Danny (dir.) *see 28 Days Later*
Bozak, Nadia 95, 97, 122
Brodber, Erna 9–13, 15–16, 19, 21, 30, 46, 167–68
Brugués, Alejandro *see Juan de los Muertos*

Cabiya, Pedro 4, 71, 80, 84–88, 138, 168
Campbell, J. Bradford 102–103, 105
capitalism
    emergence of modern 4–5, 38, 132n4, 133
    externalisation of nature *see* "Nature"
    finance/financialised 7, 9, 33, 53, 130, 157–58
    law of value and value-relationality 4, 36–39, 50, 98, 149
    as racist/racial regime 36–37, 55, 133, 133n6
    as a "seaborne phenomenon" 151–55
    systemic (potentially terminal) crisis of 1, 10, 18, 43, 51–52, 123, 126, 134, 155, 163
    as a way of organising nature 3, 8, 23, 33
    zombies as animated by "inner logic" of 21, 39, 102, 113
    see also appropriation; patriarchy; plantation; world-ecology
capitalist world-system
    American hegemony 5, 10, 43, 94, 151
    British hegemony 10, 81–83, 98, 128
    constitutive unevenness of 8, 15–18, 23, 75, 80, 108, 110, 123, 127
    critique of communism as manifested within 144, 147, 151
    as horizon of world-literature 9, 22–24, 72, 74, 93
    restructuring of by oil 97, 111, 113–14
    zombies' shifting relationship with 1, 9, 16–18, 22, 97, 115, 123, 151, 157, 161–63
    see also uneven development; world-ecology; world-literature/world-culture
the Caribbean
    ecological degradation of 5, 24, 38, 43, 44, 52, 61–66, 127

racist, colonial views of *see* primitivism
realist and regionalist texts from *see* zombies, world-cultural trajectory
uneven relationship with US core *see* capitalist world-system, constitutive unevenness of
    see also Cuba; Dominican Republic; Haiti; Jamaica; Puerto Rico
Carpentier, Alejo 26, 43–44n1, 48–49, 49n2, 109
Carson, Rachel 117
Chauvet, Marie Vieux 107, 167
    Amour, colère, folie (collection) 71–80, 162
    "Love" (novella) 72–74, 76–80
Chude-Sokei, Louis 25, 52, 102
class struggle 32, 62, 110, 161, 165
class tensions *see* gender, female zombies and gender, race and class tensions
climate change/crisis
    capitalism's responsibility for 97, 128, 132–33, 158n19, 159–60
    and the crisis of capitalism 1, 18, 128, 132, 134
    literature's capacity to represent 160–62
    uneven impact of 24, 133, 159
    and zombie texts 20, 131, 133–34, 155–57
Coates, Carrol 100, 107, 109
Cold War
    role of Green Revolution in US strategy 118
    zombies within Cold War imaginary 80, 100, 107, 110, 113, 188, 144, 147, 156
    see also communism; Cuba; US imperialism
colonialism 9, 10, 20, 30, 38, 70, 136
    zombies registering legacies of 4–5, 20, 35, 69–71, 77–88, 93, 122, 125–126, 126n1, 134, 154, 167
    see also plantation; slavery/enslavement; US imperialism

Index

commodification 2, 33, 67, 71, 89, 93, 98, 113, 140
   and commodity fetishism 15, 75, 114
   and debt fetishism 140–41
   and oil fetishism 119–20
commodity frontier(s) 17, 29, 38, 43, 61, 63, 74, 78
communism
   actually existing, critical engagements with 144–51, 161
   and collectivist zombie imaginaries 61–63, 79, 145, 164–69
   zombies and the fear of 80, 101, 106, 113, 143–44, 147, 147n11
   see also Cold War; Cuba; socialism
Cuba
   Castro, Fidel 145n10, 146, 148, 155
   Ernesto "Che" Guevara 148–51
   post-Cold War zombie films 143–55, 157–58
   "Special Period" 145–48, 155, 164
   sugar plantations in *see* American Sugar Kingdom
   see also plantation, sugar production and Haitian migrant labour

Dalleo, Raphael 26, 26n2, 43, 45, 49, 52, 53, 73, 79
Dean, Jodie 161
Deckard, Sharae 22, 134
   see also Warwick Research Collective (WReC)
Depestre, René
   "Cap'tain Zombi" 41
   The Festival of the Greasy Pole 100–101, 106–10, 122
   surrealism of 137
   on zombification 19, 29, 34, 80
Descourtilz, Michel-Étienne 6, 69
Díaz, Juno 126, 131
   "Monstro" 133–36
   see also neoliberalism, and "new zombie" effects
dispossession
   gendered 67–69, 75, 82
   land/territorial 37, 44, 53–45, 66, 67, 93, 120
Dominican Republic 11, 35, 42–45, 48, 51, 53, 134–36, 146

and Haitian–Dominican relations 51, 134, 136
   see also plantation, sugar production and Haitian migrant labour
Douglass, Frederick 52
   see also slavery/enslavement
Dunaway, Wilma 71, 74
Duvalier, François 6, 38, 73–74, 77–80, 100–101, 106–10, 146
   and Jean-Claude ("Baby Doc") 38, 106, 109–10, 126–27, 164–67

Edwards, Bryan 6–7
electricity/electrification 97–110, 122
   and medium of film 95–97
   and zombification 100–102, 105–10, 122, 125
   see also energy regimes
Ellison, Ralph 92
   Invisible Man 100–106, 110
energy regimes
   and cultural effects 3, 13, 97–99, 99n3, 100–101, 110–12, 120–21
   energetic inequality and uneven access 17, 50, 65, 75–76, 99–101, 110, 112, 116, 123
   oil hegemony 3, 23, 43, 47, 65–66, 76, 97–99, 100–23, 128, 138, 157–58
   relationship with zombie effects 17–18, 97, 99–100, 110, 111–13, 122–23, 125
   shift from coal to oil 10–11, 97–99, 99n3, 120–21
   and systemic transformation 97–98, 100, 110, 113
   see also electricity/electrification; petromodernity
Engels, Friedrich 19, 146
environmental degradation
   capitalism's "absolute general law of" 8, 155n17, 160
   and deforestation 27, 37, 46, 61–62, 78, 81, 109, 121, 134, 162
   and soil erosion/exploitation 3, 7, 11, 24, 37–38, 43, 45–46, 63–65, 78, 81, 114–15
   and zombification 19, 62, 109, 160
exploitation *see* appropriation

see also capitalism, law of value and value-relationality

Federici, Silvia 35, 71
feminism 35, 71, 73, 80
   and feminist criticism *see* Dunaway, Wilma; Fraser, Nancy; Mies, Maria; Plumwood, Val
   see also social reproduction theory (SRT)
Ferrer-Medina, Patricia 20–21, 24
Foster, John Bellamy 37, 155n17, 160
Frankétienne 80, 137
   Dézafi 165–67
Fraser, Nancy 4, 23, 35, 36
Friedan, Betty 72, 74–75
Friedmann, Harriet 112–13
Fulci, Lucio *see Zombie Flesh-Eaters*

gender
   binary conceptions of 24, 104
   female zombies and gender, race and class tensions 24, 67–94
   gendered violence 72, 79
   interlinked oppression of "women, nature and colonies" 71–80, 81–88, 167
   see also "Nature"; patriarchy; race/racism/racialisation; sexism
Ghosh, Amitav 160
global oil crisis (1973) 10, 112
   see also neoliberalism
gothic/Gothic
   American Gothic 51, 81
   colonial plantation, or "sugar Gothic" 81–82, 84, 85, 117
   gothic eco-phobia 62, 113
   use of gothic mode/effects 47, 51–52, 56, 72, 78–84, 89–90, 96, 108, 113–14, 117, 143
   monstrous-feminine gothic 78–79, 83, 90
   periodicity and "gothic spikes" 35, 143
   racialised horror and gothic anxieties 103–104
   see also irrealism; the pulps; zombie effects
Grau, Jorge (dir.) *see The Living Dead at the Manchester Morgue*

Great Depression 42–43, 52, 144
   see also Wall Street
Green Revolution 64–65, 112–114, 118, 128, 158

Haiti
   American occupation of 5, 7, 26, 29, 32, 44, 49, 61, 63, 67–69, 73, 77, 138
   Duvalier dictatorships (1957–1986) 73, 107, 110, 126
   as extraction zone for migrant labour-power 45, 61, 77
   extreme socio-ecological degradation of 27, 46, 61, 78, 125–26, 134–36, 162
   Haitian–Dominican relations *see* Dominican Republic
   Haitian earthquake (2010) 126–27, 131, 136–38
   Haitian Revolution 2, 7, 53, 83, 135, 164
   relationship to the world-system 73, 107–108, 127, 131, 133, 146
   see also plantation, sugar production and Haitian migrant labour
Haitian American Sugar Company (HASCO) 27–29, 44
Halperin, Victor *see White Zombie*
Hearn, Lafcadio 6
Henry, Paget 9
Hurston, Zora Neale 67–70, 92

I am Legend 112
I Walked with a Zombie 12, 51, 57–60, 81–82, 111, 152, 153
Industrial Revolution 4, 98, 107
industrialisation 13, 37, 52, 75, 117, 155
   and deindustrialisation 10, 128–29
   see also agriculture, industrial/industrialisation of
Invasion of the Body Snatchers
   Don Siegel (dir., 1956) original 80, 85, 89, 91, 112–13, 144–45, 147
   Philip Kaufman (dir., 1978) remake 145
irrealism
   critical, and debates around 38, 47, 66, 69, 114
   the marvellous real and *le merveilleux creole* 47, 49n2, 70, 109
   see also gothic/Gothic

Jamaica 5, 10, 15, 82, 168
James, C.L.R. 4, 71
Jameson, Fredric 15, 23, 149
Juan de los Muertos 56n7, 143–55, 157–58, 168

Kaussen, Valerie 45, 61–63
Kee, Chera 6, 144n9, 158

Laguerre, Enrique 45, 49, 61
Lauro, Sarah
   on cultural appropriation 30–33, 35, 161
   on eco-zombies 20
   on the zombie's transatlantic history 2, 6–7, 22
LeMenager, Stephanie 99, 116, 119, 120
Levin, Ira
   screen adaptations 73
   The Stepford Wives 72–75, 79–80, 85, 87, 89–92
The Living Dead at the Manchester Morgue 117–18, 137
Long American Century 2, 3, 5, 7, 17, 19, 21, 141
López, Jotacé 138, 142–43, 157
Lovecraft, H.P. 65
   and Lovecraftian race fantasies 54–57, 85–87, 134
   and the Lovecraftian Weird 85–87, 86n5, 134
Löwy, Michael 47
Lumière Brothers 120

Malthusianism 20n1, 85
Marcuse, Herbert 15, 164
Marrero Aristy, Ramón 46, 49–50, 61
Mars, Kettly 125–27
Marx, Karl 1, 20, 23, 36, 52, 36, 37, 108, 164
Marxism 149
   and Marxist accounts of the zombie 4, 12, 34–35, 112
   and Marxist literary criticism *see* Warwick Research Collective (WReC)
   see also zombie studies
Matheson, Richard (dir.) *see I am Legend*

McNally, David 2, 8, 13, 22, 112–13, 158
metabolic rifts
   and capitalist development 8, 25, 37–38, 61, 123
   and neoliberalism 127–28
   and oil 10, 13, 15, 45–46, 95, 98–99, 145
   post-capitalism, healing of 164
   and the zombie figure/zombie effects 2, 7–8, 10–15, 19, 38–39, 54, 61, 71, 95, 99, 123
Métraux, Alfred 5, 8, 21, 112
Mies, Maria 71, 74
Mitchell, Timothy 99n3
Montijo, Josué 138–40
Moore, Jason W.
   on capitalism as world-ecology 3, 25, 33, 37–38, 127–28
   on capitalism's "Cheap Nature" strategy 3, 36–37, 71, 88, 103
   on Capitalocene versus Anthropocene 18, 132–33, 132n4–5,
   on neoliberal exhaustion 127–28, 158
Moretti, Franco 22
   see also world-literary criticism
Mumford, Lewis
   The Golden Day 102–103
   Technics and Civilisation 99

"Nature"
   gendered and racialised associations 6, 13, 25, 65, 84, 92
   link with zombies/zombification 19–21, 24–25, 71
   "Nature/Culture" binary under capitalism 3, 21, 24–25, 71, 132n4, 160
   see also world-ecology
Nau, Ignace 69–70
neoliberalism
   2008 financial crisis 18, 35, 39, 138
   debt regimes *see* US imperialism, debt-based
   exhaustion and de-zombification 163–69
   ideology surrounding inequality 89–90, 130–31, 140

IMF, structural adjustment and austerity measures 10, 94, 128, 130, 138–40
impact of 1970s global crisis 10, 126–28, 130, 139, 158
impact of neoliberalisation in the Caribbean 10, 15, 126–27, 167
as itself zombified 128, 158
and "new zombie" effects 7, 18, 126–58
New Imperialism 6, 42–43, 60
see also US imperialism
Niblett, Michael
on capitalist value-relations 4, 36–38
on plot/plantation dynamics 63
on world-ecological literary criticism 22–24, 38, 114, 143

patriarchy
imperial-patriarchal anxiety around miscegenation 12, 17, 26, 54, 66, 93, 103
patriarchal nationalism and the family 45, 49, 51, 61, 63, 73, 77, 80–88
patriarchal oppression and suburban housewifisation 74–80
see also gender, female zombies and gender, race and class tensions
Peele, Jordan
Get Out 88–94
US 93
"White Zombies" 89
petromodernity
and car culture 112–13, 115
and the film industry 95–97, 119–22
and suburbia/suburbanisation 72–80, 89, 92, 101, 112
see also zombie aesthetics, and the "petro-zombie"
Pietri, Pedro 16, 130
plantation
American cotton 52–57
Caribbean sugar (US-owned) 27–30, 35, 41–54, 57–60, 61, 63
colonial British sugar 66, 81–85
Haitian coffee 70, 73, 76–77
as precursor to the Fordist neo-plantation 52, 64, 105, 118

sugar production and Haitian migrant labour 42–49, 51, 61, 77
and zombies as "beasts of burden" 5, 8, 21, 67, 108, 112
see also agriculture
Plumwood, Val 20, 24
primitivism
influence on Hispanic Caribbean writers 43–44n1, 49n2
primitivist depictions of Haiti and the Caribbean 6, 26–29, 34, 49, 52–56, 135
racialised coding of unevenness as "primitive" otherness 23
Puerto Rico 43, 46, 80–88, 100, 138–41, 143, 146
the pulps 43, 51, 54–57, 60, 71
"House in the Magnolias" (August Derleth) 55–56
"The Song of the Slaves" (Mary Wade Wellman) 56, 151–52, 152n15
"While Zombies Walked" (Thorp McClusky) 56–57

race/racism/racialisation
class and gender see gender
and conceptions of nature see "Nature"
and energy regimes 76, 99, 101–104, 110, 119
and the film industry 12, 66, 103
as inherently ecological 2–5, 10, 13, 17, 24, 43–44n1, 46, 55, 71, 75–76, 80, 83–84, 106, 133, 162, 168
and labour patterns see plantation, sugar production and Haitian migrant labour
in the "post-racial" Obama era 89–94
under and post-Jim Crow 8, 65, 102–106, 118
zombies as encoding racialised fears and fantasies 12, 17, 26, 41–43, 51–60, 66, 70–71, 83, 93, 103, 105, 122
see also capitalism, as racist/racial regime; primitivism; sexism; slavery/enslavement; zombification, and robotisation

Index

Renda, Mary
  on US occupation of Haiti 5, 29–30
  on Zora Neale Hurston 67, 67n1, 69
Robinson, Cedric 12, 41, 51, 103
Rodríguez, Luis Felipe 46–48
Romero, George A. (dir.)
  Dawn of the Dead 9–10, 13–16, 131, 139, 162
  Day of the Dead 13
  Land of the Dead 129, 131
  Night of the Living Dead 13, 15, 18, 89, 91, 110–22, 144, 168
  see also zombies, world-cultural trajectory, post-1968/post-Romero zombie effects
Roumain, Jacques
  as committed communist 61, 165
  Gouverneurs de la rosée 61–64, 79, 162, 165–67

Saint-Éloi, Rodney 133, 136–38
Seabrook, William
  influence on later zombie texts 22, 26, 26n3, 41, 43–44n1, 47, 49n2, 70
  The Magic Island 22, 26–29, 53, 55, 65, 67, 165–66
sexism 3, 9, 18, 63–64, 67, 76, 78–79, 88–90, 93, 135, 148, 152, 165
  and homo- and transphobia 148, 151n14
  and sexual violence (against Haitian women) 17, 67, 69, 73–74, 79–80, 88, 135
  and sexualisation (race- and class-based) 66, 75, 85, 87–89, 103
  and symbolic violence/enclosure 69, 78
  see also gender; patriarchy; racism
Shapiro, Stephen 2n4, 18, 24, 34–35, 134, 136, 143, 163
  see also gothic/Gothic; world-literary criticism; zombie studies
Shaviro, Steven 21, 22, 39, 113, 122
Siegel, Don *see Invasion of the Body Snatchers*
slavery/enslavement 25, 32–33, 38, 52, 81, 82, 135
  link with modern wage labour 5, 28, 48, 74, 93, 99, 102, 164

  zombie as enslaved worker 23, 36, 41
  in the zombie imaginary 4–5, 28–29, 32–33, 48–49, 54–59, 65, 68, 77, 81–82, 91, 93, 99, 102, 106, 151–54
Smith, Neil 128, 136, 162–63
social reproduction theory (SRT) 17, 23–24, 35–36, 71–72
socialism
  collective struggle and anti-capitalist critique 16, 47, 60, 149–50 161, 164
  critical zombie texts and de-zombification 162–69
  post-Cold War recommitment to in Cuban film 144–48
  see also communism
Sotomayor, Áurea María 1, 141
Szeman, Imre 112

Torres, John 21, 138, 140–42
Tourneur, Jacques (dir.) *see I Walked with a Zombie*

uneven development 29, 52, 60, 83, 100, 108, 142–43
United States *see* America
US imperialism
  9/11 and the "War on Terror" 146
  critiques of in zombie texts 47, 67–68, 68n2, 94, 99, 133–34, 144–46, 167–68
  debt-based/financial 10, 53, 73, 94, 128, 138–39, 140–43
  socio-ecological impact in the Caribbean 43–46, 61–63, 74, 78, 80, 134, 136, 138
  in Vietnam 111–12, 118
  waste imperialism 138
  see also neoliberalism; plantation, Caribbean sugar (US-owned)

Vega, Ana Lydia 71, 80
  "Miss Florence's Trunk" 80–84
Vodou 2, 43–44n1, 57–59, 70, 109
  and racist-colonial depictions of "voodoo" 26–27, 41, 54, 57–58, 70, 86, 153
  see also primitivism

Wall Street
   nature–society matrix 25, 33,
   Occupy movement 31–33, 163
   role in US imperialism 29, 32–23, 53, 138–39
   Wall Street Crash (1929) 17, 33
   see also Great Depression; neoliberalism
Wallace, Inez 55
Warwick Research Collective (WREC) 9, 15, 22–23, 29, 72
Wellman, Manly Wade see the pulps
White Zombie 41–43, 48, 51–54, 103, 162, 168
   and the birth of the US horror film 30, 51, 96–97
   as filmic translation of *The Magic Island* 26, 29
   as intertext in later zombie films 12, 66, 89, 93
   Romero's divergence from 14, 110
Whitehead, Colson 129–31, 138, 140, 156–58
Williams, Raymond 19, 163
Woods, Clyde 64–65, 118
world-ecology
   capitalism as 3, 5, 7, 18, 33, 36, 38, 51–52, 36–38, 112, 113
   and "Cheap Nature" 3, 71, 74, 88, 103, 106n6
   crisis of 18, 51–52, 158
   as horizon of world-literature/-culture 23–24, 71, 111–12
   and nature–society relations 2, 13, 24, 111, 113, 115
   and neoliberalism 33, 127–28, 132–33
   petromodern 43, 111–12, 119, 122
   and resistant zombie imaginaries 17–18, 160, 165–69
   superweeds and "nature's revolt" 157–58
   and the world-ecological unconscious 27, 29, 54, 82
   see also capitalism; environmental degradation; metabolic rifts
world-food-system 112, 143, 156–57
   and food delocalisation 10, 12, 50, 141, 143, 167
   see also neoliberalism

world-literature/world-culture
   world-literary theory and criticism 9, 21–24, 29, 38–39
   zombie as world-literary/world-cultural figure 2n3, 9, 17–18, 22, 29, 38, 110, 129, 157
   see also world-ecology, as horizon of world-literature/-culture
World Wars
   First (1914–1918) 45
   Second (1939–1945) 59, 80
Wright, Richard 92
   Native Son 61, 64–66, 91, 168
   Twelve Million Black Voices 65, 106
   Uncle Tom's Children 64
Wynter, Silvia 47, 63, 66, 71

Zombi, Jean 2
   see also Haiti; Vodou
zombie aesthetics 23, 39, 112, 113, 115, 133, 155–56
   1968 revolution in 110, 112, 113
   and the "petro-zombie" 9, 21, 110–23
   self-conscious emulations of 66, 89, 142, 144, 148, 156
   and sugar/oil aesthetics 114, 122
   and the "sugar-zombie" 8, 17, 21, 43–66, 112, 115, 120–23, 142
   zombies' disruption of genre conventions 7, 9, 17, 23, 29, 34, 47, 89, 126, 129, 146, 151
   zombification of poetic form 141–42
   see also irrealism; primitivism; world-literary criticism; zombie effects
zombie effects 7–8, 17, 23, 35, 38, 46–50, 122, 128, 144
   key periods/spikes in 7, 17–18, 24, 35, 43, 51, 70, 129, 138
   see also gothic/Gothic; zombies, world-cultural trajectory
Zombie Flesh-Eaters 152–54
zombie studies/scholarship 2, 3n5, 2n4, 5, 20, 22, 45, 135
   see also Lauro, Sarah; McNally, David; Shapiro, Stephen
zombies, world-cultural trajectory 2–9, 21, 25–26, 39, 129, 144, 151–52

appearance in British colonial writing 6–7
circulation within Caribbean regionalist/realist texts 42, 44, 46–50
as folkloric Haitian figure 2–4, 3n5, 5, 30, 34, 38
move into US core culture (via film) 2–9, 29–30, 41–43, 51, 54, 72
post-1968/post-Romero zombie effects 3, 10, 14, 89, 99, 110–15, 144, 150, 155
post-2007 proliferation of "new zombie" texts 128–32
recent zombie cli-fi and (eco-/post-) apocalypse narratives 129–31, 133–38, 151–58

zombification 2, 42, 61–63, 66, 77, 102, 104, 109, 140–42, 166–67
and de-zombification, or the potential of/for 2, 61, 63, 100, 162–69
female 17, 71, 167
and robotisation 25, 27, 52, 72, 75, 77, 103–104, 142
see also alienation; electrification; gender; slavery/enslavement